I0650761

Heigho! for a Husband.

CHAPTER I.

AT BURNHAM COURT.

 DONT see how I can refuse," mused Mrs. Raynham, uttering her thoughts aloud as she stood in the drawing-room of Burnham Court, with an open letter in her hand, and something like a frown upon her handsome face.

"Refuse what, mamma?" asked a small, slight, golden-haired girl, who was nestling in the cosy corner of a soft couch, and was amusing herself by playing with a kitten.

"This request from the executor of your father's brother. He states that I have been left joint guardian with himself of your cousin, Beatrice Burnham, and that, as he is a bachelor, he will be glad if I will invite his ward to live with me, and under my care, until she is of age."

"Dear me!" cried the golden-haired girl, pushing aside the kitten in her eagerness. "Of course she must come to us, mamma.; I have never seen her, and yet she is my first cousin. She is very rich, isn't she?"

"No; it seems that she must be quite poor," replied Mrs. Raynham, consulting the letter in her hand.

"Mr. Lascelles writes," she went on, "that my niece possesses an income of two hundred and fifty pounds a year, and of this sum he proposes that two hundred should be paid to me for her maintenance, which would

NOTICE.—With this Number is Given Away a Coloured Picture for binding with the Work.

leave her fifty pounds a year for dress and pocket-money."

"But you surely won't accept any payment from my cousin for receiving her as a guest in this house," cried Clarrie Burnham indignantly; "it would be an outrageous thing to do. Why, if I were to die to-morrow Beatrice would inherit this place, and all the money that will be mine. The idea of making her pay for living in a house that may one day be her own!"

"It is very well for you to talk in this strain," retorted Mrs. Raynham bitterly; "I am quite aware of the fact that you are counting the days and the hours that must elapse before you become mistress here, and your poor sisters and I have to seek another home; but until then you will perhaps allow me to make what provision I can for my future and theirs."

And so saying Mrs. Raynham swept from the room.

"Heigho!" yawned Clarrie Burnham wearily, when she thus found herself alone. "What a wretched thing it is to be an heiress. I have no doubt my father thought he behaved very liberally to my mother when he left her the control of his fortune, and of me after I became twenty-one, and gave her five hundred a year and the dower-house to live in until I reached my majority. But then he did not suppose that she would marry again within a year of his death, or that she would be left with four penniless daughters when she became a widow a second time; if he had thought such a condition of affairs possible, I am sure he would have taken care that she should not impoverish my property, and pinch and scrape as she does to save every sixpence she can squeeze for my half-sisters. It is perfectly wretched; but I have only another year to wait, thank Heaven, and then I shall be free—free to do as I like, and to marry Frank, if he still wants me."

The blush that came to her cheek as she murmured these last words considerably heightened her beauty, and it had not faded away before a servant opened the door and announced:

"Mr. Frank Darlington."

"Good-morning, Clarrie," said the new comer, advancing with the air of a privileged visitor, and the moment the door was closed upon the servant catching the girl in his arms in a lover-like embrace.

"How is my darling?" he added when, after a faint struggle, she was free.

"Quite well, Frank, but you must not behave in that dreadful manner; you know how angry mamma would be if she suspected that you did not keep your promise not to make love to me till I am of age. I am sure if she knew half of your goings-on she wouldn't let you come inside the house."

And as the pretty little hypocrite said this, she looked so loving and so much like a big child pleading for a kiss instead of chiding a too demonstrative lover for taking one, that Frank Darlington would have been a much more scrupulous man than he was ever likely to become if he had not accepted the mute challenge, and silenced the reproof in the most effectual manner possible.

A hand on the handle of the door startled the lovers into sudden caution, and they had assumed a suspiciously distant attitude towards each other when Clarrie's mother joined them.

However welcome Mr. Darlington might be to the heiress, it was quite evident that his presence was not so much appreciated by her parent, though Mrs. Raynham was far too cautious and too thorough a woman of the world to do more than tacitly discourage his too frequent visits.

Of course, she knew why he came to Burnham Court so often, for he made no secret of his desire to marry her eldest daughter, but she had very positively declared that she did not approve of early marriages, and that Clarrie would not marry with her consent before she was twenty-one.

But she did not forbid the young man the house, though, for consistency's sake, she exacted a promise from him that he would not try to win the heart of her daughter while she was still a minor.

She did not expect him to keep the promise he gave so readily, and in her heart she earnestly wished him to break it, for Clarrie's father, in his unbounded confidence in his wife, had made her consent to their daughter's marriage an absolute necessity if she married when still under age, the penalty of disobedience being that her mother should retain the control of the property during her lifetime, instead of yielding it up when the girl attained her majority.

So Mrs. Raynham allowed these two to meet as often as they would, and though she appeared to keep a very strict guard over her daughter, she gave Mr. Darlington so many opportunities of ignoring his promise that that shrewd young man quickly discovered the trap that it was intended he should walk into, but, while he went tantalizingly near it, he was far too wary to be caught.

"I am a very poor man, Clarrie," he said one day, with seeming candour, when the girl was pouting at his caution and his fear "of mamma," "and it is very desirable that we should wait until your mother gives her consent or you are of age; more particularly so as my father will disinherit me if I marry a wife who is penniless. Still, my darling, if you wish it, I will defy poverty and our relations and count the world well lost so that I win my darling."

A very grand sentiment, no doubt, and losing nothing in its application by the dramatic fervour with which it was uttered, though those who knew him well would not have cared to risk much on Mr. Frank Darlington being of the same mind when put to the test.

But he felt pretty safe.

No woman in her senses could ask such a sacrifice of a man, and gentle, pliant, little Clarrie, soft by nature and shallow-minded as the kitten with which she played, was utterly incapable of such self-assertion, so she submitted to be surreptitiously caressed and assured that the man whom she loved adored her, without any openly-vowed engagement existing between them.

But we must return to the drawing-room of the Court, where Mrs. Raynham, with a new scheme in her head, is talking to the lovers.

" And so you are going to town for a few days ? " she says carelessly.

" Yes," he answered smoothly, " Will you trust me to execute any commisions ? "

And he looked from mother to daughter as though asking both of them at once to make him their agent.

" Oh, I do want a piece of lace matched ! " replied Clarrie eagerly. Then, thinking she detected a blank expression of disgust upon her admirer's countenance, she added : " But I forgot that you detest shopping."

" I am afraid I should do it so badly," he replied diffidently.

" Of course you would ! " chimed in the mother. "Besides, matching lace isn't a man's work. But you can undertake a commission for me, if you like, Mr. Darlington."

The young man bowed and expressed the pleasure it would give him to be of service.

" I have a niece coming to pay us a visit of indefinite length," said the lady quietly. " She has recently lost her father—my first husband's brother—and she may have no one to travel with. You would oblige me by calling upon her while you are in town and by offering to bring her here when you return."

" With pleasure," was the reply. " I presume that I have never met the young lady ? "

" You have not met her here," said Mrs Raynham a trifle tartly, " for I have never seen her myself. Her father took the liberty of writing to expostulate with me about my second marriage when it was on the eve of taking place ; he was likewise angry with his deceased brother at the manner in which the property had been left. I replied, I have no doubt angrily, and from that time all correspondence ceased between us, but his executor writes to say he paid me the compliment of naming me as joint guardian of his daughter, and I suppose I must accept the responsibility. I presume that the poor girl has really no other female relative."

" She can't have, mamma," interrupted Clarrie, " for her mother I know was an only child, and, I believe, a great heiress."

"If her mother were an heiress, her money has taken unto itself wings," returned Mrs. Raynham disdainfully; "for the daughter is poor enough in all conscience, and you won't meet an heiress in my niece Beatrice, Mr. Darlington. But you will stay to luncheon with us," she added, as though repenting of her sneer.

"Thank you; it will give me great pleasure," was the unruffled answer.

"Then I will leave Clarrie to entertain you for a few minutes," said the elder lady as she left the room.

"Who is this new cousin?" asked Frank Darlington with a frown, as he turned to Clarrie, who expected him to indulge in a lover-like burst of delight at being again alone with her.

"She is papa's brother's daughter," was the reply; "and my first cousin. Papa and his brother you know were twins."

"Ah yes, I remember I have heard something about it. Wasn't their some doubt as to which was the oldest?"

"I think there was," returned Clarrie, "but it was decided in papa's favour long before I was born."

"So I suppose; but tell me what you know about your uncle."

"I don't know anything personally," said the girl; "for I don't think I ever saw him. He and papa quarrelled, I believe, about my father's marriage with my mother; but this I only know from hearsay, because papa died a few months after I was born, but I have always understood that Uncle Edward had a large share of the property, which he sold back again to papa, and I have also been told that he married a very rich wife, so Beatrice ought to be richer than I shall be, but she isn't."

"How do you know she is not?" asked Darlington almost brusquely.

"Because her guardian, or executor, or something, the man who wrote to mamma, I mean, said in his letter that my cousin had only two hundred and fifty pounds a year, and he offered mamma two hundred of it to let my cousin live here; and would you believe it, mamma is going to be mean enough to take it."

"I would believe anything of the meanness of Mrs. Raynham," sneered Darlington with a disdainful laugh.

Then perceiving the pained expression on Clarrie's face, he added quickly:

"Forgive me, dearest, I ought not to have said what I did. We must make excuses for your mother's unusual position, but I cannot help feeling bitter against her at times, because she keeps my own darling from me."

The darling was certainly not kept from him for the next few minutes, and as much love-sick nonsense was talked in that time as would suffice some people for an hour.

Indeed, it was only the re-entrance of Clarrie's mother, accompanied by her daughter, Geraldine, that brought these two foolish young people to their senses.

Oddly enough, though Clarrie and Geraldine were only half-sisters, they were singularly alike.

Geraldine, it is true, was two years younger than the heiress, but she was as much like her as an uncoloured copy of a picture can be like the original.

For whereas Clarrie's hair was bright and golden, Geraldine's was dull, and of the colour of tow.

Her eyes also, instead of being violet, were of a pale washed-out blue, and there was an absence of the great delicacy and refinement of feature, which was so strongly marked in the elder girl.

But for all this Geraldine had a charm of her own, and there was more brain in her little finger than in Clarrie's whole body.

She began a rattling conversation with Frank Darlington the moment she came into the room, and she carried it on without intermission, almost without interruption, until luncheon was announced.

Claribel made no attempt to check this flow of talk.

Hers was not a jealous disposition, and she was glad that Frank should be welcomed by the whole family.

At table Mr. Darlington met the other Misses Raynham, Grace and Fanny and Ruth, respectively seventeen, sixteen, and fifteen, as plain a trio as it would be possible to meet, yet all with a certain style and refinement about them, that despite their plain dresses and lack of beauty, clearly stamped them as gentlewomen.

It was a merry party that sat at the plentiful but by no means luxuriously-supplied table, for the girls all talked more or less cleverly, and the most careless observer would soon discover that, however tightly their mother might hold the purse-strings, she could not tie her daughters' tongues.

The conversation to-day turned principally upon the new cousin.

Speculations as to her appearance, and temper, and disposition, and as to how they should all get along together.

"And she is just Clarrie's age, isn't she, mamma?" asked Geraldine.

"I think so," was the reply.

"That's a bore; I'd rather she had been a little younger than me instead of older, for then I could have kept her in order more easily; but thank goodness, she isn't an heiress; two heiresses in the family would have completely extinguished us."

"I am sure I don't extinguish you," said Clarrie, with something like a pout.

"No, dear, but you would if you could," was the uncompromising reply; "but though very unlike a ball of down, Clarrie, you are not big or heavy enough to extinguish a young woman of my bulk and fibre."

"What do you mean, Geraldine?" asked the heiress, with a puzzled and half-offended expression of countenance.

"Nothing; I never mean anything," laughed Geraldine, lightly, as she rose from the table, leaving the others to follow her.

An hour later, as Frank Darlington was saying adieu, Mrs. Raynham remarked:

"Then I may rely upon you to call upon Miss Burnham and offer to bring her here when you return at the end of the week."

"Yes, certainly," was his answer; "I have taken care of her address."

"And don't flirt with her on the journey, Mr. Darlington," said Geraldine, with a gleam of mischief in her eyes. "She isn't an heiress, you know, and it might become awkward."

"I never flirt, Miss Raynham," said the young man, coldly, for he had noticed Clarrie's violet eyes flash with suddenly aroused suspicion.

"Don't you? Then I am sorry I spoke," retorted the irrepressible Geraldine. "I suppose, as you don't flirt, you were earnest in your professions of devotion to Mary Trevor."

"Really, Miss Geraldine, if I did not know your propensity for jesting, I should ask you to explain your enigmatical remarks," said the young man, with sudden anger.

"Should you? Perhaps I will do so one day."

And the girl flashed a look upon Mr. Darlington which made him feel very uneasy as he thought of it after he had ridden away.

"What did you mean by saying what you did to Frank about Mary Trevor?" asked Clarrie, when she could get hold of Geraldine alone.

"Nothing, dear; I never mean anything," laughed the other, evasively.

"She wouldn't believe me if I told her," was Geraldine's mental comment. "She would think I was only in league with mamma to prevent her from marrying him; besides, what is the use of speaking without proof; and even if I possessed proof of Frank Darlington's treachery to another woman, Clarrie is fool enough to marry him just the same.

"Ah me!" she mused, a little later; "what pitiful rubbish some women will take for a husband; but, I suppose, we can't all pick and choose. There are five of us girls to be got rid of sooner or later, and when Beatrice Burnham comes there will be a sixth. Six girls more or less eligible for matrimony, and not three well-to-do bachelors in the whole neighbourhood. What a place to live in! One might as well go into a nunnery at once as sit here and dolefully cry, 'Heigho! for a Husband!'"

CHAPTER II.

THE FIRST TUG OF WAR.

IN the drawing-room of a large, gloomy house, in one of the gloomiest though once most fashionable squares in London, sat the heroine of this story, some few days after the conversation already recorded had taken place concerning her at Burnham Court.

Beatrice Burnham is clad in deep mourning, and as she looks about the large dingy room she gives a little shiver, partly of impatience but principally of disgust.

"How I do hate to be kept waiting!" she cried at last, as she starts to her feet and begins to pace the room with restless steps. "To be kept waiting by a man, too, and by that man of all others!"

Why the particular man in question should thus excite her wrath was not by any means apparent until she spoke again.

"I do believe papa's mind was affected when he made that preposterous will," she went on with increased irritation. "The idea of leaving me to the guardianship of a young man, and to make it a stipulation that I should marry him or lose half of my fortune. Marry him, indeed! He is welcome to the money, but he isn't welcome to me. My father knew that I could never spend five minutes in the same room with Godfrey Lascelles without quarrelling with him, and yet he must insist in his will that I should marry my *bete noir*, forsooth. There is one comfort, however, Godfrey has no more love for me than I for him, in proof of which he now keeps me waiting."

She stamped her foot as she said this, and she looked at the clock angrily and impatiently; then, in a condition of intense irritation, she walked to one of the windows that looked out upon the neglected square.

As she stood there, with the grand lines of her face and figure visible in the mid-day light, you could see that she was a strikingly handsome woman.

A little above the medium height, though by no means tall, the admirable proportions of her sloping shoulders, full bust, and small rounded waist, were simply perfect. But it was the expression of her face and the proud carriage of her head which gave to Beatrice Burnham so rare a charm.

Strictly beautiful she was not, for her features were by no means regular; and yet her nose was perfect, her lips were ruby red and ripe enough to tempt the coldest woman-hater to kiss them, and though her chin was perhaps a trifle too square, the broad, straightly-pencilled brows, and the deeply sunken eyes with their heavily fringed eyelids, gave an expression of vivacity as well as a certain amount of character to a face that was alike singular and picturesque in its loveliness.

Of the colour of her eyes one would not like to be very certain. She declared they were green; people who wished to flatter her said they were dark blue; but those who excited her anger and saw her in a passion had not the least doubt but that they were black.

Her hair was dark brown, wavy, and so abundant that she scarcely knew what to do with it, and as the sunlight now glinted upon the edges and ripples of its waves and curls, turning them for the time to gold, she seemed rather like some sable-clad woman in a picture than a creature of mere flesh and blood.

A man's voice in the room coughing to attract attention made her wheel round suddenly, then her face lighted up with animation, though not altogether of a pleasurable kind, and she said brusquely:

"So you have come at last! Do you know what time it is?"

"Yes," was the equally cold answer; "it is the time I appointed for meeting you; that clock is wrong, but I have been in the house for the last half-hour; if you had enquired of the servants you would have known it."

"Oh, I was in no hurry to see you, thank you," with a half defiant toss of the head, and something like a mischievous gleam in her eye. "I see you were right," she added, consulting her watch; "this clock is fast; it's the only fast thing in the house, however; the very flies seem to have gone to sleep upon the walls, the place is so quiet and so dull."

"You will not have that complaint to make after to-morrow, Miss Burnham," said the gentleman stiffly, as he laid a bag of papers upon a table, placed a chair for her, and took another himself as far distant from hers as was possible.

"Ah! Then you have heard from my aunt?" she asked with sudden eagerness.

"Yes; there is her reply," and he handed her a letter. "You see she accepts the terms I offered her," he went on in a business-like tone, "and, therefore, while you will have a home with relatives, you will be able to feel that you are to a certain extent independent of their control."

"And you think I can't live without showing my independence and self-will?" asked Beatrice with a flash of anger.

Godfrey Lascelles shrugged his shoulders, but uttered no verbal reply.

The time was, when he was as ready to engage in a war of words with his fair antagonist as she with him; but circumstances had changed since the reading of her father's will. The antagonism between him and Beatrice, instead of being playful and more than half assumed as formerly, was now becoming real; he felt himself in a false position, he considered that she judged him unjustly and unfairly, and he was distant, cold, and angry in consequence.

Once again Beatrice read over the letter, then she folded it up as she said:

"I don't think I shall like my aunt; perhaps some of her daughters may be tolerable, but beggars can't be allowed a choice, and I have no alternative."

She looked him straight in the face as she made this last remark, uttering it in the tone of a question rather than of a statement of fact.

"SO YOU HAVE COME AT LAST! DO YOU KNOW WHAT TIME IT IS?"

But he never moved a muscle, never flinched from her steady gaze as he replied in calm even tones :

"No, you have no alternative."

Beatrice bit her lip, and for a moment her eyelids drooped, while her usually pale cheeks flushed with vexation.

But her companion did not notice these signs of feeling on her part.

He was turning over his papers, biting his lip, and thinking to himself savagely :

"She is no better, nay, she is worse than the rest of her sex; she wants to tempt me to remind her of the alternative spoken of in her father's will, that out of very spite she may flout and reject me; but no woman in the world shall have me thus at her mercy. I love the whole sex too well to trust my happiness to the care of any one of them."

Then he laughed a low jarring laugh that made Beatrice look up with sudden anger, feeling assured that he was laughing at her.

"Do you find my solitary condition so very amusing that you must laugh at it?" she asked passionately.

"I—I beg your pardon; I was not even thinking of you," he replied, with a blank expression of countenance.

"Thank you; almost as complimentary as to laugh at me; but while you sit there tumbling over those papers I am obliged to think of you, and to wonder when this interview will be over."

"I am sorry to waste your valuable time," he replied with mock humility. "I was not aware that you were in so great a hurry."

"Of course you were not; it never enters the masculine mind to suppose that a woman may have some arrangements to make before she goes into the country for a year."

"I thought all your arrangements were made," he remarked quietly.

"I suppose you thought all my gowns and bonnets were bought," she retorted sharply; not that I shall want much variety," she added with sudden sadness, as she looked at her black crape-trimmed dress.

"But now to business," she said with a sudden change in her manner; "you were going to explain to me more fully the conditions that my father imposed upon me, and," wincing as though with pain, "upon you."

"Yes," replied Mr. Lascelles calmly; "your father left a letter addressed to you and to me, the conditions of which were to have the authority of a codicil to his will. I gave you that letter yesterday, and I presume that you have read it."

"I have," she replied with a frown, "and I suppose papa had a right to do as he pleased with his own money; at the same time I cannot help wishing that he had consulted your feelings and mine a little more in the matter. I always knew you were a favourite with him, but he might have left you a handsome legacy in some other way."

"We need not discuss that part of the subject for the next twelve months, Miss Burnham," said the young man coldly; "for the present we have only to arrange for your comfort during the interval. Your late father, as you are well aware, did not like your aunt, Mrs. Raynham, but as she is your nearest and almost your only female relative, he named her as joint guardian with myself during your minority, and desired that I should write and ask her to receive you, stating that you were possessed of two hundred and fifty pounds a year, and offering her four-fifths of that amount for your maintenance."

"Yes; what could have been papa's motive for desiring it to be thought that I was poor?" asked Beatrice, looking at her companion eagerly.

"I don't know; your father entertained some peculiar ideas with regard to the influence of wealth upon certain natures, and he was anxious that, until you were your own mistress, you should be regarded as comparatively poor, but I suppose the arrangement does not suit you."

"Indeed, you are mistaken, Mr. Lascelles; I shall much prefer it; I don't want people to pretend to like me because of my money, but I suppose I need not stint myself to fifty pounds for a whole year, if I happen to want more?"

She said this with such a rueful countenance that her companion could scarcely repress a smile, though he replied gravely:

"Certainly not; if you want money write to me for it; but you will have few temptations to be lavish in your expenditure where you are going, and, unless the true condition of affairs should be suspected, it will be as well to be prudent and not yield too readily to your generous impulses."

"It is a new thing to learn that I have generous impulses," she retorted a trifle bitterly.

But he took no notice of her remark.

In his way he was quite as resolute in showing her that he did not mean to marry her as she was in making him feel that she would not accept him, only he did not yield to petty irritation or to the love of conquest, and she was too true a daughter of Eve not to feel angry with him because he did not wish to marry her, even though it might be against her will.

Of course no woman would wish to be won in spite of herself, but, at the same time, there are few women who like to have it impressed upon them that any particular man would prefer any disagreeable alternative to marriage with them.

Godfrey Lascelles attributed his companion's variable humour to the general inconsistency of her sex, and proceeded without delay to explain to her how her father's wealth had been invested.

There were shares in mines and quarries, in canals and railroads, in English and in foreign stocks, most of them bringing in good dividends, and altogether representing a total of rather more than two hundred thousand pounds.

"From the manner in which the money is invested, the total amount can easily be kept secret until the will is proved," said the young man, as he folded up his papers and returned them to the bag, "and, with your concurrence, I do not propose to prove the will for the next nine or twelve months."

"I am perfectly willing," was the stately answer. "I am quite sure you will respect papa's wishes, Mr. Lascelles, however little you may care for mine."

And so saying, the young lady pushed her chair from the table and rose to her feet.

Godfrey Lascelles looked at her questioningly, for a moment even doubtfully.

She was certainly lovely enough to make an anchorite forget his vows, and fall blindly at her feet, a slave to her beauty.

"But that beauty is only external," he thought with the bitterness that, though new to his mind, was growing daily upon him; "she has no womanly gentleness or tenderness in her nature; she could not forget herself and her own pride and vanity in love for another. No, I would rather be scourged with scorpions than be the slave of such a creature. Happily I am heart-whole, and her dead father's will cannot make me marry her."

These thoughts had passed through his brain swiftly, and he had not risen from his seat at the table when the door of the room opened and a servant announced:

"Mr. Frank Darlington."

Beatrice looked at the new comer, whose name she had not previously heard, then at her guardian, and it was Godfrey Lascelles who rose to receive the young man, and to present him to the lady.

"Mr. Darlington is a friend of Mrs. Raynham," he remarked. "You will remember, Miss Burnham, that in the letter I showed you, your aunt said a friend of hers would see you safely to the Court if you had no other escort."

"Oh, it is very kind of you, Mr. Darlington," said Beatrice, advancing, and giving her hand cordially to the new comer.

"Not at all. I shall be very glad to be of service," was the reply. "When do you propose to start for Burnham Court?"

"The day after to-morrow," was the reply.

"But Miss Burnham need not tax your kindness," here interposed Godfrey Lascelles, "for I shall consider it my duty to take her to Mrs. Raynham myself."

"It will be no tax," said Mr. Darlington suavely, "particularly, as I shall be travelling by the same route on the same day."

"Then we can all go together," said Beatrice, who noticed the frown gathering on Godfrey's brow, and who thus thought to add to his vexation.

Both of the young men bowed—an action that might mean so much or so little.

Beatrice, however, was not to be chilled, and she turned to her guardian as though he and she were the best of friends, remarking:

"You have not had luncheon, Mr. Lascelles."

"No," he replied curtly.

"Then perhaps you and Mr. Darlington will stay and join me. I do hate to eat alone."

Another bow of acquiescence; then the young lady left the room, remarking *sotto voce* :

"Supposing cook has anything to give us."

When Beatrice returned from her visit to the house-keeper's room, intending to rejoin her guests, she came in by the way of the back drawing-room, and was half-hidden by the heavy curtains.

She had thus time and opportunity to study the faces of her two guests.

Godfrey Lascelles she knew of old, but the counten-ance and general appearance of Frank Darlington puzzled her.

He was handsome enough to suit even her critical taste, but the eyes were too close together, the lips were too thin and too tightly shut at times, while there was a thickness about the neck, and the ears seemed to stand out aggressively, all of which impressed her very unfavourably.

"He looks as though he could commit murder," she thought as she watched him. "After all I am glad that Godfrey is going down to the Court with me."

Then she rejoined her guests, and devoted herself so assiduously to the entertainment of the stranger, that her guardian became disgusted.

He was politeness itself, however, though he made a point of outstaying the other man.

But when two days later Beatrice Burnham drove to the railway-station, and there met not only Frank Darlington, but her guardian, she was as much mortified as alarmed by the latter remarking :

"After all I must remain in town, for I have some business to attend to, so I must entrust Miss Burnham to your care, Mr. Darlington."

If Beatrice had followed her inclinations she would have expostulated ; but pride forbade her taking this course, and she only bowed coldly and almost haughtily as Godfrey Lascelles lifted his hat, and the train rolled out of the station.

"What a very odd fellow that Lascelles is," remarked Darlington when the young barrister was no longer in sight.

"He is peculiar, but he is very clever," retorted the girl ; with a natural desire to defend the absent.

"So I should think," was the dry rejoinder, "and rather young too, to have been appointed your guardian."

"That is a fault he will grow out of," retorted the young lady ; "but now please tell me something about my cousins—you know them all, don't you ? "

"Yes," he answered.

But though he complied with her request he would much rather have talked with her about herself.

And thus the train went on its way with its living freight, and Godfrey Lascelles returned to his chambers with a bitterness which he could not account for rankling in his heart.

CHAPTER III.

FANNY'S SECRET.

EATRICE had been at Burnham Court three days, and already the place was assuming the familiar aspect of home to her.

Mrs. Raynham was kind and courteous, even if a trifle cold, but Clarrie made up for her mother's formality by effusive demonstrations of affection, while the four other girls were in their way friendly and amiable.

Not that it would have had a very depressing effect upon our heroine had they been less cordial with her, for she had been accustomed all her life to rely so much upon her own resources for occupation and amusement, that she had become more independent of her surroundings than is usually the case with girls of her age.

Do not imagine her wanting in affection for her late father, from the fact that she grieved so little at his death; but the truth is, she had not known much of her parent.

The late Mr. Burnham had been an eccentric man.

After his wife's death he had shunned the company of women.

He had sent his little daughter out to nurse until she was old enough to go to school, and he had kept her away from his house until within a few months of his death, when he had allowed her to come home, but had provided her with the companionship of an old lady with whom she was given to understand she was to spend most of her time, and not intrude more than was absolutely necessary upon her father.

That gentleman had in the course of years become a confirmed invalid, and his valet was the only person for whose company he seemed to care, save when some old friends or Godfrey Lascelles came to see him.

For this young barrister, whose father had been an intimate friend of his youth, Marmaduke Burnham entertained a warm affection, and he always treated him as a loved son.

It had, indeed, been partly with the anticipation of his becoming his son-in-law that Mr. Burnham had allowed Beatrice to take her proper place in his household, for he fully intended that Godfrey and his daughter should marry.

But through some natural strain of perversity in the girl's disposition, she assumed from the moment they met a position of antagonism to her father's favourite that was sometimes only playful, and was sometimes very real.

I am afraid that in her heart she grudged him the love that her father bestowed upon him, and which should have been given to herself.

And then he piqued her.

He was so calm, so courteous, so self-possessed, and at the same time so undoubtedly clever that he irritated her, and insensibly drove her to do and say things to ruffle his temper or provoke him to retort.

But Godfrey Lascelles took her capricious treatment of him in very good part. He often went out of his way to amuse her and to make things more comfortable for her, and they might have ended by falling in love with each other in downright earnest, but for Mr. Burnham's somewhat sudden death, and the very outspoken conditions of his will.

If Beatrice had known the real circumstances of the case she would not have judged her father's favourite so harshly, for Mr. Burnham had at one time intended to leave the bulk of his property to Godfrey, and it was only when this circumstance came accidentally to the young man's knowledge, and he declared emphatically that he would never consent to benefit by such injustice, that the elder man had been induced to change the disposition he had made of his wealth.

This last will, however, when read had been as great a surprise to Godfrey as it was to Beatrice, and it can scarcely be said that the sensation was in any degree more pleasurable to him than to her.

But these two young people are separated now, and are not likely to jar upon each other for some time to come, and Beatrice is in new scenes, among new friends, and has, as she somewhat exultingly thinks, "the whole world before her."

It is a very small world that she meets at Burnham Court, however, and during these first three days of her stay she has not seen a single person besides the servants and the members of the family.

"Do you never go out ? Do you never have people to call and see you? Are there no shops? Is there nothing with which one can amuse one's self?" she asked impatiently of Clarrie the fourth morning after her arrival.

The little heiress opened her blue eyes in surprise at her cousin's earnestness; then she replied languidly :

"Yes we sometimes go to parties, but very rarely, because, you see, mamma doesn't invite people back again; and then we have no near neighbours of equal position, and as mamma won't keep a proper carriage we can't go and make distant calls. But we do go for long walks sometimes. I will take you for one to-day."

"As far as walking is concerned the grounds of the Court are pleasant enough," replied Beatrice carelessly; then she asked in a puzzled tone: "But how is it you all live like this, Clarrie? I can't make it out. Are you really poor?"

The little heiress laughed, though her face flushed with vexation as she replied :

"No, dear, we are anything but poor, but mamma is saving all she can during my minority; she is afraid of my marrying, and she thinks the other girls haven't a chance of doing so in this place, so she won't spend a sixpence upon us more than she is obliged to. When I come of age she means to take the others abroad to some place where, with her savings, she will be considered a wealthy woman; don't you think it is horrid?"

"Indeed I do. But tell me, who are your nearest neighbours?"

"There are the Darlingtons, who live at Holly Mount, two miles off. I dare say Frank will ride over to-day."

"Yes I understand; but Crook Abbey and Grantly Park, and Viking Grange are within half-a-dozen miles of this place," interposed Beatrice, "I hunted them out upon a county map. Are the families all away, or don't they visit you?"

"Partly both," laughed Clarrie. "Viking Grange belongs to a minor who is at present abroad; the Fernleys at Crook Abbey have some old-standing feud against us; and Sir Graham Grantly is an old bachelor, and away from the park, but when he returns he is sure to call upon us."

"But there are people of lesser note, who live near, are there not?" persisted Beatrice.

"Oh yes, there are the people in the village, and a number of small gentry and retired officers and their wives and daughters. But here comes Mr. Langdale, the rector; he will give you all the gossip of the place."

"I don't want gossip, but I do want to know where I am and amongst whom I am living," retorted Beatrice. "I want to do some good in the world. I suppose there are some poor girls in the village who would like to be taught something useful?"

"Yes, if you know anything useful to teach them," laughed Clarrie a trifle maliciously.

"I would teach them to respect themselves," retorted Beatrice emphatically.

The little heiress looked at her cousin for a moment wonderingly, then she asked:

"Does that require much teaching or learning?"

But before Beatrice could reply, Geraldine came into the room with more animation upon her expressionless face than was usual to it, and said:

"Ma wants you girls to come into the drawing-room. Mr. Langdale is there; I suspect he wishes to enlist your sympathies and assistance for a school treat."

"Our sympathies are not worth much when our purses are empty," said Claribel bitterly. "I only wish I were a man. I wouldn't be limited to thirty pounds a year for dress and pocket-money. I'd go to the Jews, if I only knew what 'going to the Jews' meant."

Beatrice laughed, then she said:

"Never mind, Clarrie. Borrow of me. I daresay I have enough for both of us, and you will be rich soon. But what makes you look so severe, Geraldine?"

"Nothing," was the brusque reply, as Miss Raynham turned upon her heel.

The cousins followed her, and a few seconds later they were in the drawing-room, and Beatrice was being introduced to the rector.

Laurence Langdale, rector of Burnham-on-Brent, was a comparatively young man. He had entered the Church as a family duty rather than from choice, and, with the secret consciousness of not having his heart entirely in his profession, he was more earnest and zealous and self-critical than a more deeply religious man might have been.

As a rule, he was not a frequent visitor at Burnham Court, for he secretly regarded Mrs. Raynham's daughters as dangerous, and he had sternly and resolutely determined that no mortal woman should tempt him into matrimony.

His visit this morning, however, was, to a certain extent, a matter of necessity, and he felt that it would be cowardly on his part to shirk it.

Despite his natural nervousness, he shook hands cordially with Clarrie, bowed to Beatrice on being introduced to her, and then, turning to Mrs. Raynham, said:

"I want to ask a favour on behalf of our school-children."

"Yes," replied the lady coldly, expecting some demand upon her purse.

"I want you to give us permission to have games and tea in the Brent meadow by the side of the fir-copse."

"Oh, of cour.e mamma will do that," said Clarrie quickly. "When I come of age, Mr. Langdale, I mean to give a treat to all the boys and girls in the village."

HE LIFTED HER HAND GALLANTLY TO HIS LIPS AND KISSED IT.

But Mrs. Raynham did not answer.

In point of fact, she was nerving herself to say "No," when she caught the eye of Beatrice fixed upon her, with surprise—almost contempt—expressed in the look.

The glance annoyed her greatly, but it likewise made her a trifle ashamed of her own meanness, and she said with some hesitation:

"I am afraid I cannot spare sufficient servants to entertain so large a company."

"We don't expect anything of the kind; we only ask for the loan of the field," replied the rector, "and," with a courteous bow, "the presence of yourself and family."

"Then you are quite welcome to it," responded the lady.

And then she began to talk rapidly about something else, lest she should be asked to subscribe to the school feast.

They all saw through her tactics, and Beatrice, who was beginning to understand her aunt's character, was meditating how to make her loosen her purse-strings, when a second visitor arrived—no other than Mr. Frank Darlington.

He was soon informed of the object of the rector's visit, and at once offered his co-operation.

"Put me down in the subscription list for a couple of guineas," he said carelessly; "and I'll ask the governor to send over some fruit for the youngsters."

"And let me give the same amount," said Beatrice, producing her purse. "Are you going to double the subscription, auntie?"

"I? No; I have so many things to subscribe to," said the present mistress of the Court with a flushed face.

"Well, you'll give one guinea at least," said her niece coolly. "Have you your purse in your pocket, aunt, or shall I lend you a sovereign? It is best to give it at once, one is so apt to forget."

"Thank you, I have my purse," was the snappishly uttered reply.

And then, to the surprise of her daughters, who likened the operation to drawing blood from a stone,

Mrs. Raynham took out a sovereign and a shilling, and handed them to the rector.

"Upon my word, Fanny, Beatrice Burnham is a brick," remarked Geraldine some time later, as the sisters were discussing this scene; "the way in which she shamed mamma into producing her purse was splendid. I am beginning to hope that she will really manage to make a change here; goodness knows it isn't before it's needed."

"No; but she needn't try to make Frank Darlington fall in love with her," was the petulant reply.

"Frank Darlington will never fall in love with anybody but himself, my dear," was the decisive reply; "and if he marries any member of our family it will be Clarrie for the sake of her money."

"I don't believe it," gasped Fanny with a pale pained face.

"What is the matter with you, Fanny?" demanded her sister sternly. "Mr. Darlington hasn't been making love to you, has he?" she went on severely.

"Making love to me? what an idea! He regards me as a child."

"And you are a child," said Geraldine emphatically, looking down from her two years seniority upon her younger sister; "but you are such a fanciful child that I am always afraid of your getting some rubbish into your head.

"I am not more likely to get rubbish into my head than you are," retorted Fanny, gaining courage as her sister's suspicions became more vague; "but for all that I don't believe Frank Darlington is in love with Clarrie."

"You had better tell her so," was the scornful reply; "but if he is nothing to you, it is of no consequence to me with whom he is in love."

And so saying Miss Geraldine walked away.

Left to herself, Fanny Raynham clasped her hands upon her breast, and while an expression of mingled pain and rapture came over her youthful face, she murmured:

"Nothing to me ! He is all the world to me ! More than mother and sisters, more than life itself. He may think me a child, and say sweet things to me as to a child, but I have a woman's heart a woman's love, and I love him. I always shall love him."

It was terrible to see this girl, so young, so slender, such a child in appearance as well as in years, excited by such strong and over-mastering passion.

But Fanny had always given her mother trouble.

She had been sent to a ladies' school because she could not be managed at home, and she had been expelled from school after spending six months there with a vaguely-written report, which but thinly concealed the fact that she had been thwarted in her efforts to elope with the dancing-master.

This escapade had been carefully hidden by her mother, and even her elder sisters did not know the precise reason of her expulsion, and, to do Fanny justice, she had for the last six months settled down with something like contentment in her home.

In an evil hour for himself, and for her also, however, Frank Darlington had observed the admiring looks with which the girl regarded him, and more out of idle vanity than from any warmer feeling, he had taken her in his arms and kissed her.

He had not meant anything by the foolish action, and of premeditated wrong we must at this stage acquit him ; indeed the little episode had altogether passed out of his mind until Fanny met him again by apparent accident, and showed very plainly by her face and manner that she had not forgotten the stolen kiss.

But Frank Darlington had other game to bring down, and he could not afford to waste time upon this foolish little girl who threw herself so often in his way.

He was but a man, however, and a weak vain man, and though he regarded himself—in this case at least—as a model of virtue, he did yield to the temptation of saying pretty things to Miss Fanny, and treating her on the very few occasions when they were alone as a petted child.

That this conduct irritated the girl, even while it fascinated her, you may be quite sure, and her misfortune was that she had no healthy occupation for her mind, and nothing to distract her from this one absorbing subject.

The advent of Beatrice into the family circle might have had a beneficial effect upon foolish Fanny if the silly girl had not become suddenly jealous of the new comer.

"I saw his eyes follow her wherever she went," muttered Mrs. Raynham's fourth daughter when thinking of the morning visit; "and though Beatrice pretends to hate men, and to scoff at the idea of a husband, I shouldn't like to give her the chance of one, particularly if I wanted him myself."

Such were Fanny's thoughts, but those of her sister Claribel were not much more satisfactory.

"Frank never tried to kiss me, though I took him out into the conservatory to give him a chance," thought the little heiress gloomily; "and he didn't even squeeze my hand when he went away; he seemed to have something on his mind all the time, and I wonder what he meant by asking Beatrice so pointedly if she had heard from Mr. Godfrey Lascelles. Well, I am not jealous of Beatrice, at any rate. She says she wouldn't marry Frank if there wasn't another man in the world; and I —I half believe her. And I am quite sure he won't ask her while I am by."

Then Miss Claribel Burnham walked to the looking-glass and gazed at her own reflection therein, and derived so much satisfaction from the performance that by the time she turned away she had quite forgotten her lover's coldness.

"It's very provoking that Beatrice and I are obliged to wear mourning this hot weather," she muttered petulantly, "though it's worse for her than for me, because black suits my style better than it does hers; besides, I can wear white with black ribbons for the school-children's fête. I was almost afraid that mamma would say something against Beatrice attending it, because of her father's recent death, but she didn't. I suppose she thought that charity covered other things besides a multitude of sins."

She laughed lightly as her thoughts ran thus, then she looked through the window down the broad carriage-drive which terminated at the lodge, hidden by the intervening trees.

Suddenly, however, her face changed, a frown contracted her smooth brow, and she cried in a tone of vexation:

"Here come Captain Trevor and Mary. Whatever can they want to call for. All the neighbourhood seems to be turning out to visit us to-day?"

Then Miss Burnham loitered about the room, arranged the golden curls upon her low broad forehead, and after giving a touch or two to her dress, went downstairs to meet these not altogether welcome visitors.

CHAPTER IV.

"THERE'S NO FOOL LIKE AN OLD FOOL."

MARY TREVOR was talking eagerly with Beatrice Burnham when Claribel entered the drawing-room.

This girl, whose name has cropped up before as having won Frank Darlington's fickle fancy, was a short plump young woman of some two or three and twenty; her strongly marked features, that were of a slightly Jewish type, with a complexion which was brown and red, yet rich and dark as any painting by Rembrandt, and her large black voluptuous eyes, shaded by long lashes, recalled Byron's description of an Eastern beauty:

> "Her soul was full of passion
> And her eyes were full of sleep."

She was more than usually animated to-day, however, for she seemed to think that she had met a kindred spirit in Beatrice, and when Clarrie joined them she was saying:

"Then you will come and see me to-morrow, Miss Burnham, and play over that piece of music with me. I am so delighted to find that we have so many ideas and tastes in common. I am sure we shall be able to help each other in our efforts to do good to others. I think that every true woman should do something towards the improvement and elevation of her sex."

"But why confine your labours to your own sex?" here chimed in Geraldine. "Don't you think that the reprobate man—I beg your pardon, Captain Trevor—claims some of your sympathies? Now we had two men here before you called this afternoon who might both be improved by female influence. Couldn't you exert the powers of your mind upon Mr. Langdale and Frank Darlington before you practised upon the rustic village girls?"

Beatrice looked at Geraldine with a quick start of interrogation, then she noticed Mary Trevor's face, and saw that it flushed and changed from pale to red, while an expression of half-subdued pain and vexation came over it.

But the girl made no reply to Geraldine's remark, and Beatrice, to cover her confusion, said lightly :

"It did not strike me that the gentlemen you name were in particular need of instruction or sympathy, Geraldine; but I believe that charity should begin at home, and that the intellectual capacities of women have been disregarded quite long enough."

"Good Heavens, Beatrice!" here interposed Mrs. Raynham, with real or affected horror, "surely you do not advocate 'women's rights' as they are called, and all the ridiculous rubbish that is screamed from so many platforms."

"I shall not plead guilty to advocating rubbish," replied Beatrice calmly; "but I suppose women have rights as well as men."

"Then I hope you will keep such pernicious opinions to yourself, my dear," returned her aunt severely; "a woman's noblest sphere in life is to be a good daughter and a good wife, to attend to the duties of her household, and to leave all public matters to her husband."

"And suppose she hasn't a husband, aunt?" asked Beatrice mischievously.

"All nice girls get husbands," returned the lady emphatically.

"Dear me, then I am afraid I am not nice, for I feel sure I never shall get a husband," sighed Beatrice. "I wonder if singing for one would be of any use."

And before anyone could stop her, she had seated herself at the piano and began to sing the chorus of a very ancient ballad, the whole of which, in its original form, she was afraid might startle some of her listeners.

> "Oh, oh, oh for a husband!
>   This is still my song.
> I will have a husband, I'll have a husband,
>   Be he old or young!"

"Beatrice!" cried Mrs. Raynham in horrified tones.

"Sir Graham Grantly and Mr. Fortescue Grantly," announced a servant, throwing open the drawing-room door and ushering in the new visitors.

Beatrice wheeled round on the music-stool and laughed in spite of herself at the dismay of her aunt and cousins, and at her own momentary vexation.

Of course she would rather not have been caught like this, but it was as well to put a bold face on the matter, and it was with a world of mischief in her beautiful face that she acknowledged the introduction to the baronet and his nephew.

Sir Graham Grantly was a tall, stout, heavy-looking man of some fifty-nine or sixty years of age, with a large round face, grey hair, and sleepy fishy-looking eyes.

As Beatrice had been informed by Claribel, the baronet was a bachelor, and as she soon discovered for herself, he did not intend to remain unmarried much longer.

Indeed, Sir Graham wanted an heir to succeed to his brand new title and to the great fortune which he had amassed himself, and with more frankness than delicacy he had of late said so.

"That was a very lively song you were singing, Miss Burnham," he said, seating himself near our heroine, whose piquant beauty stirred into unusual activity the cold organ that he called his heart.

"Yes," she replied with a smile and a very good imitation of a sigh, "it is lively, but many girls would hesitate to sing it, for the sentiment unfortunately is so often true."

"You can scarcely judge of its truth in this neighbourhood," interposed Mrs. Raynham tartly. "Four days will not admit of much experience of the kind, do you think they will, Sir Graham?" bestowing a sweet smile upon her neighbour.

"No," assented the baronet, who never understood a jest, but took all things seriously. "No; four days cannot have afforded much experience, but statistics show us that there are in the United Kingdom thousands of women who never can have husbands, and this should teach those who are married——"

" To be grateful for the inestimable blessing that has fallen to their share," laughed Beatrice as she rose from the music-stool, and crossing the room to where Captain Trevor and Fortescue Grantly sat together talking, left the baronet and her aunt to continue their conversation without her.

" Your niece seems of a merry disposition," remarked Sir Graham Grantly as he followed the girl's graceful movements with admiring eyes.

" Yes, merry enough, but dreadfully undisciplined, Sir Graham," was the reply; " I tremble for the happiness of her husband if she ever has one, she is so capricious and self-willed, and she makes such startling observations, and does such impulsive things, scarcely like a gentlewoman, I must confess. But then, poor girl, she has never known a mother's love, a mother's care, or a mother's judicious counsel. When I look at my own dear girls, Sir Graham, and think what they might have become if I had not been spared to them, I feel that I cannot thank Heaven sufficiently on their behalf."

" No doubt, madam ; no doubt," was the unexpected answer. " Devilish fine girl," he muttered to himself, putting up his glasses to regard Beatrice more critically ; " would look well at the head of a man's table—would put some new blood into the race—yes, she'll do; she'll do. She sha'n't sing for a husband for nothing. Yes, my dear, you shall have your reward."

His words, though spoken in a low tone, were quite audible to Mrs. Raynham, and she bit her lip with ill-concealed vexation, for she had always looked upon Sir Graham Grantly as a prize for one of her own daughters.

She said nothing, however.

In point of fact she was afraid to trust her voice to speak, so harsh and discordant would it have sounded and it was not until her companion turned to her and asked :

" Is your niece a young lady of fortune ? " that she was able to reply with genuine enjoyment :

"No; she has something between five and six thousand pounds, I believe."

"Ah, hem! all the better; nice little sum for pocket-money, enough to keep a husband from thinking her extravagant. My dear Mrs. Raynham, you will do me the favour of coming to dine at the Park one day next week, with your charming family."

The lady accepted graciously.

She would not say that her niece could not be of the party, because of her recent bereavement, but all the same she meant to leave her at home.

But the conversation was here interrupted by little Ruth coming forward and asking Sir Graham if he would not come to the school-children's treat.

"No, thank you, my dear," was the reply; "I am not particularly fond of noisy boys and girls."

"But we sha'n't have anything to do with the boys and girls," said Ruth with an air of importance. "Mr. Grantly and Captain Trevor are going to arrange it; we mean to make a kind of picnic of it, and have some boats on the river, or go nutting and blackberrying in the wood.

"In that case we will think about it," returned the baronet with his grandest air; "for we mean to have some garden-parties for the young people, don't we, Mrs Raynham?"

Whereupon the lady bowed, and Ruth went off to tell her sisters that she believed Sir Graham Grantly meant to marry their mother.

When the mistress of the Court heard this idea laughingly expressed later in the day, she smiled bitterly, but made no verbal protest.

Had there been the least chance of such a consummation, she would have sent Beatrice Burnham off without an hour's delay.

But Mrs. Raynham was too much a woman of the world to let vanity or self-interest blind her to the cold reality of fact.

She knew, as well as the baronet himself, that when he married, he would marry a girl young enough to be his own grand-daughter.

He did not want a companion, or a wife, so much as he wanted an heir, for, though he professed to have a great regard for his nephew he always informed the young man that he did not intend him to succeed to his property.

This being the case, Mrs. Raynham put herself out of the question, but she certainly would have liked Sir Graham to have married either Grace or Geraldine.

Perhaps the scheming mother would have managed to get her niece out of the way for a time if she had regarded her as the only obstacle to the success of her plans.

But she knew that this was not the case.

As for Beatrice herself, unconscious and utterly careless of the conquest she had made, she talked away with some animation to Mr. Fortescue Grantly until he casually remarked that Godfrey Lascelles was an intimate friend of his.

"Dear me, you know my respected guardian, do you?" asked the girl in a mocking tone.

"Your guardian?" echoed Mr. Grantly in surprise; "then you are the young lady who has given him so much trouble?"

"Am I? I didn't know that any woman could give Godfrey Lascelles any trouble," replied Beatrice with flashing eyes, and a smile that was a very near approach to a sneer.

"Didn't you?" laughed Grantly; "but you forget that Lascelles is a professed woman-hater, and therefore it must have beem embarrassing to find himself constituted the guardian of a young lady."

"He made haste to shirk his responsibilities as quickly as he could," retorted the girl; "but tell me what you think of him, Mr. Grantly; isn't he usually considered among men to be something of a braggart?"

"A braggart! By Jove, no. He is one of the most modest of men."

"Ah, I don't like modest men. I'd as soon marry a pretty man as a modest man. I should expect to see him wearing my veils and hiding his blushes behind a fan," retorted Beatrice.

"You mistake me, Miss Burnham," said Grantly in a vexed tone; "I meant that he is modest with regard to his own merits."

"When he has any merit to boast of, I will endeavour to believe in his modesty, "laughed the girl.

"Evidently he is no favourite of yours," said young Grantly with a smile.

"No, thank Heaven! just as I am no favourite of his."

"What is he like?" asked Claribel, who felt some curiosity about the man whose very name seemed to have the effect of tempting her cousin to utter some disparaging remark.

"He is like other men, my dear," replied Beatrice. "There is nothing remarkable about him; is there, Mr. Grantly?"

"Except that he is very handsome," responded the young man.

"Handsome?" echoed Claribel, glancing at her cousin.

"Yes, and more than usually clever," continued the baronet's nephew with enthsiasm.

"And how old is he?" asked the little heiress, upon whose mind a suspicion was beginning to dawn.

"Oh, something under thirty," was the reply.

"Dear me, I should like to see him," said Clarrie with another keen glance at Beatrice.

"You will do that very soon, I hope, for he is coming down to my uncle's place for some shooting this autumn," replied Mr. Grantly with a glance at Godfrey Lascelles' ward.

But if he thought to learn anything from the expression of that young lady's face, he was very much mistaken.

She gave her head a disdainful toss with just a dash of defiance in the movement, and then turned to smile her sweetest smile upon Sir Graham Grantly, who had come to her side.

"It was very safe to talk to Sir Graham," she thought, "for no one could suppose that she wanted him to fall in love with her;" and so she rattled away,

charming the old man with her lively sallies, and con-
firming him in his sudden resolution to make her his
wife.

But Beatrice never suspected the trouble she was
making for herself, and it was with a very genuine start
of surprise that she opened wide her big eyes and looked
at the grey-haired baronet, when, thinking himself
unobserved, as he was about to go away he lifted her
hand gallantly to his lips and kissed it.

"Surely the old stupid did not think I seriously
meant the words of that ridiculous song," she said to
herself wonderingly as she watched his retreating
figure.

And then she broke into a peal of mocking laughter,
which would have sadly disconcerted Sir Graham
Grantly if he had heard it and had known that he was
the subject of her merriment.

CHAPTER V.

MARY TREVOR'S TROUBLE.

IT was a scorching hot day, and as Beatrice Burnham, clad in deep mourning, walked along the dusky lane which led to Captain Trevor's abode, she could not help wishing that she lived in some country where any colour but black was regarded as the symbol of woe.

Not a breath of wind stirred the sultry air, and the sun blazed down with almost tropical fervour.

The kine stood udder deep in the cool water of the river, and the sheep lay patiently panting under the welcome shade of the trees.

Not a labourer was to be seen; a stillness that was almost oppressive lay upon the land; and our heroine experienced the strange sensation of feeling that she was the only living creature who had resolution enough to brave the fierce sun and move about as at ordinary times.

Yet even she had some doubt as to the wisdom of her proceedings, and just as she came in sight of Woodbine Villa, in which the Trevors lived, she half panted.

"I do think I am a fool for my pains in coming this afternoon; Mary will be knocked up by the heat, and she won't in the least expect me. Clarrie was more sensible than I when she suggested that I should send a note of excuse by a servant, though my private opinion is that no servant would have got as far as Woodbine Villa so soon after his midday dinner, but would have lazily gone to sleep under one of those trees, and small blame to him if he did; I feel very much inclined to do the same myself. But I am nearly at my destination, and I certainly won't walk back till the sun has gone down."

So saying, she had almost reached the garden-gate, when she paused, started violently, and uttered a low exclamation of surprise.

On the impulse of the moment, without really thinking of what she was about, Beatrice stepped back a pace or two, half-hiding herself in the deep bend of a hedge of hazel bushes.

Had she been dressed in any light colour she must have been observed, but her black dress was by no means likely to attract attention, and the man whose appearance had so startled her, after one hasty glance around, turned sharply away to the left as she was approaching the house from the right, and so did not pass her hiding-place, or perceive her proximity.

"How absurd of me! whatever made me hide myself in this ridiculous manner?" she exclaimed a few seconds later. "What is Mr. Frank Darlington to me, and what am I to him, that I should shrink away as though afraid to meet him?"

She did not answer the question though she had asked it, and there was certainly nobody else able to do so.

Indeed, she rather hastened her pace, and her hand was on the latch of the garden-gate leading to the villa, when another idea flashed across her mind.

"Somebody told me the other day," she muttered, "that the Darlingtons didn't notice the Trevors; and then, again, somebody said that Frank had been fascinated by Mary's black eyes. It is rather odd, but certainly the first story can't be true; on consideration, therefore, I won't mention having seen him, unless Mary makes some remark as to his having called. And, now I think of it, he didn't look amiable, or as though his visit had been a pleasant one."

By this time she was walking up the flower-bordered path towards the house.

The same glare of noontide heat lay upon the garden, but the house itself looked cool, shaded, and inviting, and the sound of falling water, which Beatrice knew came from a small fountain, added greatly to the sense of rest as well as to the beauty of the small and well-kept grounds.

Woodbine Villa, with the flower-gardens in which it stood, and the two fields adjoining, belonged to Captain John Trevor, who, having retired from the army upon half-pay when about five-and-forty years of age, had vegetated in this place ever since.

It happened sometimes, indeed, that the still vigorous-looking captain would weary of the calm pleasures and decidedly tame amusements of Barkham-on-Brent, and on such occasions he would pack up a small valise, start for London, and put up at a well-known bachelor's hotel but a few steps out of Piccadilly.

What Captain Trevor did with himself when thus at large his daughter did not know and never thought of asking.

From her view of life, the ways of men were strange ways, and it was useless for a girl to try to understand them.

So she gave up the puzzle as one really not worth trying to solve, and she lived among her birds and her flowers, her books and her music, indulging in some strange and fanciful theories as to the rights and duties of her sex, and which, happily for the well-being of those whom she might have influenced, she had not hitherto tried to put into practice.

Meeting what she believed to be a kindred spirit in Beatrice Burnham, however, had revivified some of Mary's pet hobbies, and the two girls seemed drawn together by a feeling of mutual attraction and sympathy which neither tried to resist.

In consequence of this sudden friendship, though Beatrice had known her new friend but a little more than a week, she had already been to the villa several times and felt perfectly at home in the place.

The wire of the bell which she pulled at the front door was broken, and consequently no servant came in answer to her summons, but one of the French windows which led into the drawing-room was slightly ajar, and Beatrice espied it.

Having no doubt as to her welcome, believing, indeed, that she was expected, Beatrice without the least hesitation pushed further open the glass door and walked boldly into the room.

There was no occupant in the drawing-room itself, but in a tiny room which was little bigger than an alcove that led out of it, and which commanded a view of an entrance to the garden at the back of the house, Beatrice thought she distinctly heard the sound of sobbing.

To think and to act were usually simultaneous with our impulsive heroine, and without pausing to consider that the person in trouble might be a stranger to herself, or that her unsolicited sympathy might be unwelcome, she quickly pushed aside the curtain which separated the alcove from the rest of the drawing-room, and to her intense surprise discovered Mary Trevor lying extended upon a couch, her face buried in a soft cushion, while she seemed to be sobbing and weeping in a manner, not loud and violent enough to be termed hysterical, but with an intensity that suggested the most heart-breaking grief.

"Mary!" cried Beatrice, in surprised and pained dismay, "what can have happened? Is your father ill, or perhaps dead?"

The girl thus addressed lifted her head and looked at her questioner for an instant with surprise and anger depicted upon her tear-stained face.

But as soon as she recognised her, the anger was succeeded by an expression that seemed almost like humiliation, and then, overcome by a variety of feelings, the wretched girl once more buried her face in the pillow and sobbed again with fresh violence.

"Mary, Mary, don't give way to your grief like this, whatever the cause may be," expostulated Beatrice, grasping her friend's shoulder. "Tell me what has happened," she went on persuasively; "perhaps I can help to relieve you, or I may be able to suggest a cure, and, in any case, you can rely upon my warm sympathy. Tell me what troubles you, dear? What is it?"

She had by this time succeeded in making Mary Trevor rise from her recumbent position and sit on the couch upon which she had been lying.

But the little brunette's face was terribly tear-stained and swollen with her unusual indulgence in passionate grief, and, even if she had desired to do so, she could not at once have suppressed the sobs that shook her frame with such violence.

"What is the matter, dear? Do tell me; has anything happened to your father?" persisted Beatrice with affectionate sympathy. "It can be no slight thing that has agitated you in this manner," she went on, "and I must share your trouble and help you to bear it; indeed I must, dear. It is the test of true friendship that we share and help to carry each other's burdens. Come, tell me, it is about your father you are grieving, isn't it? Surely he has not been unkind to you?"

Mary Trevor had sat silent during this appeal, except for the gradually subsiding sobs.

But even while she wept, she hung her head and did not utter a word, while she idly or intentionally twisted a ring round on her finger, or drew it half off, then put it back again in the place where she wore it.

Beatrice did not know the secret connected with that ring, neither did many people in Barkham-on-Brent and Mary Trevor was passionately and with angry defiance in her heart meditating whether she should confide the secret to Beatrice, and with it the cause of her present agitation, when her companion's next words suggested a much safer explanation than the truth would have been.

As Beatrice did not entertain the remotest suspicion, that her friend had a lover, and, as she invariably attributed all the pain and misery that comes to a woman to the agency of man, she jumped to the somewhat illogical conclusion that, as Mary had no husband, brother, or lover, the one man who had caused her misery must be her father.

"You won't tell me that it is so, but I more than suspect that your father is going to marry a second wife and that this is the cause of your grief and anger. Tell me, Mary, is it so?"

How easy it would have been for Mary Trevor to have answered that her father's matrimonial arrangements did not trouble her, and then to have told the whole truth.

Easy enough, in all conscience; and could she have peeped into the future and seen one tithe of the suffering it would have saved her and others, she would have hastened to reveal the true cause of her misery.

But she did not.

The risk of revealing her secret was so great, or she thought it was, that when Beatrice put into her mouth, as it were, a subject upon which she had a true story to tell, she at once seized the pretext offered her, merely colouring her tale sufficiently to account for her grief.

"Yes," she said at last, as she wiped the tear-red eyes and ceased to play with her ring—"yes, papa is going to be married—married at his time of life, and to a woman who has had two husbands already. Don't you think there ought to be some law made to prevent old people from making such fools of themselves?"

Like most amateurs, Mary Trevor greatly over-acted her part; but Beatrice was far too inexperienced to perceive it, and, even had the suspicion of unnatural vehemence crossed her mind, she would have driven it away as mean and uncharitable in herself, since Mary's intensely hot and passionate disposition made her feel and think with more fire and fervour than is usually common with simple English maidens.

Beatrice was by no means of the same kind of temperament herself, but she always took a certain amount of pride in the fact that she could enter into the feelings of others; and even where her sympathies could not reach, her wide charity and spirit of toleration could make all possible allowance.

That this harmless conceit on her part often made her the dupe of the unprincipled and the designing you may take for granted, but hitherto such persons had only aimed at the contents of the young lady's purse, and this, thanks to her ample allowance, had not affected her seriously.

So now, when Mary asked the foregoing question, Beatrice could not help laughing ere she replied:

"On the same grounds, laws should be made to prevent young people likewise from making fools of themselves. But tell me, who is your father going to marry? and is it anything more than a false alarm?"

"Oh, it is real enough," replied Mary bitterly. "But do you really not know who is to be his wife?"

"No; I shouldn't have known that he was in danger of taking one but for a remark of Clarrie's the other day," replied our heroine. "My cousin seemed to think that he was intent upon marrying somebody, and that he would have no objection to her fair self; but I know that she isn't engaged to him."

"Of course not; she likes somebody else," with a suspicious sob. "No; it's her mother whom my father means to lead to the hymeneal altar."

"What! My aunt, Mrs. Raynham!" cried Beatrice in surprise. "Surely she is not going to do anything of the kind?"

"She is going to marry my father," replied Mary bitterly. They settled the last details yesterday, and he went up to London early this morning to make arrangements for the wedding. I am glad to say they will have the decency to be married as quietly as possible."

"This news and the change it will entail affects me almost as much as it does yourself," said Beatrice thoughtfully as she passed her hand over her forehead as though to enable her to realise the situation more clearly.

"And really, Mary," she continued with a smile, "I don't think it is a matter for you to break your heart over; you will probably be married yourself one day, and then it will be a source of satisfaction for you to know that your father will not be left lonely. We ought to think of our compensations in life as well as of our losses."

"It's all very well for you to talk like this," replied Mary in a tone of vexation, "but the change can't affect you as it will affect me. I have been mistress in my father's house for the last five years, ever since my mother died, and now I shall be regarded as a nonentity, or, worse still, as an intruder, and I—I can't bear it."

And she threw herself back upon the cushions giving way to another outburst of passionate grief and despair.

Beatrice looked at her companion in wonder, and with just a shade of contempt in her heart at the thought that so much emotional grief should be indulged in for what was without disguise a purely selfish consideration.

Of course a step-mother was objectionable, particularly in theory, but when the individuals in this case were considered, it could not but be admitted that Mrs. Raynham and her daughters would lose quite as much as Captain Trevor and Mary by the proposed union.

Besides, after all, Beatrice reflected, her aunt, though cold and proud and unsympathetic, was neither unkind nor unjust, and Mary ought under the circumstances to have been glad that, since her father was determined to marry, his choice of a second wife had been made so well.

Much of this she tried to say to Mary with a view of soothing her, till at last she appeared to succeed, and the excitable girl became calm and seemingly more reasonable.

Then Beatrice heard that the projected marriage was to take place in the course of a fortnight or three weeks, and that when the happy couple had gone away together on a short honeymoon they were to return to Burnham Court and make that their home until Clarrie came of age.

" And after that time ? " asked Beatrice.

"After that—the deluge, my dear," returned Mary with a little laugh.

She had cleared her face from tears and frowns by this time, and seemed inclined to take a more cheerful and even a comic view of the situation.

" Well, there is plenty of time to consider what shall be done a year hence," said Beatrice slowly; " and for my own part I am not sorry to hear of the marriage. Of course you will come and live at the Court, and my aunt's income added to your father's will enable you to live in a larger house than this, and probably to go abroad, as I have often heard you express a desire to do. I have heard Geraldine say that it was her mother's intention to take the girls abroad when Clarrie became mistress, and you will like that, Mary."

"Yes," replied Miss Trevor slowly; "I suppose I took the gloomiest view of the case."

"Yes, but I wouldn't take the same view before my aunt, or even in speaking to your father about it, if I were you," suggested Beatrice; "so much of your comfort must naturally depend upon the way in which you behave at first; both of them will naturally wish to please and conciliate you, and they will no doubt make many concessions for the sake of amiability on your part."

"Yes," assented Mary; "I suppose they will."

But she hung her head and thought with bitter self-contempt what a despicable hypocrite she was, for, instead of expressing anger to her father when he told her of his intended marriage, she had after a momentary hesitation told him that she hoped he would be happy.

And now, but a few hours after she had said these loving words, she was telling her story in a manner which made it wear a false complexion to the girl whom she professed to love as a friend, but whom she dared not make her confidant.

Before the two girls parted that evening, however, Mary seemed to have recovered her usual cheerfulness, and it was agreed between them that Beatrice should say nothing about what Mary had told her, unless her aunt or one of her cousins first spoke of it, and then she should express her pleasure at the news, and intimate that Mary was equally well satisfied.

She had scarcely entered the entrance hall of Burnham Court, however, before Geraldine Raynham came rushing towards her like a small gale of wind, exclaiming:

"Oh, Beatrice, something dreadful has happened; I suppose you have not heard of it."

"Oh, yes, I have," replied Beatrice, with a smile, "but I don't think it is very dreadful; of course your mother has a right to marry again if she likes to do so."

"Marry!" repeated Geraldine, looking at her companion in dazed surprise.

"Yes; marry Captain Trevor, I mean," was the answer.

"Oh, yes, I see," returned Geraldine, slowly; "that is all you have heard, and, now I remember, mamma told us about her intended marriage just after you went away this afternoon; but that isn't all. About an hour ago a telegram came from a station-master at some small place between this and London. Captain Trevor had met with an accident, and this was the only address they found in his pocket. The telegram says he is seriously injured, and his friends must come to him without delay, so mamma is gone, and she left word that some of us were to break the news to Mary; but who is to do it?"

"I must," said Beatrice, resolutely, and she was turning round to retrace her steps to Woodbine Villa, when Geraldine called her back with the remark:

"Wait a minute and I'll give you the telegram to take with you."

When, however, they came to look for the paper which had caused so much consternation in the household, it could not be found; Mrs. Raynham had undoubtedly taken it with her.

"Never mind, give me the name of the place where the accident occurred," said Beatrice, impatiently.

But this was more than the girls could do. One thought it was one place, another declared the name to be thoroughly different, till Geraldine, whose head was the clearest of the whole party, suggested that nothing would be easier than to find out the place from the post-office where the telegram had been first received.

"Then pray send and get it at once," said Beatrice, anxiously; "meanwhile I will go and break the news to Mary."

"WHAT DO YOU MEAN BY COMING HERE, SPYING UPON ME AT THIS TIME OF THE NIGHT?"

No. 3.

CHAPTER VI.

ALMOST CAUGHT.

HEN Beatrice, for the second time that day, entered the front garden of Woodbine Villa, a distant clock was just striking ten.

This hour seemed comparatively early to the town-bred girl, but she knew that it was considered bed-time by most of the people in this part of the world.

"I hope Mary won't be gone to bed," she thought, as she came up close to the house. "I want to break the news to her gently, and prepare her to meet the trial with calmness and fortitude if she can."

So thinking, she looked about her, and observed that the door-like window through which she had made her entry earlier in the day was still a little open.

Still, I say; but she remembered afterwards with alarming distinctness, when the seemingly trivial circumstance had assumed a terrible significance, that this French window had been securely bolted on the inside before she came away.

There it was, unfastened now, however, and she went over and opened it still wider.

The drawing-room itself was empty of all but furniture, and it was also in darkness.

But Beatrice noticed that a faint glimmer of light, as from a shaded lamp, came from between the heavy curtains of the *portière*, and she at once jumped to the conclusion that Mary was in the alcove probably reading, or dozing, while she waited for her father.

"Poor girl," she thought, with a sigh; "she little dreams of what is in store for her."

Then she stepped into the drawing-room, and was about to announce her presence by calling her friend by name so as not to frighten her, when she distinctly heard voices from behind the curtain—the voices of a man and of a woman.

Both seemed familiar to her; one was that of her friend, Mary, and to whom the man's voice belonged did not matter.

Beatrice's one thought was of the dreadful news of which she was the bearer.

She had no desire to pry into her friend's secrets, supposing she had any; indeed, the bare idea of such a thing never crossed our heroine's mind, her one single desire being to save Mary as much pain and anxiety as was possible under the circumstances.

"Mary!" she called, in a low tone.

The low murmur of voices from behind the curtain suddenly lulled, as though the speakers were listening.

"Mary!" repeated Beatrice, more loudly and more distinctly. "Mary, I want you. It is I, Beatrice Burnham."

Suddenly, as she commenced the second call, the curtains were divided and drawn aside by a man's hands.

The figure of a man, tall, but only seen in vague outline, was visible to her, but the light, such as it was, shone behind him, and she could not see his face though he could vaguely distinguish hers.

Had there been any doubt on his mind as to her identity, her words, "It is I, Beatrice Burnham," would have dissipated it, and the next instant he had dropped the curtains, leaving her in darkness, while the sound of a glass door being sharply opened and slammed with such violence that one of the panes of glass was broken, fell upon her ear.

Beatrice stood motionless, dumbfounded, unwilling to credit the evidence of her senses; but with all the charity and allowance for others of which she had felt so proud, she could not close her eyes to the fact that there was something radically wrong here.

Mary's father was away, on that point there could be no doubt, and this tall man could not be a straightforward and honourable suitor for her friend's hand, or he would never have run away in this dastardly manner to hide himself.

Her friend! The very word seemed to give Beatrice Burnham a stab of pain.

Could she call the woman her friend who was palpably carrying on a secret intrigue, and who was receiving her lover in her father's absence, while that father was lying injured, and perhaps at death's door, longing for the presence of his daughter.

Bitterly enough did these thoughts flash through our heroine's mind, and she would without a word have turned and left the house, had the message she had come to deliver been less urgent.

She was still standing in the middle of the room, pale and irresolute, thinking it would be best to go round to the front door, rouse the servant, and state the reason of this second visit, leaving her to repeat it to her mistress, when the curtains were again drawn aside, but this time by no masculine hand, and Mary Trevor stood before her unwelcome visitor.

Her face was pale, her big black eyes blazed and scintillated with fury, and her form shook with angry passion like a tree agitated by a strong wind.

She had thrown off the shade from the lamp, and its full glare of light now fell upon the faces of the two girls, so unlike each other in form and feature, in height, in character, and temperament, that they had little or nothing in common except the sympathy of attraction that had suddenly made them friends.

But it was rather as enemies than as friends that they now met.

"What do you mean by coming here, spying upon me at this time of the night?" demanded Mary Trevor, passionately. "Who gave you the right, I say, to watch my actions and mount guard over me?"

For a second or two Beatrice did not reply, this bold defiant attitude so completely surprised her.

Spy upon her friend in whom she had believed so firmly and so implicity!

But there, it was only another illusion dispelled, and one lives through so many illusions in one's lifetime that even at the age of twenty most men and most women have felt the humiliating consciousness of having fashioned unto themselves an idol out of very common clay.

To answer Mary Trevor in the same strain and in her present mood was clearly beneath Beatrice Burnham's dignity.

Besides, the girl had assumed a position that for the moment at least was clearly unassailable. Beatrice had no right to spy upon her, and it was scarcely an excusable proceeding to come into the house through an open window instead of knocking or ringing at the house door and being announced in the ordinary manner.

Of course Beatrice might have explained that she thought the servant was in bed, that she found the window open, and that her errand was so urgent, and her confidence in Mary so implicit, that all other considerations had been forgotten or unthought of by her.

But Beatrice was too much astonished by what she had seen, and by all that this secrecy and bravado implied, to utter one word in self-defence.

She forgot for the moment her desire to save this girl from the shock of hearing of her father's accident in an abrupt manner, and she no longer thought of offering to accompany the daughter to her father's side, and she now said coldly, but with cutting distinctness and severity:

"I came to tell you, Miss Trevor, that your father, on his way back from London late this afternoon, met with a serious accident; something happened to the train in which he was travelling, and as my aunt's name and address only was found in his pockets, the people who found him naturally sent to her. She started off to him at once, being just in time to catch a train. That is the name of the place where the accident occurred," and so saying she laid a slip of paper upon a table.

Then, without another word, she turned and walked out of the house by the way she had entered it.

It is impossible to describe her feelings as she walked down through the garden and turned into the road which led to Burnham Court.

She had left her cousins with the announcement that she should travel to Wallbridge, where the accident occurred, with Mary Trevor, and with this intention she had brought a small hand-bag with her filled with trifling necessaries, and had declined the escort of a servant, being well aware that as her aunt had taken one away with her, there was not too many left in the large house to do the necessary work.

So she had waited till the messenger had come back from the post-office and had then started off in a somewhat independent manner, resolved to save Mary as much pain and fatigue and anxiety as possible.

And this was the result, this the reward for all her pains.

She hung her head sadly as she turned away from the garden gate, and she thought in her bitterness of soul that she would never believe in woman or man again.

Not a dozen steps up the road had she proceeded, however, before a small figure came running after her, panting from want of breath and from intense excitement.

"Beatrice, don't judge me harshly. I have done no wrong. You and all the world will know one day that I am pure as you are yourself. Forgive my hasty words; pity my sufferings; and oh, do believe in me just a little longer?"

"I have not judged you—at least, I have tried not to do so," replied Beatrice, with more coldness in her tone and manner than she was herself conscious of; "and you may rest satisfied that I shall be silent as to what I have seen to-night."

"It is not your silence, it is your regard and your good opinion of me that I care for," sobbed Mary, almost hysterically.

"That is yours, if you deserve it," was the chilling reply, though the speaker meant only to be strictly just.

And then, as Mary Trevor threw her arms round her neck and kissed her, though Beatrice did not repel the caress, she did not respond to it.

Few women under the same circumstances but would have acted as she did; many, indeed, would have been harsher; but for all the days of her life Beatrice Burnham will regret that she did not take the unhappy girl to her heart, return with her to the house, and remain with her until they could start together to go to Captain Trevor as she had intended.

So Beatrice walked back to Burnham Court, pained at what had happened, and in no way inclined to doubt the evidence of her senses by Mary's assertion of her innocence, and Mary was left dispirited and almost heart-broken.

What explanation Beatrice gave to her cousins for her unexpected return she scarcely knew.

They told her afterwards that she first said, in answer to their questions, that Mary was not going to her father, and then that she was; but one point she was consistent upon—she was not going herself.

The girls wondered at their cousin's *distrait* manner and at her laconic answers, but they were not greatly interested in the Trevors.

Their mother's contemplated marriage was considered objectionable by everyone of them, and though the news of Captain Trevor's accident, coming so closely upon their mother's communication, had to a certain extent silenced their opposition, it had in no way removed it.

I am afraid that in their hearts they hoped the report of his danger was not exaggerated, and whether or not his daughter went to help to nurse him was a matter of supreme indifference to themselves.

So they went to bed, some of them devoutly praying that they might be spared the infliction of a stepfather.

Breakfast was just over the next morning, when the old woman who was the Trevors' only servant came up to Burnham Court and asked to see Beatrice.

"I want to know if you can tell me what's become of Miss Mary, if you please, miss," said the old woman, respectfully. "I've heard something about the Cap'n having had an accident, and the woman at the lodge told me as how you'd come down our way a second time yesterday, and Miss Mary's gone and not said so much as a word as to when she's coming back."

"Probably she didn't know when she would be back. Of course she has gone to help my aunt to nurse your master. But what time did she start, Susan?"

"That's just what I want to know, miss."

"It is what I certainly cannot tell you," said the girl, with a slight smile. "I came to your master's house about ten o'clock. I told Miss Trevor what had happened, and I came away without having stayed more than ten minutes. But you will hear from your mistress in the course of the day."

"I'm sure I hope I shall, miss," was the dissatisfied observation, as old Susan left the room.

She did not hear from Miss Mary, however, neither did any of the inmates of the Court; but two days after the railway accident Mrs. Raynham came home, bringing her future husband with her.

The Captain's injuries had been greatly magnified, and the doctor reported him to be quite out of danger.

When asked where Mary was, there was no little surprise and displeasure expressed, but this was quickly followed by alarm and anxiety, for Mary Trevor had not gone to her father or even written to him.

Where could she have gone?

What could have become of her?

Such were the questions asked on all sides; but there was no one to answer them.

CHAPTER VII.

HE irritation that was in Captain Trevor's heart with regard to his daughter at her seeming indifference to his condition after the railway accident, gave place to anxiety when it was discovered that she had left home the very night upon which she had received the news from Beatrice Burnham.

"Of course she started off to come to me at once," said the troubled father, turning to his prospective wife for sympathy.

"So I suppose," assented Mrs. Raynham; "but why didn't she call Susan and make her help to get ready and go with her. It seems such a strange thing for a young lady like Mary to travel alone, particularly when she could take a servant with her."

"What strikes me as most peculiar," here interposed Geraldine, "is the fact that Beatrice left her home about ten minutes past ten in the evening, and the mail train to London does not pass our nearest railway-station till about half-past twelve; the consequence is that Mary had about two hours and a half in which to prepare for her journey, and yet, according to old Susan, she took nothing with her—absolutely nothing—but her hat and ulster."

Beatrice said never a word until her silence was remarked by the others, and Clarrie, who was singularly apt to ask inconvenient questions, enquired:

"What did Mary say to you, Beatie? It must have been something unpleasant, or you wouldn't have returned in the state of mind you did."

"Did I return in a 'state of mind?'" was the evasive answer.

"You know you did," was the retort. "You left here, saying you meant to go to join the mother with

Mary, and you even packed a few things in a bag which you carried with you, but you soon came back again. What made you change your mind so suddenly ? "

"Mary didn't want me," replied Beatrice, reluctantly.

"Did she tell you so?" questioned Geraldine, sharply.

"Yes," was the slowly-uttered rejoinder; "she said something to that effect, so I gave her the address at which to find her father, and came away."

Something in the girl's tone, rather than in her words, though they were vague and mysterious enough, made the rest of the party look up with eager curiosity, but Captain Trevor asked no question at the moment, and the others scarcely dared to do so.

One by one, however, they slipped out of the room, until the anxious parent and our heroine were left alone.

Then he spoke.

"Miss Burnham," he said, earnestly, "you know or suspect more about my daughter's movements than you have told us. Do you think it fair to her or to me to be so reticent ? "

Still Beatrice remained silent.

"Miss Burnham, will you not answer my question ?" said Captain Trevor, still more earnestly.

"What I can tell you is so vague and suggests so many unpleasant possibilities that I have hesitated to speak," said Beatrice; "but I will tell you what occurred the last day I saw your daughter."

Then she described her first visit to Woodbine Villa in the afternoon, not forgetting to mention the circumstance of having seen Mr. Frank Darlington leave the villa garden.

"Oh, he probably called to see me," said the Captain impatiently.

"So I supposed," was the answer, "for Mary never mentioned his name, and I forgot immediately afterwards that I had seen him."

Then she continued her narrative.

But Captain Trevor's brow darkened when he heard that his daughter attributed her violent grief to pain at and disapproval of his approaching marriage.

"False, false!" he muttered under his breath. "She told me she was glad of it."

But Beatrice scarcely heeded him.

She had a plain unvarnished tale to tell, and she told it.

In the fewest possible words, she described her second visit to the villa; how she had found the drawing-room window again ajar; how she had entered, and what she had seen. Then she told of Mary's anger, and subsequent passionate repentance and entreaty that her friend would still believe in her.

"I should never have breathed a word of this to you or to anyone," our heroine continued, "but for Mary's mysterious disappearance; but it may give you a clue wherewith to find her, and to ascertain if she is safe and happy."

"A clue! What clue?" demanded the father in a bewildered tone.

"Probably you can think of someone with whom Mary may have gone away to be married," suggested Beatrice.

But Captain Trevor shook his head. He did not know that his daughter had a single suitor.

The girl was about to make another suggestion, when, glancing through the window, she saw the man whose name was trembling upon her lips, walking by the side of her cousin Clarrie upon the grassy lawn, and looking down upon her golden head, her flower-like face, and *petite* figure with evident admiration and pleasure.

Seeing Frank Darlington thus engaged made Beatrice shrink from expressing the thought that had been growing in her mind since it was known that Mary Trevor was missing.

But the Captain, observing her involuntary start of surprise, followed her glance, and saw the man of whom she had meant to speak, and, turning away, said dejectedly:

"No; Mr. Darlington could have had nothing to do with Mary's absence from home. I am quite convinced he knows nothing about her. If he did he would not be here."

Beatrice was inclined to think so too, for of course the girl would not be foolish enough to go away alone if she went at the instigation of a lover.

But as this explanation of her sometime friend's strange disappearance was set aside, she felt more bewildered than before, for she had built up the theory in her own mind that the man she had seen in the darkened drawing-room was Frank Darlington, and that he and Mary Trevor had subsequently eloped together.

Soon after they had seen him in the garden with Clarrie, Mr. Darlington came into the house to see Captain Trevor, and to congratulate him upon his accident not being of so serious a nature as was at first reported.

The Captain seemed pleased with the attention, but Beatrice received the visitor coldly, and he was conscious that she watched the expression of his countenance with unpleasant scrutiny.

"You called at my house the day I came to grief, didn't you?" asked Captain Trevor after a time.

"I—I called one day, I know," replied the young man in a hesitating tone, while he passed his hand over his eyes, as though to collect his thoughts; but the suspicion flashed upon Beatrice that it was to hide his confusion.

"It must have been that day," persisted the Captain, "because Miss Burnham saw you come out of the garden gate."

Darlington looked up and flashed a glance of angry question upon Beatrice. Then, before she could utter a word, he said:

"Yes, I remember I did call one day last week. The weather was scorchingly hot, and I suppose all your people were asleep, for though I knocked at the door several times, I could not make anybody hear me. But how is it I didn't see you, Miss Burnham, if you saw me?"

"Because you did not look in the direction from whence I was coming, I suppose," replied Beatrice coldly. "*I* found someone in the house."

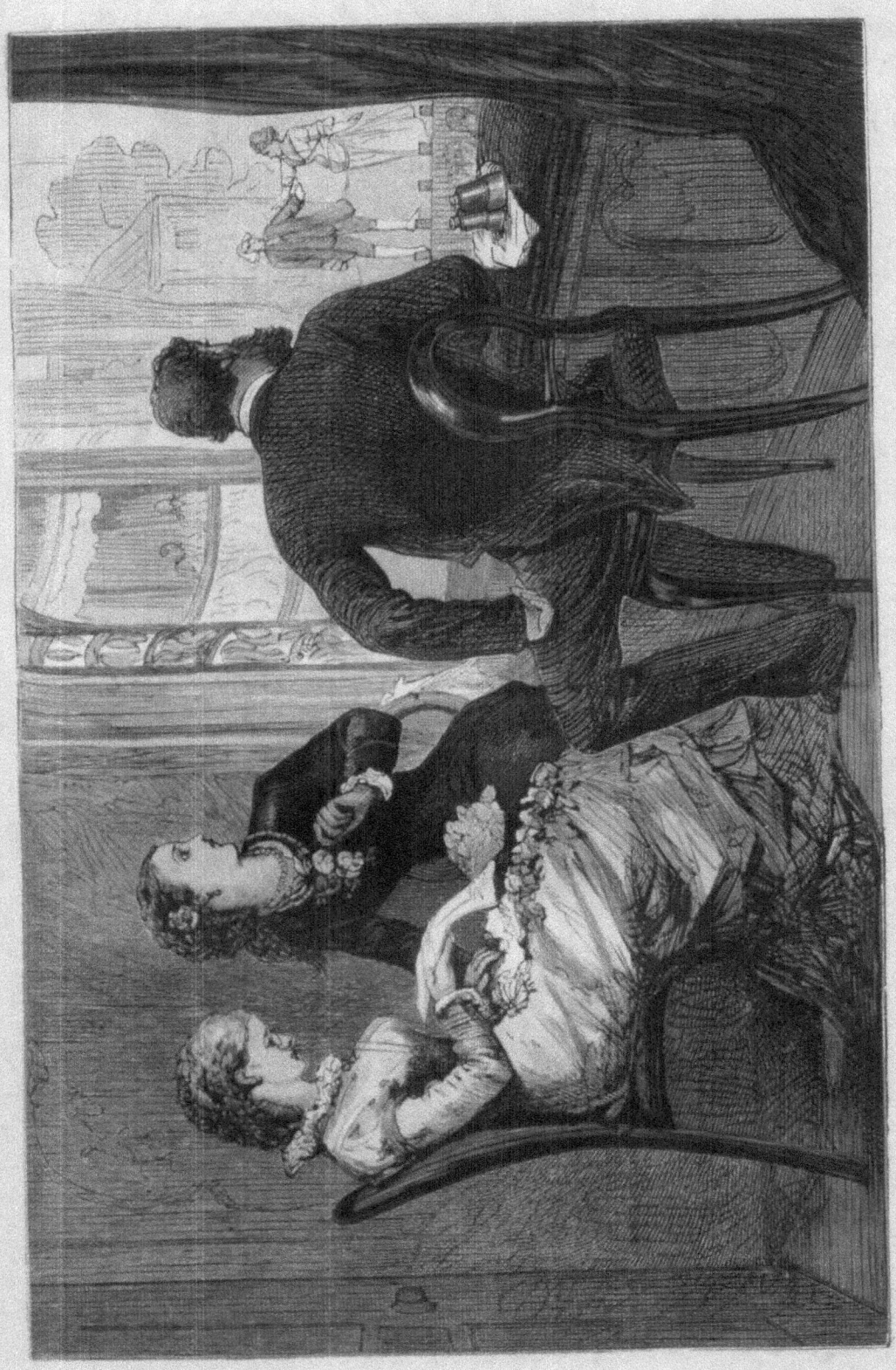

"MARY TREVOR!" WERE THE WORDS THAT ESCAPED HER LIPS.

"You were more fortunate than I," he retorted lightly. "And, by the way, when does the school fête come off?"

"I don't know," was the short abrupt reply.

"We are too anxious about my daughter to have thought or interest for anything else," here volunteered the Captain.

He was a weak man, almost effeminate in temperament, though soldierly enough in appearance. A man who never had a trouble or vexation but he must always go craving for sympathy in it from the first acquaintance he met. And now, when Beatrice would have been cautious and suspicious, and many men would have been reticent, lest Mary's reputation might unjustly suffer, he began to tell the story of his anxiety, not even forgetting to mention the mysterious lover of whom he had just heard.

Mr. Darlington, as might have been expected, expressed his extreme astonishment, but suggested at once that there could be little doubt that Miss Trevor was both well and happy. Of course it was a very imprudent thing to elope with a lover, but no doubt the happy pair were married and would come back and ask for forgiveness and Captain Trevor's blessing.

"But why didn't she leave a note behind when she went away? or why hasn't she written?" questioned the elder man fretfully.

"Who can find a reason for a woman's whims?" laughed Darlington in a manner that jarred upon his listeners.

No one attempted a retort.

Beatrice disdained to reply, and the re-entrance of Mrs. Raynham and her daughters Clarrie and Fanny gave a different turn to the conversation.

Our heroine, sitting a trifle apart from the rest of the company, could not help being interested by the contrast between the two half-sisters.

Clarrie, as we have already explained, was exceedingly pretty, with golden hair and violet-blue eyes, but Fanny, who lacked the delicacy and bright colouring of the heiress of Burnham Court, had dark-brown eyes, almost black in their passion and intensity, though her hair was light-coloured and dull as any of her sisters.

It was well known to Beatrice also that while Clarrie scarcely seemed to think of her undoubted beauty, Fanny, who was almost plain, was as full of vanity as a travelling balloon is full of gas, while, from many remarks which she had made on the appearance of others, it could readily be inferred that she considered herself the best-looking of the family.

Sitting and watching these two girls, while Frank Darlington went through the difficult task of talking to both of them, some glimmer of the true condition of affairs passed through our heroine's mind.

"If I were Aunt Raynham I should send Miss Fanny away from home for a time," was her mental conclusion; "she is just at the age when a girl is apt to make a fool of herself, and she is feeding that coxcomb's vanity to an alarming extent by her too evident admiration. I must interfere if only for the honour of my sex."

Then she said aloud:

"Clarrie, have you been able to tell Mr. Darlington when the school fête is to take place?"

"Yes, it is arranged for Tuesday next," was the answer.

"That will be delightful, particularly if the weather is fine," continued Beatrice, "but don't you think it would be nice to engage a fiddler or two, so that the boys and girls could have some real dancing instead of playing at kiss-in-the-ring and such boisterous games. A real country dance or two and Sir Roger de Coverly is in my opinion twenty times more amusing."

"I like to see them play at kiss-in-the-ring and enjoy themselves in their own way," here asserted Miss Fanny, who felt that it was her half-cousin's intention to ignore her and keep her out of the discussion.

"Do you. Then I pity your taste, my dear, was the irritating reply; "but what is your opinion, Mr. Darlington?"

"I quite agree with you," was the prompt answer; "a little music would be a great addition, and I will see about procuring it."

Whereupon Miss Fanny suddenly sprang to her feet, gave a little stamp upon the carpet, then walked to one of the windows.

None of her companions seemed to notice her annoyance, and some minutes later Darlington said with a repressed yawn:

"The day has been very hot, but it is getting cooler now; would you two like a pull on the river for an hour?"

"I should," cried Clarrie eagerly, turning to her cousin a glance of entreaty.

"So should I," assented Beatrice.

"Then will you put on your hats," said the young man; "I can manage to pull two of you easily."

Then he turned to talk to Captain Trevor, for Miss Fanny, hearing something about a small boating-party, had come back to his side hoping to be asked to join it.

Mr. Darlington had nothing further from his thoughts, however, than the idea of making love to Miss Fanny, particularly in the presence of others, and he resolved now, not for the first time, unfortunately, that he would not again be tempted into saying sweet foolish things to one who was after all a mere child.

So Fanny stood by with a swelling heart and burning cheeks, angry with the man she loved, and furiously jealous of Beatrice, whom she believed to be angling for Frank.

She would scarcely have entertained the same opinion had she seen Beatrice an hour afterwards as she sat in the stern of the boat by Clarrie's side, her eyes fixed dreamily on the sluggish river, or upon the green foliage on the river's banks, wandering off at times to the soft blue summer's sky, looking at anything but the man before her, who, despite his struggles to resist her influence and his efforts to dislike her, was slowly but surely becoming fascinated by her.

"She is poor," he thought a dozen times a day, "poor as a parson's daughter, and. I must have money with my wife, or I would marry her and make her love me in spite of herself."

Marrying Miss Beatrice Burnham, however, against her will would not have been an easy task, and Mr. Godfrey Lascelles, if he had had Darlington's interests at heart, would very soon have told him so.

As it was, however, the young man plied his sculls lazily, the soft languor of the summer evening influencing even him, and as he slowly propelled the boat along with its living burden, and watched the changing faces of the two girls seated opposite to him, he felt with a man's egotism that the choice between them remained with him.

One represented wealth and influence, the other love and domestic happiness.

And as he thus mused, a fiendish thought came into his mind, a thought which, if the girls could have read it, would have shown how utterly and completely regardless of the feelings of others he was when his own interests and inclinations were concerned.

As he thus rowed along with the two girls who had for the time trusted themselves to his care, he suddenly remembered that Burnham Court would belong to Beatrice if Clarrie were dead, and that in winning her under these circumstances he would be possessing himself of wealth as well as gratifying his love.

Only to a man whose practice and principle in life was the consideration of self could such a vile plan as now framed itself in his mind have been possible.

He looked at Clarrie Burnham, with the love-light in her eyes, with the sun shining on the rich ripples of her golden hair, and with her soft sweet face that looked more like that of a child than of a grown-up woman.

Then his eyes rested upon Beatrice, and the fascination of her darker and more picturesque beauty fired his selfish soul.

His decision was made.

It was a risk, of course, a risk even to himself, but people who play for high stakes must stand to lose something when they hope to win much.

Besides—but his reflections went no further in this direction.

He knew the part of the river upon which he was rowing well.

The stream just here was deep, there were several dangerous holes about, and the weeds on either bank were thick and tangled.

Still, a good swimmer might save himself and one other if thrown suddenly into the water, and Frank Darlington knew that he was a very good swimmer indeed.

"But I couldn't save two frightened women," he thought grimly; "particularly if I didn't try."

At this moment Beatrice cried in alarm:

"Take care, Mr. Darlington, you'll have us over."

He started, seemed to be flurried, dipped one of his oars too deeply, caught it in the thick weeds that made this place so dangerous, and the next instant the occupants of the little boat were struggling in the water.

Clarrie shrieked wildly, crying:

"Frank, Frank, save me!"

And she caught hold of one of the sculls and tried to keep her head above the dreadful water.

But Frank paid no heed to the woman who hoped to be his wife; it was Beatrice whose side he struck out for, and whom he tried to save.

"Look after Clarrie—I can swim," were the words that fell upon his astonished ears.

And even as he hesitated to obey the injunction, the splash of oars and the sound of voices sounded upon the air, and the next moment a boat rowed by two pairs of strong arms turned the sharp bend of the river, and Frank Darlington knew that his devilish trick must fail.

Then, and not till then, he swam to Clarrie's side. If he could not kill her this time he might as well take the credit of saving her.

CHAPTER VIII.

A NEW SUSPICION.

WO men who had so opportunely arrived upon the spot which a very few minutes later would have been the scene of a tragedy, first of all helped Beatrice to the river's bank, and then while one of them remained with her to assist her out of the water, the other returned to the assistance of Frank Darlington and the now insensible Clarrie.

To get the latter into the light narrow boat was no easy matter, but the task was at length accomplished, and the whole party were soon safely on *terra firma.*

It was not until Beatrice saw that her cousin was safe and in a fair way towards recovery that the familiarity of the voices of those who had come to their rescue struck her, and she looked at their faces, and recognised, though scarcely with surprise, Godfrey Lascelles and Mr. Fortescue Grantly.

"I thought I knew your voice," she said, addressing her guardian, who had remained on the bank with her while his companion had returned to help the others. "What a pity you came so soon; a few minutes more and you might have been relieved of the burden my father imposed upon you, for though I can swim in deep water my feet and dress got entangled in those weeds, and I should never have reached this spot unaided."

"Then I ought to be thankful that we were in time to save you," replied Godfrey gravely.

"Perhaps it is well to be thankful for small mercies," retorted Beatrice; "but do let us get my cousin home. I am afraid the shock and fright may seriously injure her. How does she seem, Mr. Grantly?"

As she asked this question she turned to the baronet's nephew, who was assiduously attending to the young heiress.

"She is coming round," was the reply; "but I quite agree with you, the sooner we get her back to the Court the better. I can't imagine how the accident happened."

"Oh, I can," retorted the young lady. "Mr. Darlington seemed as though he thought we wanted a bath, and so upset us on purpose. You didn't see a ghost at the moment, did you, Mr. Darlington?"

"A ghost!" repeated the young man, his face becoming deathly pale at the suggestion.

"Yes; the ghost of a young woman with big burning eyes and flowing black hair. Such a one, I am told, haunts the wood opposite; but see, Clarrie is conscious. Let us get her into a boat and take her home, her mother will be frantic with anxiety."

And she knelt down by her cousin's side, and tried to cheer and soothe her.

But Clarrie had only eyes for her treacherous lover, and only felt confidence and assurance of safety when he was by her side and held her hand in his own.

Seeing which, Grantly and Lascelles returned to their own boat in order to secure the one which had been upset, but had been prevented from drifting far away by some tall rushes which arrested its course.

The boat and sculls were soon recovered, though the cushions were irretrievably lost, and then the question arose as to the manner in which they should divide the party.

"One of you gentlemen had better come in the large boat with us," said Beatrice decisively. "We cannot rely again upon Mr. Darlington's nerves, and if the other will keep near us in the other boat we cannot very well come to grief a second time."

A suggestion that was at once carried out, and Frank Darlington, though he winced under the cutting words from the young lady's tongue, made no retort and offered no protest.

If Clarrie had reproached him, he would have felt that he deserved all she could say; but to be stung by the woman for whose sake and to win whom he had been ready to commit murder, seemed a refinement of punishment, while Godfrey Lascelles' presence in the boat did not add to his comfort.

But few words were uttered on their way back to Burnham Court.

Clarrie was too frightened and exhausted to do more than lean her head upon her cousin's shoulder, her eyes but half-open and her cheeks wan and colourless.

Fortunately the evening was so warm that the drenching the girls had sustained was not likely to injure them, particularly as Grantly and Lascelles had taken off their dry coats and wrapped them round the girls' shoulders.

As for Beatrice, she looked as calm and collected as usual; but her deep searching grey eyes seemed to regard Frank Darlington curiously, and when, as they sometimes chanced to do, they rested upon Godfrey Lascelles, their expression changed, I might almost say softened, and then the eyes wandered off to the moon that was now rising to their right, while the dying daylight was not yet lost on their left.

How calm, and still, and peaceful all around them seemed; the birds and insects had gone to sleep, only the splash of oars broke with musical regularity the deep silence that prevailed, and Beatrice, as she saw Godfrey Lascelles' eyes fixed upon her face, let her own eyelids droop, and seemed to sleep.

"What a contrast between him and that man Darlington," she thought reflectively; "when one is alone with the latter the very air seems charged with duplicity and unrest, while with the other—well, I suppose poor papa was right; he is a man to be loved or hated as one's fancy takes one, but he is a man undoubtedly to be trusted."

Perhaps by way of illustrating this opinion, Miss Beatrice, when the boat reached the landing-steps, took no individual notice of her guardian, but, with the careless remark:

"I think you had better all of you come up to the house," led the way, having first of all resigned Clarrie to the care of Mr. Darlington.

"You risked your own life to save mine," murmured the little heiress, clinging heavily to her false lover's arm.

"Hush! darling," he whispered in reply; "whose life should I risk my own so readily for as yours?"

She pressed his arm tightly, and when she spoke again it was to say in low and tremulous tones:

"My life is yours, Frank, whenever you like to claim it; I care nothing whatever for money in comparison with your love."

"Darling!" was his safe and vague rejoinder.

And thus they walked up to the house, Beatrice, with a cavalier on each side, preceding them.

If Clarrie had not been so weakly, and so idiotically in love with this worthless wretch, she would have noticed even now how he hastened her pace to keep up with the trio before them, and how he scarcely heeded what she said in his anxiety to overhear the conversation of those a few paces ahead.

But she did not; she thought he was walking so quickly to prevent her from catching cold, and she attributed his silence to the emotion he must feel at her escape from a watery grave.

Mrs. Raynham met them on their arrival at Burnham Court.

She was pale and anxious, and when she heard what had happened, she was inclined to blame the two girls for the danger they had encountered, rather than to express thankfulness for their escape.

Her introduction to Mr. Godfrey Lascelles diverted her thoughts, however, into another channel, and she even stretched her hospitality so far as to invite him to stay for a day or two at the Court.

It was rather a relief, therefore, to her economical soul when Godfrey explained to her that he was the guest of Sir Graham Grantly, and was at present on a visit at Grantly Park.

Then Mrs. Raynham made some verbal excuse to young Grantly, in addition to the written one she had sent, explaining why she and her family had been prevented from dining at the Park as previously arranged, after which the two young men took their departure, Frank Darlington having already gone.

The next morning Clarrie remained in bed, she was really not well enough to get up, for the shock her nervous system had sustained was greater than any of her family at first supposed.

Feverish as she was, however, she would dress and come down to the drawing-room directly after luncheon in the expectation of Frank Darlington riding over to see her.

Sir Graham Grantly with his nephew and Mr. Lascelles certainly did call and make a long stay, but Clarrie could not help feeling that the attraction which brought them was Beatrice, and that, though they showed a polite interest in herself, they really cared but very little about her.

Not that this would have troubled her had Frank only come to sun himself in her presence, and assure her of his unchanging love ; but he came not, the other visitors departed, and Mrs. Raynham, perceiving her daughter's nervous and excited condition, insisted upon her return to bed.

The next morning a note was brought from Frank Darlington to Clarrie's mother by a mounted groom, enquiring after the health of her eldest daughter and niece, and regretting the writer's inability to ask the question in person as he had been laid up the previous day and would be obliged to start for town in the course of a few hours.

To this Mrs. Raynham sent a courteous and satisfactory reply, and then for several days Clarrie heard no more of her by no means ardent lover.

Meanwhile Captain Trevor was sufficiently recovered to return to his own house, and begin to make a search for his daughter.

But he had not been at home more than a couple of days when a letter bearing the London postmark, and in his daughter's handwriting, though partially disguised, was brought to him.

The letter itself contained a plea for forgiveness, an assurance that the writer was well and happy, that her husband was all she could desire, and she hoped soon to introduce him to her father.

All this was satisfactory as far as it went, but the letter contained no address or name, and was simply signed " Mary."

A more suspicious man than Captain Trevor would at once have put the matter in the hands of detectives, and have tried to trace the missing girl, but he did nothing of the kind.

It is true that he would have liked to know more about his daughter, whom she had married, and where she was living; but the captain was of a very easy-going disposition, he believed that all he wished to learn would be told him in time, and, provided Mary was happy, he assured himself that he was satisfied.

Indeed, when he came to think the matter over, he could not but acknowledge that it was very fortunate that Mary had got married at this time.

Mrs. Raynham might smile sweetly and say she liked Mary, and would be glad to act the part of a real mother to her, and Mary might express herself satisfied at the prospect of her father's marriage, but the captain had seen too much of the world to believe the arrangement would work well; Mrs. Raynham had too many daughters of her own to make the acquisition of a step-daughter at all desirable, and it was with a very decided feeling of relief that the middle-aged suitor walked up to Burnham Court with the welcome letter.

To say that Mrs. Raynham would have taken the same easy-going view as did Mary's father, had the letter concerned one of her own daughters, would not be true, indeed her keen eyes and feminine instinct discovered many flaws in it, and she more than half doubted that it was written by Mary herself.

However, she gave no expression to these doubts. Whatever Mary Trevor had done, she had done of her own free will, and, provided the girl's father was satisfied, his future wife saw no necessity for casting a cloud upon his contentment.

So she smiled, and even jested, and said Mary was a sly puss to run away with some mysterious stranger, while so many girls in the neighbourhood could not find a husband; and she treated the letter as undoubtedly genuine, and the marriage as such a certainty, that any lingering doubts which Captain Trevor might have felt were completely dissipated.

The person who was least satisfied with this letter, which she was allowed to read, was Beatrice Burnham.

She had reproached herself many times for her hardness of heart in not responding to poor Mary's last caress, and when she read the written words, that were so unlike, in tone and expression, the manner and thought of her friend, she decided at once in her mind that the letter was a forgery.

In he usual outspoken way, she was about to say so, when she caught her aunt's eyes, and the warning expression of that lady's face arrested the words upon her lips.

When they were alone, however, some time later in the day, Beatrice said suddenly:

"Aunt, I don't believe Mary Trevor wrote that letter to her father."

"Nor do I," was the quiet answer.

"Then who could have written it?" asked the girl with rapidly-growing suspicion.

"I don't know—I cannot even surmise," replied Mrs. Raynham, gravely; "but the handwriting, though like Mary's, scarcely strikes me as being hers, and the words used are more like those of a man trying to imitate a woman's way of thought and expression than of gushing, effusive, passionate Mary Trevor."

"Yes, that is my own feeling," assented Beatrice reflectively; "but if our suspicions are correct, there is something more than an elopement in this. There is some tragedy, which it is our duty to bring to light."

IMPORTANT! *Presented gratis with this Number:* ANOTHER BEAUTIFUL COLOURED PLATE *for Binding with the Work.*

HE LOOKED AT CLARRIE BURNHAM WITH THE LOVE-LIGHT IN HER EYES.

NO. 4.

"If Mary were married," pursued Beatrice, "why should she write in this vague strain; and if she is not married, why should she write at all?"

"My dear Beatrice, how very outspoken you are for a girl of your age—an unmarried girl, too! I assure you it is most unbecoming, and I have intended to tell you of it many times."

"I am afraid that I am past cure in that respect, aunt," replied the girl gravely, "for I never can understand the use of closing one's eyes to glaring facts. But with regard to poor Mary Trevor—what can be done?"

"Nothing," was the reply.

"Nothing!" repeated Beatrice.

"No, nothing for the present," continued Mrs. Raynham. "Perhaps she, or the person who has written in her name, will write again; then we shall have some ground to go upon. At present we have nothing."

"We have all the information from that source that we are ever likely to have, I am convinced," said Beatrice, resolutely, "and I am determined to sift the matter thoroughly. Do you think you can manage to get hold of that letter for me for an hour or two, aunt?"

"For what purpose do you want it?" asked that lady, suspiciously.

"To show to Mr. Lascelles; you know he is a barrister and a man of the world, and his opinion may be worth something."

"Mr. Lascelles!" and Mrs. Raynham contracted her brows as she repeated the name; then she asked suddenly:

"Are you and Mr. Lascelles engaged to be married?"

"Married! Heaven forbid!" was the quick response.

"Then you have neither of you any intention of the kind," persisted Mrs. Raynham.

"I can answer for myself, and he can answer quickly enough for himself. Why, only the usages of society make us barely civil to each other, aunt."

"So I perceive, but that is a very dangerous sign; if you had been calmly friendly with each other, I should not have thought of such a connection."

"Don't think of it now, aunt; but help me to find out what has become of poor Mary Trevor."

"There is time enough for that, Beatrice; but, in the meanwhile, it is desirable that we should understand each other. You perceive, I presume, that Sir Graham Grantly means to propose to you?"

"Good Heavens, aunt! If it were not unladylike, I should be inclined to say, 'Confound the men!' What do I care who proposes to me and who doesn't? I may sing, 'Heigho! for a husband,' but I don't mean to take one for all that. And now, will you get hold of that letter for me for an hour or two?"

"Yes, I will; but here comes Sir Graham Grantly himself."

CHAPTER IX.

ASSURANCE.

SIR GRAHAM GRANTLY was a man who prided himself upon never being beaten.

Throughout the whole of his life he been singularly successful.

Whatever he had touched in the way of business had turned to money, and every speculation he joined—be it ever so risky—had invariably become a success.

Such a continued run of prosperity would be apt to spoil the most forbearing and generous nature, and Sir Graham Grantly had never much generosity or forbearance to injure.

He was indeed a purse-proud man; proud of his invariable success, proud of himself, proud of his fine house and grounds, and prouder than all of his title.

This baronetcy had been given him partly as payment for some political influence he possessed, but ostensibly for the successful construction of a suspension bridge that was looked upon as one of the greatest triumphs of engineering in modern times.

That Sir Graham had earned his title as he had earned his money, there could be no possible doubt, and now he meant to settle down at Grantly Park to enjoy his success. But a man of this kind who is ambitious of social distinction wants a wife.

He can dress his wife out in purple and fine linen, he can hang diamonds from her ears and upon her neck, he can load her with wealth, surround her with elegance, talk of "her ladyship" as of the most exalted woman under the sun, and yet feel all the time that she is but a reflection of his own importance and of his own glory.

So Sir Graham Grantly wanted a wife. Not a wife who would be loving and obedient, and whose highest ambition was to make his home a kind of earthly paradise and his life calmly happy, but a wife whose ambition should surpass his own.

A woman who would carry herself with the pride and dignity of a young queen.

One upon whom jewels and fine raiment would seem but her natural adornment, and who would thus add to his importance by never abating one jot of her own.

And such a woman he believed he had found in Beatrice Burnham.

She was young yet, it is true, but this was a fault that time would cure, and she came of a good old county family—which was far preferable to the man who did not wish to be eclipsed by his wife, than if she had belonged to one of the noblest houses in the land.

So there was everything in Beatrice's favour, nothing against her so far as the baronet knew, and he had firmly made up his mind that she was to be his wife.

Of course she would require a certain amount of wooing—that was the worst of matrimony. You could not approach it as you could any other contract, and having bargained for terms, get the matter settled out of hand.

But, despite his liking for having his own way as expeditiously as possible, Sir Graham Grantly was a great stickler for propriety and for doing things in the most correct manner possible, and, therefore, he was prepared to go through all the delay and vexation of wooing and courting.

He came into the drawing-room of the Court to-day carrying a bouquet of choice flowers which his groom had brought over from Grantly Park, and with much unusual *empressement* he presented the floral tribute to Miss Beatrice Burnham.

With great gravity Beatrice accepted the flowers, admired their beauty and their rich perfume, placed them in a vase, and then, to use her own simile, sat " demure as a cat," listening to the baronet's pompous sentences and heavy compliments until Mr. Fortescue

Grantly and Godfrey Lascelles arrived, when the spirit of mischief broke out in our capricious heroine, and she began, according to her aunt's subsequent account, to flirt with young Grantly most outrageously.

But the Baronet was not to be discouraged by any such freaks of fancy.

To take notice of his nephew was, Sir Graham Grantly considered, a kind of indirect compliment paid to himself, for, of course, no woman in her senses would think of marrying an almost penniless barrister, when a rich baronet stood by ready to lead her to the altar.

Besides the, baronet was consoled for Beatrice's neglect by Geraldine, who, if not pretty, was most undoubtedly clever.

Not that Sir Graham Grantly admired clever women, he thought them a mistake, a kind of anomaly in nature, but he would go so far as to admit that they did help to fill up half an hour pleasantly sometimes, and on this ground they were to be tolerated.

Perhaps the person who least approved of what was going on was Mr. Godfrey Lascelles.

From words which the baronet had spoken, and from his own personal observation, he saw what the rich man's intention was, and he mentally congratulated Beatrice on being in a position whence she could not be tempted by wealth.

Indeed, the baronet's suit found no favour in the young man's eyes, though he would have scouted as indignantly as would Beatrice herself, the idea that he himself wished to marry his own ward.

He was he told himself and told others, a confirmed bachelor, and the woman was not yet born who could tempt him into matrimony.

The baronet had been disappointed in his dinner-party through Mrs. Raynham's sudden call to Captain Trevor's assistance, when it was feared he would die, but he had made up his mind to give two or three entertainments to the ladies of Burnham Court, and the first failure did not daunt him.

He stated his desire now with a frankness that had in it something of ostentation, and if Mrs. Raynham had not had that slight explanation with her niece half an hour previously she would have felt inclined to resent the tone of condescension and evident patronage with which Sir Graham Grantly seemed to be taking her family under his special protection.

But Mrs. Raynham was a clever woman. A woman who could control her temper and hold her hand, and she calculated with some craftiness that the baronet meant to have a wife, and that if he could not get the girl he wanted, he would be most likely to take the first he could get after his first rebuff.

So she smiled, and said she knew that the girls would enjoy garden-parties and a ball, such as Sir Graham proposed to give, but they must not forget that Beatrice and Clarrie were in deep mourning, and it would be quite impossible for the former to attend any entertainment of any kind at present.

Then Geraldine chimed in.

"What you say is quite true, mamma, but couldn't we get up a quiet picnic with only one or two people besides Sir Graham and his friends? Surely there can be no objection to such a mild form of dissipation, and Beatrice has never yet seen Everly Priory. I think a picnic would be of all things the most delightful."

"A capital idea Miss Geraldine," said the baronet with a glance of approval at her animated countenance. "What do you say, Mrs. Raynham? What do you say, Miss Beatrice?"

Both ladies expressed their approval of the idea, and Sir Graham Grantly entered into the proposed arrangement with more eagerness than he had felt for many a long year.

It was of no use wasting time in a long wooing, he thought; he would find an opportunity at the picnic of informing Beatrice Burnham of the honour he intended to confer upon her, and then the matter could be settled and the wedding could take place as soon as the necessary period of her mourning would allow.

So he talked the matter over, arranged the day and the manner in which the party should reach the Priory, wrote down the names of the few guests it was proposed to invite, and promised the ladies that if the weather should prove fine they should have a day of unbroken pleasure.

"What a pity poor Mary Trevor won't be here to go with us," said Beatrice with a sigh when the baronet and his nephew and guest had gone away.

"Yes," assented Clarrie. "Mary always enjoyed a picnic immensely. I wonder where she is now. I wonder if Frank will be back in time to be of the party."

Beatrice glanced at her cousin quickly and suspiciously.

It was odd that Clarrie should mention the names of Mary and Frank in the same breath, and Beatrice wondered for the moment if there had been any purpose in so doing.

But no, Clarrie had no doubt or suspicion of her lover, and it was only because the two happened to be absent that she had thought of linking their names together.

In prospect of this picnic and the possibilities that might arise from it, Mrs. Raynham was politic enough to loosen her purse-strings.

Pretty girls look all the prettier in new and fresh costumes, and the improvement is still more perceptible when nature has not been too bountiful to the girls themselves.

Of course, for Beatrice and Clarrie there was little or no choice.

Beatrice must wear black with a certain amount of crape, and Clarrie might wear white, provided she half covered herself with black ribbons.

But for the other girls, mourning was only in the very slightest degree necessary.

"Complimentary mourning, at the very utmost," remarked Mrs. Raynham when in consultation with her daughters, "and in these days almost anything may be called complimentary mourning."

A remark that was treated with the utmost elasticity, and the four Misses Raynham were provided with new dresses which were certainly not white, and in which there was not a trace of black.

Blue, indeed, was the prevailing hue; and blue as we all know is the colour of hope.

But the appointed day came, and punctual as the clock Sir Graham Grantly in an open carriage, and followed by an empty one of like proportions, arrived at Burnham Court.

He had previously arranged to come in this manner and to overtake the rest of the party at a given place of rendezvous.

Captain Trevor had left the Court and gone to his own house to reside for the short period that was to elapse before his marriage, and he also was to be of the picnic party, but was to drive to the Priory in a small pony-carriage with one of the younger girls.

At the last moment there was some discussion upon this point, and greatly to her disgust Miss Fanny was told off to drive with her future step-father.

" Will Frank be there? " was the thought in Clarrie's heart as they drove away.

And the same eager hope was in the heart of her foolish half-sister as she sat in gloomy silence by the old soldier's side.

The answer met them in the person of Mr. Frank Darlington himself, as, mounted upon horseback, he rode up to the side of the carriages, and greeted the party from Burnham Court, just as they had reached the gates of Grantly Park.

He looked as careless and handsome as though he had never had anything to trouble or annoy him, and he enquired earnestly after the health of Beatrice and Clarrie, and declared himself delighted to hear that they had not seriously suffered from the upset on the river.

Fanny he did not look for and did not want to see; but the poor foolish girl was watching him jealously, and eagerly anxious to attract his attention as any moth is to fly to the flame that fascinates and destroys it.

The picnic party, after all, was a large one, for Sir Graham had found that when he began to send out invitations there were so many people that he ought to invite, if he invited anyone, that having once begun he scarcely knew where to stop.

It was a good couple of hours' drive to Everley Priory, and it was thus fully two o'clock before the by this time hungry party reached their destination.

But Sir Graham Grantly never did things by halves when he began to do them.

A competent staff of servants had been on the spot for the last two hours, and an ample luncheon was spread out in the part of the ruins that had once been the monks refectory.

Mrs. Raynham glanced over the well-covered cloth, noticed that all the delicacies of the season had been plentifully provided, then quietly accepted the arm that Fortescue Grantly offered her, Sir Graham having somewhat ostentatiously appropriated Beatrice.

The baronet had got up the picnic specially for Beatrice, and he seemed to wish that everyone present should know it, and he took very good care to impress the fact upon the young lady herself.

Indeed, the marked attention from the purse-proud old man made our heroine very uncomfortable, yet she scarcely knew how to repulse or resent it, for he was her host, and he told her calmly in words as well as by looks, that this entertainment was for her benefit.

" What an old nuisance he is," was the girls mental comment ; " if I don't put a stop to his absurdity he will be proposing to me, and then there will be a scene. I must get somebody else to keep close to me, so that this old stupid doesn't get a chance to make a fool of himself. Who shall it be? His nephew dare not do it, and he would be sent off if he tried to devote himself to me. If Godfrey Lascelles had any sense I might utilise him, but he hasn't, and he would be worse than useless."

Then her eyes wandered over the faces of the assembled guests, many of whom were strangers to her, until they encountered those of Frank Darlington, fixed with strange earnestness upon her own face.

Much to her own vexation Beatrice felt herself blush, her eyes drooped, and for a few seconds she seemed as much confused as any love-sick girl who had half-betrayed her cherished secret.

But the feeling in Beatrice Burnham's heart was not a pleasurable one.

She was not by any means in love with Frank Darlington; nay, so far from it was she that she distrusted and disliked him, but his deeply-passionate glance had made her flush and turn hot and cold, and she felt angry with him for being able to move her so.

Whether or not he misinterpreted her confusion it is hard to say, but scarcely was luncheon over than he sought her side, and managed to keep close to her despite the baronet's efforts to get rid of him.

"If I could only get away from both of them I should be so glad," thought Beatrice, with something like irritation. "Clarrie will be ready to tear my eyes out for keeping her admirer from her side, and Sir Graham is becoming simply intolerable."

At this juncture she caught her aunt's glance, and that lady signalled that she wanted her.

Here was her opportunity, and with a hasty—

"Excuse me a minute, I want to speak to my aunt," she left the two gentleman and walked over to Mrs. Raynham's side.

For a few minutes the two ladies talked together very earnestly, then they walked away from the rest of the party, and when Mrs. Raynham was again seen by Sir Graham Grantly, she was alone.

"We seem to have lost your niece, madam," said the baronet in a tone of irritation.

"Lost her!" repeated Mrs. Raynham, opening her eyes in well-acted surprise; "not at all. I left her with my daughter Geraldine, and your nephew and her guardian, Mr. Lascelles."

"Her guardian, indeed," growled Sir Graham; "her father must have been mad to leave her to the guardianship of so young a man."

"So one would think unless he wished him to marry her," replied the lady quietly.

"Marry her!" cried the irate baronet, rapidly losing his temper. "I mean to marry her myself, Mrs. Raynham."

"Dear me!" said the lady sweetly, yet with a good spice of covert malice in her tone; "how very unkind of Beatrice not to have told me; pray accept my congratulations, Sir Graham. My niece is a charming girl, and will make you a most excellent wife. Still, I must scold her for being so reticent with me."

And she was turning away as though to seek her niece when Sir Graham said with some awkwardness:

"Mrs. Raynham, wait a minute if you please. I—I have not yet proposed to Miss Beatrice; I am just going to do so."

"Oh!"

It was all that the lady said, but there was a volume of meaning in the sound.

But Sir Graham did not heed it, or rather he would not heed it.

The exclamation seemed to suggest doubt as to his success, and Sir Graham Grantly was a man to whom doubt was intolerable.

Without another word, therefore, he strode past Mrs. Raynham in the direction in which he supposed Beatrice Burnham to be.

The baronet had screwed up his courage for the occasion, and he was not a little surprised to find that any courage should be needed.

But then, as he told himself, he had never proposed to a woman before; so, encouraging himself by repeating the well-known lines:

> He either fears his fate too much,
> Or his desert is small;
> Who will not put it to the touch,
> And win or lose it all,

he walked on for a few steps at a somewhat rapid pace, then pulled up suddenly, for Beatrice Burnham stood before him—alone.

CHAPTER X.

HOW HE FARED IN HIS WOOING.

"ISS BEATRICE, will you be my wife?" This was the speech that all Sir Graham Grantly's well-prepared sentences had suddenly reduced themselves to.

"Marry you!" repeated the girl, looking up saucily at his flushed face; "No, thank you, Sir Graham; I like you much better as a friend than I should as a husband."

"You think I am jesting," he said hurriedly, "and I can quite understand that you should take such a view of my proposal, but I am not, I assure you; I am in sober earnest. I don't need a wife who is rich, nor one of high rank; I want a wife who will devote herself to my interests and to me; and, dear Beatrice, I believe I have found her."

And he took her white hand in his own, and was lifting it to his lips, when she withdrew it quietly, but very decidedly, as she replied:

"I have no doubt you will find many girls who would be glad to accept you, Sir Graham, but I have no inclination for matrimony."

"No inclination!" echoed the baronet. "I heard you the first time we met singing, 'Oh, for a husband!'"

Beatrice blushed; then she laughed heartily as she said:

"Evidently you have not heard the whole of that ancient ballad, Sir Graham, or you would not refer to it on the present occasion; but I may as well tell you that one of the verses ends with this addition to the chorus:

'I will have a husband! I'll have a husband!
But he must be young.'"

And with another laugh, Miss Beatrice Burnham darted away.

Sir Graham Grantly stood where she had left him, like a man spell-bound.

Refused! Was it possible! Refused by an almost penniless girl! Refused, when he had more than once announced his intention of marrying her!

It was incredible; he could not believe it! And he looked and felt like a man who was the victim of some horrible dream.

Suddenly the terrible spell is broken; a girl's voice sounds upon his ear, and he looks up to perceive Geraldine Raynham standing before him with evident concern and sympathy in her face.

Geraldine is looking her very best to-day. She has fastened some rosebuds in her hat and at her throat, and, until the last few minutes, she has been talking in an animated strain to Fortescue Grantly, who is just the very least bit in love with her.

So Miss Geraldine's eyes are bright, her cheeks are flushed, and she looks at this moment far handsomer than she has ever done in her life before.

So the baronet thinks, as she asks in tender tones, and with evident sympathy in her manner:

"Are you unwell, Sir Graham? Can I get anything for you, or will you lean upon me for a few steps? There is a stone seat close by."

"Thank you, my dear;" and taking her at her word, he placed his hand somewhat heavily upon her shoulder.

But she did not flinch; in this way they walked a few paces till they reached a stone bench, upon which the baronet sank heavily.

"Let me fetch some water," said Geraldine, and she was starting to do so when her companion said eagerly:

"No, don't go. I am better; I want you to stay with me; I want to talk to you."

"Yes," she said, quietly taking the seat he pointed to at his side.

She knew now what was coming as well as he did.

Of course she was surprised, for she had no more expected a proposal from the owner of Grantly Park than he had an hour before intended to make it.

But she rapidly counted up in her own mind the losses and gains of such a match, and before Sir Graham had really begun to speak her decision was made.

"Do you think I am a very old man, Miss Geraldine?" he asked in an almost plaintive tone.

"Old!" repeated the girl, opening her pale blue eyes wider than was her wont; "certainly not. You don't seem old to me. I never once thought about your age; there are some people so nice that one never asks whether they are old or young."

"Yes, you are right," he assented with a sigh of relief; "that is what I have always felt when I have been with young people. That is what I feel with you, my dear—a sort of companionship, a feeling of close sympathy that makes me forget all difference of age between us."

"Like his impudence!" was Geraldine's mental comment, but aloud she said:

"It is very kind of you to feel so, Sir Graham."

"No, it is not kind," he went on lowly, and in what he believed was a very sentimental tone; "it is more than kindness, it is the craving of a soul for sympathy and love. Yes, for love. Geraldine, do you think, my dear, that you could love me?"

"Oh, Sir Graham! I——"

Then Miss Geraldine covered her face with her hands, which was about the safest course she could pursue.

She was a young woman who possessed a lively sense of the ridiculous, and it was to smother her laughter, not to hide her blushes, that she turned her face away.

But the baronet felt that he was in no danger of a refusal this time, and the big arm was clasped round the girl's slender waist, while he drew her unresisting form to his ample breast.

"And you think I can make you happy, my child!" he asked with more tenderness than Beatrice would have believed him capable of.

"I am quite sure of it, Sir Graham," she replied softly, "if you think that I shall be all that you can desire in a wife."

"More than I deserve, very probably, my dear," he replied a trifle sharply; "a man's desires sometimes run ahead of his judgment."

Geraldine asked for no explanation of this remark, for she knew very well of whom and of what he was thinking.

In point of fact, she had overheard his proposal to Beatrice, and that young lady's cutting retort.

Real compassion for the disappointed suitor, and the half-amused feeling that a heart might be caught in the rebound, had made her step forward and offer her sympathy, and she had now no more feeling of jealousy towards Beatrice than she had of doubt as to the wisdom of the step she had taken.

"It will be a capital thing for mamma and the girls," she mused; "for they will have a home with me when Clarrie becomes mistress of the Court. That is, the girls will, for, of course, if mamma marries again, she must live with her husband."

Then her thoughts wandered off to Fortescue Grantly, and she gave just one little sigh at the thought of what perhaps might have been.

And meanwhile Sir Graham was expounding his views of matrimony to somewhat dull ears.

"As a rule, I do not like clever women, Geraldine, and you know, my dear, you are clever; but, with a little mutual concession, I daresay we shall get along together."

"Yes," she assented absently.

"I want you to be the mistress of my house, to take the lead in society as my wife, to dress well, and to—to —be everything that a devoted wife should be to a husband."

"Yes," the girl said again.

She had scarcely heard him, and she had not observed how he floundered and paused when he was about to speak of the olive-branches which he hoped to see round his table in the years to come.

She only knew that he kissed her, and that she did not like it, and wondered if he would often do that kind of thing, and he was still sitting with his arm encircling her when a low cry of anger and surprise made her look up suddenly, to find her mother before her.

Her natural impulse was to start to her feet and escape from the embracing arm, but Sir Graham Grantly was equal to the occasion, and held her tightly.

"We were coming to seek you, Mrs. Raynham," he said a trifle pompously, "but you have found us. You know what this means, I presume. I have the honour of asking you to give me your daughter's hand."

And as he rose to his feet, he held Geraldine's hand in his own.

Mrs. Raynham was taken by surprise, but she did not say so.

Neither did she seem to be overwhelmed with the prospect of her daughter's good fortune.

On the contrary, now the fish was caught, and could not decently get away, it was just as well to let him understand that he was not to consider himself such a wonderful prize, after all.

Mrs. Raynham was strong upon the subject of good family, and upon this point the baronet was most weak.

She herself came of a good stock, and both of her husbands could show a good descent; and thus, in giving one of her daughters to a self-made man, she wished him to feel that he took from her hands what was of far more value than his money.

Sir Graham did not quite like this view of the case, but, downright and masterful as he was by nature, he was no match for Mrs. Raynham's subtle courtesy and quiet assumption of superiority.

On one point, however, the baronet felt that he ought to be satisfied. He had determined to be engaged to be married before he went back to Grantly Park that night —and he was engaged.

But he rather regretted his precipitation when, some time later, he came upon Beatrice Burnham, surrounded by a group of young men and girls, to whom she was talking brightly and gaily.

She seemed to have quite forgotten the baronet's proposal, or to treat it as a light jest, for she smiled when she perceived him, made some pleasant remark, and pointed out a vacant seat not far from her own.

But the baronet was not to be thus mollified, and he turned coldly away to talk to Geraldine.

Then he noticed with a pang how plain his *fiancée* was.

The light had gone out of her eyes, the colour from her cheeks, and he thought for a moment disdainfully that no amount of fine clothing would make her a leader of fashion or her husband a man whom other men would envy.

This was the first failure in the whole course of a successful life, and it was likely to prove the beginning of a change of fortune.

But the baronet was a man to whom success was so essential that he would never admit himself to be beaten, and he at once resolved to make the best of the situation.

Meanwhile, there are other members of our party whom it may perhaps be as well to look after.

Fortescue Grantly, as we have seen, had been flirting with Geraldine, and had half persuaded himself that he was in love with her, while Godfrey Lascelles, with a firm belief in the safety of numbers, had strolled away from the rest of the party with Claribel Burnham and her half-sister, Grace Raynham.

Grace was seventeen—one year younger than Geraldine, and not one whit better-looking, so she formed a good foil to Clarrie, who was alike rich and beautiful.

I am afraid that Clarrie would have managed to excuse herself from accompanying Grace and the young barrister to the Monk's Well, for which they were bound, if she could have caught sight of Frank Darlington and been sure of securing his attention.

But Frank was nowhere to be seen; nor, for the matter of that, was Fanny.

Nobody missed Fanny, however.

Even Mrs. Raynham, who looked pretty sharply after her girls, and who held it as part of her social creed that if a girl went wrong in any way before her marriage, it was the fault of her mother, and if she compromised herself after marriage, the blame lay with her husband, even this uncompromising matron did not observe the absence from her brood of the most dangerously inflammable member of it.

Frank Darlington took no notice of Fanny. At any rate, no more than he bestowed upon her younger sister.

He wished to forget the foolish girl, and to ignore the love passages that had occurred between them.

But Fanny was mad and reckless.

She was consumed with jealousy and passion, the latter feeling being no more like love than a piece of black shining coal is like the clear crystal diamond.

Thus, though Darlington tried to avoid her, and not to hear the whispered words she uttered when he passed, or to let his eyes rest upon her when she sought his glance, she followed him desperately, and resolutely determined that he should talk to her, that he should spend some of the day in her company.

Once, when he was standing by himself, she went up to him, and said in low half-threatening tones :

" You must manage to take a walk with me, Frank ; I have something to say to you."

He bowed his head and said nothing, but he mentally cursed his own folly in allowing himself to drift into such a dangerous position.

Some time later, however, fearing that Fanny might make up some scene if he did not listen to her, he told her where to meet him, and then set off to walk to a wood that was not far distant.

No one observed him, and not one of the party saw the silly girl a few minutes later take the same path ; but he went and Fanny followed him, and both of them had cause to the end of their days to regret that stolen meeting.

" And you will always love me, Frank? " she said with flashing eyes as they parted.

"Always!" he repeated huskily.

But he did not return with her, neither did he rejoin the picnic party.

Cursing his own folly, he started off to walk back to his father's house.

His groom would bring back his horse to the stables, and no one would, perhaps, miss him, except Clarrie.

Poor Clarrie!

He almost felt in his heart to pity her for loving so devotedly a man so weak and erring as himself.

Bad as he was, he had sufficient conscience left to avoid her presence for the rest of this day, and so he walked home, along the dusty roads, through the heavily ploughed fields; thoughts of Fanny Raynham giving place at length to the still more serious subject of Mary Trevor.

What those thoughts were it is hard to say; but the perspiration stood out in large cold beads upon his brow, and he carefully avoided one thick copse of trees. through which it would have been the shortest way to pass, as though it had been haunted.

"I can't stand this any longer," he thought as he reached home; "I can't and I won't. I'll have an understanding with Clarrie, and then I'll go away for a time. However much I may prefer Beatrice, I must marry Clarrie for the sake of her money, unless I can first get rid of her and win her cousin; but I must keep out of Fanny's way, and then if she tells her story no one will believe her; happily, I have been wise enough not to write a single line to her. Little fool that she is, I feel as though I could kill her for dragging me into such a dilemma."

And, meanwhile, Fanny was in the seventh heaven of delight.

Frank was hers. He could not desert her now, and Clarrie's fortune, and Beatrice's fascinations would, she felt assured, be insufficient to win him from her.

So the picnic passed off, but its influence on many who were present at it was abiding.

CHAPTER XI.

"I LOVE YOU!"

HOUGH Mrs. Raynham had not appeared to be overwhelmed with gratification at the proposed union between Sir Graham Grantly and her daughter Geraldine, there was, in point of fact, much quiet jubilation in the family over the matter.

"I hope you will be happy, my dear," said the girl's mother, after she had discussed some of the advantages which the marriage would bring; "Sir Graham is a very difficult man to get along with."

"Very difficult, mamma," replied Geraldine with a laugh that was almost a sneer; "but then a penniless girl can't expect to marry ten thousand a year and a brand new title without some slight drawbacks to the value of her prize."

"That is quite true, my dear; but I wish you had a little more love for your future husband; it would make your life so much more pleasant for you, and there are so many things which with affection would not feel irksome, but that otherwise are apt to gall you."

"Yes, I know all that," said the girl a trifle regretfully; "but how can I love such a self-inflated piece of humanity as Sir Graham Grantly? Why, he doesn't even love me?"

"My dear, you must be mistaken. The fact of his proposing to you is proof to the contrary."

"Is it?" and again the girl laughed unpleasantly. "He proposed to me because Beatrice laughed at him. I heard the whole conversation; but don't let us talk about it. I am going to marry him, and have no doubt I shall make quite as good a wife as he deserves."

"Very much better, I hope, dear; but though I am anxious for the match to take place, I have seen so much misery, and even disgrace, when there has been no pretence of affection on either side that I tremble for your happiness."

"Then don't tremble any more, mamma, for there will be plenty of pretence on both sides. Sir Graham is too proud, and believes too firmly in himself to admit at any time that he has made a blunder, and I—I am not a beauty, you know, mamma, and I have had no love experiences to stand between me and my grey-haired husband. If he is moderately kind to me, I shall seem very fond of him, and the seeming may one day become a reality."

Mrs. Raynham sighed. She loved Geraldine better perhaps than any of her other children, and she had fancied more than once during the last week that the girl had looked, with eyes that softened and cheeks that flushed, upon Godfrey Lascelles when he had addressed her. But the mother was too wise a woman to express this suspicion. It was above all things necessary that her daughters should marry, and Geraldine's success would, without doubt, have its influence upon the fortunes of her sisters.

After this one conversation, therefore, both mother and daughter tacitly avoided the subject of sentiment or love.

No ardent lover, however, could be more impatient for the day of his nuptials to arrive than was Sir Graham Grantly.

The day after the picnic he drove over to Burnham Court to talk to his *fiancée* and her mother, and to have the day fixed for his marriage.

"I don't see why we should lose any time," he said in his masterful way; "there will be no need for marriage settlements in our case, for I have no doubt my wife can trust to my generosity for providing for her."

Geraldine said nothing, but her mother here interfered promptly with the remark :

"No one who knows you would doubt your generosity, Sir Graham, but in this case I have a duty to perform; my daughter is—pardon me—many years younger than yourself, and much of your property is, I believe, in land, which could only come to her by will."

"Certainly, madam; it has been my ambition to become a large landowner, and I have bought up land whenever I could do so. It is my ambition to found a family, Mrs. Raynham, but I am quite rich enough to provide for my wife without impoverishing my children."

"Of course, Sir Graham, I quite understand that, and therefore I wish proper settlements to be made; indeed, no daughter of mine will marry with my consent without settlements."

Sir Graham looked hot and restive.

Geraldine had strolled away to the further end of the room, leaving her mother and lover to fight out the matter in hand together.

She had not the least doubt as to which would win, and her anticipations were verified, for after a short but decisive discussion it was agreed that settlements should be at once drawn up giving Geraldine, when she became Lady Grantly, five hundred a year as pin-money during her husband's lifetime, and a jointure of three thousand a year at his death.

"So you will not be dependent upon his caprice, and he can't leave you penniless," said Mrs. Raynham with an emphatic nod of the head.

Whereupon Geraldine expressed her satisfaction, and then the two ladies began seriously to discuss the details of the bride's trousseau, for the wedding was to take place in the course of a month or six weeks at latest.

But meanwhile the school treat, of which we heard almost immediately after Beatrice arrived at Burham Court, is about to come off.

From some cause or other it had been postponed, and the children at one time feared they were going to be defrauded of it altogether.

After all, however, it had only been delayed, and the Wednesday of the week following the eventful picnic saw the Brent meadow prepared with a marquée, and several small tents. All was now bustle and preparation.

The entertainment about to take place in the Brent meadow was not an ordinary Sunday-school treat, for, partly through the influence of Beatrice and Clarrie, partly through an unwonted outburst of liberality on the part of Mrs. Raynham, and principally because when one or two persons begin to do a generous thing others must follow their example, the present gathering had become more like a garden-party than a Sunday-school festival.

Frank Darlington had not yet gone away to London; and he, despite his resolutions on the subject, had persuaded his father to send a hamper of fruit for the children's feast.

Sir Graham Grantly, hearing of what was meditated at Holly Mount, sent not only fruit but flowers to grace the occasion.

Malicious people were not wanting who hinted that Mrs. Raynham was giving a large and successful entertainment at very small cost to herself, but that lady could afford to despise such ill-natured comments.

She had allowed herself to be dragged into it very much against her will, but as the whole affair was a decided success, she was quite willing to accept the satisfaction which success always brings with it.

Indeed, Mrs. Raynham was beginning to think that she had been exceptionally fortunate of late.

Beatrice Burnham's two hundred a year was a nice addition to her income; then the way to her own marriage was made smoother by the considerate, though mysterious withdrawal of Mary Trevor from the neighbourhood; and lastly, Geraldine's engagement to Sir Graham Grantley was a matter to be satisfied with.

To-day, however, another possible piece of good fortune came up before the scheming mother's eyes.

AND WITH ANOTHER LAUGH, MISS BEATRICE BURNHAM DARTED AWAY.

No. 5.

The rector, who was known to be a good match if he could only be caught, seemed to be more than usually attentive to Beatrice and to Grace.

It is true that Grace was only seventeen, and that some of the attention shown her might be meant for her cousin, still Mrs. Raynham was not as suspicious of Beatrice as she had at first been.

A girl who could refuse a wealthy baronet, and who afterwards, when he was engaged to another girl, could treat him with the calm careless friendliness which our heroine displayed, could not be very formidable as a rival unless her heart were engaged in the matter, and in that case, Mrs. Raynham felt that it would be as well for the girl's rival to retire from the lists at the commencement.

Indeed, an exaggerated estimate of the power which Beatrice's wit and beauty could exercise over the masculine mind had taken hold of Mrs. Raynham, and she respected, even if she slightly feared, her niece accordingly.

But meanwhile the entertainment of the school, and of many of Mr. Langdale's older parishioners continues; and while others are looking after the comfort of the junior members of the party, Beatrice is in the marquée busy dispensing tea and other liquid refreshments.

Suddenly a voice, the clear accents of which she knows full well, says :

"Miss Beatrice, may I beg a cup of tea?"

"Can Mr. Lascelles beg for anything?" she asked, trying to speak lightly and to smile even while she poured out the tea he asked for.

"Surely; why not?" he asked, thrown off his guard.

"Demanding things as a right seems to come more naturally to some people than begging for them," she retorted, handing him the cup.

"And you think I am one of those people?" he asked a trifle too eagerly.

"Does not conscience make the cap fit?" she enquired evasively.

"Certainly not," he replied with a frown. "There are things that I have not dared to beg for, still less to demand."

But Beatrice turned away resolutely and would not look at him, though she could not resist the temptation of saying, by way of a parting shot:

"How your friends must misjudge you, Mr. Lascelles."

"You do, at any rate," he replied bitterly.

She made no answer, possibly she did not hear him, but Frank Darlington, standing close by, watching the faces of the speakers and hearing what they said, felt his heart swell till it seemed ready to burst with envy and jealousy.

"She loves him," he groaned inaudibly; "that is why she flouts us all; she loves him, but she is of such a proud untameable nature that she will not admit her love, but will rather die than let him suspect it. Oh, to win the heart of such a woman were a triumph indeed. What care I for the fruit that falls ripe and unbidden into my hand; it is the apple that grows on the topmost branch of the tree and that one risks one's neck to reach that a man covets. I can well sympathise with our mother Eve when she risked the loss of Eden to taste the forbidden fruit. By my soul, I would risk all the present and the future to win that girl's love and to call her my own!"

"What are you saying so earnestly, dearest?"

The questioner was Fanny Raynham, and she clasped her small hand upon one of his.

He started as if he had been stung, shook himself as though he would pull himself together with an effort, then said sharply and crossly, though in a low subdued tone:

"I wish you wouldn't make a fool of yourself, and in public too; how do you know who is looking on, or what people will think of your caressing my hand in that manner? If you have no regard for me, have a little for yourself, for goodness sake."

And he was turning away but she arrested him with pleading eagerness, saying:

"But, Frank, you have never spoken to me to-day. How do you think I can bear it? You treat me worse than as a stranger; you treat me as though you hated me."

"I believe I do hate you," he replied brutally.

Then he turned on his heel and joined a group of people, amongst whom were her mother and Clarrie, and before them she dared not speak to him as she had just done.

But Beatrice Burnham had watched the girl's face while this conversation was taking place.

She had seen with dismay the pleading familiarity which characterised the girl's expression and actions, and though she could not hear the words uttered, and she was very far from guessing the truth, she felt certain that there was falsehood and treachery being practised upon Fanny or Clarrie, or upon both.

So impressed was she with this conviction that although she and Fanny never had got along well together, she could not resist the temptation of going up to the girl's side, laying her hand upon her shoulder, and saying:

"Are you not well, dear? You look so pale."

"I am well enough," replied Fanny brusquely, while her face flushed. "Have you been watching me?" she added suspiciously.

Beatrice could scarcely suppress a smile at the absurdity of the girl's question, but she answered quietly:

"Everybody in the tent was watching you, for that matter. I suppose you and Mr. Darlington have been quarrelling—he and I quarrel whenever we speak, for that matter."

"Do you?" retorted Fanny savagely; "some people would like to quarrel with him in the same manner; but we are not all so clever as you are."

"You are certainly not so clever in keeping your temper," replied Beatrice calmly; and as for Mr. Darlington, I have always understood that he was engaged to your sister Clarrie."

"Then you have understood what isn't true," replied Fanny hotly; he is not engaged to Claribel."

"Indeed! Then is he engaged to you?" asked Beatrice in surprise.

"That is my business," was the reply.

Whereupon Miss Fanny Raynham walked away, with her head well thrown back and with much dignity of manner.

"Dear me, this looks serious," thought Beatrice anxiously; "surely the man cannot have been villain enough to make love to such a child; as for marrying her, I think I know the man too well to believe he would throw aside Clarrie's fortune for any woman. No; Mr. Darlington thinks first of his pocket, next of his inclinations, and lastly of the feelings of others."

She was pondering over this question when a voice at her side said in a bantering tone:

"A penny for your thoughts, Miss Burnham?"

She glanced up and saw that the speaker was Frank Darlington himself.

On the impulse of the moment, and with her usual outspoken candour, she said:

"You shall have them without the penny; I was wondering if it could be possible that you are engaged to Fanny Raynham?"

"Engaged to that child!" and he laughed disdainfully.

But Beatrice fixed her eyes upon him with cold enquiry; to laugh at the idea of an engagement was not to deny it.

Seeing which, his own face became grave; a mad wild hope came into his heart, and he said emphatically and steadily:

"No, Miss Burnham; I am not engaged to anybody."

"But Clarrie," she said impulsively, without thought, and wishing she could recall the two words the moment they were uttered.

"I am not engaged to Clarrie," he replied steadily. "I proposed to her, it is true, some time ago; but her mother refused her consent even to an engagement between us. I might have asked her again when she was her own mistress, but that a stronger and a nobler woman has won my heart. Beatrice, you know whom I mean; you know that I love you."

They happened to be alone at the minute, and he would have taken her hand in his own, and, had she submitted, would have desecrated it by pressing the fair fingers to his false lips.

But she stepped back, and said coldly, and with proud disdain:

"I am only interested in the welfare of my cousins, Mr. Darlington. Clarrie, no doubt, can take care of herself; but I think it is unmanly to play with the feelings of such a child as Fanny."

"I have not played with her feelings; I swear I have not. And Beatrice, I love you," he cried passionately.

"Such love as yours is easily transferred," she replied contemptuously; "and even if it were better worth having than it is, it would find no acceptance from me. The man is not born who shall make me his slave."

"Slave!" he repeated. "It is a wife I seek, not a slave."

"In your case the terms would be identical," she replied scornfully.

Then, perceiving he was about to persist in his unwelcome suit, and catching sight of Godfrey Lascelles at the entrance of the marquee, she called him to stay, and, with an inclination of the head to her discomfited suitor, she went and joined the barrister.

"I was afraid I was interrupting an interesting conversation," said Lascelles, with more feeling than he usually showed.

"You came most opportunely," she replied; and I want you to help me."

"Certainly, if I can. What do you want?"

"I want a sharp detective."

"A detective! What on earth can you want of a detective?"

"I will tell you," she said, "if you will come for a stroll in the wood."

He bowed, and walked on by her side in silence.

For the moment he was far from sure that this young lady who was his ward was in her right senses.

CHAPTER XII.

"HE WILL NOT MARRY YOU."

 tell you it is the same man! I recognised his figure as he stood that night holding back the curtains in the darkened room, his form reflected by the lamp that was behind him. The effect was almost the same as he stood with his back to the entrance of the tent; I could swear to him."

Such were the vehement words which Beatrice Burnham poured into the astonished ears of Godfrey Lascelles.

She had told him of Mary Trevor's strange behaviour, and still stranger disappearance; she had expressed the conviction that had slowly been dawning upon her that Frank Darlington was the mysterious lover who had lured her away from home.

Godfrey had listened in silence, but now when he spoke his words seemed like a breath of cold wind upon her fevered brain.

"And supposing you are right, what do you prove?" he asked calmly.

"What do I prove!" repeated Beatrice with growing excitement. "I prove that he is a villain."

"I don't even see that," was the quiet response. "You don't suggest that the girl was taken away by violence; you believe her to have been a free agent."

"Yes; but I don't believe that letter which her father received was written by her."

"Even supposing it was not, you don't wish to imply that he has murdered her?"

"Murdered! Oh no!"

The idea was so horrible that her first natural impulse was to repudiate it.

"Well, then, what would you have; what do you want to do?" he asked quietly.

"I want to expose him so that he shall not make love to every woman he meets, nor delude every silly girl who will listen to him."

"Why? Has he tried to delude you?" he asked with a piercing glance.

"Delude me!" she repeated with ineffable scorn. "Do I look like a woman whom a man of that type could treat lightly?"

She paused as she asked this question, and looked him full in the face, and he smiled with just a little pain and regret in the smile as he replied:

"He would be a daring man who presumed to love you, and little better than a madman who pretended to do so."

Beatrice contracted her brows with anger, and her face flushed with vexation.

She had not been fishing for a compliment, but she had not expected such an answer as this, and she was annoyed accordingly.

So much annoyed, indeed, that she said, without thought and with some heat:

"Yet Mr. Darlington was mad enough to pretend to love me. He cannot have found out that I am not so poor as I am believed to be, can he?"

"I don't think he can have done so; and, after all, it may be but daring on his part, and he may really love you. It is possible."

"But not probable," she retorted, stung by his tone and manner; "and I must say that I expected a little more help and sympathy from you, Mr. Lascelles."

"My help and sympathy are both at your service, Miss Burnham, but I must know in what way I can help you, and on what ground I can offer sympathy. At present you don't seem to have suffered much, except," with a smile, "in the way of a slight ruffling of your temper."

Beatrice gave her shoulders a little shake of impatience, for her temper was ruffled, and she did not like to be told of it, but she knew that the man by her side might be relied upon to help her if she needed help, and recovering her usual good-humour with a little laugh, she said :

"You know my temper is not my strong point, and I have been very much put out to-day ; but seriously, I am a little alarmed about one of my cousins and this Mr. Darlington's influence upon her. The more I think the matter over the more convinced I am that Mary Trevor was married ; and if it should be as I suspect that she was married to this man, for the protection of other women it ought to be known."

"Yet you are in no danger from him yourself ?" asked Godfrey, curiously.

"I! Really, Mr. Lascelles, I wish you wouldn't put me in a passion," she said, in a tone that showed she was so near this condition that he could scarcely repress a smile. "I despise and dislike that man so intensely," she went on, "that professions of love from him seem worse than insults from anyone else, but as I told you just now, I am anxious for the happiness of one of my cousins ; and also, I want to find Mary Trevor. What I want in the first place is a quiet clever detective ; will you find such a man for me ?"

"Certainly I will," he replied, promptly ; "but to succeed in this matter we must be very secret ; after your last conversation with Mr. Darlington, no matter what the subject may have been," he said, with a peculiar smile, "he will be doubtful of you, and if he has anything really to hide he will have you watched ; therefore it will be better that you and the detective should not meet, or that if you do so you should come to London to see him. You can write down the main facts for me, can't you, and let me have a photograph of the young lady who is missing ?"

"Yes," replied Beatrice, "I have Mary's photograph, and I can supply a written description of colour, expression, and manner, which no portrait would convey ; but I should like to see the detective sooner or later, Mr. Lascelles."

"You shall, but you will have to come to town to do so ; I never like to undertake a matter in which I do not see the road to success."

" I know it, and that is why I wished to secure your help," she said, eagerly.

Then, remembering all her words might seem to imply, she blushed deeply, turned away her head, and tried to think of some other topic of conversation.

She need not have troubled herself, however ; Godfrey Lascelles had no more intention of pressing his suit, or even of trying to woo her, than she had of offering herself to him.

Her father's will had been a greater disappointment to him than to her.

He could have accepted a handsome legacy from the old man who had regarded him as a son, but he could not take the greater part of the recluse's fortune to the detriment of the natural heiress, neither could he attempt to force the girl to marry him to obtain possession of the money that would have been such a marvellous help to him in his career.

There was the chance, of course, that Beatrice would refuse him and thus give him the right to claim half of her father's fortune, but Godfrey Lascelles was a very proud man, and he felt that he could not take the money at such a price.

They had walked along the narrow pathway through the wood for some time in silence, when they suddenly came upon a sentimental couple who had evidently come here to get away from the rest of their dear fellow-creatures.

Beatrice would have passed on without even looking at them, but Godfrey was not so fastidious, and a low exclamation from him made the young lady use her eyes also.

The couple were Sir Graham Grantly and Geraldine Raynham, and directly she observed Beatrice and her companion, the girl sprang to her feet glad of any excuse to shake off the attentions of her elderly lover.

" Oh, Beatrice," she said, coming towards her, " you must be tired with attending to those troublesome children, and the weather is still so dreadfully hot that Sir Graham and I strolled here for the sake of the shade."

Beatrice made a suitable reply, but meanwhile the baronet had scrambled awkwardly to his feet, muttering:

"So that is the young jackanapes for whom she refused me; I was almost sure it was Fortescue who had cut me out, and it would have been bad for him if it had been."

Godfrey seemed not to hear this muttered soliloquy, and Geraldine had meanwhile whispered to Beatrice:

"Let us leave the men together, I want to talk to you; I am rather troubled about Fanny."

"I have been very much troubled about Fanny," said Beatrice, seriously; "but let us walk this way and talk the matter over, probably we can help each other."

So the two girls walked away leaving the gentlemen to return to the meadow, and then Beatrice learnt what she had not known before, namely, that it had been reported more than once that even while Frank Darlington was an avowed suitor for Clarrie's hand he was making professions of love to Mary Trevor.

"We will unmask him," said Beatrice, resolutely; "if ever I felt intent upon hunting down a dangerous animal I do now in exposing this man."

"Yes; but what are we to do about Fanny?" asked Geraldine, anxiously. "You don't know how hard and unforgiving mamma can be to a girl who compromises herself in any way. She has had a great deal of trouble with Fanny already, but I am sure that if she found she had done anything really wrong she would turn the child out of the house and close the door in her face. You don't know how resolute my mother can be where any question of disgrace is concerned. I have heard her say that if her right hand offended her she would cut it off and cast it from her, and that she would cast away an unworthy child quite as remorselessly."

"Well, let us hope she will not be put to the test," said Beatrice, soothingly. "I think if we could get Fanny away from Mr. Darlington's influence for a time, it would be the best thing that could happen. Do you know any people to whom she could be sent?"

"Yes, I know where she could be sent; but the question is, would she be willing to go? And would

mamma insist upon her doing so without an explanation?
You see, Fanny is very much like mamma—exceedingly
difficult to manage."

"I can understand that; and I don't think it will be
possible to send her away until after your wedding.
But we will keep a sharp look-out upon her. If we
could get Mr. Darlington out of the way it would
answer our purpose quite as well. At any rate, I will
try it."

"I wish you would," said Geraldine, with a sigh.
Then she exclaimed suddenly, though in a low
frightened tone: "Isn't that Fanny whom I see yonder
through the trees?"

"Yes; and Mr. Darlington is with her. He seems to
be scolding her, and she is crying and pleading to him
for something. I don't like the look of affairs at all."

"Nor do I," said Geraldine, while her face seemed to
gather upon it some of her mother's sternness.

"See, he is leaving her," she went on, watching the
couple through the leafy branches of the intervening
trees. "I will go to her alone, Beatrice; I am her
sister, and can speak to her with more authority than
you can."

"Yes, go to her, but don't be hard on the child,"
said the elder girl, gently; "convince her of his utter
worthlessness, then she must cease to care for him."

But Geraldine made no reply, she knew her sister's
character better than Beatrice, and was well aware that
gentle measures would have no effect upon her. Therefore she wished to have no witness to the interview
which she knew would be a stormy one.

Nor upon this point was she mistaken. Fanny wept
and entreated, defied and protested, but Geraldine was
resolute, and though she did not learn the terrible truth,
she ascertained quite enough to be sure that weakness
on her part at this juncture would be little better than
a crime.

Thus, before the sisters left the wood Fanny had
promised to express her willingness to go for a long
visit to her uncle, Dr. Raynham, at Rawfell Rectory, if
she were invited.

"But I don't want to go till after your wedding," pleaded Fanny, tearfully.

"If you behave well you shall not," was the answer. "I intend to ask Uncle Raynham and Ursula to the wedding, and you can go back to the rectory with them; but, remember, no more unmaidenly pleading to Frank Darlington, or I will tell our mother, as sure as you are living."

"He said he loved me, and so he did till Beatrice Burnham came," sobbed Fanny, passionately.

"Don't talk such nonsense," retorted Geraldine; "Beatrice would not pick him up with a pair of tongs; and of one thing you may be quite certain, he will not marry you; he laughed the idea to scorn this very day."

"Who told you so? Who asked him?" demanded Fanny, her pale blue eyes flashing with sudden rage.

"Never mind who told me, such is the fact. And now, if I were you, I would go home; your face is not in a very attractive condition."

"I am going home," was the sullen reply, "and I wish I could go away from this place, and never see any of you again."

"That is a very sensible wish," sneered Geraldine, "especially as you have brought this disgrace upon yourself."

"Disgrace! What disgrace?" and Fanny's face became white.

"The disgrace of throwing yourself at a man who cares nothing for you," replied Geraldine, turning away disdainfully.

She did not see Fanny's face; she did not hear the girl's low despairing cry of "Disgrace—I am indeed disgraced!"

Half-an-hour later, however, there was a sudden alarm raised.

Someone had seen a girl get into a boat, push out into the middle of the river, then jump deliberately into the water.

"And it's one of the young ladies at the Court," said a little girl who had witnessed the rash deed. "I knowed her by her dress."

CHAPTER XIII.

THE BLACK SHEEP OF THE FOLD.

IT was Fanny Raynham who had thus taken her life in her hand to fling it away as something worthless and utterly done with.

Fortescue Grantly in pretty much the same mood of disappointment as herself, though not so mad or so desperate, was leaning against a tree near the river's bank, repeating cynically the words of the Preacher:

"All is vanity and vexation of spirit," when his attention was attracted by the movements of one of the Raynham girls, whom he recognised by her style of dress.

Very idly and dreamily he watched her as she got into a boat and seemed as though she meant to indulge in a solitary row on the water, but she had not taken more than two or three strokes before his experienced eye detected the fact that she did know how to manage a boat.

"Fools rush in where angels fear to tread," he muttered; "I suppose some of us will have to go to her assistance directly, or she will drift among the reeds on either bank and stick there."

But his meditations presently took a new form, and he uttered a low cry of horror, as he saw the girl, when she had reached the middle of the stream, quietly throw over her sculls, stand up, and, without a moment's hesitation, leap into the river.

So quiet and matter-of-fact did the proceeding appear, and there was such an utter absence of excitement or tragedy about it, that the full meaning of the mad leap did not for the moment strike the young man, and he muttered contemptuously:

"The little fool wants to create a sensation by taking a bath with her clothes on, I suppose."

The next moment, however, he realised that it was no mere bath that was being indulged in, but a desperate effort to destroy life.

In an instant Fortescue Grantly had thrown off his coat, and was running at a swift pace towards the river's bank.

There was not time to get a boat, but he was a strong and powerful swimmer, and a few vigorous strokes brought him to the spot where reckless Fanny had already sunk twice since her mad leap.

She came up a third time and he caught her, and held her head above the water; then he tried to swim for the boat from which she had leaped, but it was drifting away, and he found it no easy matter to reach the bank weighted as he was with the girl who was now completely unconscious.

But he managed to keep afloat. Help was at hand, and in a very few minutes more he and his burden were safely brought to shore.

Of course Mrs. Raynham was in a sad state of mind.

She could not imagine what sudden madness had seized her daughter; indeed, she refused to believe that the girl who had so deliberately attempted suicide was her daughter, until she had seen the reprehensible young person's face, and could no longer find an excuse for doubting.

But there was no sympathy, no leniency in Mrs. Raynham's heart as she looked on the face of the erring girl.

In the secret recesses of her own heart she wished that the girl had succeeded in her wicked attempt upon her own life, for Fanny must either have been very mad or very bad to have felt tempted to commit such a crime.

It was not her mother's hand, therefore, that was most ready in trying to revive the girl, but that of Beatrice Burnham.

She did not shrink from the erring creature, and her charity was wide and deep enough to make her hope and almost believe that it was some sudden madness or temporary disappointment, and not lasting disgrace that had driven the unhappy girl to seek death just as life had opened out to her.

But Fanny Raynham's mad act completely put an end to all further enjoyment for the rest of the party.

An accident that had not terminated fatally might have been regarded as a romantic incident, and been talked about and treated accordingly, but this attempt at self-destruction had been too cool and too deliberate for any gloss to be put upon it.

Sir Graham Grantly, particularly, looked grave over the matter.

He was about to marry Geraldine, not for her beauty or because he loved her, but partly because in his momentary need for sympathy he had received it from her, and principally, he told himself, because her family was an ancient one, and had no stain upon it.

To marry a girl whose sister had brought disgrace upon the name she bore was a piece of generosity and self-devotion of which Sir Graham was by no means capable; he expected his marriage to add to his importance, and not to shield anyone weaker or more needing social recognition than himself.

"There is always danger in marrying into a family of girls," he mused, "and yet, what is one to do? Boys are as bad in their way, though the way may be different, and when they do kick over the traces they are apt to make more row with their misdeeds than women do. The most comfortable thing would be to get hold of a girl who hadn't a relative in the world, then there couldn't be any danger of suffering by the connection."

So the baronet reflected, feeling no sympathy for the family upon which this anxiety had fallen, caring for nothing except in so far as it affected himself.

At Burnham Court the pain and terror which Fanny's mad act occasioned, are past description.

Geraldine and Beatrice avoided looking at each other, lest their tell-tale eyes should reveal the terrible dread that ever and again crept into their hearts.

Clarrie went about wringing her hands and wondering how Fanny could be so wicked as to endanger her own life, and spoil the pleasure of so many people, while Grace and Ruth looked on stupidly, and wondered aimlessly what it all meant, and incontinently got in the way of other people when they tried to make themselves useful.

Mrs. Raynham was the only person who seemed calm and almost indifferent, but those who knew her face well, saw by the contraction of the brows and the tightly-drawn mouth, that though she said little she thought much, and that Fanny would have a hard time of it if she recovered.

The "if" was soon set aside.

Life was too strong in the undisciplined girl to be so easily extinguished, and by the next morning she had quite recovered, and was in her usual state of health.

A message was sent to her by her mother, however, ordering her to keep her room, and a little before noon, when her household duties had all been attended to, Mrs. Raynham went herself to Fanny's room.

What passed between mother and daughter on this occasion only they themselves knew; subsequent events showed, however, that the girl did not give the true reason for her mad act, and also that she was so frightened and overawed by her parent's attitude, that she readily made promises which she had neither the power nor the inclination to perform.

The story given out, however, was that Fanny had quarrelled with one of her sisters, had been sharply spoken to by her mother, and in a consequent fit of temper had tried to drown herself.

"What a very uncomfortable young lady to have anything to do with!" remarked Sir Graham Grantly when this story was told him.

"She is," assented Mrs. Raynham with a sigh. "She has given me more trouble than all the others put together."

"I should advise a strict school for a couple of years," said the baronet grimly.

"I have threatened her with something of the kind," was the reply; "but directly after your marriage she will go on a long visit to her uncle, Dr. Raynham, at

Rawfell Rectory, and I trust that the complete change and the companionship of her cousin Ursula will have a beneficial effect upon her."

"And give her a piece of advice from me, madam. Tell her to kill herself outright the next time she makes the attempt—not to half do it, and set her friends wondering and her enemies saying malicious things about her. I am more than half inclined to tell you one or two things I have heard."

"Don't, Sir Graham," expostulated the lady. "Of course they are false, and it will only give me unnecessary pain and vexation. I have really very little to complain of with Fanny, except that she is so passionate and hot-tempered, and that is a fault she will grow out of. She is but a child—only just sixteen—and we cannot expect old heads on young shoulders."

This was said in such a tone of dignified rebuke, as well as of entreaty, that Sir Graham Grantly felt himself silenced, and though he came to the Court that morning with the full intention of demanding an explanation, and, if it were not quite satisfactory, of shuffling out of his engagement, he found himself, where Mrs. Raynham was concerned, pretty well twisted round that clever lady's fingers.

"I suppose the girl really made the attempt out of spite and temper," he mused, "and that there is nothing in the stories I have heard but sheer malice and the love of gossip. It is quite evident, however, that they don't mean to let me slip out of my engagement, and after all, I don't know that I am sorry for it. When Geraldine is my wife I can cut her family if I find it desirable."

With this amiable conclusion, the baronet smoothed out the frowns from his face just in time to greet Geraldine, who at that moment entered the room.

A young lady endowed with more romance and less common sense than Miss Raynham might have felt disappointed and even angry at the demeanour and tone of her future husband.

But Geraldine put no fictitious gloss upon the matter. She was marrying for a home of her own, for a position, for a good private income during her husband's lifetime, and for a comfortable jointure at his death.

Naturally enough, she would have liked a little love and romance wherewith to gild the pill, but love and romance in connection with Sir Graham Grantly were too incongruous to be thought of, and she wisely made up her mind not to make him or herself appear ridiculous.

She was bright and clever and amiable as usual this morning, and she consulted him as to the colour and style of some of the dresses that were to form her trousseau; and having received a hint from her mother, she made no mention of Fanny until the baronet himself did so.

"Oh, don't say anything about her," she cried impatiently, "she is a most trying girl, she will do anything for the sake of getting her own way and of creating a sensation. I shall be very glad when she goes away to Uncle Raynham's; perhaps they will be able to do something with her—we can't."

"Your uncle lives in Yorkshire, doesn't he?" asked the baronet.

"Yes, in such a wild, bleak, desolate place; the scenery is very fine for those who like that kind of thing, but I don't. I am so glad you are going to take me to Italy for my honeymoon, Sir Graham; I hope we shall remain there a long time."

"There is no place to me like my own house," said Sir Graham pompously; "I hate hotel life and the mixed lot of people one comes in contact with, and I shall be glad to get back to Grantly Park after a month's absence, as I dare say you will."

Geraldine did not pout and fret at this speech as Clarrie under similar circumstances would have done; but as her half-sister came into the room she turned to make some remark to her and include her in her conversation.

"How weary I am of this place! How I do long to get away to the sea-side," said Clarrie in tones of discontent a few seconds after she had greeted the baronet. "We never do go away in the autumn like other people, and I am beginning to hate this place."

"That is very absurd," said Geraldine, "you won't hate the Court when you are mistress of it; but I dare say mamma is open to persuasion; you know she can't go away for a week or two."

"Oh, I don't want to go till you are married, but I should like to start immediately after you go away. I must arrange something of the kind with Beatrice, she has much more influence with mamma than I have."

"Your cousin seems to be a wonderful young lady," said Sir Graham with a sneer.

Clarrie looked at the self-made man in surprise; she knew nothing of his unsuccessful suit, and she had been under the impression that Beatrice was a favourite with everybody.

The baronet's face told her nothing however, but looking out on the lawn she saw the subject of their conversation walking slowly by the side of Fortescue Grantly, with whom she was talking and laughing brightly.

"You see I am not the only person who thinks Beatrice wonderful," said Clarrie, pointing with a smile to the couple in view. "Mr. Grantly is evidently quite of my opinion."

But Sir Graham's face grew black and threatening. The idea of his nephew carrying off the prize he himself had failed to win was intolerable to him, and in the heat of his anger he said hastily:

"He had better not entangle himself in that quarter if he expects anything from me."

"Really, Sir Graham, what objection can you have to my cousin?" demanded Clarrie indignantly.

"It is quite sufficient that I have an objection," returned the baronet with offensive haughtiness; "my nephew with my consent shall never marry your cousin."

"I don't suppose she particularly wants him," retorted Clarrie with a toss of her golden curls; "if she did you may be sure she would have him, and your opposition, Sir Graham, would only give an added charm to the prize."

And with a still more defiant toss of the aforesaid curls, Miss Clarrie Burnham went off to join the couple in the garden.

"What very disagreeable sisters you have, Geraldine," said the grey-haired suitor testily; "I hope, when we are married, we shall not see much of them; and as for your cousin, I think her a most forward young person."

"Do you?" asked Geraldine demurely.

She was resolved that no provocation should make her quarrel with the man whom she was engaged to marry, and she had no doubt whatever as to the wisdom of the advice that you should first catch your hare before you attempt to cook him.

The upshot of all these petty discontents was, however, that the baronet, with his likes and dislikes, his selfishness and his fear of doing good to anybody, made himself so disagreeable that it became doubtful if many people would be found to come to his wedding; and it was, therefore, felt to be a relief all round when Geraldine suggested that the ceremony should be a very quiet one, without bridesmaids, guests, or wedding favours.

"But what about your uncle and cousin?" asked the baronet testily.

"Oh, uncle can marry us, assisted by Mr. Langdale," was the reply; "and as for Ursula, she will come to church with the other girls; she is as quiet as a nun."

So it was arranged, not to the bridegroom's satisfaction, it must be confessed, but greatly to the comfort of the bride.

In point of fact she was afraid of a scene with Fanny.

If any guests were invited, Frank Darlington—who had gone off to London the day after the attempted suicide—must be of the number; and that he would come, Geraldine had not the least doubt.

But if this man and Fanny could be kept apart until the latter went away into Yorkshire, then the bride-elect believed that all danger would be avoided.

Of course she did not know that it was like locking the stable door when the steed was stolen.

So the marriage about which there had been so much talk passed off very quietly.

Fortescue Grantly was his uncle's best man; the Rev. Dr. Raynham, the uncle of the bride, assisted by the clergyman of the parish, performed the ceremony; and only Beatrice and Ursula were of the party, besides the sisters of the bride, her mother, and Captain Trevor.

The latter was looking pale and worn. His own marriage should have come off about this time; but he was every day becoming more anxious about his daughter, from whom no further news had been received.

But the wedding itself and the breakfast that followed were soon got through, and the bride and bridegroom departed on the most unromantic of honeymoons, leaving behind them all the elements of bright romance and darkest tragedy.

A week later Captain Trevor and Mrs. Raynham met at Burnham Church in the early morning and came back to the Court husband and wife.

But meanwhile Fanny had been sent off to Yorkshire with her relatives, and Beatrice and Clarrie Burnham had succeeded in inducing the mother of the latter to allow them and the other two girls to go off to some quiet spot by the seaside.

A chaperon had been easily provided, and Mr. and Mrs. Trevor were to join the girls before they returned to Burnham Court.

All of these arrangements seemed reasonable and satisfactory enough; but perhaps the person to whom they gave the most quiet satisfaction was our heroine, Beatrice.

As yet the passion-flower of love had scarcely taken root in her heart, and even her anxiety for others was for the moment allayed, for Godfrey Lascelles had reported that he believed the detective he had engaged was on the track of Mary Trevor.

CHAPTER XIV.

LADY GRANTLY CARRIES HER POINT.

IX months have passed since Sir Graham Grantly's wedding, and during that time neither he nor his youthful wife have found the state of matrimony a condition of perfect happiness.

In marrying a wife, Sir Graham, with a coarseness that was ingrained in his nature, seemed to think that he was only taking, in a legal manner, a woman who should be a kind of upper servant in his house; who should sit at the head of his table, entertain his guests, wear the costly dresses and ornaments with which he chose to provide her, and be the mother of his children. But the first, and all-essential qualification in this white slave was, according to her master, obedience.

It was a pity that the baronet had not insisted more upon this point before he took the lady to church, because he and she might then have exchanged views upon the subject that would have prevented a great deal of subsequent misapprehension.

Sir Graham Grantly did not do this, but he ever afterwards declared that when a woman went to church and promised to obey the man she took for her husband, it was her solemn duty to do so.

Her ladyship, however, insisted that her promise of obedience was just as binding and no more so than her husband's vow to worship her, and to endow her with all his worldly goods, and that in so far as he kept his part of the contract she would keep hers.

It was in vain that Sir Graham said, with more emphasis than politeness, that this was sheer trifling and a distortion of the meaning of the words of the ceremony; my lady could be quite as obstinate as he, and was, in truth, quite as fond of having her own way.

In truth, obedience is not one of the chief attributes of the British matron, particularly when her husband is some forty years older than herself, and possesses none of the qualities necessary to win his wife's heart. Sir Graham never tried to win his wife's affection, such an effort would have seemed to him undignified.

It was her duty to love him as it was her duty to obey him, and failing in either particular was on her part a heinous offence.

Of course Lady Grantly was not a happy woman; who could be happy with such a man for a husband?

But she was not miserable, or disappointed, or discontented.

She had not hoped for anything very much better than she had really got, and hers was one of those strong self-contained natures which, although capable of a great love and of infinite devotion, can yet go through life without their hearts being stirred by a breath of passion, and who can do their duty calmly and steadily as though duty were the sole aim and end of life.

And Lady Grantly did her duty, according to her reading of it, towards her husband.

His house was always well ordered, and she was herself always exquisitely dressed.

She was smiling and courteous to him and to his guests, and she never, even under the greatest provocation, lost her temper before a third person.

My lady, however, was trying and obstinate enough in her way.

She was really a clever woman, and had she been driven to earn her own bread, she would, without doubt, have excelled in whatever work she undertook to do.

But the now happily exploded creed that no lady must work for money, and that she loses her claim to be a gentlewoman, because she earns her daily bread, still held sway over Mrs. Raynham and her daughters, and thus it happened with Geraldine as with so many millions of women before her time—she had married for independence when she would ten thousand times rather have earned it.

"A PENNY FOR YOUR THOUGHTS, MISS BURNHAM?"

Being a clever woman, and having had but few opportunities of cultivating her inborn talent, Geraldine no sooner became Lady Grantly than she determined to follow the natural bent of her own inclinations.

She was courteous to her husband's friends, but she likewise had friends of her own.

People who had souls above drainage, cattle-breeding, and turnips, and who could talk intelligently of art, and literature, and science, subjects which the baronet detested.

Her ladyship read a great deal also.

She must have all the new books and magazines from town, and she interested herself in all the topics of the day, taking much more interest in the proceedings of Parliament than in those of her cook and dairy-maid.

Not that the cook and dairy-maid were neglected; Sir Graham would have had more excuse for his grumbling if they had been.

But a sensible woman can attend to all the details of her household, be it large or small, and yet have time for more intellectual pursuits.

The misfortune of this ill-assorted pair was that while Sir Graham could not bear to see his wife with a book or a pen in her hand—he had an idea that she always ought to be at work upon some useless piece of fancy work or other—she, on her part, disliked to use a needle, except for some absolutely necessary purpose.

A weaker woman than Geraldine would have sunk under the wearying "nagging" ways of her husband; but, though it would be untrue to say they did not annoy and worry her, she endured them with great calmness and equanimity, regarding them as part of the price to be paid for her comfortable settlement and other advantages.

All this time Geraldine did not see Fanny, and she only occasionally heard of her.

From some perverse idea that Geraldine was the real instigator of her banishment, Fanny Raynham cherished a deep resentment against Sir Graham's wife, and though she had as yet found no opportunity of showing it except by silence, she did this pretty resolutely.

From Ursula, however, with whom she kept up an irregular correspondence, Geraldine learnt that Fanny had at first moped a good deal, and had wandered about over the moors and fells alone, shunning even the society of her cousin, but after a time this morbid mood changed, and she developed as great a desire for society as she had lately shown for solitude.

And then came at wide intervals hints rather than complaints of Fanny's conduct, till Geraldine grew alarmed with the conviction that there was still further trouble in store for them from this quarter.

Thus matters had gone on until one morning, some seven months after her own marriage, Lady Grantly received a letter from her cousin Ursula which seemed to confirm her worst anticipations.

"MY DEAR GERALDINE,"—the rector's daughter wrote—"It is most important that I should see you or your mother without delay about Fanny. I should like either of you to see your sister also, but I think it desirable that she should not know that you intend doing so. I have not written to my aunt because I am a little afraid of her harshness towards Fanny, but will leave you to show her this if you think it best to do so and to urge her to come here without delay if you cannot manage to come yourself. Write by return of post and tell me what you will do. The matter admits of no delay. My father does not know I have written, and I have only our old housekeeper to advise me. Come if you possibly can, but don't telegraph; a telegram in this out-of-the-way place would cause remark and attention. Anxiously awaiting your reply, I am your affectionate cousin, URSULA RAYNHAM."

"I shall go, of course, and I shall start to-day," said Lady Grantly, as she laid down the letter on the table before her. "The question is, how to dispose of my amiable lord and master. I suppose I must ask him to go with me, but I would very much rather he remained at home and let me take Beatrice Burnham; she would be worth twenty of him in any trouble or perplexity."

She said all this to herself, but a heavy step outside the door warned her that Sir Graham was at hand, come, as she disdainfully thought, to pry into the contents of her letters.

Having nothing to hide, however, she never moved, except to greet him with a little smile and to ask:

"Any news this morning, dear?"

"News? No. What do you want with news? I hate news," was the snappish reply. "I should like to live in a place where a newspaper never penetrated."

"Then I should like you to live there alone, dear," was the placid rejoinder.

Having said this she glanced again at her letters.

"You ask for news, but I should think it is you who have news, Lady Grantly, with such a pile of correspondence; you will soon be wanting a letter-bag to yourself at this rate.

"Thank you, dear; there is no necessity. I never receive a letter that you should not read," said her ladyship quietly. "Indeed, there is one here that I was coming to consult you about," she added, taking up her cousin's letter and handing it to him.

Sir Graham took the open sheet of note-paper gingerly between his thumb and finger, as though he thought it would explode in his hands.

Experience had taught him that when his wife said she wanted to consult him about anything, she had almost invariably made up her mind as to the course she would take beforehand, and all that was really required of him was to assent to it.

Still, in these days, when a man may not tyrannise to an unlimited extent over his own wife, and when a woman has not only a will of her own, but knows how to use it, the fact of being appealed to gives a semblance of authority, and as Sir Graham Grantly could not have the substance of power, he thought it best to seem satisfied with the shadow.

"Well," he asked, when he had read the letter through, "what do you want me to say?"

"I want you to say whether you will go with me yourself, or whether I shall ask Beatrice Burnham to be my companion and take a maid with us."

"Go with you! Ask Beatrice Burnham to be your companion! Surely, Lady Grantly, you are not so mad as to think of going to the wilds of Yorkshire because your cousin asks you to come, and because your sister, who is sure to disgrace us sooner or later, shows a morbid anxiety to lose no time about it?"

"I certainly do mean to go, dear," said the young wife in her quiet even tones, "and it is just the question whether you will go with me or not."

"But why not send your mother?" protested the baronet, feeling, however, that he was losing ground at every word. "She is the proper person to look after her own daughters," he went on. "Fanny won't pay any attention to what you may say."

"I think she will," was the answer. "At any rate, I mean to try. I can summon mamma if I fail myself. Besides, I feel to a great extent responsible for Fanny being where she is. It was partly in consequence of a sharp discussion with me that she tried to drown herself, and it was I who suggested that she should be sent to Rawfell, so I feel in a degree morally responsible for her."

"Then I hope you won't undertake any more such responsibilities," snapped Sir Graham. "Your sole duty in life is towards me, and it does not suit me to go to Yorkshire this week."

"Very well, dear; don't put yourself out of the way in the least on my account. Beatrice and I can manage very well, with Saunders to take our tickets and look after our luggage."

"I tell you you cannot go," said the husband, resolved to fight for mastery on this matter. "You have invited a lot of people to the house," he went on, "and though I detest the whole set of writers and painters, still decency alone makes it necessary that we should be at home to receive them."

"I don't see the necessity," replied Geraldine with a yawn. "I must write some notes to say I am unexpectedly called into the north, but hope to see our friends on my return. And now, dear, would you mind getting me a railway guide. I want to see how the trains run."

"But, Geraldine, I said you could not go," said her husband resolutely.

"You know I never recognise the word 'can't,'" was the lady's placid answer. "But if you won't find me the railway-guide I can get it for myself. Ah, there is the breakfast-bell, and I am famished!"

So saying her ladyship rose to her feet, gathered up her letters, and then led the way to the breakfast-room, her husband sulkily following.

Sir Graham Grantly was beaten and he knew it. Unless he locked his wife up—a high-handed proceeding that even he did not dare to attempt—she would go to her uncle's house whether he went with her or not.

But for the fact that defeat is always unpleasant, Sir Graham would have been in no way averse to taking the journey into Yorkshire.

He and his wife had not been away from Grantly Park since they returned from their honeymoon, and the baronet was getting a little tired of admiring his own possessions.

As also they would have to pass through London, both in going to Yorkshire and returning, a few days might be very pleasantly spent in the metropolis.

And then it occurred to Geraldine's husband that he might save his own dignity, and seem, after all, not to have been beaten, by saying that he had business in town that must be attended to in the course of the week.

"Then you could look after your business on our way back," said the lady quietly.

She had become accustomed to her husband's tactics of surrender, and like a wise woman always met him half-way in overcoming the difficulty.

"I do not propose to stay more than a few days at Rawfell," she continued.

"In that case I may as well go with you," he grunted. "I don't approve of my wife wandering about the country alone."

For one brief instant Geraldine felt tempted to wind her arms round the neck of her husband and kiss him gratefully for his concession; but the temptation quickly passed away.

Memory recalled to her mind how such a demonstration on her part had once been met, and she had then resolved never to repeat it.

The result of this domestic controversy was, however, that Sir Graham and Lady Grantly started that very morning for Rawfell, that no letter went before them to announce their intended arrival, and that in the hurry of departure Geraldine forgot to send over to Burnham Court to say where she and her husband were going; so that foolish Fanny, despite all her precautions, stood a very good chance this time of being taken unawares.

CHAPTER XV.

THIRST FOR ADMIRATION.

RAWFELL RECTORY is situated in the North Riding of Yorkshire, and in one of the most bleak and desolate parts of England.

The summers here are short, and the winters long and dreary, and when Fanny Raynham left her home in Sussex, to travel with her uncle and cousin to their home in the North, she seemed to leave all the beauty and warmth of summer behind her, as well as every prospect of hope and happiness.

For the first night after leaving Burnham Court, Dr. Raynham and the two girls remained in London, and Fanny was more than tempted to elude the vigilance of her relatives in the great metropolis, and drift away from them, losing herself in the ever-moving stream of life, which always seemed hurrying along in the busy streets.

Indeed, she did try her scheme so far as to go some two hundred yards from the hotel where her relatives were staying, but here her courage failed her.

She became frightened, she began to realise that every man, woman, and child, in the crowd she joined seemed to be going somewhere, and to know where they were going; but for herself, she could do nothing but drift on and on till the lights grew dim and the crowds thinner, until weary, homeless, and exhausted, she found herself by the banks of the dark silent river.

As these thoughts coursed rapidly through her mind, she smiled bitterly, then she said in low cynical tones, the words being meant only for herself:

"No; I needn't come to that yet. I took one cold plunge, and it proved a failure, but others shall suffer the heartache as well as myself before I will try the efficacy of cold water again to wash out the past."

Then she turned and walked slowly back to the hotel, her brief absence not having been noticed by Ursula.

It was part of the misfortune of Fanny Raynham's career that she should at this critical time have been consigned to the care of two such people as her uncle Herbert and her cousin Ursula.

A better man than Dr. Herbert Raynham never breathed.

He was a man of an intensely grateful disposition, and having been indebted to his late brother, Fanny's father, for the living he held, he would have considered it his duty to give shelter to the whole of that brother's family had they required it.

When, therefore, it had been suggested to him that a change from Sussex to Yorkshire might do Fanny good, he had replied cordially and sincerely that they would be glad for her to make the rectory her home as long as ever she would do so.

But the reverend doctor having said this and consigned the girl to the care of his daughter, thought no more of Fanny, and troubled himself no more about her.

He was to all intents and purposes a book-worm, and though he preached twice each Sunday to a large congregation who came from many miles round to listen to his eloquent and soul-stirring appeals, his parishoners knew very little of him, save from his exhortations from the pulpit, for he kept a curate to do all his visiting and parish work, while he shut himself up in his study or wandered about over the bleak desolate moors, always with a book in his hand, and not unfrequently pausing to harangue an attentive if not intelligent flock of black-faced sheep who stood in mute wonder to listen to him.

But the rector of Rawfell was neither idle nor aimless.

His popularity as a preacher had not been gained without much labour, practice, and study, and besides his published sermons, which where many, he was the author of several popular books which, oddly enough, had brought him at various times considerable sums of money.

So there was nothing to be said against the rector, and his daughter could have truthfully given him the character of being a most amiable person to live in the same house with, but at the same time he was not the best of all possible guardians for a self-willed, passionate, shallow-natured girl of sixteen like Fanny.

And for this simple reason, that instead of looking after her he simply left her alone to follow her own devices.

Fanny's mother knew that this would be the case, but she consoled herself with the reflection that in such an out-of-the-way place her daughter would find few if any opportunities for mischief.

As though, where the inclination exists, opportunity cannot always be found.

Ursula Raynham was a tall, thin, severe-looking girl of some one or two and twenty.

A girl who, if she had been a Roman Catholic, would have entered a nunnery, but who, having been brought up a Protestant, was so anxious about her fitness for another world that she took but slight interest in the duties and none in the pomps and vanities of the world in which she found herself.

But she was kind-hearted like her father, and sweet-tempered, and, to do her justice, she tried very hard at first to interest Fanny in the routine of household cares and mild enjoyments that made up the round of her own daily life.

Fanny, however, was not to be so influenced. She wandered about the rectory for the first day or two after her arrival, taking stock of the place and evidently not thinking much of it.

Compared with Burnham Court, the strongly-built square edifice, with all its barns and out-houses, was a very inferior place, and Fanny chose to forget in making her invidious comparison that Burnham Court had never belonged to the Raynhams, and that very soon it would no longer be a home for them.

But Rawfell Rectory was not a place to be despised, and a lover of the wild and picturesque might have found much beauty in the brown moorland stretching away to Great Shunmor Fell that is considerably more than two thousand feet high.

Ursula Raynham was never tired of the rugged beauty of the neighbourhood, and she took her cousin to see Hardrew Force, the famous waterfall, and tried to interest her in the natural features of the country around.

Fanny failed to respond, however.

She complained of the cold, sat wrapped up in shawls near the huge blazing fire, declared that the dialect which the common people used was vile, and that she could not understand it, and exasperated the old house-keeper beyond expression by making her repeat her words over and over again before she would admit that she knew what she meant.

All these were small things enough, but they showed the spirit and temper in which Fanny had come to her new home.

Sunday brought a change, however.

On Sunday there were people to look at her, and therefore it was worth while putting on a pretty dress and a stylish hat, and if it did nothing more than make the other girls who saw her jealous, still even that was something to achieve.

Then, also the curate was an interesting specimen of humanity, because he was unmarried, and there were a few other young men, more or less good-looking, some of them sons of the neighbouring gentry, others of large manufacturers and well-to-do farmers; for many people who were not Mr. Raynham's parishioners, drove from long distances to hear him preach.

But these Sundays were disappointing to Fanny, although they afforded her a little pleasing excitement.

The curate had only eyes and ears for Ursula, and the people who loitered about the churchyard when the service was over, to speak to the rector and his daughter, showed no great desire to become better acquainted with the light-haired, plain-faced girl who seemed to give herself great airs as though she were a person of consequence.

Once Ursula had introduced her cousin to some people of very good standing in the neighbourhood, but Miss Fanny had behaved in such a disdainful manner that Ursula felt vexed and mortified, and did not again repeat the experiment.

Before Fanny had been at Rawfell Rectory a week, she had secretly written to Frank Darlington, and begged him to write to her in return.

But no answer came to her impassioned epistle, and she became restless and irritable, and desperate enough for any wild deed.

Her old seat by the fireside had no longer a charm for her, and she would wander out over the moors, braving the cold wind, thinking madly of her own weakness and of Frank Darlington's indifference.

One day the spirit of mischief, induced no doubt by idleness, led her to do something which would have considerably scandalised her sister Geraldine.

She seized pen, ink, and paper, and wrote a long letter to Fortescue Grantly.

It is true that she never had written to the young man before, and had never received a line from him, and save for the doubtful service he had rendered her in pulling her out of the river when she tried to drown herself, he would probably not remember her distinctly, except as one of the "Raynham girls."

Still, Fanny could not think at the moment of any other man with whom she could get up the mildest flirtation, even upon paper, and she determined to try her luck in this quarter.

"DEAR MR. GRANTLY,"—she wrote—"I can't say that I am grateful to you for pulling me out of the river when my sister Geraldine—now your respected aunt—tormented me so much that I scarcely knew what I did, and so threw myself into the water, because as punishment for my fault she has banished me to this region, so wild and desolate that one is only surprised to find such a place in England. Still, as your intention in rescuing me from the Brent was kind, politeness requires that

I should thank you; my gratitude, however, is very much of the same character as that described by a Frenchman 'a lively sense of favours to come,' and if you would make the life you have saved, simply tolerable, you will write me a letter full of gossip, telling me any news you may have heard, well-founded or not, about my sisters and their admirers, not forgetting Sir Graham Grantly and his bride, or my cousin Beatrice and her youthful guardian. I could write so much about the horror of this place that you might almost want to come and see it. With nice company the wild scenery might be enjoyable, but, alas! I am alone. Can you wonder that my gratitude is of such a doubtful quality?"

She signed this, read it over once or twice, laughed with malicious pleasure to think how wild with indignation her mother and Geraldine would be if they could look over her shoulder and read this daring epistle, and then she put it in an envelope and sealed and directed it.

She knew she would have no difficulty in giving it to the postman, for neither her uncle nor her cousin had been warned to look after her correspondence.

So the letter went on its way, and greatly surprised the recipient of such an unexpected favour, but by return of post came a reply, that, under the circumstances, Fanny considered to be very satisfactory.

It will not be forgotten, perhaps, that Fortescue Grantly was himself in a discontented mood when he watched Fanny leap from the boat into the river on the occasion of the school fête.

The young man considered that he had been badly used, for though he had really not breathed one word of love to Geraldine, he considered that his attentions plainly indicated that he meant to do so.

He was still smarting under this sense of wrong, when Fanny's letter reached him, and her evident resentment against Geraldine found a responsive echo in his heart, and though he did feel a little surprised at receiving a letter from this young lady, and also at the tone of it, he, under the circumstances, answered it more cordially than he would otherwise have done.

So Fanny gained her point.

Without the possession of one half of the natural talent of her sister Geraldine, Fanny had a certain amount of boldness, dash, and brilliancy of her own which was glittering and attractive enough for those who cared little for more sterling qualities.

Having opened the campaign as it were, and initiated the correspondence, Miss Fanny brought all the resources of her restless fertile brain to the task of writing clever sparkling letters that should seem to the reader as though they were dashed off as the natural outpouring of her imprisoned soul.

Fortescue Grantly would have been in no slight degree surprised if he had seen how many times the letters which reached him were written and re-written, scratched, corrected, and copied before the were confided to the post.

The result was altogether satisfactory, however. His fair correspondent told him how she had wandered alone to Hardrew Force, the famous waterfall which was frozen for the first time this winter, and was now a vast stalagmite of ice between eighty and ninety feet high.

And then she told him of the rude uncouth people among whom she found herself, of the whitewashed cottages in the dales, looking like white stones in the distance, of the dark peat-stained streams and brooks, seeming to merit their name of "Hell becks," that rushed down the sides of the hills with such maddening haste to the valleys and dells below.

All this she described graphically, with all the vivid realism of an eye-witness, and sometimes she would enclose a bit of moss, a tiny flower, or a sprig of fern, and ask him to to tell her its scientific name.

These letters were very interesting to the young barrister as he sat and read them in his handsome chambers in the Inner Temple, looking out upon the gardens, the Thames Embankment, and the lazy muddy river beyond.

More than once he thought of sharing the pleasure he derived from them with Godfrey Lascelles, but he remembered that his friend had spoken almost contemptuously on one occasion when Fanny had tried to attract attention to herself, and he shrank from exposing his fair correspondent to the remarks which her somewhat forward behaviour might seem to warrant.

Not that he himself considered her conduct unmaidenly, but he was quite conscious that Lascelles might do so.

After this correspondence had lasted a little over a month, Fanny ventured upon new ground.

"I want you to do something for me," she wrote; "I want you to find out what kind of a young man my cousin, Archibald Raynham, is.

"Odd that I should know nothing about him, except what his people here tell me, isn't it?

"But the fact is, I have never seen my Cousin Archie, and he is coming home at Christmas, and I want to be prepared, lest he should be the intolerable piece of perfection he is so often described to be. Ursula tells me that he will probably bring one or two friends home with him when he comes; I wish you were one of them. I enclose Archie's address, and I may add that he is a member of a club to which you may belong—the 'Regency.'"

She added much more which he scarcely heeded at the time.

He quite understood her suggestion that he should make her cousin's acquaintance, and manage to get invited down to Rawfell Rectory for the Christmas, and the idea suited him.

Above all things he wished to avoid being the guest of his uncle and Lady Grantly, as he knew he would be expected to be.

If he could plead a prior engagement Sir Graham could not take offence, and even if he did so, what mattered it.

Without doubt an heir to the purse-proud baronet would soon be born, and then, as Fortescue thought bitterly, his own prospects would be utterly worthless.

So that evening Fortescue Grantly strolled into the club, of which, as Fanny knew, he was a member, seated himself near Archibald Raynham, whom he also knew by sight.

He did not know that young Raynham wished to make his acquaintance, though Fanny had gathered as much from her cousin's letters to his sister, and this had suggested to her active mind the plan that was now being carried out.

Foreigners talk of the stiffness and unsociability of Englishmen both at home and abroad, but when two Englishmen are sitting close to each other on the same divan smoking, and wish to become acquainted with each other, nothing is more simple than to ask for or offer a paper or magazine, and by some casual remark open up a conversation.

This indeed really happened.

Grantly spoke first, Raynham replied, and rather enlarged on the subject, and then a conversation ensued which ended in becoming personal.

Grantly asked if his companion was in any way connected with the Raynhams of Burnham Court, one of whom was now Lady Grantly.

The other replied that he was first cousin to her ladyship, and would have been present at her wedding but for an accident.

So the two young men talked on, smoking many cigars, and getting through a good deal of the evening, until Grantly suddenly remembered that he had invited two or three men to come round to his rooms.

"You had better come with me if you have nothing better to do," said Fortescue Grantly as he rose to his feet; "there are one or two men coming whom you may like to know."

Raynham at once accepted the invitation, and the two young men strolled off together as though they were old friends.

We will not accompany them, indeed it is only necessary to remark at this juncture that Fanny's plan was completely successful.

Before Christmas came, Fortescue Grantly and Archibald Raynham were fast friends, and the former had promised to travel with the latter to his home in Yorkshire.

"I don't know what kind of amusement we can offer you," said Archie doubtfully as they were discussing the proposed visit; "but I have a rebellious little cousin there who may be entertaining, and there is also my sister."

"Oh, I shall get along very well," was the answer; "and I believe I know the cousin in question."

Then in reply to Raynham's enquiry, Fortescue told the story of the girl's leap into the river.

"Well, there must be pluck at the bottom of that, or else some unpleasant secret," muttered Raynham, uttering his thoughts aloud.

But Grantly made no reply.

CHAPTER XVI.

FROM BAD TO WORSE.

ANNY RAYNHAM had her hands pretty full at this time.

Christmas had come and had gone with its abundance of cheer and its rude merry-makings, but there were no balls nor parties in this far away northern rectory such as she had been used to at this time of the year.

Her uncle's parish extended over twelve miles of moorland, mountain, bog, and dale, and though there were miners and cotters, and a few farmers, making a goodly number of parishioners all told, the few gentry among the number seemed to live at the greatest distance, while the almost ascetic life which Ursula and her father had lived, shut them out more even than distance could do from any form of gaiety and excitement.

But the arrival of the two young men did make a difference in the family circle, and also in the way in which Christmas was spent at the rectory.

The rector himself left his study much more frequently than usual, for he liked to talk about the current topics of the day with his son and Fortescue Grantly.

He had also just engaged a new curate, in whom he was much interested, and he would certainly have occupied the whole attention of the three young men had they been willing to be so far victimised.

But two of them, at any rate, found metal more attractive than the discourse of the eloquent Churchman.

Fortescue Grantly had come here, really in the first place because Fanny had asked him, and next, because he had nothing better to do.

Coming on Fanny's invitation, however, he naturally felt it his duty to pay some more than ordinary attention to that young lady, and it was quite evident from her manner that she expected it.

On the other hand, however, he could not help admiring Ursula Raynham.

It was not only that she was so much handsomer than her cousin, for that she might easily have been and still have possessed no great claims to beauty, but her character was so grand, her disposition was so generous and so unselfish, that no one could live in the same house with her a week without realising with something like reverence that she was a woman of no ordinary type.

Fanny keenly felt the difference between Ursula and herself, and this made her more reckless than she would otherwise have been.

At any rate she now tried the difficult game of winning the love and monopolising the attention of three men at one and the same time.

Two she might have managed, and if she had left the curate to Ursula, probably no one would have grumbled, but Fanny's greed of admiration spoilt her game.

Fortescue Grantly, after flirting with the young lady for a day or two, quietly resigned his place by her side and devoted himself to Ursula, and the curate was not very long in following his example.

Thus Fanny, greatly to her disgust, was left to the guardianship of her cousin Archie.

Not that the party broke up or separated, for they made long excursions together to places of interest, but Fanny's object always seemed to be to get away with her companion for the time, from the vicinity of the others.

The winter so far had been particularly mild, after that one visitation of frost about which Fanny wrote to Fortescue. There had been neither ice nor snow, and old people shook their heads and talked gloomily about a green yule-tide making a full kirkyard.

In consequence of the mildness of the weather the party at the rectory were enabled to walk and drive about more than would otherwise have been the case, and the day before Fortescue was to return to London it was arranged that they should pay a visit to Butter Tubbs Pass, a wild rugged road which runs over the ridge of hills between Muker and Hawes.

The curate was engaged about parish business, the rector was busy with his sermon for the following Sunday, and thus the four young people were left to make the excursion together.

Archie drove the gig, which just held four persons, to Muker, and having refreshed themselves there, and left the horse in safe keeping, they set off for their long and difficult walk.

Over and over again the girls paused to admire the wild and extensive mountain views which lie between Great Shumnor Fell and Lovely Seat, but Archie warned them that the days were short and the distance not inconsiderable, particularly as they would have to return by the way they came.

The Butter Tubs are six or seven deep holes in the limestone a little below the Swalesdale side of the summit of the pass.

One or two have pillars like basaltic columns, while others are very deep, and have bright green ferns growing on the sides, and are half hidden by the juniper bushes which grow about their tops.

But here Fanny Raynham began to indulge in what her companions regarded as a fit of temporary insanity, she seemed to lose all consciousness of danger.

"What a capital place to kill oneself in," she cried recklessly as she started to explore what was really a dangerous spot; "if one rolled down here one would never come up again."

"Fanny, don't be so wicked," cried Ursula in alarm. "Stand still; another step may be fatal. Do you hear me? Are you mad?"

In her excitement Ursula had also descended to a perilous position, but she had caught Fanny firmly by the arm, so firmly that if one girl fell over the precipice that yawned beneath them the other must inevitably go also.

For one moment Fanny turned and looked in her cousin's face.

There was a mocking vengeful demon in her heart, urging her not to die alone, while despair told her that only death could save her from disgrace.

In that one moment Ursula knew that it was more than reckless bravado that made her cousin act like this, and she incautiously asked:

"Fanny, what have you done that makes you wish to die?"

The question drove all hesitation from the mind of the maddened girl, and making a desperate clutch at Ursula, she tried to fling herself and her intended victim into the dark void below.

Tried, but the effort came one second too late, though but for Ursula's clinging grasp Fanny must have gone over the precipice herself.

It was Fortescue Grantly's arm that clasped Ursula's slender waist, while with the other hand he clung to a fragment of rock that enabled him to withstand the effect of Fanny's mad jerk.

A minute later, Archie was helping to drag the girls to a place of safety, and Fanny, ashamed but not repentant, offered no further resistance.

Ursula was the most agitated of the party, she trembled and became hysterical, and it required all the efforts of Fortescue Grantly and of her brother to calm her.

As for Fanny, she did what was perhaps the best thing she could do under the circumstances, she went into a fit of the sulks.

But they were none of them inclined to talk.

Even the young men had received too great a shock to readily get over it.

Fanny's reckless desire to throw away her own life seemed bad enough, but her determined effort to drag Ursula with her to destruction, filled them with horror.

Almost in silence they made their way back to Muker, Ursula leaning heavily upon Grantly's arm the whole way.

The rector's daughter was terribly shaken.

The look on Fanny's face haunted her. It seemed such a revelation of guilt and determined despair that she could not persuade herself, as the two men did, that her cousin was mad.

"She is not mad—she is bad," was the sorrowful conclusion to which Ursula could not help coming. "I wonder if any earthly power can arouse her to the danger of her condition, and induce her to repent."

And yet Ursula never for one moment suspected the real truth.

But a chill had come over the whole party.

In silence they drove back to the rectory, and directly they reached the house, Fanny walked straight up to her own room and locked herself in.

She did not come downstairs again that night, but she did not hesitate to ring the bell and order tea and some meat to be sent up to her.

Hers was by no means the nature to sit and mope and starve, and she was getting utterly careless of what other people thought of her.

She had tried to make Fortescue Grantly propose to her, and had failed, and when she had fooled Archie on to a declaration, and she had responded on condition that he would take her away and marry her secretly, he had positively refused to do anything of the kind.

"There's nothing for either of us to be ashamed of," he said sturdily, "and I don't mean to behave as if I thought there was. I mean to take my wife to church in broad daylight, and before all my friends when I am married."

And he stuck to this despite all her pleas and excuses till she saw that nothing she could say would move him.

"As though I should marry the lout except to screen myself," she muttered savagely; "but if he won't have me secretly he can't have me at all."

That night Archibald Raynham stated his intention of starting for London in the morning with Fortescue Grantly, and the two young men held a consultation with Ursula as to what had better be done with Fanny.

"I think she is mad and ought to be put under proper restraint," said the rector's son positively, "and with your consent I will speak to my father about her."

But Ursula, with the weakness born of kindness, said quickly :

"No, it isn't necessary. I don't think she is at all mad, she will be better again when we are here alone."

Her brother was silenced, but not convinced.

The next morning he and Grantly started for London.

More than once had Fortescue tried to say a few quiet words to Ursula, and each time had some trivial circumstance occurred to prevent it.

And now he went away with her brother, his heart beating with love, though his lips were silent.

While she, when the carriage drove away, went to her own room to calm her disappointment, and reason away the pain that was in her heart.

Alas! how easily things go wrong.

Fortescue Grantly wrote the next day to Ursula, telling her of his love, and offering her his hand.

But the letter never reached her. It fell into Fanny's hands, and though she saw the mistake that had been made in the destination of the epistle, she did not give give it to the woman for whom it was intended, neither did she return it to the writer.

"Perhaps he will take her silence for displeasure, and won't write again," she thought with malicious pleasure in her eyes.

She was right in her surmise.

Fortesue Grantly did not write again, and poor Ursula thought he had won her heart, only to let her know how worthless he thought it.

But a day of reckoning was coming to Miss Fanny, and as it drew near she became more wild and desperate.

It was a casual remark made by one of the labouring women to another of her own class about Fanny, and which Ursula overheard, which first startled the rector's daughter into action.

And then she wrote to Lady Grantly as already described.

But no answer came to this letter, and every hour seemed to deepen the anxiety that weighed upon poor Ursula, while Fanny, on the contrary, had developed a cheerfulness that was unusual for her.

Suddenly, one afternoon, when the mists were coming over the valley, a carriage drove up to the rectory gate.

"Sir Graham and Lady Grantly," cried Ursula in glad surprise, as she ran out to greet the guests.

She did not pause to look at Fanny's face, and so did not perceive how the girl turned white, reeled, then roused herself and fled from the house by one of the back doors as though pursued by the furies.

"YOU SEE I AM NOT THE ONLY PERSON WHO THINKS BEATRICE WONDERFUL," SAID CLARRIE.

CHAPTER XVII.

IN THE WOOD.

E have neglected our heroine for a long time, but in point of fact nothing of any great importance has happened to Beatrice Burnham during these long autumn and winter months.

She went to the sea-side with Clarrie and the two Burnham girls, Grace and Ruth, while Mrs. Raynham was spending her third honeymoon, and when Captain Trevor and his new wife joined them they all returned to Burnham Court.

During all this time no definite information had been obtained of Mary Trevor.

Twice had Beatrice gone up to London on the plea of being sent for by her father's lawyer and Mr. Lascelles, but in reality to see the detective whom Godfrey had engaged to discover the missing girl.

But though there had been a great deal of talk and a considerable sum of money spent, nothing of importance had really been discovered.

More than once the detective had been on an utterly false scent, and the last time Beatrice had gone to London, it had been to identify a young woman whom the human blood-hound was positively convinced was the girl they wanted.

Of course he was mistaken, and the man's professional pride was not a little wounded by the contemptuous manner in which Beatrice turned to Godfrey Lascelles, and said:

"That girl is no more like Mary Trevor than she is like me."

"You see Longridge never saw Mary Trevor," replied the young barrister in an apologetic manner.

"No; but he has her portrait," was the retort; "and just look at the big oriental-looking eyes, and the almost Jewish cast of countenance of poor Mary, and then think of the small pinched features and little beady black eyes of the girl we have just been to see."

"The likeness is not striking, certainly," replied God - frey with a smile; "but what do you wish to have done ? No girl answering the description of your missing friend left Burnham-on-Brent the night when you last saw Miss Trevor, nor on the following day, and the same can be said of the two nearest railway-stations, the next on the road to London, and next beyond Burnham. Longridge has taken care to be very sure upon these points."

"That may be," said Beatrice impatiently, "still she might have left Burnham-on-Brent without travelling by rail, but I don't think it is of any use hunting for Mary herself, a woman is so easily hidden or disguised, or frightened into keeping out of the way, that she may elude us for years; what we must do is to keep a very close watch upon Mr. Frank Darlington."

"It is very easy to talk about keeping a watch upon a young man," said Godfrey dubiously, "but it isn't an easy thing to do, nor is it exactly fair to the man him- self unless there is something really suspicious about his conduct."

"I consider that there is something more than suspi- cious," returned Beatrice positively. "I am convinced that he is the man whom I saw that night in Captain Trevor's drawing-room, and besides that, I have my suspicions about his conduct towards another girl, and I should like to have him watched for the next few months."

"You seem to take a great interest in this Mr. Dar- lington," said Godfrey with growing irritation.

"I do; I take as much interest in him as I should in a snake that had got loose in a room where I and my friends were seated. I have a vital interest in knowing what part of the room he is in, what he is doing, and where he is going to strike; for that the snake will strike is as certain as that he is a snake."

"You are a woman of terribly strong prejudices, Miss Burnham !" said Lascelles, looking at her in curious surprise.

"Do you think so ?" she asked indifferently.

"Yes—one would think this man had done you some great injury," he went on curiously.

"No, he has not done me any wrong," was the calm reply, "because I have not given him the power; but I fear he may have wronged some who are dear to me, and I mean to have him watched."

She announced this intention in such an emphatic manner and with such a resolute expression of countenance that Godfrey laughed as he said :

"If you will, you will; but I hope you won't take it into your head one day to have me watched."

For a moment she looked at him; then she turned away her eyes as she said :

"No, I should never do that. You are a man to be trusted or to be carefully avoided."

"You might say the last of Mr. Darlington, I should think," he said, but half pleased by the doubtful compliment.

"Not at all," she returned quickly. "There are some animals that you cannot avoid and that you must keep a strict guard against. But don't let us discuss the matter any more. Will you give instructions to the detective or shall I ?"

"I think you had better do so," he said with a smile, "for I confess I don't quite like the idea."

Beatrice laughed.

She had no such scruples herself.

In her heart she had made up her mind that Frank Darlington was a villain who had decoyed Mary Trevor from her home, had made love surreptitiously to foolish Fanny, and who would marry Claribel solely for her money, while he at the same time would like to get hold of herself. And taking this estimate of his character and intentions, Beatrice had resolved to thwart the man as much as possible and to thoroughly unmask him.

Mr. Longridge was by no means difficult to manage when Beatrice set him upon this new track.

The payment was sure, and the matter seemed to be all plain sailing.

Seeking for an unknown woman of whose movements he had no clue, was a very much more unsatisfactory piece of work than keeping a sharp look out upon the movements of a young man who could be found at any moment, so the detective began his new work with alacrity.

It promised to be a long engagement also if he were to keep guard upon Mr. Darlington until he discovered something which connected him with the disappearance of Mary Trevor.

Frank Darlington was at this time living in London.

The Darlingtons of Holly Mount were not a wealthy family, and Frank was not the only nor the eldest son, his brother, who would succeed to the estate, being an invalid and a cripple, whose life was principally spent in his bed-room, or the library, or in a bath chair, in which he was wheeled about in the grounds.

Indeed, few people outside the gates of Holly Mount ever saw Arthur Darlington, and even the few visitors who called but rarely caught a glimpse of him, his extreme sensitiveness with regard to his personal appearance making him shun the society of strangers.

In consequence of the seclusion in which his brother lived, Frank Darlington was often regarded by outsiders as his father's heir; but the old squire never fostered this delusion. All his love was given to his crippled boy, and he fondly believed that Arthur would one day grow strong and robust, marry, and have children, as his ancestors had done.

Frank had, in his heart, long looked forward to his brother's death, and to the certainty of one day becoming the possessor of Holly Mount.

He was naturally of an extravagant disposition, and the squire hated extravagance.

Also, he was indolent, and disliked tying himself to any profession, and he always managed to prove his unfitness for any pursuit that his father set him to.

His last attempt at finding a suitable occupation, however, bid fair to be successful.

With some difficulty Frank had persuaded his father to buy him a partnership in a small but highly respectable firm of merchants doing business with the islands in the Eastern Archipelago, which brought in large profits at small risk.

Frank himself had very little to do with buying or selling.

He went down to the City every morning, getting to the office between eleven and twelve.

Here he talked with the head clerk, who brought letters and papers for his signature, talked of various things of which Mr. Darlington himself had but little knowledge, and was himself indispensable when certain merchants came in to transact business with the young stranger, who was for the time the representative of the firm, the real head of the establishment being on the Continent in consequence of ill-health.

There were a good many cigars smoked and some wine drank on these occasions, but the business could have been transacted as well without Frank Darlington as with him, though he left the City about three o'clock every day, persuading himself that he had really done a good day's work.

He was making a decent income at any rate, and this was the point that mostly concerned his father.

What the young man did for the rest of the day and in the evenings does not interest us, at least at present.

Mr. Longridge soon made himself acquainted with all the little details of Frank Darlington's life, and in the furtherance of his enquiries he even went so far as to make the acquaintance of the daughter of the landlady in whose house the young man lodged.

From her, however, he gleaned but little. Mr. Darlington had very few visitors, and none of the fair sex.

He never dined at home, and he belonged to a couple of clubs, which was just what the detective would have expected.

"It seems to me that Miss Burnham is spending a lot of money for nothing," said Mr. Longridge when making his weekly report to Godfrey Lascelles, "but I 'spose she knows her own business best."

"Yes, I suppose so," assented the barrister as he handed the man his money. "She seems to have formed some theory on the subject, and she may be right after all; it is impossible to tell whether she is or not, and in any case she can afford to indulge her whims even if they are more costly than this is likely to be."

"And, after all, she may be right, sir; it's surprising how women do sometimes jump at things that it would take a man a twelvemonth to ferret out. I remember a case now——"

But Godfrey Lascelles, who had already been favoured with more than one narration of Mr. Longridge's cases, here cut the conversation short by saying he had an engagement, and in this way he got rid of his weekly visitor.

"I shall not be sorry when my guardianship of this unsatisfactory young lady ends," thought the young barrister when the detective had left him; "she is altogether perplexing and disappointing. If she were penniless, and less fond of having her own way on every possible occasion, something might be made out of her, but as she is, he would be a bold man who would dare to marry her; I, for one, would as soon put my head in a noose and hang myself—it would come to that sooner or later."

Then he turned to the pile of papers that lay on a table near him, and tried to forget Beatrice Burnham and everything connected with her.

Meanwhile Mr. Longridge had returned to his post.

He was getting rather negligent of late, and was almost thinking of taking a short holiday when he observed an empty cab drive up to the door of Mr. Darlington's lodgings, and that gentleman, with a small valise in his hand, get into it.

"Ah! going into the country, perhaps," muttered the detective; "well, I must go too, though it's rather a nuisance at such short notice."

And so muttering, the man hailed a passing cab, and directed the driver to follow the one ahead of them.

It was not a long drive.

Frank Darlington was lodging in South Belgravia, and the cab which he had entered took him to Victoria station, where he alighted.

Even in the short space of time occupied by the ride a change had taken place in the appearance of the man whom Clarrie Burnham was so ready to marry, and whom her half-sister Fanny so madly loved.

He had exchanged his fashionable ulster for a short shabby-looking overcoat; a thick scarf loosely wound round his throat hid the lower part of his face, and his low-crowned hat was slouched over his eyes, altogether altering his appearance.

In a moment all the detective's faculties were on the alert.

He could not be mistaken in his man, for he had taken the number of the cab, and moreover, the disguise was not so complete but that anyone knowing Frank Darlington well by sight, and looking for him, would recognise him easily.

"This is a rum start," muttered Longridge as he kept close to his man as he walked to the booking-office and heard him ask for a ticket for Brookfield, which the detective recognised as being a station about five miles short of Burnham-on-Brent.

Longridge himself took his ticket for the latter place.

He could alight at Brookfield or could go on to Burnham as might be necessary.

"I should think he was going home on a visit to his father if he hadn't got himself up in such queer style in the cab," mused the man, "but he can't be going to Holly Mount in that coat."

Then the detective got into the next carriage to the one which the man he was following had entered, for Mr. Darlington had tipped the guard to ensure his having the compartment to himself.

Holly Mount, as Mr. Longridge knew, was about halfway between Burnham-on-Brent and Brookfield, and though the Darlingtons were in the habit of using the Burnham station because of the greater facilities it offered for driving to or from the Mount, still, if one did not object to a good walk, Brookfield did quite as well.

At each stoppage of the train on that journey, Mr. Longridge managed to alight, if only for a few seconds, just to see that his man was quite safe.

Arrived at Brookfield, Frank Darlington alighted, gave up his ticket, and hurried out of the station as though afraid of being recognised.

Longridge likewise left the train and the station, but he did so in a more leisurely manner, and the man he was following was already some distance ahead when the detective got into the country road.

"I must put my best foot forward if I want to keep up with the fellow," mused the man; "what a desperate hurry he is in; and by the powers, how the wind does blow."

It was March, and the atmosphere seemed cold, keen, and frosty, as though it had been December.

There had been no rain or snow for the past fortnight, and the roads were dry and white and dusty, and the keen east wind seemed to fray the traveller's skin, and to cut through his clothing like a knife, while the very marrow in his bones seemed to freeze with the intense cold.

Yet onward, unheeding the wind or the cold, Frank Darlington walked, his head held down partly to shield his face from the bitter blast, but principally to hide it from any chance passer-by whom he might meet.

A fever was in his veins, a gnawing terror in his heart, and he looked neither to the right nor to the left, until, having walked fully four miles he came to the outskirts of a wood that was not very far from Burnham Court.

Here he paused and looked about him nervously, but no one was in sight.

The detective was hidden by the trunk of a tree, and even had he not been, Darlington would scarcely have feared the man.

Indeed, his real dread was not of any living creature, but of the horror that was in his own heart.

Having entered the wood, Darlington's first action was to place his valise in the hollow of a tree, where he would be able to find it again, and then he went on through the wood unencumbered, but with nervous hesitating steps, and, could the detective have seen his face, he would have perceived that it was pale with terror, and that great beads of perspiration stood upon his brow.

He would also have noticed that as Darlington proceeded upon what was evidently a search for something, he started at every sound, and the shrill wind as it tossed about the branches of the leafless trees and howled dismally through their trunks, seemed to make him tremble as though with ague.

But the detective dared not approach the man he was watching, for fear of being observed.

The trees were by no means close together, and the absence of foliage made it possible for anyone to be seen quite distinctly even at some little distance.

It is true there was a path through the wood; and Longridge kept as near this path as was practicable, but hiding himself behind trees as he got nearer to the man whose every movement he expected to reveal some tragic secret.

At last Darlington stopped at what appeared like a wide deep trench, that, after running along for some little distance, reached the deep sluggish river that bounded one side of the wood.

Here he looked about him fearfully, but with a strange appearance of anxiety and eagerness, then throwing himself on his hands and knees, and muttering, "It must be near here," he began to search about for something which either he had lost or had buried.

"I must see what he is up to," grunted the detective desperately; "yes, I must, and I will."

Then he crept cautiously along, using all possible care to hide himself, but at every step getting nearer to Darlington and to his dreadful secret.

"Yes, it must have been carried away by the flood."

And Frank Darlington, as he said this aloud, though he was speaking to himself, and believed that no human being was near him, rose to his feet and looked at the deep trench in which he stood with anxious scrutiny.

The ditch was dry enough now, for there had been no rain for a long time, and the wind and the frost had made the earth hard and dusty, but there were signs about of the action of water at some not very distant date, and Darlington remembered that the winter had been a very wet and stormy one, and that he had heard in his letters from home of great damage having been done in the neighbourhood by the overflowing of the Brent through the floods.

Looking carefully about him also, it was quite evident that Brent Wood had suffered from the inundation.

The roots of trees had been laid bare while the ditch had evidently been the bed of a torrent.

"Yes," mused Darlington, leaning against the trunk of a tree, and looking down at the place he had been searching so carefully, "it must have been swept into the river by the heavy rains, and carried away, and I need have no further misgivings. I can't have been mistaken in the spot, but I will go over the whole ground once more. It was night when it was done, but yet I knew the place well."

He walked slowly and thoughtfully, his eyes bent upon the ground until he came to the river's bank, and he shuddered as he detected a great roll of weeds that might have been a human body swathed like a mummy, lying in the reeds, a few yards lower down the river.

Although he was greatly interested in this mass, his interest seemed of a horrible nature, for he threw stones at it and strove to reach it and touch it with his walking-stick.

But when, after much effort, he succeeded in getting near enough to the shapeless heap, and had convinced himself that it was nothing but an accumulation of wood and mud, and grass and reeds, he laughed bitterly and even loudly at his own fears, and turned back with almost jaunty cheerfulness to take a last look at the trench in which he had been first interested.

He found nothing here, however, but instead of being disappointed he seemed greatly pleased, like a man from whose mind some great load of terror had been lifted, and when he came to the head of the trench he sprang up to the level ground with such cheerful buoyancy that Mr. Longridge, starting back to hide himself behind a tree, made a rustling sound and for a moment alarmed the man who had believed himself to be quite alone.

Only for a moment, however; one glance around satisfied him that the sound was caused by the wind and magnified by his own guilty fears; then the beloved of Clarrie Burnham walked briskly back to the spot where he had secreted his valise.

From this he took out a clothes-brush, with which he soon removed the dust and stains from his clothes.

Then, enchanging his shabby overcoat for his ulster and removing the muffler from the lower part of his face, he was to all appearance the Frank Darlington of old.

"Humph!" grunted the detective. "Going to his father's house, I suppose, or else to Burnham Court. I must follow him, I reckon, and by the time I get back here the daylight will be gone. Well, the wood won't run away nor the ditch neither, though what he came to find wasn't here. I wonder what it could have been, now?"

Mr. Longridge was right in his surmise.

Frank Darlington was going to his father's house.

The detective followed him to the lodge gate of Holly Mount, where he saw the young man hand over his valise to the lodge-keeper and then himself walk up to the house.

"He means to stay a day or two, and he knows that the bag is locked," muttered the detective. "But I must keep an eye on him till he gets safely back to town. He's harmless and reg'lar going enough there. It's down here, as it seems to me, that he is up to his pranks."

Then Mr. Longridge went off to secure a bed for himself at the nearest roadside inn, to obtain such substantial refreshment as he needed, and to pick up such local gossip about the big families in the neighbourhood as he could get hold of.

The next morning, quite early, however, Mr. Longridge made his way back to Brent Wood.

Long and patiently he went over the same ground as Frank Darlington had hunted over the previous day.

The detective, however, not being in such a hurry and not really knowing what he was looking for, met with much more success than did the man who had gone before him.

At the bottom of one part of the trench, covered with sand that had been washed down over it by the rains, but had been trampled loose by Darlington the previous evening, Longridge made a discovery.

As he was moving this sand about with the point of his stick something yellow and bright attracted his attention, and stooping down, he picked up a woman's gold earring.

" By the powers! "—his favourite oath—" this is a queer thing to find in such a place. 'Tisn't what Mr. Frank Darlington was a-looking for, I'll be bound ; but it's a pretty thing in its way. I wonder if I can find the fellow of it ? "

The " fellow " of it, however, could not be discovered, and after spending a full hour in the trench and on the sides of it without any further result, Mr. Longridge sat down to examine his prize.

It was a handsome earring of bright dark gold, in the form of an old Greek or Etruscan urn, and it bore at the back two letters besides the hall-mark of the gold.

" Eighteen carat, E. and F.," was what Mr. Longridge read, and he quickly made out the letters as referring to the jewellers' name.

" Edwards and Foster," he muttered, " yes, that's clear enough; this 'ere trinket was made and sold by them ; but no doubt they've sold thousands of the same pattern. But there are the church bells ringing, and Mr. Frank Darlington is sure to be at church, so I must be there too."

And he went and saw Mr. Frank Darlington in the Holly Mount pew with his father.

He also saw the family from Burnham Court, Beatrice among the number, but he took very good care that the young lady did not see him.

Frank Darlington might meet him dozens of times and not know his face again, or be even conscious that he was the same man who so often passed him, but once let the squire's son see him talking to Beatrice, or observe that he was recognised by her, and he would be marked as dangerous from that time forward.

So the detective kept well out of sight, though he saw the glad flush of pleasure on Clarrie Burnham's pretty face when Darlington came to her side in the churchyard after the service was over, and held her hand in his own for a second or two longer, perhaps, than was necessary.

He also noticed that though Beatrice bowed to the young man, she did so stiffly and coldly, then turned away to rejoin other friends, and walk home.

The next morning the detective expected to return to town, but such was not Mr. Darlington's intention.

He strolled about with his father, and near the bath-chair in which his brother was wheeled, smoking and chatting, as though no office in the City knew him or had any claim upon his time, but in the afternoon he went out on horseback dressed with exceptional care, and Longridge, who followed him, soon ascertained that his destination was Burnham Court.

"He's gone a-courting of that young woman with the yellow hair. I wonder what Miss Beatrice Burnham will say to that," was the detective's reflection.

CHAPTER XVIII.

GOING TO BE MARRIED.

FTER much shilly-shallying, Frank Darlington had determined to marry Claribel Burnham.

He would have preferred Beatrice, nay, he would have given his very soul for Beatrice could she have been purchased with such a worthless commodity.

But having come to the conclusion that the girl was not to be won, and that as she was poor, he could not afford to win her, Frank Darlington had decided to carry off the little heiress before a rival appeared upon the scene.

For in very truth Mr. Frank Darlington was in sore need of money.

To all outward appearance the young man was very well off, and should have had money in hand besides being out of debt.

His father had bought him the partnership in the City business, and had paid his debts, and had informed his hopeful son that this was all he meant to do for him.

It was enough, too, if Frank had not been bitten by the unfortunate mania for gambling. But he was a confirmed gambler.

Sometimes he won, but oftener than not he lost, and only the previous week his losses had been so heavy that he did not know how to raise the money to meet them.

Of course, he knew that Clarrie could not help him, for she would not come of age for another two months, but he thought he would be able to gain time if it was known that he was going to marry the heiress of Burnham Court, and even if time could not be obtained from those who demanded settlement of their claims, he could without doubt raise the money if he could only be sure of paying it back within some definite time.

He was conscious that he had neglected Clarrie during the last six or eight months, and that he had once made up his mind that he would not marry her, but he had great faith in his own power over the little heiress, and he had not the least doubt that he would be gladly welcomed whenever he liked to return to his allegiance.

On the day when the detective followed him, he rode up to Burnham Court and boldly enquired for Miss Claribel.

The servant who had known him as a frequent visitor, showed him without a moment's hesitation into the small drawing-room, in which Clarrie Burnham was seated alone, pretending to be engaged with some fancy-work, but in truth playing with the last new family of kittens with which her favourite cat had presented her.

"Oh, Frank!" she cried in delighted tones, rising to her feet, and letting the soft little creatures roll upon the floor at her feet. "I am so glad to see you; mamma has gone out."

"So much the better, dear; I want to talk with you alone."

Then he took her two hands in his own, looked down into her deep blue eyes for a moment with a searching passionate gaze, such as he could so readily call up into his own, and then, reading all he sought to read, and even more, he drew her gently to his breast and folded her in his arms.

Claribel made no resistance.

It was not the first time she had nestled to his breast like a weary child, and as he led her back to her seat on the couch, she murmured:

"Oh, Frank, I thought you had ceased to love me."

"Foolish child, as though I ever could cease to love you," he replied, passing his hand caressingly over her bright golden hair.

"But you never came near me," she pouted, "and—and you haven't been in love with anybody else, have you, Frank?"

She asked this question so suddenly, and withdrew herself from his embrace in such a decided way, that the unprincipled schemer was for the moment taken aback, and he became confused, and stammered:

"In love with somebody else; what do you mean?"

"Well, I don't quite know what I mean," was the undecided response; "but Geraldine has hinted all kinds of things about you, and Beatrice, though she hasn't said so much, has really made me feel more certain that you were not true to me."

"I really am much obliged to Lady Grantly and to your amiable cousin," he said hotly, thinking that his safest course was to seem to get into a rage. "Of what, pray, do they accuse me?" he asked, rising to his feet assuming a tone of virtuous indignation that had its well-calculated effect upon Clarrie.

"Oh, don't get angry, Frank," she pleaded anxiously; "Beatrice doesn't accuse you of anything, except that she says you are not good enough for me."

"Well, she's right enough there," he said, sullenly throwing himself down on the furthest corner of the couch on which she was sitting. "And what does Lady Grantly say about me?" he went on.

"Oh, Geraldine says frightful things. She says first of all that you made love to Mary Trevor, and that she believes you know more about her than you care to tell."

She did not see how white his face became, and how even his lips became colourless, nor could she know that his tongue was so parched and dry that he could not for a moment compel its utterance.

When he could speak, however, he managed to ask:

"Is that the only improbable thing she accuses me of?"

"No, and it isn't the worst," faltered the little heiress; "she says—don't look so dreadful, Frank—she says you have been making love to Fanny, and that is why Fanny tried to drown herself, and why she is sent away from home."

"Upon my word your sister gives me a charming character; doesn't she likewise credit me with being in love with herself?"

"No, but she says you wouldn't look at me if it were not for my money, and if Beatrice would marry you."

"And you believe all this scandal?" he asked, rising to his feet in seeming sorrow rather than anger, and looking as though he meant to leave her."

"I don't, Frank, indeed I don't; only say it isn't true, just tell me it isn't true."

"I shall not condescend to do anything of the kind," he replied, assuming the appearance of injured inno- cence. "I came down from London on purpose to ask you to be my wife, and to beg you to fix the earliest day after your birthday for our marriage; but, of course, if you believe that I only want to marry you because of your fortune, and that I have been making love to your friend, your sister, and your cousin—in point of fact, to every woman I came near, I should not think of humiliating myself by an attempt at justification."

And he was moving towards the door when she sprang to his side, clasped his hands, and pleaded:

"Oh, Frank, I don't believe it. Don't be so hard and cruel, you will break my heart between you; don't go away, don't leave me, Frank.

So she entreated, and after a time he condescended to be induced to resume his seat on the sofa, and to re- turn to the question of their marriage.

But he was on his dignity, was Mr. Frank Darlington, and every suggestion he made had to be assented to without amendment or hesitation.

Beatrice Burnham, coming into the room believing Clarrie to be there alone, was not a little astonished to find Mr. Darlington also, and her surprise was increased when Clarrie, with evident triumph, informed her that they were shortly to be married.

She managed to murmur some words of congratula- tion, then, more disturbed than she cared to show, she left the room and the house, and hastened down to the post-office, intending to telegraph to London.

In turning quickly into a lane, however, just outside the lodge gates of Burnham Court, she ran against a man who was loitering there.

"Mr. Longridge!"

"Hush!" he said cautiously; "you must not seem to know me here."

"But I must speak with you," she said positively; "I was just going to telegraph to town to tell you to meet me. Something has occurred."

"Yes; something has occurred," he replied quietly. "Did you ever see that before?"

And he showed her the earring, scarcely thinking it likely that she would recognise it.

But she uttered a low cry, and said:

"It belonged to Mary Trevor; I gave her the pair."

"Then we must have a long talk together, miss, and I will be at Mr. Lascelles' chambers to-morrow at two o'clock, if that will suit you—but here comes my man."

"I will be there," was all the girl could say before Mr. Longridge had walked briskly away, and, though she continued her walk slowly as though still going to the town, she knew that Frank Darlington on horseback was just behind her.

CHAPTER XIX.

CATCHING AT A STRAW.

F Frank Darlington had been wise he would have allowed Beatrice to keep well ahead of him without attempting to join her, but the temptation to look into her eyes and to talk to her alone for a few minutes was too great to be resisted, so he made his horse quicken his pace, and in a few seconds was at her side.

"You are going into the town, Miss Beatrice?" he asked, compelling her to pause and look at him.

"Yes," she replied briefly, pursuing her way.

"Can I execute any commission for you?" he next asked, dismounting from his horse and walking by her side.

"No, thank you," she returned coolly. "I don't suppose you are very clever in matching wools and silks."

"But you don't use many wools and silks," he said suspiciously. It is Clarrie who fritters away her life in such useless work."

"As you are going to marry Clarrie, I think it would be in better taste for you to admire her habits than to find fault with them," was the severe rejoinder.

"And whose fault is it that I am going to marry Clarrie?" he asked hotly.

"Her own, I am afraid," was the reply, with a bitter laugh.

The laugh irritated him, and he said hastily:

"It is not her fault. If you had accepted me——"

But she stopped him sharply and quickly as she said:

"Mr. Darlington, if you have a grain of self-respect left you will not revert to this subject again. As I told you once, no power under heaven would make me accept you. Good afternoon."

And with a cold bow she walked on quickly, leaving him to remount and take the road which branched off in the direction of Holly Mount.

"I wonder why she hates me so intensely, and why I am fool enough to care," the young man mused as he sprang into the saddle and galloped off at a swift pace towards his father's house.

But he got no answer to either question, and then he tried to dismiss the subject from his mind, and to think of the very substantial advantages that would accrue to him as the husband of Clarrie Burnham.

"I shall get the rest of the family out of the house, of course," he thought, "and I shall have a jolly good income after a time; but I wish I knew how to get hold of five hundred pounds next week. I would pledge the rental of the Burnham estate for a whole year if I could see my way through my present difficulties."

As he could not see his way out of the difficulties in which he had involved himself, the horse had a bad time of it for the next ten minutes—a circumstance that was unfortunate, because Mr. Darlington, senior, happened to witness the outburst of temper, and he rode up to his son's side, hot and furious.

"Confound you, sir! don't you know when you are on a decent piece of horseflesh? Thrash your own horses and not mine. You'll not get a mount out of my stables again for many a long day, I can tell you."

"The beast is vicious, sir," said the younger man mendaciously.

"He isn't half as vicious as the beast that bestrides him," was the furious answer. "That roan cost me two hundred pounds, and there you are taking it out of him as though he were a tradesman's hack."

"I am sorry to have vexed you, sir, but you shall have a better horse in his stead before six months are over, I promise you."

"Humph!" grunted the squire; "and where are you going to get a better horse?"

"Buy one," was the short reply. "I am going to marry Clarrie Burnham on the first of June."

"Ah, I thought as much, and a nice life you'll lead her. There's one comfort, however; you can't gamble away the whole of her property; it's too carefully settled for you to make much havoc with it."

"Still I have no doubt I shall be able to afford you a hunter within the time I have named," was the cool reply.

He was more disturbed than he wished his father to perceive at the allusion to gambling, for he had fondly believed that this particular vice of his was unknown to his parent.

"Better pay your debts," grunted the squire, "than talk of making presents. You have a goodly crop of them again if half of what I have just heard is true, and you'll not get another sixpence out of me to pay them, so I tell you."

With which the squire shook up his reins, and started off at a good pace, leaving his son to follow him.

Frank Darlington indulged in some very unfilial thoughts even if he did not give vent to disrespectful language as he rode after his parent.

Despite his father's declaration that he would not advance him another shilling, Frank had fully calculated upon being able to induce him to do so when he heard that a marriage was definitely arranged between himself and Clarrie Burnham.

And so he might have done but for his unlucky fit of temper with his horse.

All this Frank knew from past experience, and he felt it would be an utter waste of time to attempt to sooth his irate parent.

Once, it is true, he thought of asking his brother Arthur to accept a bill for him for three months for the five hundred pounds he so sorely needed, telling him the certainty he had of meeting it when due as he would have been master of Burnham Court for a whole month before the money could be wanted.

But a moment's reflection convinced him that this would not do.

Arthur would be almost sure to refuse to help him in the way desired, and he might also make things very unpleasant.

So he reflected, coming to no conclusion as to what was to be done to meet his liabilities; but he went back to town that night, having promised to be in the City the following morning.

He was hungry when he reached town, and knowing there would be nothing in the shape of dinner for him at his lodgings, he went into the dining-rooms attached to Victoria Station.

Having given his orders he looked about him and recognised Fortescue Grantly, who was sitting alone at the next table.

They shook hands, exchanged a few commonplace observations, then Grantly said:

"I have been defrauded of my dinner by my uncle, who went into Yorkshire a short time ago with his wife."

"Indeed!" said Darlington; "did you expect them here?"

"Not in this place, but they were to have been in London some time to-day, and intended to start for the Park by the six o'clock train this evening, and I was to meet them and see them off, so I have been kicking my heels outside on the platform for two mortal hours, until I gave them up, and came in to feed."

"What part of Yorkshire were they in?" asked Frank with seeming carelessness.

"A place not far from Hawes, called Rawfell Rectory; Dr. Raynham is Rector of Rawfell, and they went to see him, and Fanny Raynham, one of Lady Grantly's sisters, is staying there."

"Ah, I suppose there was no special cause for their going; it seems such an odd place to visit at this time of the year."

"Yes, doesn't it. I was there at Christmas, but I was not sorry to get away. Fanny Raynham gave us a scare, and if it had not been that her cousins begged me to be silent, I should have represented her conduct to her uncle, and have suggested that she should be put under proper restraint."

Then, in answer to Darlington's questions, Fortescue Grantly described Fanny's conduct in Butter Tubs Pass, asserting his belief that she quite meant to kill herself and Ursula.

"A very dangerous young lady," was Darlington's comment; "I always thought she was a little mad."

But the story of Fanny's suicidal tendencies quite spoilt Mr. Darlington's appetite, and he felt certain that something unusual had occurred, or Sir Graham Grantly and his wife would not have gone to Rawfell.

The immediate result of this conversation was that Darlington attached himself for the rest of the evening to young Grantly, and ultimately accompanied him to his chambers in the Temple.

"You seem to have a comfortable den here," he remarked, looking critically around.

"Yes," assented the other absently.

Then, as he took up some letters and papers from the table he exclaimed : "I thought as much, a telegram from my uncle and also a letter. The telegram must have come a few minutes after I went out this morning. By Jove, what can have happened ? "

As he said this he threw down the baronet's letter, staring at it in wonder, then took it up again and read it over carefully.

"Nothing serious the matter, I hope ? " asked Darlington, who saw that he was not favoured with the contents of the epistle.

"No ; at least I hope not," was the dubious reply, "but I can't make it out; it seems that Fanny Raynham has bolted, and they think she has come to me."

"To you ? That is a splendid joke," and Darlington laughed uproariously.

But Fortescue Grantly did not quite see the fun in the suggestion which so tickled his companion's fancy, and he frankly said so.

Not long after this, however, he took his leave, saying he was tired, and had important business to attend to in the morning, and it was not until he had been gone some time, and Godfrey Lascelles had sauntered into the room that Fortescue Grantly missed his uncle's letter.

FOR ONE MOMENT FANNY TURNED AND LOOKED IN HER COUSIN'S FACE.

No. 8.

"I wanted you to read it," said Fortescue, hunting among the papers that lay strewed about the writing-table; "what can I have done with it?"

And he turned over everything again, but with the same result.

"Who have you had with you here?" questioned Lascelles.

"Only Frank Darlington; by the way, he has invited me to his wedding; he is going to marry Clarrie Burnham on the first of June."

"Is he? Perhaps that explains a communication that reached me this afternoon; but can't you find your uncle's letter?"

"No; and I also miss a letter of my own that I wrote to Moon and Filby, the solicitors. They were to send for it to-night, or early in the morning—that is why I wrote it in readiness; I'll swear it was lying there when I came in with Darlington, for I remember thinking I need not have been in such a hurry to get it ready."

"It's very odd," was Godfrey Lascelles comment. Yet neither of the men gave expression to the but too natural thought that rose in their minds.

Meanwhile, Darlington went back to his own lodgings in no enviable frame of mind.

Though he had been accepted by Clarrie Burnham as her future husband, and though the date of his marriage with the heiress was fixed, he felt that this had been anything but a satisfactory day.

"That little fool Fanny Raynham will give me some trouble yet," he thought gloomily. "And then there is that five hundred pounds to be raised; I wonder if I really can manage it?"

What he wished to manage was not very clear, but certain it is that Mr. Darlington sat up more than half the night, writing over and over again two names that were not his own, and when he was at length satisfied with his performance, the pale grey dawn was breaking over the metropolis.

Yet no one would have guessed that the young man had passed a disturbed night when he came the next morning to the City, looking, to use his own expression, as "fresh as paint."

He told everyone with whom he was sufficiently intimate about his approaching marriage, as though he were the very happiest of expectant bridegrooms, and he went through all the details of business jauntily, and talked of large transactions as though they had been trifles.

"I couldn't very well refuse to cash the bill, as he will soon be a kind of connection, and I already owe him a good turn," Frank Darlington observed that afternoon as he was discussing a glass of wine with a member of a well-known firm of bill-brokers; "but its rather a heavy pull upon me at present, so you must make as liberal terms as you can with me, Cohen; the uncle is good for half-a-million."

"Yes, it's odd that he should put his name to a bill; I shouldn't have thought he would have done it for his own son."

But Darlington only laughed as he said:

"My dear Cohen, he has married a wife, and she is no bad imitation of a shrew, and she interferes in everything. I have had some experience of my lady, I can tell you."

"Ah yes; I have heard something of the kind," replied Cohen, satisfied with the explanation; and then the terms of discount and commission were arranged, and the sum of six hundred pounds changed hands, Mr. Cohen taking as security a bill payable three months after date, drawn by Fortescue Grantly, accepted by Graham Grantly, Bart., and endorsed by Frank Edward Darlington."

Three months was really more time than he required, he told himself, but it was as well to be safe, and not to be tied to a day or two, and after all, there was the sense of not having been under obligation to anybody, that was in itself satisfactory, and he walked into his club that night, met the men to whom he had lost so much money, and paid them carelessly, as though such a sum were of no consequence to him.

Here again he announced that he was going to marry an heiress, and he even went so far as to show one or two intimate friends a costly ring set with opals which he had purchased to send to her.

The next morning he posted it to Clarric Burnham with a letter as warm in its tone as the opal was fiery in its hue.

But there is another girl who has an interest in Frank Darlington's matrimonial arrangements—one who is at this moment a fugitive and an outcast, destitute and almost mad.

CHAPTER XX.

FLIGHT.

NE must needs pity Fanny Raynham as a poor erring creature suffering the consequences of her own wickedness and folly, but except upon these grounds no woman could have been very much less deserving of piety.

There were few good traits in this girl's character. She had no impulsive generosity, none of that quick sympathy for others that sometimes makes an observer sigh with pity for those who have swerved from the straight and narrow path of virtue.

On the contrary, she was thoroughly selfish, and was always ready to sacrifice those who were kindest to her, if by so doing she could save herself a moment's pain.

But pure, unalloyed selfishness is not always profitable, and Fanny had certainly not found it so.

She had no real friend at the rectory, for she had never tried to make one, and she had repelled both her cousin and the old housekeeper when they sought to gain her confidence.

What she meant to do was clear enough in her own mind. But the unexpected arrival of Sir Graham and Lady Grantly completely upset Fanny's plans.

She simply dared not stand before Geraldine and meet her cold keen gaze.

What wonder, therefore, that she rushed out of the rectory by the back door, clutching a thick plaid shawl that hung on a hook in one of the passages, and with this as her only covering for head and shoulders, passed unobserved into the wood-yard at the back of the house.

Here she stood for a few seconds like a hunted creature, her heart beating wildly, and her head dazed and bewildered with terror and with the overwhelming consciousness of shame.

Yes, Geraldine's sudden arrival had brought back to Fanny Raynham all the old feelings and instincts of her class, and though in her case it was the education and training she had undergone rather than a natural regard for personal purity that opened her eyes to the depth to which she had fallen, still the awakening was not the less terrible, nor the less complete.

"It is too late," she moaned in her sudden humiliation; "I must not kill myself as I once thought to do. No, I must go away and destroy my identity, forget who I am and what I am. Surely the world is big enough for a girl like me to hide herself in, so that neither friend nor foe may find her.

There was no reckless bravado in this.

She was only facing her destiny, the destiny she had brought upon herself, but as she thus realised her position, a dull despairing apathy came upon her, an utter indifference as to what might happen, provided only that she could get away and keep away from all who knew her.

Evening had been closing in when she rushed out of the rectory drawing-room, and in the ten minutes in which she had been hidden in the wood-yard, the darkness had increased.

It would not be safe for her to remain here much longer, for if her absence were observed, and they began to look for her, she must soon be discovered.

She half wished that she had gone to her room in the first instance, and that she had been able to pack up one or two articles of clothing, and also to take with her the little money she possessed.

But it was too late for that now, she had not a moment to loose, so drawing the shawl she had appropriated over her head and shoulders, after the fashion that women who work in factories often attire themselves, Fanny Raynham walked slowly and hopelessly away from the house which for so many months past had given her shelter.

The night air was cold, the road was dark, and a drizzling mist-like rain filled the atmosphere with unpleasant moisture.

But the girl did not feel the damp, and was almost unconscious of the darkness.

On she walked steadily, in an apathetic, dazed kind of way.

If she had one idea more clearly defined than another, it was to get to London, because in the great city, better than anywhere else, she believed she could more completely conceal herself.

But her brain had become torpid, she no longer thought clearly or rationally.

Like some wounded animal that seeks to get away into a quiet corner to die, she went blindly forward.

And so she trudged on, mile after mile, until the lights of a railway station attracted her attention, and she went in like a woman walking in her sleep, and asked for ticket for London.

She did not say what class, but the booking clerk observing the shawl on her head, and taking her for a working-woman, gave her a third-class ticket and named the fare.

Fanny put her hand in her pocket, took out four shillings and some odd pence, which was all her store, and said blankly, and with a stupid expression on her plain face :

"This is all I have; how far on the way will it take me?"

The man grumbled and muttered something, but she paid no heed to him, she quietly took the ticket he handed her, and without taking the trouble to pick up the few pence that were over and above the price of the ticket, she walked on to the platform and waited for the train.

Her manner, though quiet, was so strange that the booking-clerk spoke to one of the officials, and suggested that she had better be looked after, or she would travel on to London without paying her full fare.

The hint was not unnecessary, for when the train came into the station, poor Fanny, from habit was getting into a first-class carriage, when a porter roughly demanded to see her ticket, and then she was hustled with but scant ceremony into a third-class compartment.

But she did not resent the want of civility as she would have done the day before.

It seemed not to be herself who was treated in this harsh way, and who was suffering so much for her own folly, but somebody else whom she was standing near, and for whom she felt a great pity, but whom she was quite powerless to assist.

So she submitted to it all with silent patience, but with what seemed to other people like sullen sulkiness.

Some remarks were made to her by her fellow-passengers, but she did not answer them. She closed her eyes and pretended to sleep until the pretence became a reality, and for a time she lost all consciousness of the place she was in and of what she was flying from.

She was roused from this happy condition, however, by a rough hand shaking her shoulder, and a voice in broad Yorkshire dialect demanding to see her ticket.

"Out you go," said the man. "That ticket won't take you no further."

And the wretched girl, only half awake, was made to leave the carriage, and the train went on without her.

Not that it much mattered where she alighted, seeing that she had no definite purpose in view.

If she had managed to reach London she would not have attempted to find Frank Darlington, for she had come to the bitter conclusion that nothing she could say to him in the way of expostulation or entreaty would induce him to marry her.

Suspiciously watched by the railway officials she tottered rather than walked out of the station, and got on to the high road.

The train in which she had travelled was a slow one, and it was past ten o'clock when she thus set off upon her aimless tramp.

Also the mist had developed into a smart rain, and it came down as though it meant to last all night.

There was nothing about the girl to denote that she belonged to a higher class than that of working people, except her speech and the tone of her voice, and she never uttered a word more than she was obliged to.

Besides the plaid shawl, which belonged to the house-keeper at the rectory, she had on a navy-blue serge dress, with plain linen collar and cuffs, a pebble brooch being used to fasten the former, while her watch and one or two ornaments she sometimes wore, were left behind on her dressing-table.

Had Beatrice or Clarrie been in this plight, their beauty, and a certain air of distinction that was observable in both, might have prevented them from passing unobserved through a crowd; but Fanny was fair, and sallow, and plain, and she was likewise too young to impress a looker-on with a sense of her importance.

All these natural drawbacks would be advantages in their way if she is to succeed in her plan of losing herself among the seething mass of those who yearly go down to unknown graves.

Mile after mile, and hour after hour, the wretched girl walked on, the pitiless rain making her woollen garments heavy, and thus adding to her fatigue, but in no degree making her think of turning back to friends and shelter.

Though she had only been away from Rawfell Rectory a few hours, it seemed to her dazed mind as if half a lifetime had passed since she had known the comfort of a home.

She was hungry, too, and as the hours went by, and the morning broke, she felt as though she must lie down by the roadside and die.

But carts came along, going to the great manufacturing town to which her own steps were unconsciously tending, and for very shame she could not sit down to be stared at while it was physically possible to walk.

A man's voice, rough and uncouth, but with the intention of kindness in it, asked her if he should give her a lift.

Her first impulse was to refuse, but she was so utterly weary that pride gave way to fatigue, and with an almost inaudible "Thank you," she submitted to be helped up into the cart.

The drenched condition of her garments excited the man's pity, and he was also a man who liked to hear himself and others talk, so he began to ply the girl with questions about whence she came, where she was going, and whom she belonged to, till at length finding that she either did not answer him, or was so brief and curt in her replies that he could learn nothing about her, he grew impatient and let her alone for a while.

"Dang the baggage, she might be civil and sociable," he growled after a time; "if she ain't I don't see why my Dobbin should carry her for nort."

Then he began again.

"What did you say your name was, my lass?"

"I didn't say; and my name has nothing to do with you," she replied sharply, irritated beyond endurance by the man's persistence.

"That's true enough, my lass; and I aint got nort to do with you, so p'r'aps you'll get down from this cart; Dobbin don't like to carry noane but civil people."

She complied sullenly and in silence, but as the man went on his way whistling he felt rather small as he looked behind and saw the desolate girl wearily trudging along the road, when she might as well have ridden without the least inconvenience to Dobbin.

He solaced himself with the reflection, however, that people who wanted to get along in the world should keep a civil tongue for those who were willing to help them, and he soon after forgot all about poor Fanny.

As for the girl herself, she walked along wearily and drearily, her limbs tottering and her brain in a whirl.

She was no longer cold or hungry, but her blood was on fire and her limbs were scorched with heat, while her joints ached with cold, and she felt at every step as though she must lie down in the wet road and sleep.

That was the overpowering desire that was upon her —to sleep.

Her lips were hot and dry, her throat was parched and burning; with water falling upon her and drenching her to the skin, she seemed not to be able to get a drop to drink until she came to a trough where they watered horses, and there she plunged her hands and face into the liquid eagerly.

But the cold shock only seemed to add to the intensity of the fire that consumed her, and she walked on again like a woman pursued by some haunting dread rather than like one anxious to reach a given destination.

Question her now, and she knows not where she is, whence she came, or whither she is going.

Her ill-balanced mind has given way under the strain put upon it; her brain is consumed with fever, and she is no longer responsible for her words or actions.

But still she walks on.

Mechanically now and unsteadily, like a woman under the influence of alcohol.

She has reached the outskirts of a great and busy town, and there are men and women and children about going to their work, who stare at her, some of them coldly and with contempt, others with something like pity in their faces.

But they are too intent on their own business to pause for her.

The end of this phase of her life is not far off, however.

In crossing a road she stumbles and falls, just as a dog-cart, driven at a rapid pace, dashes round the corner.

There is a cry, a rush of feet, and the sound of many voices, and then the insensible girl is picked up by kindly hands, and carried into a doctor's house close by.

No bones are broken, but her condition demands immediate attention; and still insensible, Fanny Burnham is placed in a cab and taken off to the workhouse.

Who she is nobody knows; and, cruel as it may sound, nobody cares.

CHAPTER XXI.

A FALSE SCENT.

"I AM glad you have come," said Ursula Raynham, leading Lady Grantly into the drawing-room closely followed by the baronet. "I expected a letter from you this morning, and was quite disappointed at not getting one."

"I didn't write because I determined to start directly I received your letter yesterday morning," replied Lady Grantly; "but Sir Graham wished to remain in London last night, otherwise we should have been here before a letter could have reached you."

"It has been a very disagreeable journey," interposed Sir Graham Grantly gloomily. "I would rather have paid a hundred pounds than have taken it."

Ursula looked at the baronet with something like wonder in her big brown eyes, but she made no comment, though Lady Grantly said quickly:

"There was no necessity for Sir Graham to come, and I told him so, Beatrice Burnham would have accompanied me, I have no doubt, but now we are here we will forget the horrors of the journey; so tell me, Ursula, how is my uncle, and where is Fanny?"

"Papa is quite well, thank you, dear," was the reply, "and Fanny was here a few minutes ago; she knows you are come. Let me show you to your room, probably she will join us.

And so saying she led the young wife upstairs, leaving Sir Graham to give orders about his luggage, divest himself of his wraps, and gradually thaw in temper as well as temperature before the drawing-room fire.

He was soon joined by the rector, who was as much pleased as surprised by the arrival of his unexpected guest, and his hospitable instincts made him take Sir Graham off to his study, while he himself paid a visit to his cellar, and came back armed with a bottle of choice wine upon which he set much store.

It was an unusual thing for the baronet or the rector to drink wine at this hour of the day, but the journey from London had been long and cold for the former, and the latter had been feeling hipped and out of sorts, and was glad of the arrival of a guest and an excuse for a little unusual indulgence.

Consequently when the two ladies returned to the drawing-room, they heard from the housekeeper what had become of the two gentlemen, but they did not find Fanny.

"I will go to her room and look for her," said Ursula.

And she went, but she soon came back saying she was not there.

Then the servants were questioned, but they had none of them seen the young lady, and Geraldine was beginning to feel a little alarmed when Ursula said :

"Oh, it is nothing for Fanny to go off and hide herself for hours at a time ; but I am surprised at her doing so when she saw you arrive, but she will come into dinner you may be sure."

"P'r'aps she's gone down in the valley to see her friend Granny Jowet," suggested the old housekeeper grimly.

But Lady Grantly frowned so darkly that the woman did not pursue the subject.

Arrived at Rawfell Rectory, Geraldine began to think she had been rather precipitate in coming here in such hot haste, and she was prepared to judge Fanny very leniently, believing that the dullness of the place had driven her sister to act with less prudence and consideration than she might otherwise have shown.

Indeed, her ladyship was beginning to look about her critically, to think Ursula uncharitable and hasty in her judgments, and she was getting quite ready to receive Fanny with open arms.

But no Fanny came, and when the dinner-gong sounded, and Ursula felt sure that her cousin would put in an appearance, the truant's place remained empty.

Sir Graham Grantly was far too hungry and too irritable for his wife to second Ursula's suggestion that they should wait for Fanny, so the meal was served, though the two ladies ate but little.

In point of fact, both of them were getting alarmed, for the conviction was growing upon them that Fanny had run away from her uncle's house to avoid meeting her sister.

As the evening wore on, and messengers who had been sent in various directions to seek the missing girl came back without having obtained any news of her, Ursula summoned up sufficient courage to repeat to Geraldine some of the remarks she had overheard concerning Fanny, and her own fears that they were not ill-founded.

But Geraldine, with that unreasonable perversity from which even clever women are not exempt, refused to listen to any suggestion against her sister's honour or purity, though she herself was puzzled for an excuse for Fanny's conduct in hiding herself from her.

That was a terrible night for the inhabitants of Rawfell Rectory.

Lady Grantly would not be persuaded to go to bed till her sister was discovered, and Sir Graham lost both patience and temper, and audibly expressed a wish that the whole Raynham family had been exterminated before he had married a member of it.

But no one paid much heed to his mutterings, for, as the hours went on, the conviction forced itself slowly on the minds of the waiting watchers that Fanny Raynham had made a third attempt upon her own life, and this time had succeeded in destroying it.

So the morning dawned, wet and cold, with the rain falling in steady persistent streams, and men were sent out to search the pools, and the lake, and the fell-side, and every other dangerous spot where the missing girl could have " met with an accident."

Later on, however, news was brought to the rectory that Miss Fanny had been seen at the railway-station, some five miles off, the previous night.

A woman living in the valley had recognised her, and had wondered to see the rector's niece with a shawl pinned over her head like a factory lass, and had mentioned the circumstance to a neighbour on her return home a couple of hours later.

The mention of a railway-station dissipated all thoughts of suicide from the minds of Fanny's relatives.

"I told you so!" Sir Graham Grantly said, with irritating bluster. "Miss Fanny loves her life too well to endanger it except for the sake of effect. If she thought you were looking at her, she'd pretend she wanted to kill herself, but if she is left alone she will be as cautious as anyone. I wonder if there is a man at the bottom of all this queer behaviour; did the woman who saw her at the railway-station say she was alone?"

The answer was in the affirmative; but the rector suggested that he and the baronet should go to the railway-station in question and make enquiries about the lost girl; and, though Sir Graham had a great objection to going out in wet weather, he assented to the arrangement, principally because his wife said his going was useless.

Poor Lady Grantly had gone through a good many changes of opinion and of sentiment since her arrival at the rectory, but I think the most terrible sensation of all to her was the knowledge that Fanny had intentionally run away because she would not meet her.

"She has something to hide," was the conviction that forced itself upon her mind, "and that something must be what Ursula has suggested; but how can it have happened? who can be the author of this terrible disgrace?"

Her mind wandered back over the past, and she remembered Fanny's infatuation for Frank Darlington, but she could not recollect anything answering to it on his side, and she was scarcely inclined to accredit him with being the cause of her sister's strange behaviour.

Suddenly a thought struck her, and she said to Ursula :

"I think we had better look over Fanny's boxes and examine any letters we may find there ; we may discover a clue to her singular conduct."

"Yes," assented Ursula reluctantly ; "but don't you think we had better wait, or that you should read her letters alone. I have a great aversion to prying into Fanny's secrets."

"Perhaps you are right," said Lady Grantly in a tone of relief. "I will go to her room, but if I don't find her keys, I may want assistance to break the locks open."

"One of the servants will help you if you ring," was the answer.

Then Ursula went to a recess in the window, from whence she could watch the road and see anyone who might be coming to the house, and Geraldine went to search Fanny's room.

"I know that Fortescue used to write to her before he came here at Christmas," was Ursula's thought, "and I could not bear to read his letters to her, even though he is nothing to me."

So the rector's daughter stood watching the falling rain, and looking out upon the long wide valley over which the rain mists hung, making it look even more bleak and desolate than usual.

She thought of her own life and of the lives of those who were dear to her, and she thought sadly that rain and mist were probably the truest emblems of what was before her.

And in one of the rooms above, Geraldine was poring over a packet of letters and a diary that Fanny had kept with more or less regularity.

The letters were principally from Fortescue Grantly, but though they were friendly, and some of them were even sentimental in tone, there was not a hint or suggestion in them that could connect the writer with Fanny's present conduct.

Except the last, which was of comparatively recent date, and contained a distinct offer of marriage.

Geraldine read this letter over two or three times, and it puzzled her.

Its tone was unlike that of the others, it was more formal and more deferential, as though the writer were not on such intimate terms with his correspondent as he had previously been, for most of the earlier letters had been commenced with "My dear Miss Fanny," and this began "My dear Miss Raynham."

The writer spoke of his pleasant visit and of the hospitality he had met with, alluded to the young lady's cousin in what seemed to be a sad and pitying tone, and spoke of Archie as though Archie had been Fanny's brother.

But though this letter puzzled Geraldine, there was nothing in it to show her that it had fallen into hands for which it was not intended, and though Ursula and Archibald as well as Fanny herself would have seen at once from the allusions it contained for whom it was intended, Geraldine herself had not a suspicion of the real truth.

"I wonder if she accepted him?" she mused, "and I wonder if he will still marry her."

Then a brilliant idea took possession of her ladyship's mind, and, with an impulsiveness that was characteristic of her, she jumped to the conclusion that Fanny had gone off to Fortescue Grantly directly she saw his uncle arrive at the rectory.

"Poor girl, how we have misjudged her," was the sister's pitying remark. "I shall not tell Ursula precisely what I have discovered, but I shall give her to understand that her judgment of Fanny has been quite erroneous and unfounded, and that I expect she will soon become Sir Graham's niece by marriage. As it happens, I am glad that Ursula did not come up to read these letters with me."

Then her ladyship took up the diary and opened it.

Now Fanny did not write a very legible hand to begin with, and Lady Grantly having jumped to a conclusion, was but little curious to decipher the record of her sister's daily life, while some of the entries were enough to daunt a more patient investigator than was Geraldine Grantly.

Here is the first that met her eyes as she opened the volume:

"Boiled beef for dinner—a thing I detest. Ursula busy making flannel petticoats for the old women in the parish, as though they couldn't make them for themselves. Wanted me to help her, but I declined; then she suggested that I should take some grapes to a sick girl, as though I were not sick enough myself—sick enough of this place, at any rate. I know I shall run away or do something desperate if my mother and Geraldine keep me here much longer. I hate them both. Nothing happened for the day—nothing does happen here."

Two or three more entries like this, and Geraldine closed the book and tied it up in a parcel with the packet of letters.

It might be worth looking through at another time, but now it seemed to throw no light upon Fanny's flight.

By the time the rector and Sir Graham returned, Lady Grantly had quite made up her mind as to the course she would take. At present, at least, she would not admit even her husband into her confidence, but she would say that she had looked over Fanny's papers and letters, that she was convinced she knew what had become of her, and then she would get Sir Graham to telegraph to his nephew to meet them.

Her certainty of finding her sister with Fortescue received a slight shock when her uncle and husband returned from the railway-station with the information that Fanny had certainly applied at the railway-station they had been to for a ticket for London, but not having sufficient money in her pocket to pay for it, had been supplied with one which would take her within a few miles of Leeds.

"She would no doubt sell some of the trinkets which I know she brought from home with her, and so get on to London," said her ladyship quickly.

And having herself made the suggestion she was herself ready to believe that it was quite logical and reasonable.

To Ursula, Geraldine asserted her belief that Fanny had gone away to be married, saying that she had found letters which confirmed this supposition, and that no doubt Fanny had started off in the mad manner she had done because Sir Graham should not have an opportunity of preventing the marriage.

"I know that my husband thinks Fortescue must marry a woman with money," Lady Grantly continued, "and he knows that Fanny hasn't a penny."

"But surely Mr. Grantly would not ask Fanny to compromise herself in this manner," expostulated Ursula.

"I don't say that he did ask her, and I fear she acted on the impulse of the moment," was the answer, "but he was certainly engaged to her; I have the letter in which he distinctly asks her to be his wife."

Ursula's heart sank, and her lips seemed to refuse to move in obedience to her will. Until this moment she did not know how she had hugged the belief to her heart that Fortescue Grantly loved her and that he would one day come to her and tell her so.

And now she learnt that he had all the time been engaged to another woman, that he had never loved her, and that her heart had been given to him unsought.

"Thank Heaven no one knows of my weakness but myself," was the first thought that came to console her.

And she turned away to hide her pale face and the expression of agony that could not be entirely kept out of it.

But Lady Grantly was too much absorbed with thoughts of her missing sister to pay any heed to a slight change of tone or manner in her cousin, and she at once announced her intention of starting for London.

"And I wish you would send to your nephew Fortescue and tell him to meet us," her ladyship said in as careless a tone as she could assume; "I have no doubt he can help us to find Fanny."

Sir Graham assented; he thought he should be glad to get away from Rawfell on any terms, so he wrote a brief note to his nephew, telling him to meet him at Victoria Station the evening of the following day.

But the baronet and his wife did not leave Rawfell that day as they intended.

The weather which had been wet and windy enough in the morning, developed as the day went on into a terrible storm, and Sir Graham, who had taken a chill on his drive to the station, now experienced a decided tendency to sore throat, and declared it was more than his life was worth to travel in this condition.

So Geraldine had to curb her impatience as well as she could, and as a kind of vent to her excited feelings, she did what she had previously resolved not to do, she told him that she did not believe the slander about Fanny to be true, but that she was quite convinced she had gone to London to Fortescue, who was engaged to marry her.

This put poor Sir Graham into a terrible condition of mind and body. Illness and impotent rage took entire possession of him. His wife might believe what she liked; he had made enquiries about Fanny, and to put the case mildly he was convinced that her lady-ship's opinion was wrong.

His wife's suggestion therefore put it into the old man's head that a clandestine marriage between the young couple had taken place with the object of cheating him, and without a word to Geraldine, he shut himself in his own room and wrote a furious letter to his nephew.

In his anger the baronet was not very clear or lucid in his expressions, but the name of Fanny Raynham and the words intrigue and secret marriage crept up more than once and puzzled the recipient not a little as we have seen.

This letter was too late to catch the night post, but it went away in the early morning, and, as we know, it reached Fortescue's hands at the same time as the telegram despatched later, the latter telling him to be at a certain hotel to meet his uncle the following morning instead of at the time and place previously appointed. For Sir Graham's cold was a little better, his wife's impatience to meet her sister was very great, and thus the second day after Fanny's flight they took their departure from Rawfell Rectory, and Ursula was left alone with the one great disappointment of her life.

CHAPTER XXII.

BAFFLED.

" HERE is Fanny? Tell me that she is safe and well, and everything that has passed shall be forgiven."

Such were the words with which Lady Grantly met Fortescue as he came into the room in the hotel where she was staying, the morning after her arrival.

Before the young man could control his astonishment to reply, however, Sir Graham rose from his seat, and said, in his pompous dictatorial tones:

"Indeed, Lady Grantly, you are promising much more than you can perform. I distinctly refuse to forgive anything."

"Perhaps, sir, you will let me know what you have to forgive?" asked Fortescue sternly, and with flashing eyes. "You and Lady Grantly seem to be labouring under some very strange delusion with regard to me."

"We are looking for my sister Fanny. She came to London to join you," said Geraldine, promptly enough, but with a new doubt in her mind.

"To join me!" repeated the young man, with a hard laugh; "why should I be selected for the honour of such a visit? Personally, I have no particular interest in Miss Fanny Raynham, except as your sister, my dear aunt."

There was a mocking sneer in his voice, and Geraldine shrank back as though he had struck her, for she remembered she had herself once thought it possible she might become this young man's wife.

It was Sir Graham, however, who next spoke, and in his blustering manner asked:

"Is it true that you have married Fanny Raynham?"

"Most certainly it is not true," was the indignant answer; "she is the very last girl in the world that I should think of marrying."

"But you proposed to her," here interposed Geraldine positively.

"I am sorry to contradict you, Lady Grantly," was the cold though courteous reply, "I never proposed to either of your sisters."

"Perhaps you will deny that this is your hand-writing?" said Geraldine, irritated beyond all control, and throwing a letter towards him.

Fortescue Grantly picked it up from the carpet, opened it, and a new light came over his face as he recognised his unanswered letter, and he said, in more earnest though in milder tones than he had previously used:

"Yes; this letter was written by me. May I ask where you obtained it?"

"I found it among other letters from you to my sister Fanny," was the disdainful reply; "and you tell me you never proposed to her."

"I repeat the assertion," was the dignified answer. "This letter was not addressed to Fanny, but to Ursula Raynham, a woman as unlike your sister as light is unlike darkness."

"By Jove, he's right there," interposed the baronet. "I should not have minded marrying Ursula myself."

Lady Grantly tossed her head contemptuously, but in silence, while Fortescue Grantly continued:

"That letter was written by me, but it was never answered. From what you tell me, I can but suppose it never reached your cousin's hands, and your sister knew well enough it was not intended for her. Perhaps you would like to read it, sir."

And he handed the epistle to his uncle. Sir Graham put on his spectacles, and sat down to enjoy the novel treat of seeing how another man can make a fool of himself on paper.

But he did not sneer at the offer of marriage. There was a certain manliness of tone in the composition that struck the baronet, and won his admiration, and as he folded it up he said:

"Very prettily put, my boy—send it to her; she'll have you, I'll be bound, but she's an awful bad match. Old Raynham won't cut up well, I feel convinced, and there is a son somewhere isn't there?"

But Geraldine's patience was quite exhausted, and she asked imperatively:

"You say that letter was not intended for Fanny; but what made you write to Fanny at all? I found a whole bundle of your letters in her desk."

"I wrote to your sister because she first wrote to me," replied Fortescue, "but if you read her letters or mine, you will find there is nothing more than friendly gossip in them, but even those ceased before this one addressed to your cousin was written."

"But where is Fanny?" asked Geraldine almost frantically.

"At Rawfell Rectory, for aught I know," was the answer.

"She is not. She ran away from there. I believed she came to you. What shall I do. My poor sister!"

Lady Grantly, despite her affectation of strong-mindedness, sank upon a chair, and began to sob and cry with such utter *abandon* that Fortescue feared she was becoming hysterical. Sir Graham sat blankly and helplessly looking at her.

His wife in tears was a phenomenon which he had never previously witnessed, and the sensation was not only novel but embarrassing. More than once during their brief married life, Sir Graham Grantly had tried to bring tears to his wife's eyes, but she had invariably taken care to avoid such an exhibition of weakness, and now, because she could not find her sister, who was, according to the baronet's opinion, as little worth finding as any sister could be, she was as distressed and agitated as the most sensitive of her sex could have been. At length, however, the sight became unbearable. Somewhere in a remote corner of his cold heart there was a feeling near akin to softness and sympathy, and he now rose heavily from his seat, walked over to where his wife sat, and dabbing a handkerchief in her face, rather than wiping the tears from her eyes, said:

"Come, Geraldine, don't be a baby, crying won't bring the girl back again. I thought it was a mad notion of yours that Fortescue had tempted her to fly to him. Why should he do it? If he had wanted to marry the girl there was no one to say him 'nay' but me, and I dare say I might have been induced to consent under certain conditions."

It was well, perhaps, that the baronet did not look at his nephew's face as he made this remark, or he might have perceived a smile upon it that would have given rise to a suspicion that his consent would not have been asked.

But his words roused the lady, who dried her eyes, and said apologetically to her husband's nephew:

"I could not help breaking down, I had so made up my mind that Fanny was safe with you, and now we have to begin our search over again, and nobody seems to know what has become of my poor sister."

Fortescue's sympathies were aroused; he asked several questions, and the replies told him of Ursula's letter, the journey to the north, Fanny's flight, and Geraldine's discovery of the letters, and of the theory she had built up on their contents.

But when the young man hinted that, perhaps, Fanny had made a third, and this time successful, attempt upon her life, the suggestion was at once disposed of by the account of how she had been traced to a railway-station, and thence to a village within a few miles of Leeds, and how there was reason to believe she would arrive there penniless.

"Then your only course is to go there to seek her," said young Grantly promptly.

"OH, FRANK! I AM SO GLAD TO SEE YOU."

"You have lost much precious time," the young man went on, "and it will be well to send to your mother, and think of any friends to whom your sister can have gone."

"Of course, of course; a very sensible suggestion," said Sir Graham, who was longing for the comfort of his own house. "Fanny would naturally go to Burnham Court; her place is with her mother, and after all, Geraldine, you would have no authority over your sister, and if she refused to do as you wished, you could not compel obedience from her."

"But mamma is so hard, and if Fanny has been foolish, or imprudent in any way, our mother will never forgive her."

"Your mother was never hard with you," replied the baronet severely; "and she is really the proper person to look after her daughter."

Then, perceiving that her ladyship was hovering between obedience and rebellion, and seeing also an avenue of escape from responsibility and exertion for himself, he added in the tone of a man actuated by the best and noblest feeling:

"I must insist, my dear, that we go at once to your mother, and acquaint her with all the facts of the case that have come to our knowledge. If Fanny is with her, all the better; if she is not, there will be time enough then to decide what steps are the best to be taken to find her."

"You don't know mamma," objected Geraldine, feebly looking to Fortescue for sympathy and support, in opposition to his uncle.

But she found none, for the young barrister said gravely:

"I think my uncle is quite right; from the little I have seen of your sister I do not believe she would submit to be controlled or influenced by you, and it must not be forgotten that if she is not with your mother or at her uncle's house, every day she is missing adds to the difficulty of finding her, and helps to compromise her more seriously."

"I suppose you are right," replied her ladyship dejectedly; "but Fanny did not run away from me to go home, of that I am quite convinced."

"No; I fear she is not at the Court," was the answer. "I met Darlington last night, and he had just come up from Sussex; he was full of his approaching marriage to your sister Claribel. He came back to my chambers with me, and I showed him my uncle's letter, which I found awaiting me, and that puzzled me not a little; I think we even talked about Fanny, and if she had been at Burnham Court he would have been sure to have mentioned it."

"Then it is evidently useless for us to go there," said Lady Grantly in a tone of relief; "it will be much better for us to go back to Yorkshire and try to trace my sister from the station where she must have alighted; don't you think so, Mr. Grantly?"

But Mr. Grantly did not think so, neither did Sir Graham, and my lady found that she could not always have her own way, and that whatever happened afterwards there was nothing now for her but to go and see her mother, and then return to Grantly Park.

But she was far too dispirited to try to keep up even an appearance of cheerfulness, and murmuring some slight excuse for leaving them, Lady Grantly went off to her bed-room.

"Ah!" groaned the baronet, when he found himself alone with his nephew, "this comes of marrying into a family of girls; there is one gone to the bad, and nobody can say how many of the others will follow her pernicious example."

"But do you really think the girl has got into any serious difficulty, sir?" asked Fortescue gravely.

"Think—I am sure of it," was the reply. "I made enquiries myself," Sir Graham went on; "and country folks are more outspoken to a man than they are to a woman. I have no doubt as to what has happened, I was only furious to think you had been the cause; and now I mean to get home as soon as I can, and leave the girl's mother to look after her. I am sorry I wrote to you in the tone I did, Fortescue, and I wish you'd come back with us and stay a few days."

"Thank you, uncle; but I can't leave London at present, for I am rather busy; and as for the letter, of course it was written under a misapprehension. Oddly enough, however, I have lost it. I can't find it anywhere."

"What is it that you have lost?" asked Lady Grantly, who re-entered the room at this point.

More with a desire to avoid talking about Fanny than because he attached any importance to the loss of the letter and of the legal opinion which he had had to write out a second time, Fortescue Grantly described how he had waited at Victoria Station the previous night, how he met Frank Darlington, and what had happened at his chambers.

But he was not very animated in his description, and his listeners were not very attentive.

Sir Graham was thinking of the business that he had not attended to, and that he had meant to remain in London a few days to transact, and he was resolving not to allude to it, lest it should give his wife an opportunity and excuse for delaying the meeting with her mother, perhaps of avoiding the explanation altogether, and Lady Grantly was wondering how she could in the first place get hold of Beatrice Burnham, and consult with her about poor Fanny.

So Fortescue talked to almost deaf ears, though what he said was well remembered afterwards by at least one of his listeners.

Soon after this the young barrister took his leave, the luggage was sent off to Victoria Station, and my lady found that, despite her anxiety, she must do a little shopping.

In point of fact, self-willed and self-reliant as Geraldine could be with her husband, she was decidedly afraid to meet her mother with such a tale to unfold, and she loitered and wasted time in so many ways that it was five o'clock when they reached the railway-station, and they had only just time to catch the express.

"This is lucky," said Sir Graham, looking out of the carriage window; "with good fortune we shall reach the Court at eight o'clock, in time for dinner. I wish I had thought of telegraphing for the carriage to meet us. I'll do so the first place we stop at."

His wife made no reply.

Her mind was too full of anxiety to allow her to pay much heed to her husband's babble, and she did not notice his sudden cry of surprise, or the way in which he almost threw himself back in the carriage to avoid recognition.

And yet his cause for doing so was very simple.

A young lady in the next carriage was saying good-bye to a young gentleman, who had evidently come to see her off, and she was leaning out of the window for a last word, just as the train was on the move.

"Beatrice Burnham, by all that is blue," muttered the baronet savagely; "parting with Godfrey Lascelles too; came to town on purpose to meet him, I have no doubt. I never quite believed in that girl; she was too saucy by half. She has more influence over my wife than I at all approve of. I would forbid Geraldine to be on friendly terms with her, if I thought she'd obey me, but I doubt it, and then I should be in a very false position; but if I don't keep a sharp look-out on them now my lady will be off with this adventuress to look for Miss Fanny whether I consent or not."

So the baronet pondered, and for fear of being recognised by Beatrice he did not get out of the train to telegraph for a carriage to meet him as he intended.

"Probably we shall be able to get a fly," he thought by way of excuse for his change of purpose; "in any case, I'll risk it."

He did risk it, and on arriving at Burnham-on-Brent found that the only cab at the station had been previously ordered.

"I would offer to share it with you, if you were going to the Court," said Beatrice, touching Lady Grantly lightly on the shoulder.

"That is where we are going," said Geraldine with a bright expression of countenance; "and oh, I am so glad to meet you!"

"And I to see you," said Beatrice; "I was wondering what had become of you!"

Then the two girls got into the cab, and Sir Graham sulkily followed.

He disliked Beatrice Burnham exceedingly, still she might have been polite enough to speak to him.

In point of fact, she was unconscious that she had not done so, but she was almost as anxious to talk to Geraldine as the baronet's wife was to confer with her.

"But I will put a spoke in their wheel," muttered Sir Graham gloomily. "I will talk to Fanny's mother before my wife can say a word; she is a woman of the world, and will pay some heed to what I say, if only for her own sake."

CHAPTER XXIII.

CLARRIE'S DANGER.

SIR GRAHAM GRANTLY had told his story, and Mrs. Trevor—as Fanny's mother was now called—was simply speechless with indignation and shame.

That a daughter of hers should have created a scandal and have left such terrible doubt as to her conduct behind her, seemed to this proud stern woman next to impossible, and yet, knowing Fanny as she did, she could not persuade herself that the story was untrue."

"She is no longer a daughter of mine," said the proud stern woman in the low concentrated tone of strongly repressed feeling, "and I shall take no step to find her; she shall never cross the threshold of my door again, her name shall be forbidden to be uttered under my roof, and the fact that I ever had such a child shall be blotted out of my memory.

So slowly did the outraged mother speak, and so low was the tone in which she thus cast away her child, that Sir Graham was a little alarmed, and he said hastily:

"I didn't think you would take it in this way; I thought you would go and look for her, and make sure that she was in a place of safety; I am afraid Geraldine will not rest quietly till Fanny is found."

"Geraldine is your wife, Sir Graham," said Mrs. Trevor coldly, "and when she married you she passed beyond my control; it is for you to influence her."

"I wish I could influence her," said the baronet ruefully; "but she seems to me to possess more than her share of the family wilfulness. I was first of all dragged into Yorkshire post-haste, then I was hurried back to London, now I am brought here, and what next is to follow I cannot conjecture, and all because my wife has some quixotic idea about saving her sister."

"From what you tell me I should think she was past saving," said the lady sternly; "and if Geraldine has any consideration for you or for herself, she will leave the wretched girl to her fate. Such passion-tossed creatures find their level sooner or later, and if it is in a nameless grave, the world is well rid of them, and they should be forgotten speedily."

"Don't you think your creed is a hard one, Mrs. Trevor?" asked Sir Graham, who was not himself remarkable for the charity which covereth a multitude of sins.

"Hard or soft, it is my creed and I will follow it," she replied coldly; "if my right hand offend me I will cut it off and cast it from me. I would have no mercy upon myself, and I will have none upon another. We will consider the subject disposed of, if you please, Sir Graham; and there is the dinner-bell."

So saying, Mrs. Trevor led the way to the dining-room, where they were almost immediately joined by Captain Trevor, Clarrie and Beatrice Burnham, Lady Grantly, and her two younger sisters.

The captain was beginning to look old and careworn. His second marriage had not been altogether a success; he was anxious and troubled at times about the silence of his daughter and the mystery that enshrouded her; while his wife's complaints at soon having to leave Burnham Court to go and live in his small house, did not in any degree add to his comfort.

But he tried to seem cheerful this evening, and to atone for the frigid silence and absent-mindedness of his wife by his own genial conversation.

In these efforts he was only partially successful, however.

The ladies were all of them very silent and ate but little.

Sir Graham, however, felt that until now he had never properly appreciated his host, and he was not sorry when the ladies rose from the table and he and the captain were left in conference together.

Directly they had entered the drawing-room Lady Grantly stepped to her mother's side and said in a low tone:

"Mamma, I want to have a little talk with you; shall we go to your room?"

Mrs. Trevor looked at her daughter calmly, almost coldly, then she asked:

"Do you want to talk to me about Fanny?"

"Yes," was the hesitating reply.

"Then there is no necessity for going to my room," was the stern reply; "for I have something to say to you and to the rest of the girls."

She raised her voice as she said this, and Beatrice, who had been talking to Clarrie and Grace and Ruth with the intention of leaving Geraldine and her mother undisturbed, felt that her audience was leaving her, so she also turned to listen.

"Girls," said Mrs. Trevor in clear incisive tones, "your sister Fanny has disgraced herself and me and all of you. Henceforth she is to me and to you as one that is dead—for aught I know she is dead, but her name is never to be mentioned again in my hearing. I positively forbid it."

"But, mamma," expostulated Geraldine hotly.

Mrs. Trevor lifted her hand to impose silence, then she said:

"You are married and beyond my control, Geraldine, but you will obey me in this matter if we are to remain friends."

"Really, mamma, I think you are very unjust," here broke out Lady Grantly impetuously; "you might, at any rate, listen to me."

"You compel me to leave the room," said the mother with unbending sternness as she suited the action to the word, leaving the girls to themselves.

"What has Fanny done?" asked Clarrie anxiously, while her own cheek paled with some undefined dread.

"I cannot exactly say what she has done," replied Geraldine evasively, "and I am afraid mamma is right in saying she has disgraced us; but even if it is so, mamma need not be so hard and so unfeeling, she might at least make some effort to reclaim her."

"I think mamma is quite right," said Clarrie in what seemed a strangely callous tone from one who was usually so soft and sympathetic; "I told Frank yesterday how you attributed Fanny's strange behaviour to him, and he was furiously indignant. She always was a bad unruly girl."

But Beatrice and Geraldine had uttered a simultaneous "Ah!" and their eyes met.

Clarrie's jealous observation had brought things back to their minds that might otherwise have been forgotten, and they for the moment were afraid to speak lest they should give expression to the suspicion that as soon as it had birth became a certainty.

It was Geraldine who some minutes later took Clarrie aside and asked earnestly:

"If Frank Darlington is the cause of Fanny's disgrace, Clarrie, you won't marry him, will you?"

The heiress of Burnham Court looked at her half-sister for an instant in dumb bewilderment.

Lady Grantly's horrible suggestion seemed to have deprived her of the power of speech.

For a second or two the girl seem to fight for breath, then a violent fit of coughing came on, and before it ceased the handkerchief which she had pressed to her lips was dyed red with blood.

Beatrice and Geraldine, who had both been trying to soothe the excited girl, became pale when they saw the hue of the bright fluid, while Grace ran from the room screaming wildly:

"Mamma, mamma! Clarrie has broken a blood-vessel."

It was but too true.

The heiress of Burnham Court and the affianced wife of Frank Darlington had broken a blood-vessel, and the doctor who was summoned in all haste looked very grave, said that she must be kept quiet and free from all excitement, as, if the hæmorrhage broke out again, the result would in all probability be fatal.

So that evening, while Frank Darlington was showing the opal ring he had purchased for Clarrie to a friend at his club, Clarrie herself was lying in bed in a critical condition, and his chances of ever becoming master of Burnham Court were suddenly become almost worthless.

Sir Graham and his wife drove back to Grantly Park that night almost in silence.

Only once did the baronet break it by asking abruptly:

"If Clarrie dies, who will the Court and estate go to?"

"To Beatrice," was the answer; "it was always a doubtful question whether her father or Clarrie's had most right to it."

"Ah, I remember now."

Then he relapsed into silence, but he thought bitterly that he would gladly give half of his own fortune to restore Clarrie to health.

It would, indeed, be added gall and bitterness to the dissatisfaction of his married life if the woman who had refused him should, without aid from him, become really wealthy.

For he did not know any more than the inmates of the Court that Beatrice, instead of being poor, was, in point of fact, a very great heiress indeed.

All through that night Mrs. Trevor sat alone by the bedside of her eldest daughter.

She had refused the offers of Beatrice and Geraldine to share the watch with her, and she sat there now, patient as the time itself, and sleepless as fate.

Very bitter were the thoughts of this proud imperious woman as she sat there so silent and tearless.

Like scenes in a panorama, her past life seemed to come back to her from the time that she clasped as a babe in her arms the fair girl who lay there so calm and motionless with a face as colourless as the pillow upon which it rested.

How proud she had been of that beautiful baby, and how happy she was in her first husband's love!

And then came death and desolation—soon forgotten, however—and her second marriage followed.

But she was jealous of the child by whose father's will she only retained her position and wealth for a limited time, and then came other children for whom she felt grasping and greedy, and of this second family the one who had been her favourite and of whom she had hoped the most was Fanny.

She thought of these shattered hopes bitterly through those long watches of the night; but she was not like many mothers who by deliberate choice cling to the very blackest of the sheep in their folds.

What she told Sir Graham was strictly true. She would have had no mercy upon herself, and she had none to bestow upon her erring daughter.

It seemed, in looking back to this time, as though she had then buried two of her daughters—her fairest and her best beloved.

But though the bitterness of death entered into the mother's heart, Clarrie did not die then.

On the contrary, she was better the next morning and able to sit up in bed and to take some food languidly, and she showed a good deal of vexation when no letter came to her from her absent lover.

Late in the day, however, Darlington's opal ring came, accompanied by the letter he had written, and Clarrie put the flashing jewels on her finger, admired the white hand with its new ornament, and pressed the letter to her breast when she had read it over and over again with glowing eagerness.

But for the girl's anxiety and disappointment in the morning, Mrs. Trevor would not have given her daughter the letter and packet, and, as it was, she feared the excitement might be dangerous.

But she was mistaken. Happiness rarely kills, and from this time forward Clarrie began to mend most wonderfully.

For such a gentle impressionable creature, Clarrie was very determined, and even resentful upon one point. She would not see her sister, Lady Grantly, when she came to the Court.

"Tell her that she nearly killed me, and that I never wish to see her again," she said with dangerous energy, and for the first time in her life she persisted in her determination.

Mrs. Trevor said nothing about the letter she had received from Darlington.

Its tone and manner annoyed her beyond expression, but she was, as he knew, powerless to resent it.

By the date he had fixed for his marriage with Clarrie her tenure of power at the Court would have ceased, and though he asked her to remain where she was for the wedding, he did so rather in the manner of a man conferring a favour than of asking one.

"His triumph will be short lived," mused the mother, resentfully but sorrowfully. "Clarrie's life at the best will not be a long one, and if she dies childless he will not even have a life-interest in the estate."

But she uttered never a word of her anger or of her fears.

Clarrie's death and the failure of Darlington's mercenary designs would bring the sad mother no satisfaction, for the house of which she had so long been the mistress would then pass into the possession of her niece.

So poor Mrs. Trevor had to sit and suffer in silence, not daring to hope for anything, lest what she wished for might come, and be the worst that could happen for her.

As for Beatrice, she found herself in a painfully delicate position.

Had she not been the one person who would materially benefit by Clarrie's death, she would unflinchingly have warned her against a marriage with Frank Darlington, and have given her such reasons against it as must, in her opinion, have broken off the match.

But Clarrie's life seemed to hang upon her love for this worthless man, and our heroine, who was so often singing "Heigho! for a husband," and yet scoffing at every man who came as a candidate for her favour, could not help wondering what subtle charm or hidden fascination Squire Darlington's youngest son possessed to make two girls in one family so weakly and foolishly in love with him.

For Miss Beatrice was a very observant young person, and she had seen quite enough to convince her that, whatever might be said to the contrary, Frank Darlington was the author of Fanny's misery and of Fanny's flight from her friends.

In her heart also Beatrice believed that this man had married Mary Trevor, and had murdered her, but she could get no real or tangible proof of this, and the crime was of far too terrible a nature to be spoken of unless it could be brought home to the perpetrator.

Still the very suspicion that the man whom her cousin was about to marry was such a miscreant made the girl silent and wretched, and though she would not refuse her help in preparing for the wedding, she went about the house "looking," as Clarrie peevishly expressed it, "as though she had just come from a funeral."

But time waits for no one, and the days and the weeks went by.

Clarrie was getting stronger, more like her usual self, and if she had any doubt about the wisdom of the step she was so near taking, she resolutely put it aside and would not attempt to face it.

As for the triumphant lover, he came down from London on flying visits, sometimes remaining for a day, sometimes only for an hour or two, but always devoted and tender to the girl who was so soon to become his wife, whatever his words or bearing might be to the rest of her family.

Lady Grantly came to the house once after Clarrie was taken ill, but she was received so coldly by her mother, and her half-sister refused to admit her with such evident aversion, that the baronet's wife felt no inclination to repeat her visit.

"I am determined to find Fanny," she said to Beatrice as she took her leave on this occasion. "My mother and Clarrie and my husband may say what they like; I am not going to abandon my sister to please them."

"I should say and do the same if she were my sister," was the reply, "and if I can help you in any way, be sure you let me know."

"I will," said Lady Grantly.

But no appeal for help came.

No news reached the Court of the lost and erring girl, and Claribel Burnham's twenty-first birthday arrived.

It had been the intention of the young heiress to celebrate her coming of age with much feasting and rejoicing, but as the time drew near she felt unequal to the task, and she readily agreed to her lover's suggestion that they should keep up the double event on their wedding-day.

Thus the all-important morning came, and Darlington, who had been staying at the Court for the night, felt as he rose that morning that Fortune was in his favour, and he no longer need care for friend or foe.

"A few hours more, and I shall be master here," he thought, as he looked out of his bedroom window, "and then my father and my hunchbacked brother will find I am not a man to be snubbed with impunity."

CHAPTER XXIV.

IN A WORKHOUSE.

HE was not pretty to look at, and the ill-fitting, unbecoming workhouse clothes in which she was clad, would have made even a handsome girl look plain and uninteresting.

Also she had been very ill, "nigh unto death's door," the old pauper women, who acted as nurses, told her; she is still in the workhouse infirmary, too weak to walk across a room without assistance.

It is Fanny Raynham, and she is on the road to getting strong in body, though her silent sullen manner, and the vague uncertain answers she gives to the questions asked her, make the people who come in contact with her think that her mind is affected.

There is a method in her madness, however, if she is mad.

When questioned as to her name, she said it was "Fanny Richards," because she remembered that her linen was marked "F. R.," and, when asked about her place of residence, she said she had come from London, but she had no home and no friends.

And beyond this they could learn nothing from her.

The great burden of shame that was upon her when she fled from Rawfell Rectory no longer weighed upon her heart or conscience, for the innocent proof of her error had not lived to see the light.

Slowly it was beginning to dawn upon the unfortunate girl's mind that life might be worth living even now, but she was still at war with her own heart, and she has many a hard lesson yet to learn before the path of virtue and duty will seem worth striving to regain.

She is sitting in a listless weary attitude, thinking how hard the seats are, how bare the boards, how ugly and uninviting is every object that meets her eye, and then she contrasts the ward she is in with the reception-rooms of Burnham Court and Grantly Park, and she sighs regretfully, wondering whether her feet will ever tread soft carpets again, and whether or not she will once more experience the luxury of soft couches and easy-chairs.

Her thoughts are disturbed by the entrance of the matron, a tall, thin, sallow-faced woman, possessed of a pair of keen black eyes that seemed to look through every person or thing they rested upon.

But it was not Mrs. Crabtree's eyes only that denoted the sharp restless inflexibility of her character.

Her mouth was straight, a mere slit across the lower part of her face; her lips were thin, and looked like two red threads drawn across a double row of large, yellow, savage teeth; but her chin was square and heavy as the chin of a man, and anyone studying the woman could see that she was of no ordinary type.

There was a flutter among the pauper women as the matron came into the ward, as though the poor creatures, old and young, were at school, and their governess had just returned to the class-room.

But Fanny Raynham did not move or stir.

She had not been here long enough to appreciate Mrs. Crabtree's importance; she forgot that she was herself a pauper, and naturally regarded the matron as her social inferior, and she never raised an eyelash as the woman with a fixed steady gaze on the girl's pale face came towards her.

This indifference irritated the matron, and she paused before the chair upon which the invalid was seated, and said in a clear incisive tone:

"Fanny Raynham, you are wanted."

"The girl's face became very pale, then it flushed slowly and her heart seemed to stand still for a moment with terror.

But she did not lose her presence of mind, and she replied slowly and with seeming carelessness:

"I said my name was Fanny Richards."

"Come, come, that kind of thing won't do with me," said the woman roughly. "You're found out; you've ·_____"

Then she paused abruptly.

The expression of Fanny's face was something startling in such a place and under such circumstances.

This black sheep had always been the most haughty and overbearing of Mrs. Raynham's children, and the servants at the Court had often complained that "Miss Fanny treated them as though they were dogs."

Certainly an excess of courtesy and consideration for the feelings of others was not among the young lady's weaknesses, and now she looked at the workhouse mistress as a princess might have glanced at an offensive beggar, while she said coldly and disdainfully:

"You are forgetting yourself, I think."

For a moment Mrs. Crabtree was speechless with rage, but the expression of Fanny's face had recalled another face to her, the face of someone whom she had just left, and triumph and cupidity alike made her restrain the torrent of sharp words that rose to her tongue, and, to the unbounded surprise of the other inmates in the ward, she turned upon her heel, and, without a word, walked out of the room.

No sooner was she gone than a buzz of voices rose on every side, and all eyes were fixed on the audacious girl who had "muzzled Mother Crab," as they termed the workhouse mistress.

But Fanny heeded them not.

She had closed her eyes and was wondering who could want her, and how she could get away from this place without being recognised.

Suddenly the chatter ceased, and the lull of sound caused the fugitive from Rawfell Rectory to open her eyes to ascertain the cause.

Escape was impossible now, and denial was utterly useless, for there, in the doorway, standing by the side of the matron, was Lady Grantly.

Fanny Raynham felt humiliated enough to have satisfied even her mother.

Her pauper clothing seemed to burn and scorch her, and what had been revolting enough to her own taste and sense of comfort previously now seemed part of herself, to drag her down to its coarse common level, to make her no better than an outcast among outcasts, a pauper among paupers, creating a moral and social gulf between herself and her sister, which no love on the part of one, or repentance on the part of the other, could ever completely bridge over.

She uttered no word of recognition, and she gave no sign of pleasure or of aversion, but she seemed to shrink and shrivel into her chair as though she hoped the earth would open and swallow her; her head fell forward, and though she had not really fainted, a state of unconsciousness, half real and half assumed, came over her, and for the time at any rate enabled her to avoid anything like an explanation.

A few words were spoken in a low tone by Lady Grantly to the matron, and then two strong pauper women were called, and they carried Fanny out of the sick ward down to the matron's private sitting-room.

Here some wine was given to the girl, who would have been glad never to have opened her eyes again, and after a time even Fanny's obstinacy was conquered, and she was obliged to look upon her sister's face.

"I am going to take you away with me," said Lady Grantly decidedly; "you must have been mad to come to such a place."

"I did not come; I was brought," was the sullen answer. "Some accident happened, I think, but I haven't taken the trouble to enquire."

"Well, this is no place for you," said her ladyship briefly; then turning to the matron she said: "I will pay any expense that may have been incurred on behalf of my sister, and now will you bring her own clothes, please, and let her be dressed in them."

The woman, who believed she saw a handsome present for herself as well as payment to the parish, went out of the room to give the necessary orders, and the two sisters were left alone.

"You'd much better leave me where I am, Geraldine," said Fanny gloomily when the door had closed upon Mrs. Crabtree; "you don't know what made me run away from the rectory, and wander to this town."

"I do know," was the sad reply, "and I feel bitterly grieved and deeply humiliated to think a sister of mine should have fallen so low, but to leave you here will not mend the past, and there may be better things hoped for from you, I trust, in the future."

"I am not sure that I shall ever be any good to myself or to anybody," said Fanny, gloomily; "besides, where do you mean to take me—will my mother let me come home?"

"No; mamma forbids us to mention your name," was the answer.

"Ah!" and the girl caught her breath with a gasp; "then my disgrace is known?"

"It is suspected, not known," was the evasive reply.

"Then you don't propose to take me to your own house?" asked Fanny quickly.

"No; Sir Graham would not have it, and it is a matter I could not insist upon. Neither could I take you back to uncle and Ursula, for I do not believe they would receive you; but I will place you in a respectable home and provide for you, if you will trust to me."

"I don't suppose I have any choice," was the ungracious answer. "And so mamma has forbidden my name to be mentioned, has she?"

"Yes; but she may relent after Clarrie is married, and when I can get her more to myself than I have done lately."

"When Clarrie is married?" repeated Fanny, knitting her brows in a dark frown. "Whom is she going to marry?"

"Her old lover, Frank Darlington, of course."

"Frank Darlington!" repeated Fanny, her eyes blazing with rage and her cheeks suddenly aflame with passion. "Do you know, Geraldine," she went on hotly and furiously, "that it was Frank Darlington who made me what I am, and who brought me to this miserable degraded condition?"

"I suspected he was the cause of it," said Lady Grantly sadly.

"You suspected it, and yet you allowed Clarrie to engage herself to marry him," continued Fanny, all her anger suddenly directed against Geraldine. "I won't go with you," she went on recklessly. "If you have so little regard for me as to let this marriage take place, I shall hate you, and I won't accept a kindness at your hands. If Frank marries Clarrie my only hope of future happiness will be gone."

"Listen to me," said Geraldine sternly.

Then she told the excited girl what she had said about her to Clarrie; how her half-sister's life was endangered in consequence, and how Clarrie had refused to see her since that evening, and had not even invited her or Sir Graham to the wedding.

"And when does the wedding take place?" asked Fanny, with a relapse into her former sullenness.

"This day week," was the reply. "I have spent an age of time and large sums of money in tracking you to this place."

"And yet it did not cost much to bring me here," said the girl with cynical bitterness; "but you must send out and buy me a hat of some kind, for I left Rawfell without one."

"It is fortunate that you did, it was by the shawl you took to cover your head that the detective and I traced you."

"Detective!" repeated Fanny, frowning again; then she asked maliciously: "What does your amiable husband say to your leaving him to look for me?"

"Many things not complimentary to you or to me either," was the answer; "but don't talk in this tone, Fanny; ah, here comes the matron."

And Lady Grantly with an expression of relief rose to her feet, and begged Mrs. Crabtree to have Fanny dressed as quickly as possible, as she was anxious to get away.

Half an hour later, and Fanny and her sister were in a train travelling rapidly to London.

The runaway was still terribly weak, though the excitement she was labouring under, and the change that had suddenly come over her prospects, had given her for a time a fictitious strength, and she was so much more cheerful than Geraldine anticipated, and, truth to tell, the baronet's wife was more than a little disgusted.

Weak and ill though she might be, she was just the same Fanny Raynham as of old, impatient of control, regardless of the feelings as well as of the opinions of others, and as ready as she had ever been to sacrifice the comfort of everybody else to ensure her own.

She was in no way grateful to Lady Grantly for what she had done, or what she was going to do for her, and she was by no means pleased when she found that her sister intended to place her under the care of a former governess of her own, who had had a small legacy left her by the parent of a pupil, and who now lived in a detached villa at Tulse Hill.

"Miss Harper is glad to add to her income," said Lady Grantly by way of explanation, "for she lost some money a little while ago by the failure of a bank, and she is likewise in want of a companion. She wrote to me a few weeks ago, asking if I could recommend some young lady to come and live with her, so I wrote off at once directly I knew where you were to be found, and she agreed to receive you."

"Does she know anything about my running away from Rawfell?" asked Fanny gloomily.

"No; she believes you come straight from uncle's house, and to complete the deception, your boxes will be ready to pick up and take along with you when we reach London. I detest telling lies, but I have had to utter a few on your behalf, Fanny."

Lady Grantly said this with a sigh; but Fanny, not having the same regard for the truth as her sister, quoted in a mocking tone from Marmion:

> "Oh what a tangled web we weave
> When first we practice to deceive."

Geraldine looked at her sister in pain and surprise.

Then she bit her lip to keep back the scathing words of rebuke and indignation she was tempted to utter.

Already she was beginning to repent that she had not left Fanny for a time to earn experience in the secure refuge in which fate had flung her.

A large dose of workhouse discipline and workhouse fare would surely have made her more grateful for comfort and freedom.

In point of fact, however, Fanny had not experienced privation, or felt the want of freedom; illness had taken away her appetite and had procured her luxuries, which in such a place she would otherwise have failed to get, and the same cause had likewise made it impossible for her to go out of doors.

She was critical and captious enough now, however, and when the sisters reached Miss Harper's house at Tulse Hill, Fanny exclaimed with disdain:

"What a horrid pokey little hole. Am I really to live there?"

At this Geraldine's last grain of patience entirely disappeared, and she replied indignantly:

"Remembering whence you have come and the people with whom I found you, I think you might be grateful for any decent shelter, but if you prefer the care of Mrs. Crabtree, you are quite welcome to return to it. I am compromising myself, as it is, by bringing you here under false pretences."

Fanny looked at her sister, saw that she was in earnest, and conscious that she was the only person in the world who at this moment could or would help her, she said more gently:

"I dare say you think I am very ungrateful, Geraldine, but I must rattle on as I do. If I stop to think I shall go mad."

Lady Grantly was subdued at once; her sympathies were appealed to, and she gently pressed her sister's hand, then led the way into the house.

An hour later Sir Graham Grantly's wife started for the Park, where he was impatiently expecting her.

She had made every possible arrangement for her sister's comfort, and besides impressing upon her the necessity for getting strong and well, she had, at Fanny's request, given her five pounds.

"And Clarrie is really to be married next Tuesday?" asked Fanny as her sister was leaving her.

"Yes," was the reply; "and I don't see that you or I can do anything to prevent it. The doctors say that sudden excitement will kill her, and it is useless to appeal to Frank Darlington. He is only marrying her for her money."

"And you are not going to be at the wedding?" questioned Fanny persistently.

"No; we are not invited, and we would not go if we were. There is going to be a grand fête, I hear, for Clarrie will celebrate her coming of age as well as her marriage."

Then Lady Grantly went away.

But as Fanny turned from the window, having watched her sister get into a cab, she muttered to herself:

"If you are not there, I will be, and it will go hard with all of us if I don't put an end to their merry-making."

SIR GRAHAM SAT BLANKLY AND HELPLESSLY LOOKING AT HER.

CHAPTER XXV.

HER BRIDAL MORN.

LARRIE BURNHAM was looking very pale this morning when her mother came into her room, bringing with her own hands the early cup of tea which the heiress was in the habit of being roused to drink.

"It is for the last time," she said with a sad smile when her daughter expostulated at her taking so much trouble.

"Yes, I suppose it is, mamma," replied the girl with a shiver, but I don't feel at all as though it were my wedding-day, and I have had such horrible dreams during the night.

"Dreams go by contraries," said the mother, assuming a cheerfulness she was far from feeling; "I suppose you thought you were fighting with the lawyers over again?"

"No, I did not dream about them, but I do think it is very hard that I can't do what I like with the money and estate papa left me, now I am of age, don't you, mamma?"

"No, my dear, I cannot say that I do," was the grave reply; "your father and your grandfather had both of them the right to leave their property with any conditions attached that they considered desirable, and I might quite as reasonably complain that I had not been fairly dealt with."

"I suppose you are right," assented the girl with a sigh, "but I should have liked to give Frank a proof of my entire confidence in him by giving him absolute control over all I possess; I think it places a wife in such a very false position for all the money to belong to her, and for her husband not to be able to sell an acre of land without her consent."

"I don't think it makes any difference when the husband and wife are one," replied the mother gravely —"one in mutual confidence and in aim and purpose —but in your case, dear, not an acre of this land could be sold even with your consent."

"No, that is what Frank was saying, mamma, and he seemed quite vexed the other day when the lawyer explained how matters stood; he said there ought to have been a large accumulation during my minority, and that you ought to have nursed and improved the property for me instead of squeezing all you could out of it."

"I don't know that I am interested in Frank Darlington's opinion when the expression of it is dictated by such mercenary motives. I daresay he is disappointed to find he cannot squander your father's property as he would like to do, and I for your own sake wish you had been going to marry any other man, my child. Had your choice fallen upon Fortescue Grantly, or Mr. Godfrey Lascelles, or even upon our rector, I should have felt more confidence in your future happiness."

"Yes, I know you are all against Frank," retorted Clarrie hotly; "Beatrice detests him. By the way, mamma, has Fanny been found yet?"

Mrs. Trevor turned and looked at her eldest daughter, then she said slowly:

"Yes; Geraldine wrote to say that Fanny was in London."

"Ah!" and a startled look came into Clarrie's eyes. But with a resolute effort she conquered herself. Then she said: "I don't want to see her or to hear anything about her. I believe you are all in league to set me against Frank and to prevent my marrying him; but I will have him, in spite of everything and everybody, and I will give him every penny I can control. My will is drawn up, and the moment I come home from church I shall sign it."

The mother looked at her daughter curiously. Such a change had come over the girl that it was difficult to realize it.

She had grown irritable and suspicious during the last few months, and this morning her hand was hot and feverish, and her breathing seemed laboured and irregular.

Clarrie's evident ill-health arrested the sharp words that trembled on her mother's tongue, and instead of uttering them, Mrs. Trevor said kindly, but gravely :

"Do as you like, my dear; but if I were you I would try to sleep for an hour, and if you dream at all, dream of Frank's perfections. I remember that when your father and I were married we talked and thought of the happy life we would lead together, not of the disposition of money or lands, or wills or settlements."

"I cannot sleep," returned Clarrie in irritable tones; "and when I dream, I dream of Fanny. I wish she had never been born. Frank always gets furious with me when I mention her name."

"Then I would not mention it if I were you," remarked the mother coldly as she rose from her seat and left the room.

"What a brute I am !" groaned Clarrie with sudden repentance, when she found herself alone. "But they all irritate me so," she went on, trying to make excuses for herself. "Frank grumbles because my fortune amounts to nothing more than the income from the estate; but that income isn't a trifle, as I ventured to tell him; three thousand a year is not a bad dowry for a man who has nothing to get with a wife. If it were not for the conditions in papa's will we might sell some of the farms; but while Beatrice lives we can't do that, and Beatrice herself doesn't seem pleased at my marriage, and she isn't half as nice and kind as she used to be."

The girl whose wedding-morning had opened so inauspiciously, was silent after this for a time, and she tried to follow her mother's advice and compose herself to sleep; but her mind was too active and too troubled for refreshing slumber to draw the curtain of temporary oblivion over it, and she at length started up restlessly and with a kind of terror upon her, exclaiming :

"I can endure this no longer. I'll get up and dress. I see Fanny's face everywhere. The wretched girl seems to haunt me. I wonder what has really happened? Frank will tell me nothing. He gets in a passion and says if I doubt him he will leave me; and my mother and Beatrice look as though something had happened that they were afraid to tell me of. Oh, it is cruel of them all, and I am so miserable!"

She shed a few tears in self pity; then she rang for her maid and began to dress.

Miss Claribel's maid was a new institution at Burnham Court, for until her majority the heiress had been treated like her half-sisters, and one servant had waited upon the whole of them.

Now, Miss Clarrie had a maid to herself, and this young person came in obedience to the summons, and fussed about and saw that the bath was ready, and did all that was necessary for her mistress's comfort.

But no one else came near the intended bride, and when her toilette was more than half complete she began to ask questions about the other members of the family.

"The captain and the mistress and the two young ladies are going to have breakfast together as usual," replied the maid; "but Mr. Darlington and Miss Beatrice have both ordered breakfast in their own rooms, and I suppose you'll have yours here, miss?"

"Yes," was the reply, and she felt inclined to send and ask Beatrice to join her.

Pride, however, kept her from doing so. Her cousin had avoided her of late, she had refused to be one of the bridesmaids, and though she had not announced her intention of absenting herself from church during the ceremony, Claribel was by no means certain that she would join the wedding-party.

"All my relatives are simply horrid," grumbled Clarrie angrily as she sat down to her solitary breakfast; "to think that this is my last meal before I am married, and yet I have to eat it alone."

No one heard this petulant remark, and she knew quite well when she uttered it that it was unreasonable.

She could have joined the family party at the breakfast-table, or she could have invited anyone in the house to come to her room and join her, and even Beatrice, grieved and disappointed as she was, would not have refused the invitation.

But Clarrie's conversation with her mother had not made that lady inclined to repeat her visit to her daughter's room, and it had also made her discourage Grace and Ruth from going.

So the poor peevish heiress ate her breakfast alone.

A very sorry breakfast, but then Clarrie's appetite had not been worth much since that evening when Geraldine, after her return from Rawfell Rectory, had spoken about Fanny, and the consequent excitement had caused Claribel to break a blood-vessel.

Indeed, from that night could be dated the complete change, and that not a change for the better, in the mind, heart, and temper of the young mistress of Burnham Court.

As a natural result, she had alienated the affections of those with whom she lived, and her mother and cousin, with the rest of the household, were only waiting until the marriage should take place, before leaving the Court with the intention of allowing a long time to elapse before they favoured its owner again with their presence.

So the morning wore on.

Breakfast was unusually early to allow plenty of time for dressing afterwards, and when the meal was over, Mrs. Trevor walked into the large dining-room to look at the table upon which the cake and many of the things for the wedding-breakfast were already laid.

The mother's heart was sad. She had been married three times herself, and she had been present as a guest at many weddings, but never before had she felt the same sinking at heart, the same presage of evil, that weighed so heavily upon her now.

In sheer depression of spirit, she went up to her own room, shut herself in, and gave way to a violent fit of weeping.

The weakness was so unusual in this strong-nerved, strong-willed woman, that the consequent prostration was greater in her case than it would have been with most women, and when her tears and sobs ceased, she fell into a sleep so deep and lethargic that it was rather like a condition of coma that of natural repose.

Her husband came and knocked at the door, but receiving no reply, and finding it fastened on the inside, went away.

Beatrice came some time later, wishing to ask her aunt a question, but she also knocked in vain, and went away at length in some perplexity.

Time was passing at an alarming rate. In less than half an hour the bridesmaids, who, with Grace and Ruth, were to attend the bride, would arrive, and many of the servants were absolutely doing nothing, waiting for orders.

"I think we ought to break the door open, uncle," said Beatrice to Captain Trevor, as he stood in dire perplexity outside his wife's room. "Aunt may have fainted, or she may be dead for aught we know. Shall I call some of the men-servants?"

"I don't know. She may be very angry with us if we do, and yet——"

The temporary master of Burnham Court was greatly troubled in mind. Since Clarrie had attained her majority he had felt something like an intruder in the house, and he scarcely liked to give orders for a door to be broken open without his step-daughter's leave.

He hinted something of the kind to Beatrice, but this young lady was of far too decided a character to pay much heed to such scruples, and at the suggestion that Clarrie should be consulted she said:

"Pray don't do anything of the kind, uncle. It will only upset her for the day. Let us ascertain first of all what has happened before we alarm her."

And so saying, the young lady walked down the corridor of that wing of the mansion, and returned a few minutes later with two sturdy workmen, whom she directed to force open the door.

This order was more easily given than executed, however.

Burnham Court had been built under the supervision of a former owner, and by conscientious workmen, and

neither the hinges nor the lock of the door would yield
to force.

The noise made in the attempt, however, roused the
sleeper—it might have waked the dead, could the dead
ever have been waked by earthly sounds—and just as
there was a consultation about breaking in one of the
oak panels, the key turned in the lock, the door opened,
and Mrs. Trevor, pale, tear-stained, only half-awake,
and looking many years older than when she left the
breakfast-table, stood before them.

"What is the meaning of this uproar?" she asked
dreamily and vaguely.

"We were alarmed about you, aunt," replied her
niece; then turning to the servants she said: "You
can go now, tell the housekeeper I will come to her
directly."

Then she followed her aunt into the room, while the
bewildered husband and frightened daughters came in
anxiously after her.

"What is the matter, auntie?" asked our heroine
tenderly; "are you feeling ill?"

"Yes," was the reply; "my head is so strange, I
cannot go to church to-day. Clarrie will not be married;
I—I—forbid it."

The last words were the utterances of a sleeper, for
Mrs. Trevor had sunk down again upon the couch from
whence she had risen, and had fallen off once more into
her trance-like condition.

"Was your mother ever like this before to-day?"
asked Beatrice of Grace anxiously.

"I don't know," was the reply; "I have never seen
her so."

"But I have heard Clarrie and Geraldine say that
mamma frightened them, she was so like a dead
woman herself when papa died," here interposed
Ruth.

Meanwhile Captain Trevor was examining his wife's
pulse, and an added gravity came over his face, as he
said :

"We must send for a doctor, I don't like her
condition at all."

So the doctor was sent for, and anxiety about Mrs. Trevor was so great, that everybody forgot for the moment that this was Claribel Burnham's wedding-day.

Suddenly Beatrice remembered it, and she said in troubled tones to Captain Trevor:

"Some one ought to tell Clarrie; she cannot be married while her mother is in this condition!"

"Will you go and talk to her?" was the reply; "I am afraid she will be very much put out."

"We are all put out for that matter," returned the girl, who doubted whether her cousin and Darlington would consent to postpone the wedding; "but our being put out doesn't make aunt any better. Yes, I will go and tell her."

And she went.

Claribel Burnham was in her large elegantly-furnished bedroom, standing before the long pier-glass, looking at, or more correctly speaking, admiring her own reflection.

And well worthy of admiration was the blonde beauty, who attired in the delicate costly dress stood before the glass.

For Clarrie was already clad in her wedding garments.

Her gown was of white satin with a rich ivory tint, half covered with lace and tulle and orange-blossoms.

A wreath of real orange-blossom, sending forth its strong perfume, crowned her golden curls.

On her neck and in her ears were pearls, the gift of the bridegroom—pearls that were not yet paid for— while she wore on her finger the fiery opal ring.

Nothing but the bridal veil was needed to complete her toilette, and it yet wanted nearly an hour to the time when it was necessary for her to be ready to start for church.

"So you have condescended to come to me at last?" she said as Beatrice came into the room; "I was beginning to think my amiable relatives were going to cut me without even waiting until I am married."

She had not turned her head to look at Beatrice as she uttered this unamiable speech, but, receiving no reply, she glanced at her cousin, and, observing that she wore an ordinary morning dress, she asked with more anger now than petulance:

"Aren't you late? You are not dressed. Don't you mean to go to church with us?"

"You are very early," was the evasive reply, "it is only half-past ten; but something has happened, Clarrie, that I fear will put off your wedding; your mother has been taken ill."

"I knew it—I knew something would happen. I knew one of you would do something to keep me from marrying Frank," cried the little heiress passionately; "but you sha'n't succeed," she went on with flushed cheeks and flashing eyes, "I will marry him to-day even if you all lie dead or dying about me."

"In that case I have nothing more to say, except that you must be mad or very bad," said Beatrice severely, "but I have been so disappointed in you, Clarrie, that I am scarcely surprised at anything you say or do now. However, if you have no consideration for your mother, I have; under present circumstances I shall certainly not be present at your marriage, and I would ask you for decency's sake to have everything as quiet as possible."

And so saying, Beatrice was leaving the room, when Clarrie, in a state of nervous excitement that was bringing her very near to a condition of hysteria, placed herself before her.

"It is you and all the rest of you who are cruel to me," she cried in anger, doing her best to keep back a sob; "here on my wedding morning not one of you has come near me, and I have had to be dressed for my marriage by a paid servant; how would you like that, Beatrice, with a mother and sisters and cousin living in your house? Would you call that kindness? Do you think such conduct would soften your heart to any of them?"

"I am not aware of any necessity for softness of heart," was the cold reply; "we none of us want anything from you, Clarrie, and if Mr. Darlington has put such ideas in your head, pray dismiss them at once. I will tell you now what has hitherto been kept secret—I am as rich as you are; nay, my fortune is larger than yours, and what enhances its value is that when I come of age, in a month's time, it will be at my own command, and I can spend every shilling of if I like."

"You are rich!" gasped Clarrie; "does Frank know it?"

"Not that I am aware of," was the coldly-uttered reply; "but my poverty or wealth can never make any difference to Mr. Darlington. Your accusation of un-kindness, however, is unfounded. Your mother came to you this morning, and from what I heard of your recep-tion of her, I was not inclined to follow her example. But you will not be much longer troubled with the presence of your mother and sisters, or of myself; directly my aunt is well enough to travel I shall induce her to come to my house in town."

And Beatrice was again about to leave the room, when Clarrie caught hold of her dress as she asked eagerly:

"You are not going to talk to Frank, are you?"

"Certainly not. Why should I speak to Mr. Dar-lington? He is nothing to me—worse than nothing, for he has changed you from a loving gentle girl, into a suspicious, cold-hearted, jealous woman."

Without another word Beatrice walked past her cousin and returned to her aunt.

For a few seconds Clarrie stood silent, angry, and yet troubled in heart.

Then she said, half aloud:

"I will talk to Frank and ask him what is to be done. I don't want to set them all against me."

Then, forgetful of the bridal dress she wore, she walked downstairs till she met a servant, of whom she asked if Mr. Darlington had left his room.

"Yes, miss, he is in the small drawing-room by the conservatory," was the reply.

And Clarrie walked thither, but as she came outside the open glass door, she heard a man and woman talking, and she recognised the voices of Frank and of Fanny.

CHAPTER XXVI.

WHAT FANNY DID AT BURNHAM COURT.

FANNY RAYNHAM seemed to have settled down calmly and contentedly in her new home.

Miss Harper was a lady of an uncertain age, who had done some hard work in her time in teaching the young idea how to shoot, and she now considered she was entitled to take her ease, and devote a portion of her thoughts to a more sentimental and romantic view of life than she had hitherto indulged in.

For Miss Harper had never had a lover until within a few weeks of Fanny's arrival at Tulse Hill, and now the lady, who was certainly a long way past her first youth, experienced the novel sensation of having a suitor.

Mr. Marsham, the lover in question, was a widower of some seven or eight and fifty, with a large family of girls, who were sadly in need of maternal management.

He had become acquainted with the ex-governess through her taking the villa in which she now resided. It formed part of a large property of which he had the management, and in taking the single lady as a tenant, and in superintending repairs and alterations of the house, the couple had almost insensibly glided from business terms to those of friendship, and from friendship to a still warmer state of feeling.

Mr. Marsham was a well-to-do man, and he had ascertained that Miss Harper, despite her bad investment of some of her money, was still possessed of a very comfortable income, and thus, with more celerity than younger couples show in such matters, he proposed after a two months' acquaintance, was accepted, and, as the marriage was not to take place immediately, he came three times a week to see his *fiancée*, drink strong tea, and eat a hot supper.

These visits gave Fanny Raynham more liberty to keep her own room than she might otherwise have obtained, for when Miss Harper was favoured with the presence of her future husband, she could get along very well without any other companion.

Miss Fanny, indeed, turned up her nose at the auctioneer and estate agent, and showed her resentment at his being invited to sit down in the same room with her, by quickly pleading fatigue and walking off to her own apartment.

But Fanny was becoming stronger every day, she ate, drank, and slept well, and she went for a short walk early every morning, for the first week accompanied by the housemaid, to whom she was more liberal in the way of presents than was her wont to be.

In all this Fanny had a very definite purpose, and when, the seventh morning after her arrival at Elm Villa, she rose about five o'clock, dressed herself, and went downstairs quietly and stealthily, she felt quite strong enough to take the journey to Burnham Court.

She had bribed Sarah to say to Miss Harper, when that lady made her appearance downstairs between eleven and twelve o'clock, as was her custom, that she had gone with Miss Fanny for her morning walk as usual, that the young lady had felt tired after her breakfast, and was lying down, having begged she should not be disturbed.

To carry out the deception, Fanny locked her bedroom door, taking the key with her, and remarking to the servant, who had expressed some doubt about the proceeding :

I shall be back before evening, unless I have some very good news ; and in that case, I shall telegraph." The young lady walked off, hailing the first cab she met, and directing the man to drive to London Bridge railway-station.

She had made all her calculations beforehand, and was in very good time for an early train to Burnham-on-Brent.

Also, she had so attired herself that no one who had previously known her was likely to recognise her at a casual glance.

The events of the last year had changed Fanny Raynham considerably.

She looked five years older than when she went to that picnic where Sir Graham Grantly proposed—first to Beatrice, then to Geraldine—the day from whence might be dated a change in her own life.

Fanny forgot her recent illness, and even her present weakness, when she found herself at the railway-station.

A wild excitement was in her blood, though she looked so quiet and so calm, and a diabolical purpose was in her heart.

Her object this morning was to stop Frank and Clarrie from being married.

She had firmly resolved to see both of them, to tell her story, and make a wild appeal for justice and for mercy, and, failing to get satisfaction from either, she meant to join the bridal party in the church, and there tell publicly the story of her wrongs.

That her taking this last mad step would alienate even Geraldine from her she knew quite well, but she was as utterly reckless as she was blindly vindictive, and the one short sharp spell of adversity she had experienced had failed to teach her any useful lesson.

In this frame of mind she reached Burnham Court, and avoiding the lodge-gate, where she would have been recognised, she entered the grounds, and hidden by the leafy trees—everyone of which she knew so well—made her way up to the house.

The servants were either busy with their several duties or were waiting for orders from their mistress, who at this time was in her own room, the door of which her husband was trying to force open, so that Fanny entered the house unobserved.

Reaching a small drawing-room through a conservatory, she sank upon a couch, partly overcome with exhaustion and weakness, and also for the moment doubtful as to what her next step should be.

"This is the room Clarrie used to spend most of her time in," she mused; "if Frank comes to see her before he goes to church, he will be sure to be shown in here. I did not dare to go to Holly Mount to see him, for his father and brother would say I was mad; but I would give the world to see him before I talk to Clarrie; the difficulty of meeting them together, except in church, never occurred to me until this moment."

But time is passing, and she thinks bitterly that she might as well have remained in London as come here, unless she acts, and acts quickly.

"I will go straight to Clarrie's room," she decided, rising to her feet and taking a step towards the door; "she at least shall know the truth and the whole truth."

At that moment a man's voice, coming from the conservatory, reached her.

She knew the voice well, too well for her peace of mind.

He was singing, or rather humming to himself:

> "Sigh no more, ladies, sigh no more;
>   Men were deceivers ever.
> One foot in sea, and one on shore,
>   To one thing constant never."

And as he sang he came towards the drawing-room.

She did not advance a step to meet him. A rush of feeling was in her heart which seemed as though it would burst.

Her eyes swam, there was a buzzing in her ears, and she clutched the back of a chair to keep herself from falling.

And Frank Darlington, without the faintest misgiving, entered.

Frank Darlington started with surprise as he came forward from among the bright flowers into the half-darkened room and saw a lady, who seemed to him a stranger.

He did not recognise her until she spoke; but the tone of voice in which she said "Frank," filled him with dismay.

"Fanny!" he cried, unwisely showing his true state of feeling. "What do you do here?" he continued excitedly; "have you come to ruin me?"

"What do I do here?" she repeated. "Where should I be but in the same house with my mother and sisters?"

"But something has happened to you, or rather, I don't mean that—Clarrie is jealous of you; all kinds of things have been said about you and me. Do go away, Fanny, only for to-day, and I will do anything you wish afterwards—I swear that I will."

"Will you marry me?" she asked calmly, almost coldly.

"Marry you!" he repeated, aghast; "do you know what you are talking about?"

"Oh yes; I know quite well, she replied with a bitter smile; "I know that you expect to marry Clarrie Burnham to day, and I also know that I am come to the wedding. But before you start for church, Clarrie and my mother shall know what you have been to me—what you have made me—and if, after that, you still go to be married, I will follow you and repeat the story to a large audience."

"You are mad. This will be utter destruction to both of us," cried Darlington, frantically.

"I mean to ruin you," she replied icily. "You seem to think nothing of having ruined me."

But Darlington paid no heed to her words. He was pacing the room with troubled steps and with darkly-contracted brows.

Every moment that this girl stayed here imperilled the probability of his marriage and the success of his plans.

"You must go away at once—you shall go," he cried determinedly. "I am desperate, and you don't know of what a desperate man is capable. Promise me you will go away silently, or——"

But she had sprang to the bell, and, with her hand upon the knob, she laughed mockingly and derisively.

"Or what?" she asked. "Pray let me know the penalty if I refuse to obey you."

For a moment he struggled with his own impotent fury, then he changed his tactics.

Threats were useless. He must—he must succeed by entreaties and promises, or he must fail.

"Fanny, you used to love me," he said in a tone of reproach.

"Yes, I used to," she replied. "I gave you very unmistakable proof of my love."

"And now you have ceased to care for me?" he asked.

"I don't care to see you another woman's husband," she replied sullenly.

"But, Fanny, I cannot marry you—at least, I cannot marry you now," he said dejectedly. "I am miserably poor, I have no prospects, and I am heavily in debt. My position—my very liberty depends upon my marrying a rich woman, and Clarrie is rich, though her confounded money is so tied up that I can't get hold of much of it. Still, my marriage with her will give me enough to save me; and listen, Fanny, Clarrie cannot live long, and when she dies I will marry you. I swear by all that is holy that I will, Fanny, if you will only go away quietly and without anyone seeing you now."

"Thank you. I am not a fool to be deluded by such worthless vows," she replied disdainfully. "If you marry Clarrie you cannot afterwards legally marry me, for she is my half-sister. Besides, why should Clarrie die? She is young, and she takes care enough of herself. She is as likely to live as you or I."

"On what condition will you go away from this house in silence?" he asked desperately. "Tell me your terms, but don't lose more time, for Heaven's sake."

"I will go if you go with me," she replied steadily. "No, I am not afraid of you," she went on, observing a murderous gleam in his eyes. "If you will go away with me now, and marry me as soon as the law will permit, I will be silent for your sake as well as my own."

"Would you marry a felon?" he asked wildly.

"No," she involuntarily replied, shrinking back; "but you are not a felon," she went on, recovering from her surprise.

"I am not, but I shall be if I marry you," he said gloomily. "I told you I was in debt, but now I must tell you more. I was hard pressed, and I used another man's name to help me out of the difficulty. There is no danger if I have money in time, but if I have not, it will be ruin."

"You have forged another man's name," said Fanny, steadily and reflectively.

"That is what the law calls it," he answered sullenly.

She reflected for a moment.

Never was Fanny Raynham nearer to an act of self-sacrifice than at this moment.

One word of regret for her own disgraced condition, one word of tenderness, or a hint that he still loved her, and she would have gone away intending to spare him, even if her mercy had been in vain. But there was not one.

He thought only of himself; he would have sacrificed her and ten thousand like her, could he but ensure his own safety.

The moment of possible yielding upon her part passed, and she said resolutely:

"You will go with me now, or I shall remain. We can arrange for the future afterwards."

"Very well; if I must I must," he said with dogged despair. "But I warn you that you had better go alone."

"I told you, and I tell you again, I am not afraid of you," replied Fanny dauntlessly. "Come."

And she was about to walk out into the hall, when he said hurriedly:

"We will go this way—we don't want all the world to see us."

And he turned to step into the conservatory, but he started back with a cry.

Ready dressed in her bridal robes, and white as the pearls around her throat, Claribel Burnham stood, or rather leaned, against a statue.

The reproach in her eyes, and the pallor of her face, did not startle him so much as her gasping efforts to speak.

Only for a second or two, however, did this struggle last. Then a stream of bright red fluid burst from between her parted lips, and the shimmering satin dress was stained with her life's blood.

CHAPTER XXVII.

DASHED FROM HIS LIPS.

 "GO! you have murdered her and ruined me!"

And Frank Darlington, as he said this in a low stern voice, waved Fanny from his presence, while with the other arm he supported Clarrie.

The girl was frightened, and wanted to render some assistance, but again she was sternly bidden to go away and hide herself, and somewhat cowed at the tone and manner of the man whom a few minutes before she seemed to have conquered, she slowly and reluctantly obeyed.

To lay the dying girl upon a couch, to ring the bell furiously and summon immediate assistance, was Darlington's next step.

The doctor who had been summoned to attend Clarrie's mother was in the house, and came to the girl at once.

But the case was beyond his skill, and, before he could reach her side, Claribel Burnham had ceased to breathe.

What a shock her sudden death was to all the girl's friends it is impossible to describe.

They knew that any excitement would bring about this fatal result, and they had all tried as far as it had been in any way possible, to keep from her anything that could worry and agitate her.

Of course they had not been as successful as they desired to be, and Beatrice and Mrs. Trevor blamed themselves for not having exercised more patience and forbearance with the girl who was now beyond their love and their resentment.

Frank Darlington was so completely prostrated that even Beatrice felt inclined to pity him.

When she came to think the matter over calmly, she took some comfort from the conviction that Frank and Claribel had quarrelled, and that her cousin's death had not been caused by the angry words that had passed between the girl and herself.

For certainly more than twenty minutes had elapsed between her leaving Clarrie's room and the breaking of the blood-vessel.

Darlington said truly enough when questioned on the subject, that he had met Claribel by the statue where the blood-stains were to be seen on the ground, that she was gasping as though in pain, and trying to speak, but that her utterance was choked by the hemorrhage which burst from her mouth, and then all was over.

The sad news spread like wildfire.

More than half of the guests bidden to the wedding had already assembled in the church, and the messenger bearing the gloomy tidings passed under triumphal arches and along flower-decked paths to tell the story of how these preparations were in vain.

Poor Mrs. Trevor completely collapsed when she knew that her eldest child was dead, and she fell into a low fever, a condition fraught with much danger to a woman of her decided and energetic temperament.

Everything devolved upon Beatrice.

The servants came to her for orders, Captain Trevor and the two girls looked to her for directions and for sympathy, while one man at least in that house remembered that the inheritance of Clarrie Burnham would now fall to her cousin Beatrice.

This circumstance had not yet been thought of by the girl herself, or by the rest of the household, but Frank Darlington had very good cause for thinking of it.

Had Clarrie lived but a few hours longer, just long enough to become his wife and to sign the will, the contents of which she had made him acquainted with, or even had she signed it while still unmarried, he would have been saved from the ruin that now impended over him.

She had died without making that one poor signature, however, and he was left in a worse plight than when he had first asked the girl to marry him.

The agony of mind he suffered might very well be mistaken by those about him for grief at the loss of the woman who had loved him so truly and so well.

But he did not deceive himself.

A hundred Clarries might have died; a whole city full of people might have been destroyed, and he would not have been so frenzied as he now was at the prospect of that forged bill becoming due.

More than once during that dreadful day he thought of taking his own life.

Death seemed the only possible escape for him.

He got out his razors and looked at their sharp edges, but he covered them up again with a shudder.

The very sight of them seemed to recall Clarrie's last moments and the sickening smell of blood that will haunt his memory for many a long day.

Besides, with all the possible ills that might befall him, he was not tired of life.

The world was a very beautiful world. The mere sensation of living in it was pleasant, and if he could only tide over his present difficulty there was much keen enjoyment still to be got out of life.

Late in the day, just as he was trying to come to some decision as to his movements, feeling it impossible to remain much longer at Burnham Court, a servant came over from Holly Mount with a letter from his father, telling him he would be quite welcome at home if he cared to come.

It was not a very cordial epistle, and it had cost Arthur Darlington some trouble to induce his father to write at all, but Holly Mount was clearly the place for the squire's son under the circumstances, and Frank was only too glad to pocket his pride and to accept the hand held out to him.

Certainly it was not much like the triumph he had promised himself when he looked out of his window over the park at Burnham Court that morning, and instead of this being the luckiest day of his life it was in point of fact, the most unfortunate, and he had no choice but to bend his head to the storm.

So the inmates of the Court, who had learnt to dread him as the future master of the place, were relieved of his presence, and he went away unregretted by a single person.

No one at the Court knew of Fanny's visit and no one suspected it until Lady Grantly, hearing the sad news, came over to see her mother and offer to stay and help to nurse her.

It was she who said to Beatrice privately:

"I don't believe the story that man tells about Clarrie's death. Are you sure that Fanny and Clarrie did not meet?"

"I am sure of nothing," was the reply; "but I don't think Fanny can have been here."

"Then I think she has been here," said Geraldine gravely. "I received a telegram from Miss Harper, in whose charge I left my sister, saying that Fanny had gone out early in the morning and had not returned, and asking if I knew anything about her. I replied in great alarm, but just as I was leaving home to come here a second message came, saying that Fanny had returned, ill and faint, and had gone straight to bed, refusing to give any account of herself."

"It is very singular," replied Beatrice, "let us go into the room where Clarrie died; if your sister has been there to-day she may have left some trace behind."

So together they entered the small drawing-room.

Geraldine shuddered as she saw the dark stain upon the carpet which marked where Clarrie had been carried from the conservatory to the couch, but, close to the fire-place, near to the bell-handle, they found what they sought.

A piece of cambric marked "Fanny," and with the number nine under the name.

"I thought so," said Geraldine with a sigh, as she put the handkerchief in her pocket. "I feared Fanny was taking the matter too quietly not to mean mischief. This is one of a dozen handkerchiefs I gave her only a week ago; now what is to be done."

But Beatrice shook her head as she replied that she could offer no suggestion.

Clarrie's death had not been due to violence, nor, as far as they knew, to foul play, and no good was to be gained by dragging "the family skeleton," as they had begun to regard Fanny's disgrace, into the light.

So Geraldine took the compromising handkerchief away with her when she left the Court to return to Grantly Park.

Here she found her husband in a great fume.

He made no warm professions of affection for his wife, but he hated to be left alone, and he chose to consider himself slighted and neglected when she absented herself for an hour from his side, though he grumbled persistently enough when asked to accompany her.

But the baronet was more out of sorts than usual this evening, this condition being induced by the knowledge that Beatrice would become the mistress of Burnham Court in consequence of Clarrie's death.

He had hoped, and even believed, that she would go away from the neighbourhood when her cousin married, and that he should be troubled by the sight of her beautiful mocking face no more.

"And now she will live permanently among us," he groaned.

He knew he should meet with no sympathy from his wife on this ground, so he wisely refrained from alluding to his grievance, but he asked a great number of questions, and grumbled and grunted over the replies, and altogether he made himself as unpleasant and disagreeable as he possibly could, until Geraldine lost her patience with him, and remarked curtly:

"I am going to town to-morrow to purchase my mourning."

"I shall go with you," he said promptly.

"And I also mean to go and see Fanny," she went on resolutely.

To this he made no reply, a circumstance which she took as a bad sign, for he would either thwart her, or, what was almost as bad, would insist upon accompanying her.

But she consoled herself with the reflection that every condition of life has its drawbacks, and that a plain girl without fortune could not expect to marry a wealthy baronet, and not find that he was himself anything but perfect as a husband.

So she accepted the situation as philosophically as she could, and very rarely allowed her temper to be ruffled.

And meanwhile Fanny had got back to Tulse Hill to find her absence discovered, Sarah, the housemaid, in tears and under notice to leave, and Miss Harper in a state of nervous agitation that would have reduced her to a swoon or to a condition of hysteria if Mr. Marsham had only been at hand to help to revive her.

But it was not Mr. Marsham's time for coming to Elm Villa, and the ex-governess was thinking of sending for him when Fanny put in an appearance.

The truant herself was weak, and pale, and trembling.

Only strong resolution had kept her up in the morning, and Clarrie's death had been a shock to her.

A shock that had gained in intensity the longer she reflected upon it, and the more so as she realised that she herself had been the cause of the tragedy.

To say she was really sorry would be overstating her condition of feeling, for Fanny was really sorry for nobody but herself; but Clarrie's sudden death had weakened her own hold upon Frank Darlington, and his own confession of having committed forgery convinced her that he would not marry a woman who, like herself, was penniless.

If she could at any time go to him with the price of his redemption from danger and disgrace in her hands, then she felt she might demand that he should marry her with some chance of being listened to, but under no other condition could any appeal benefit her.

As she was even more unlikely to be able to do this than was Frank Darlington to find the means to extricate himself, she seemed to loose heart and hope and spirit, and to have no care as to what other people thought or said about her.

"SO YOU HAVE CONDESCENDED TO COME TO ME AT LAST?" SHE SAID AS BEATRICE CAME INTO THE ROOM.

In this frame of mind she disdained to tell the story which she had invented to account for her absence from the villa for some nine or ten hours; but remarking that she had been to see a friend, and felt ill, tired, and hungry, she went to bed desiring that some tea and a chop should be sent up to her.

Judging Lady Grantly's anxiety by her own, Miss Harper sent off a second telegram to her ladyship, and then, feeling it impossible to remain quiet after such an agitating day, the good lady put on her bonnet and walked round to Mr. Marsham's office to take counsel with him as to what she ought to do with her former pupil.

As they could not very well talk of such delicate matters in the office, Mr. Marsham left his business for the rest of the day to his head clerk and returned with Miss Harper to the villa.

And the result of their conversation was, that the date of their own marriage was fixed earlier than was at first intended, and thus, as a necessary consequence, Lady Grantly would have to find another home for her sister.

When Fanny was informed of this arrangement the following morning, she made no comment, and never uttered a word of congratulation or vexation.

That the arrangement could affect herself she never considered, for Geraldine, no doubt, paid handsomely for her residence here, and the same amount of money would procure her a home elsewhere.

What was troubling this scheming young woman's mind was the possibility of getting hold of a sum of money sufficiently large to tempt Frank to marry her.

She was still puzzling over this insoluble problem when Lady Grantly arrived at the house.

" I can only stay with you a few minutes," said her ladyship hurriedly, as she came into her sister's room. " Sir Graham is waiting for me."

" I wonder he spares you out of his sight," sneered Fanny, who was in anything but an amiable mood. " It must be a delightful sensation to be an old man's darling."

"I prefer it to being a young man's slave or a worthless man's toy," retorted Geraldine severely. "But I did not come here to-day to talk about myself. You know, I presume, what brought me to town?"

"How should I know?" was the snappish answer.

"Your visit yesterday morning to Burnham Court might have helped you to guess my errand," was the steady reply.

"Ah, then it is known that I was there? Well, I don't care," in a defiant tone. "It wasn't my fault that Clarrie was listening in the conservatory while I was talking with Frank. But for her being there he would have come to London with me."

"Would he?" And Lady Grantly face darkened, and a stern expression came over her features; but she said steadily and calmly: "I suppose you know that Clarrie is dead?"

"I hoped so," was the answer.

And Fanny's face lighted up with triumph.

Lady Grantly felt repelled and disgusted by her sister's heartlessness, and she now said coldly and resolutely:

"It is time we understood each other, Fanny. I am the only friend you have in the world. My husband and mother are both of them averse to my speaking to you or helping you in any possible way, and I am myself beginning to think that it is a mere waste of time on my part to try to reclaim you. By your confession, it seems you have been running after Frank Darlington again, and he and you together are morally guilty of having killed poor Clarrie. Now you must promise me never to speak to that man again, or I shall wash my hands of you. Will you make the promise and keep it?"

"No, I won't," was the defiant reply. "I believe that Frank will marry me, and I will never rest until he does so."

"Poor foolish moth!" said Geraldine with pitying contempt. "Frank Darlington will no more marry you than he will marry me. Nay, if I were a widow he might be glad to take me for the sake of my money.;

but you have no money, and never can have any. We
have not a relative in the world who will be likely
to leave you a sixpence."

"That is true," sighed Fanny gloomily; "but if I
only had money Frank would marry me."

"'If' is a small word, but in this case it means a
great deal," retorted Geraldine with contemptuous
bitterness.

"I don't know that it does mean a great deal," said
Fanny with considerable irritation. "I wish you would
listen to me Geraldine, and not say all the nasty things
you can think of."

Lady Grantly shrugged her shoulders, threw herself
into a chair, and with a provoking smile, said:

"Proceed, but make your story brief. I am pressed
for time, and I don't know when we shall meet
again."

Fanny was inclined to indulge in a little more ill-
humour, but something in her sister's tone and manner
warned her that she had tried her forbearance to its
utmost limit, so she put a curb upon her tongue, and in
a few words she made Geraldine acquainted with the
substance of her conversation with Frank Darlington
the previous day.

"It cannot be such a very large sum of money
that he wants, can it?" she went on persuasively.

"How can I say?" was the cold reply. "A man
who will forge the name of another would not be
particular with regard to the amount. But why have
you told me this, Fanny?"

"Because I thought you might provide the money,
and consider it a cheap way of getting me off your
hands," was the boldly uttered answer.

Geraldine laughed bitterly as she rose to her
feet, and pulled on her gloves in a calm leisurely
manner.

"I have no desire to compound a felony," she said
calmly, "or to see you married to a forger; and though
you seem to forget the fact, I am not made of money.
If you have nothing more reasonable to suggest I will
go. I have given orders about your mourning."

"Then you will not find the money for me?" demanded Fanny, losing her self-control, and standing before Geraldine in a threatening attitude.

But Geraldine had no fear of man or of woman in her heart, and she fixed her cold grey eyes steadily upon Fanny's as she said sternly:

"I will not spend one sixpence in helping Frank Darlington to marry you, and if you and he repeat the folly and wickedness of the past, I will use the information you have given me this morning to hunt him down and convict him."

Fanny shrank back with sudden dismay as she recognised the weapon she had placed in Geraldine's hands, and before she could recover from her consternation her sister had left the room.

"Everybody turns against me," she groaned bitterly as she realised that even Geraldine had deserted her, "and now I have put Frank in her power, though after all it doesn't matter much, she doesn't know whose name he has forged. I wonder if he would be very angry with me if he knew that I had told her."

She little thought that if he had known of her indiscreet confidence, Mr. Frank Darlington would without delay have left the country.

But the bill will not be due for nearly a month yet, and Frank is not quite without hope of meeting it.

CHAPTER XXVIII.

FACING HIS DANGER.

HE funeral is over!

All that is mortal of Claribel Burnham has been consigned to the tomb, and the mourners have returned to the Court and are assembled in the long drawing-room.

Frank Darlington is there.

He has assumed the position of chief mourner, and he almost ostentatiously speaks of the dead girl as though she had been his exclusive property.

The deceased had left no duly executed will, although she had had one drawn up ready for signature, and the man who would have benefited by it hoped in his heart that the new heiress would insist upon carrying out the conditions of the unsigned document.

So, under other circumstances and in favour of any other man, Beatrice Burnham would have done, for, as we know, she was rich enough to be able to spare a few thousands without feeling the loss.

But her natural dislike and distrust of this man were intensified by her knowledge of his conduct towards Fanny, and the conviction she entertained that he was in some way connected with the strange disappearance of Mary Trevor, and added to this was the fixed belief that he was only going to marry Clarrie for the sake of her wealth.

Thus, as a natural consequence, Beatrice, who was by no means exempt from many of the weaknesses of her sex, took a malicious pleasure in noticing the expectation and subsequent disappointment which Darlington could not completely hide.

She was grieved at Clarrie's death, but she was glad that the prize for which the young man would have married her cousin had slipped from his grasp, and she showed no anger when Godfrey Lascelles incidently remarked, in Darlington's hearing, that the Burnham estate would not represent one half of Miss Burnham's fortune.

This, indeed, was the manner in which the truth came out that Beatrice was one of the greatest heiresses in England.

But there was one man who, though not present at the funeral, mourned Clarrie Burnham's death more than all her relations and friends together, and this was Arthur Darlington, the deformed son and heir of the owner of Holly Mount.

Poor Arthur could not remember the time since he had known Clarrie and had not loved her.

To him she was the most lovely of her sex, the most perfectly beautiful both in mind and body; and preposterous as the idea might have appeared to others, he at one time believed that she loved him.

And so she did in a calm sisterly manner, but not in the fashion that she loved his handsome, worthless brother.

What agonies the poor deformed youth suffered—but suffered in silence—none can tell.

He knew his brother's character thoroughly, and was well aware that he did not really love the young heiress, though it was pretty certain he would marry her if no wealthier prize came in his way, and thus Arthur had suffered the pangs of despised love, added to the mortification of being passed over for one so utterly unworthy.

But though Clarrie would never have been his wife, Arthur Darlington mourned for her sincerely; and his grief, added to a severe cold he had caught, prostrated him to such an extent that the doctors looked grave, and the squire became exceedingly anxious.

Frank, however, took heart over his difficulties when he learnt his brother's critical condition.

Here was the chance of another avenue of escape open to him.

If Arthur died he would be his father's heir, and surely the heir of the owner of Holly Mount would be able to raise six hundred pounds to escape from penal servitude.

It was worth waiting and hoping for at any rate, and though Beatrice Burnham showed no sign of any intention of carrying out her late cousin's wishes, he still believed that something would occur to save him.

"If I could only carry off the proud beauty herself, and compel her to marry me," he thought gloomily, "then I could laugh at them all, for the fortune her father left her is, I believe, untrammelled by conditions."

He knew nothing of the stipulation that Beatrice should marry Godfrey Lascelles, or give him half her fortune.

But even this would not have affected him. Half a loaf is better than no bread, and the half loaf in this case would have represented no inconsiderable trifle.

The amount of brotherly affection he showed at this time was so great as to arose suspicion in the squire's mind.

The old man had formed the lowest possible estimate of his youngest son's character, and there were few acts of baseness or of treachery of which he did not believe him capable.

As a natural consequence, Squire Darlington kept such a strict watch and ward over his eldest born that Frank, who quickly detected that he had been watched, found it convenient to have very pressing business in town, and with many expressions of anxious solicitude he left the Mount.

In London, however, a host of difficulties met him.

He had left town to marry an heiress, and he had been by no means troubled with notions of economy with such a prospect before him; but now the day of reckoning could not be long evaded, and he felt bewildered and helpless as he contemplated his position.

"If I could but renew that infernal bill that Cohen holds, I might make the others wait for a time," he mused, sitting in his office in the City and savagely biting his nails. "I wonder how it can be managed. I must not excite suspicion, however, or the whole affair will come out, and then nothing can save me."

He spent the rest of this day pondering over the matter, and the next morning he went to the office of the wealthy Jew, having his plans already made.

But here a serious disappointment met him. Mr. Cohen was in Germany, and the date of his return was doubtful.

Frank did not dare to ask a question about the bill. It might be in the safe of the money-lenders, or it might have been negotiated or paid away with less questionable securities, and, except that he had made it payable at his own bank, it would be almost impossible for him to trace it.

In much perplexity, and with all his plans upset by Cohen's absence, he walked away from the money-lender's office gloomily, his head downcast, and neither looking to the right nor the left until he was pulled up short by coming in violent collision with some person.

"Confound you!"

"I beg your pardon."

"Grantly!"

"Darlington!"

Such were the exclamations that escaped the two men as they thus met.

"You in the City?" said Frank when he and Fortescue Grantly had shaken hands.

"Yes. I don't often get so far east," was the reply; "but business brings me here this morning. By the way, I was very sorry to hear of Clarrie Burnham's death; it must have been an awful shock to you."

"It was; don't talk of it. Good morning." Then they separated.

A few minutes later, however, Darlington turned round in the crowd, and followed Fortescue closely enough to keep him well in sight.

"By Jove! if he hasn't gone to Cohen's," he groaned; "but it can't be about that bill; it won't be due for the next fortnight, and no one can have given him notice of it."

And solacing himself with this reflection, he went back to his own office.

He was, however, too troubled in mind to make even a pretence of attending to business, and after an hour of miserable restlessness he seized his hat and strolled out into the busy thoroughfare.

For a time he wandered on, not heeding whither his steps led him, until he found himself under the shadow of St. Paul's.

Frank Darlington did not go into the cathedral, but turned sharply to the left and passed under an archway leading to Doctors' Commons.

There was no fixed motive in his mind when he came here.

It was rather the desire to get away from the noise and crowd of the busy street, than any more clearly-defined intention, that made him take this turning.

He had not proceeded half-a-dozen steps, however, before a man accosted him.

" Want a license, sir; this way, sir," and the tout, who was dressed in a long white apron, and wore a brass badge, took Frank persuasively by the arm, while another man similarly attired tried to carry him off from his first captor.

With some of the recklessness that had often driven him to play for high stakes, Darlington submitted to be led off to the proctor's office.

He knew very well what he was about; he believed that it was a hundred chances to one that he was throwing away a few pounds, but he reflected that this sum would not make much difference to him in the long run, whether he won or lost, and in his present desperate condition it was just as well to be prepared for all emergencies.

So when he left Doctors' Commons he carried away with him a license authorising any clerk in Holy Orders to join together in the bonds of matrimony, Frank Darlington, of Holly Mount, Sussex, and Beatrice Burnham, of Burnham Court, in the same county. That the young lady whose name figured in this document would have been furiously indignant had she known of it, we may readily take for granted, but it was just one of those things not likely to come to her knowledge, unless she was powerless to help or to save herself.

With this paper in his pocket, to obtain which he had made a false oath, Darlington once more joined the busy stream of life that was tending westward.

He had crossed Farringdon-street, had walked up Fleet-street, and was just about to pass the end of Middle Temple-lane, when he had to pause while a four-wheeled cab came out from the gateway.

The persons in the vehicle were too busy talking to take any notice of him, but he started back with genuine surprise and a desire to escape observation as he recognised Beatrice Burnham, Godfrey Lascelles, and an old lady, whom Clarrie used playfully to call her cousin's dragon, and who usually met the young lady at the railway-station when she came up to town, went about with her as her chaperon, and parted from her when she was on her way back to Burnham Court.

Beatrice was talking earnestly to Lascelles as the cab came out of the gateway, and Darlington experienced a keen pang of jealousy, for, despite his intrigues and his engagements, Beatrice exercised such a spell over him that he would have counted the whole world well lost if he might win her.

"I wonder if she loves that fellow?" was the question that now tormented him as he watched the cab pass through Temple Bar towards the Strand.

Then another thought struck him, and he hailed a hansom and directed the driver to follow the four-wheeled cab.

The man had no difficulty in doing this, for the first cab went straight to Victoria Station, and there the whole party alighted.

Mrs. Gray was evidently a model chaperon, she knew that it was expected of her to be seen and not heard, so she looked industriously after certain parcels that were tobe taken down to the Court by the young heiress, while Beatrice and Godfrey stood by the wooden gateway that led to the platform, talking and waiting for it to be opened.

Darlington, who felt ready to risk anything so that he might hear their conversation, took out a newspaper from his pocket, and, standing with his back to the couple, seemed to be intently reading.

Of course there was the danger that they might recognise him at any moment, but he kept his face turned away from them and well hidden, and there was nothing peculiar in his dress or attitude to attract their attention.

"And you really think you are not throwing away your money on a wild-goose chase?" Lascelles was asking cynically.

"I am sure of it," was Beatrice's emphatic reply; "I am quite convinced that we are on the track of Mary Trevor, and I shall never rest until I have found her."

It was well that Frank Darlington's face was hidden from view as these words fell upon his ears, otherwise the ghastly pallor that came over it would have startled even the most indifferent observer.

"And you are going to the North this week?" Lascelles next asked, changing the subject.

"Yes, I am going on a visit to some of my mother's relatives, but first I shall go to Rawfell Rectory. I took a great fancy to Ursula Raynham when she came to Geraldine's wedding, and I promised one day to visit her. I hear she is not in very good health, so I shall probably remain there a week, then I shall go on to the Riggsworths; the Court has become insufferable to me since Clarrie died."

"You will soon get over that. Do you want to see me about any business as you pass through London?"

"Thank you, no," she answered in a slow deliberate tone.

"If you do, you can write or telegraph; you go on Friday, don't you?"

"Yes, I shall arrive here about twelve o'clock. Mrs. Gray will meet me, and will see me off from King's Cross about five o'clock."

"Does she travel with you?" was his next question.

"Certainly not. Imagine my having Mrs. Gray tacked to my skirts for the next three or four weeks."

"Then, I suppose, you will take a maid with you," he remarked.

"Indeed, I shall do nothing of the kind. I can take care of myself wherever I go; why should I be bothered with a maid?"

"Your position makes it desirable, I think."

"My position is what it always has been, and papa took good care I shouldn't have a maid while he lived; I was never quite certain that my father would not leave me without the traditional shilling, but with the injunction to earn my own living."

"You do your father an injustice, Miss Burnham; but here comes your train, so we shall be able to part to-day without quarrelling."

A few minutes later and the train containing Beatrice Burnham rolled out of the station, Godfrey Lascelles put Mrs. Gray into a cab, and then feeling uncomfortably restless he walked all the way back to the Temple.

And Frank Darlington with a face much paler than usual walked slowly and thoughtfully to his lodgings.

"I cannot have more at stake than I now have," he thought gloomily; "and she travels alone. She must be arrested in her dangerous enquiries at any price; if she will marry me, well. If she will not——"

He did not finish the sentence, but if ever there was murder in a man's heart, it was in that of Frank Darlington as he thought of what he had heard and of what it all meant to him.

CHAPTER XXIX.

CAPTURED.

EATRICE BURNHAM was piqued.

She had come to London according to her stated intention, had arrived at Victoria Station on this particular Friday, and, after spending several hours with Mrs. Gray in shopping, had just said good-bye to that useful personage who had seen her safely into the train at King's Cross.

But she had not seen Godfrey Lascelles.

It is true that she had not sent him either a letter or a telegram requesting him to meet her, and that there was no particular business upon which it was necessary for her to consult him, but for all that she had quite expected to find him at either of the railway stations waiting for her.

And he had not put in an appearance. She would not have admitted it for the world, but she certainly did loiter at Victoria for a full quarter of an hour longer than was necessary after her arrival, and she reached King's-cross a good half hour earlier than she would otherwise have done, in the expectation that somebody would be there waiting for her.

But she was disappointed; she looked about, but she saw no face that she knew, and it was not until the bell rang that she reluctantly took her seat in the carriage.

An old gentleman and a middle-aged lady were in the compartment when she took her place in it, and she thought she would have their company the whole of the journey, but they both got out at Peterborough, and, as no one else entered the carriage she began to feel solitary and to wish that she really had brought a maid or some companion with her.

Evening had set in, and the light from the lamp was not bright enough to make reading pleasant or easy, so Beatrice closed her book, and composed herself in a corner to sleep.

How long she slept she did not know, but she was roused by the closing of the carriage door, and, looking up, she saw that a man had entered the compartment.

Our heroine was by no means of a nervous disposition, but, despite her self-confidence, she did feel vexed with herself for not having bribed the guard to keep anyone else out of the carriage after her two fellow-travellers had left it.

For the man who had just come in was not satisfied with the vacant seats near the door, but came up to the further end of the carriage, and seated himself opposite to the girl.

Beatrice contracted her brows, and she felt so annoyed that she would not look at the man, but she did not feel inclined to move, or to show any fear of him, so she re-opened her book and began to read.

Suddenly she gave a start of surprise, for the man was speaking, and she recognised his voice.

"Miss Beatrice, who would have expected to meet you here?"

And Frank Darlington held out his hand, and affected the most genuine surprise.

Very coldly and reluctantly Beatrice gave him her gloved hand.

"Are you going to Scotland?" he asked, finding she did not echo his expression of surprise.

"No. Are you?" she asked.

"Oh dear no!" he answered. "I am going to Raw-fell Rectory on a visit to the Raynhams."

"Indeed!" said Beatrice in genuine dismay.

She did not say that her destination was the same.

In point of fact she resolved at the moment that she would not go to Rawfell, but would at once pay a visit to her mother's relatives, leaving it an open question whether she went to the Raynhams later on or not.

It was easy enough to make this resolution, but when she came to think of how it was to be carried out the matter was by no means so clear.

If she did not go direct to Rawfell as already arranged, she would have to change her course and to go to an hotel, and this, for a girl travelling alone, is by no means a simple or easy matter.

So she reluctantly came to the conclusion that she had better go on straight to Rawfell Rectory, even though she left it again the following day.

Several times while they were travelling, at the rate of forty miles an hour, Darlington walked to the further window and looked out.

"We seem to be going at a good pace," he remarked ; "but the journey is a long one. By the way, you have not told me where you are going."

"No, I supposed you knew," she replied coldly.

"How should I know ?" he asked in well-affected surprise.

"Because I also am going to Rawfell," she answered.

"Dear me ; then you must be the young lady I was asked to take care of. Dr. Raynham did not mention any name, and I pleaded pressure of business ; under the circumstances I have been more fortunate than I deserve."

"That might very well be," responded Beatrice dryly.

But she was vexed with herself immediately after she had uttered the words.

To make even a disagreeable remark was to imply a certain amount of familiarity, and she wished to keep him at the most frigid distance possible.

He siezed the opportunity, however, and said sadly :

"I get more than I deserve in the way of misfortune and disappointment."

She made no reply.

But he was not to be kept quiet by her silence.

He plied her with questions about Mrs. Trevor and those she had left behind at Burnham Court ; he asked how long she was going to stay at Rawfell ; and then, finding all her replies more or less vague and unsatisfactory, he began to discuss some of the current topics of the day.

Not a word of love, not a glance of admiration, not a hint that could offend her escaped him, and much as the girl disliked him, good breeding alone kept her from unnecessarily showing it.

And thus hour after hour passed by. Morning was breaking, and Beatrice remembered afterwards that as they drew nearer to their destination Darlington became nervous and restless and ill at ease.

In the pale grey dawn of coming day they slackened speed, and Darlington said:

"This was the station I was told to alight at. A carriage will be in readiness to take us to Rawfell, which is still some distance."

"That is not the way I am going," said Beatrice decidedly, looking at the name of the station they were approaching and then at her Bradshaw. "I go on ten miles further, and there will be someone there to meet me."

He made no reply, but he stood with his back to her, and she was conscious of a strong strange odour pervading the carriage.

The next instant a handkerchief was pressed over her mouth and nostrils and held firmly there.

She struggled desperately and tried to hold her breath, so that she should not inhale the powerful drug with which he sought to deaden her senses, but he was a strong man and had far too much at stake to be gentle or to consider whether or not he hurt her, and he soon knew that he had conquered and that she was helpless in his hands.

Not that she entirely lost consciousness, but the power of speech and of independent action deserted her.

The train stopped and Darlington alighted, called a porter, and said:

"Just help me to lift out my wife, she has been taken ill; a carriage will be outside waiting for us. No, there is no luggage except what we have with us, the rest has been sent on."

Then he and the man lifted the helpless girl and carried her through the station, where a modest-looking brougham was quietly standing.

The train had stopped by signal, and therefore only waited two or three minutes, and directly it was gone the station-master went out to offer the hospitality of his house to the sick lady ; but before he could reach the carriage it had started, so there was nothing left for him but to question the porter.

"She seemed faint and white," said the man.

"And the gentleman said she was his wife ? " questioned the official.

"Yes, and they was both in mourning," was the conclusive answer.

And then neither of the men thought any more of the circumstance—at least, at the time.

The effect of the drug did not last long, and Beatrice had not been carried more than à mile before she regained her power of speech.

Darlington, who thought he knew her character well, was expecting an outburst of rage and scorn as soon as she could use her tongue. He was not a little surprised therefore, at her asking faintly though quietly ·

"Where are you taking me ? "

"To a place where you will be kindly treated," he answered quickly.

"And why are you taking me anywhere against my will ? " was her next question.

"I want to teach you to love me," he replied, taking her hand and pressing it to his lips.

"Love you ! "

And she laughed.

Not loudly or defiantly, or with any effort, but as though the idea were really amusing, and could excite nothing but mirth.

"Yes," he said, irritated beyond self-control; "is it such a very difficult lesson to learn ? "

"To me, an impossible one," she replied with the same absence of angry temper.

"The result will be the same," he said doggedly, "for I mean to marry you."

"It is very kind of you, I am sure," and again she laughed. "It is refreshing to discover that the days of romance have not entirely departed. I feel quite like a heroine. Imagine a girl being taken out of a train and carried away, whether she desires it or not, in this prosaic nineteenth century."

He made no reply, and she leaned back in the carriage, and seemed to be absorbed in thought.

Darlington was uneasy.

It would have pleased him better had his captive been wild and excited, had she stormed and threatened him, or had she wept and begged that he would set her free.

But her quietly amused manner of treating the whole matter as a good joke greatly disconcerted him.

He had been so terribly in earnest himself; he had felt that this woman was such a prize if won, and such a dangerous enemy if not under his influence and control, that he had worked himself up to the terrible resolution that she must become his wife or he must silence her for ever.

And now she was at his side, and was his prisoner, and he felt more positively afraid of her than ever.

Leaning back in the carriage, and to all appearance so indifferent as to her destination, Beatrice was, nevertheless, taking very careful notice of the road along which they were travelling.

Her apparent absence of fright was in no way feigned.

She was not in the least degree afraid that Darlington would force her into a marriage with him, because she was quite resolved she would not marry him, and she had no fear of violence at his hands, for she thought he lacked both the incentive and the courage necessary for such conduct.

In point of fact she made the mistake of underestimating her danger, for, despite his many professions of love, she believed that Darlington only wanted her for her money, and next, she believed him to be completely ignorant of her search for Mary Trevor.

This last point, indeed, was her greatest danger, for neither love nor greed would have nerved Darlington to abduct her, if fear as to what she might discover about Mary Trevor had not been added as an incentive.

And meanwhile the brougham, with one strong horse in it, was going on at a good pace, and Beatrice calculated that they must have travelled at least five miles of country that was naturally wild, and that would have been bleak and gloomy at any other time of the year.

It was desolate enough even now, for in their drive they had not passed a single man or woman, and though the day was still young Beatrice was surprised not to have observed people going to their work in the fields.

At length the road dipped and the carriage descended into a valley where three or four whitewashed cottages nestled against the hillside, though at some little distance apart.

The carriage pulled up before the garden gate of the first cottage from the neglected road, and Darlington alighted and held out his hand to help her to follow.

"Thank you, I prefer remaining where I am," she said, looking at him coldly and disdainfully.

"You cannot remain where you are," he said darkly; "if you don't come with me quietly you will compel me to use force."

"If you lay hands upon me, my shrieks shall resound through the valley," she said, while her eyes blazed with anger.

"I will soon get over that difficulty," he said in a threatening tone.

Then he called to the driver to come and keep guard at the carriage-door, while he himself went into the house.

"Now," thought Beatrice, "is my time."

And she took out her purse, and wrapped three sovereigns in a piece of paper upon which she hastily scrawled the address of Godfrey Lascelles.

Then she said to the man who stood by the door:

"Don't seem to be listening to me, but you will find some money and an address underneath the cushion. Keep the money, but let the gentleman whose address is on the paper know where I am. If you do this, and he finds me within a couple of days, you shall have a hundred pounds."

"It's very fine to promise, ma'am; but your husband——"

"I have no husband, I am not married, but I am very rich, and this man wants my money. If you doubt me go to the man whose name I have written down, and tell him that Beatrice Burnham has been carried off by violence. Ah——"

She stopped talking, for she saw Frank Darlington coming from the cottage accompanied by two big-boned Yorkshire women, beautifully clean, but looking as hard and uncompromising as their native fells.

"This is the lady," said Darlington, pointing to Beatrice.

The foremost of the two women spoke in a harsh dialect, though her words were not meant to be uncivil, as she asked the girl to come into the house.

"Yes, I will come," said Beatrice readily, "but I warn you that I am brought here against my will, and that in making me a prisoner you are breaking the law."

Then she stepped from the carriage, and ignoring Darlington altogether she walked up to the cottage-door between her two female warders.

Then she passed through the low porch and entered the kitchen, or house-place, which the two grim females used as a living-room.

Early as was the hour a fire burned in the grate, a kettle hissed on the hob, and a three-legged crock containing porridge steamed as though almost ready for use.

Beatrice observed all this, and she also noticed that the room was wonderfully clean, that a border of the stone floor as well as the walls were stencilled, and that what wood there was about the place was scrubbed till it was as white as milk.

Her inspection, however, was cut short by Darlington, who said:

"I am obliged to leave you now, my dear, but I will return in the course of a day or two, when I hope you will have changed your mind, and in the meantime don't you think it will be advisable for you to wear your wedding-ring?"

So saying he took a plain gold ring from his pocket and offered it to her.

She looked at him for a moment scornfully, then she laughed disdainfully as she asked:

"Have you been telling these people that I am your wife?"

He did not answer her, though he asked with a frown:

"Will you take your ring?"

"The ring is not mine; I have no right to wear such a ring, and I never shall acquire that right from you, Mr. Darlington. But pray don't make any excuses for leaving me; I shall be glad never to see your face again."

Then she turned away, and taking a chair, seated herself near the fire, for though it was summer, the early morning air was cold and chilly.

Darlington looked at her for a moment, a variety of conflicting feelings agitating his breast, then, with a sign to the eldest of the sisters to follow him, he turned and left the room.

CHAPTER XXX.

TRYING TO BE BRAVE.

THE conversation between Darlington and the eldest of the big-boned women was a long one, but at last it was over, and Beatrice, sitting in such a position that she could command a view of the window, saw the man she had most reason to dread walk down the garden-path, enter the brougham, and drive away.

"Thank Heaven I am not to be annoyed by the presence of that man," was her mental comment.

Then she took off her gloves and hat, and said to the woman who had remained in the kitchen with her:

"I wish you would show me to a room where I can have a good wash; I feel dusty and tired after my journey."

The woman made no reply except to leave the room, probably to confer with her sister, for the two shortly returned, and, requesting the girl to follow her, the eldest led the way to what looked like a kind of cupboard, the door of which being opened disclosed a narrow staircase which she was bidden to ascend.

Beatrice did not like the look of the place, but after the first momentary hesitation she followed the woman, who had already ascended the steep staircase.

There were two rooms upstairs, and into the best of these Beatrice Burnham was led.

Everything was as spotlessly clean as whitewash and soap and water and constant washing and scrubbing could make it, but the boards were bare, and could not boast of a single strip of carpet.

A trestle bedstead with a home-made mattress—the tick filled with chaff instead of feathers—stood against one of the four walls, and though the sheets upon it like everything else in the place were spotlessly clean, they were, it must be confessed, terribly coarse, and Beatrice gave a little shudder as she realised that she would be expected to sleep between them.

"I wonder for which of my particular sins I am doomed to sleep in sackcloth," she muttered *sotto voce,* then she asked aloud:

"Did the man who brought me here see this room before he engaged it?"

The hard-looking woman's face slightly flushed, and she frowned angrily as she said:

"We are single women, and no man comes into our sleeping rooms."

"That is a comfort at any rate," replied the girl; "and I don't suppose he quite knew what he was consigning me to."

"It is clean," said the woman aggressively.

"Beautifully clean," was the reply; "but it isn't soft or pretty. But can't you give me more water than that?" and the girl looked ruefully at a pint of liquid provided for her ablutions.

"You can have a tub full if you like," was the growling response.

"Then I should like a tub full if you please, the biggest tub you have, but don't take the trouble to bring it yourself; hire somebody else to wait upon me, and pay them out of this. I want a cold bath every morning."

And so saying she handed the woman a sovereign.

Miss Jex looked at the gold coin, then at the donor.

She bit it between her teeth, then looked at it again as she asked:

"Have you many more like this?"

"Next month I shall be worth as much gold as would fill this room," replied Beatrice, looking round the small apartment; "that is why the man who brought me here against my will wants to marry me; but he won't succeed; I believe he has a wife already."

"He says you are his wife," said the woman shortly.

"It would puzzle him to prove it," returned Beatrice with a short laugh; "and men don't usually run away with their own wives. What reason does he give you for bringing me here?"

IN HER BRIDAL ROBES AND WHITE AS THE PEARLS ROUND HER THROAT, CLARIBEL BURNHAM STOOD, OR RATHER LEANED, AGAINST A STATUE.

No. 12.

"He says you want to run away with another man," Miss Jex replied.

"Bah! what a flimsy story. I should have thought he could have invented something more probable and more plausible. Can you read?"

"No."

"Can the other woman read?"

"No," was again snapped out like the snarl of a dog.

Miss Jex was as proud as she was ignorant and mercenary, and she thought that Beatrice was trying to humiliate her; this the girl quickly perceived, for she hastened to say:

"I only asked the question because if you could read I would prove to you that what I say is true; but will you send me some water now, I am tired and dusty, and so hungry."

A request that the woman silently complied with, bringing up her largest washing-tub, and filling it with water from a neighbouring well.

It was a very slow process, however, and a full hour elapsed before Beatrice, who happened to have her dressing-case with her, got through her ablutions, made her toilette, and descended to the kitchen.

Here she found two tables spread, one for herself, the other for her two keepers.

"You'll not like porridge, I'm thinking," said Miss Jex the elder.

"No, thank you," was the reply; "I should like some tea or coffee, and some toast and an egg."

Coffee was not forthcoming, but an egg with fresh butter and home made bread was, and Beatrice made a hearty meal, though she could not help perceiving that the grim sisters rather seemed to resent her refusal to eat the same oatmeal diet as themselves.

But Beatrice did not care whether they were pleased or displeased.

She was wondering how she could escape from them.

Her first intention had been to offer them a larger bribe than Darlington could have promised, for she was well provided with money, and would not have hesitated to part with a considerable sum to regain her freedom, but something in the elder woman's eyes when she clutched the piece of gold, and asked if she had much more, convinced her that the money would be taken, and the conditions for which it was given would not be complied with, so she resolved to try to outwit her gaolers instead of turning the wards of her prison lock with a golden key.

When breakfast was over the girl said:

"As I haven't slept for the night, I think I will go and lie down for an hour or two; you won't let me be disturbed, will you?"

"No; if you are wanted we will call you ourselves," was the answer.

Then Beatrice went up again to the bare comfortless room, threw herself upon the bed and tried to sleep.

But sleep would not visit her, and instead of losing consciousness, her brain seemed in a nervously excited condition.

She closed her eyes, and her sense of sound became keener than it had ever been before.

Outside the house not a whisper broke the deep silence, but from the room below came the buzz of voices, indistinct at first, though after a time she could make out what the speakers said.

"I believe she's got lots of money," said one sister.

"'Twould be well if we could get hold of some of it," said the other.

"'Twouldn't be worth doing unless we got all," said the first speaker.

"Maybe she'd give it to us to get away," said the voice which the listener recognised as belonging to the woman whom her sister called "Sall."

"Augh!" said the elder of the two, "I don't mean to let her go; dead folks tell no tales."

"But there's the man," objected the younger sister; "he'll come and want to know what's become of her; and whether she's his wife or not, if she's half as rich as she told you, he'll not rest till he's found out."

"I doubt it," said Miss Jex significantly; "there's more than love or money in the matter. Before he went away he said, with a look on his face that I'll not forget, that he must find her here when he came back—find her alive or dead."

"Then you think he wants to be rid of her?"

"If she won't do as he wants her to do. He's a dangerous man to cross because he thinks only of what's good and pleasant for himself."

"And you'll let him find her dead when he comes for her?" questioned Sall.

"No. I'll let him find us all gone if she's got enough with her to make it worth our while," was the answer. "I'm tired of this place, and I'd like to go to America."

"So would I," said her sister; "but I much doubt she ain't got enough for that."

"I'll see," said Miss Jex, "if she's asleep, I can soon find out what's in her pocket."

"And if she wakes up in the middle?" suggested the more timid of the two.

No verbal reply reached the strained ears of the agonised listener, but some significant action must have followed, for Sall said in frightened tones:

"No; don't do it till night comes; I can't abear that daylight should look in on such a thing; and besides, we can get away without being seen at night, and we can't in the day time."

"I'm going to see if it's worth our while," said Miss Jex doggedly.

Then Beatrice heard the cupboard-like door cautiously opened and for the moment her heart seemed to stand still.

Her terror did not last long, however.

Before the woman had crept half way up the stairs Beatrice Burnham had sprang from the rude bed, seated herself on the solitary chair by the window, had snatched out from her dressing-bag a large dagger-like knife which she held with seeming carelessness in the right hand as she turned over the leaves of a magazine with her left hand.

Her attitude though unstudied and quickly assumed was a natural one, and the would-be murderess, creeping up the stairs, and cautiously opening the door, started with something like fear as she looked at the empty bed. Then she saw the graceful but black-robed figure by the window.

"Come in, I am not asleep," said Beatrice quietly, while she let the magazine rest upon her lap as she toyed with her formidable-looking paper-knife.

"I—I thought I'd have a talk with you, ma'am," said the woman, trying to hide her confusion.

"Yes," assented the girl courteously; "take a seat on the bed, I am not rich in chairs."

The woman complied, though she felt annoyed at the assumption that the room for the time belonged to any-one but herself.

"You don't want to stay here longer than you can help, I suppose," began Miss Jex.

"Well no," I don't find it so particularly comfort-able," was the answer, "and moreover, my friends, who were expecting me, will be anxious about me."

"And who may your friends be?"

"The friends I was going to are the Rev. Dr. Rayn-ham, of Rawfell Rectory, and his daughter. Rawfell is about five miles from here, I think."

"It's more than that, it's seven," was the answer, though the woman could have bitten off her tongue with vexation the moment she had made the admission.

"I know it isn't far off," said Beatrice with seeming indifference, "and they and my other friends will find me sooner or later. But I warn you," she added, looking steadily at her companion, "that you will have to pay heavily for your part in this affair. I am brought here against my will by a scoundrel who wants to get hold of my fortune, and I am detained here by you who render yourself liable to punishment as Mr. Darlington's accomplice."

"I don't know nothing about the matter except that a gentleman asked me to take care of his wife, and then he brought you here," said the woman sullenly; "but if you ain't his wife, and if you like to pay me well, I'll let you go."

Beatrice felt her heart throb with hope, but she remembered the conversation she had just listened to, and she said cautiously:

"I am quite willing to pay you handsomely. How much do you want?"

"Have you got the matter of fifty pounds about you?" asked the woman.

"About me, no! The idea of my carrying fifty pounds about with me when I am going on a short visit to friends. I can get fifty pounds by writing for it to my trustee, or if you like to come with me to Rawfell Rectory, Dr. Raynham will let me have the money."

"Then you don't carry a lot of money about with you?"

"I carry a pound or two with me, of course; I have given you one and I think I have two more, but I can always get money by writing for it."

"I wish I could," said the woman gloomily; "if you could pay me fifty pounds, I'd let you go."

"I can pay you if you will go with me to Rawfell, or if you will post a letter to London for me," was the reply; "but I can't coin money here any more than you can."

The woman rose to her feet.

For a moment Beatrice did not feel sure that she did not mean to spring upon her, and it required all the girl's nerve and self-control to enable her to retain her seat, and play with her knife so carelessly.

She showed no sign of fear, no consciousness that the woman before her was ready to strangle her for a few pieces of gold.

Once, indeed, she half smiled upon her would-be murderess, and the woman, slightly cowed and somewhat abashed, muttered something about "talking it over with Sall," and so left the room.

But Beatrice was still their prisoner, and her heart sank in her breast as she remembered that even if the driver of the brougham communicated at once with Godfrey Lascelles, one or two days at least must elapse before he could come to her rescue.

One or two days! And the grim sisters had talked of ending her life that very night!

CHAPTER XXXI.

GODFREY'S PRESENTIMENTS.

ODFREY LASCELLES sat alone in his chambers in the Inner Temple.

He was trying to concentrate his thoughts upon some legal work before him, but the effort was not successful, as you could perceive if you watched him.

A dreamy faraway look would cover over his face and soften the keen glance of his eyes, and he would remain like this for a little time, and then he would rouse himself angrily, would get up and pace the room with impatient footsteps, and then set himself resolutely to work again.

But his attention would flag, his mind would wander, and his thoughts would drift off again to a matter that was not in the papers or in the law books before him.

At length he pushed away his work and muttered with genuine vexation:

"Confound the girl! I can't get her out of my head. Why should I trouble about her? She goes her own way; she is, to all intents and purposes, her own mistress, and my guardianship means little more than the numerous opportunities it gives her for treating me with discourtesy."

He threw himself into a low chair by the window which commanded a view of the river, and he watched the steamboats and the craft on the water with a dreamy, purposeless gaze.

But even this soon wearied him. A troubled feeling was in his mind; a vague, undefinable presentiment of evil, as though some great misfortune were hanging over him, and as though Beatrice Burnham were in some way or other connected with it.

"I can't stand it any longer. I'll go out and see if I can shake off this unpleasant feeling;" and he caught up his hat and had reached the door when he met two men who were coming to his rooms to see him.

One of them was Fortescue Grantly, and he introduced his companion as Mr. Archibald Raynham.

The two young men had heard of each other, though they had never before met, and Godfrey went back into his sitting-room, asking them to follow him.

He was glad that Grantly had brought young Raynham with him, for he felt sure that he should now hear something about Beatrice, but, at the same time, the sense of depression would not leave him.

They had seated themselves, and Godfrey had offered his visitors some claret-cup, for the day was hot and sultry, when Raynham said carelessly:

"I came to see you this afternoon, Lascelles, at the request of my father and sister; they are anxious about Miss Burnham."

"What has happened to her? She is not ill, is she?"

"That is just what they don't know," was the reply. "She was to have arrived at Rawfell three days ago. Her luggage reached the rectory, but she never put in an appearance. It seems that they grew anxious, and telegraphed to Burnham Court, but the answer they received only increased their alarm, for Miss Burnham had started for Yorkshire at the time arranged. Then my people sent to me, asking me to come to you and ascertain if you knew anything of the young lady's movements."

"No, I know nothing whatever about her," said Lascelles in genuine alarm.

"Then you did not see her last Friday when she came to town?" questioned Raynham.

"No; I knew she was to pass through London that day, and I told her if she wanted to see me to write or telegraph, and I would meet her; but she did neither, and I have not seen or heard from her."

"It is very mysterious," said Raynham, who began to think the matter was more serious than he had at first considered it; "one would imagine she started from King's Cross, because the luggage went on with her name upon the boxes, with the word 'passenger,' and my father's address."

"We can ascertain that quickly," said Lascelles; "I will go or send at once to the old lady who chaperons Miss Burnham when she comes to town. I suggested, when she talked of going to Yorkshire, that she ought to take Mrs. Gray or a maid with her."

"Where does this Mrs. Gray live?" asked Raynham.

"In Guildford Street, Bloomsbury. I will take a cab and go to her at once."

"And I will go with you," said Ursula's brother promptly.

"I don't seem to be of any use at present," said Fortescue Grantly, rising to his feet, "but if I can help you in any way, pray let me know. In the meanwhile I will telegraph to my uncle's wife; she and Beatrice Burnham were firm friends, and she may know something of her movements."

"Do," said Lascelles; "I am more alarmed than I can express. The girl is so self-willed, and so independent in her thoughts and actions, that there is always danger of her getting into some difficulty."

Then the young men parted, Fortescue to telegraph to Lady Grantly, and Lascelles and Raynham to seek Mrs. Gray.

They found that useful lady in her rooms at the top storey of a handsome house, seated near the open window with her parrot, her favourite cat, and her afternoon tea.

She was very much flustered at the appearance of visitors, and she was still more disturbed when she learned what had brought them there.

With much more repetition of detail than was necessary, she told the two young men how she and Beatrice had spent the previous Friday, and how she had seen the girl and her luggage off by the train.

"I expected to have had a letter from her yesterday," the old lady went on, "for I was to have sent her a dinner-dress that was not finished on Friday, but I

wasn't alarmed at no letter coming, for Miss Beatrice
never did make much fuss about what she wore."

But the young men were not interested in the dinner-
dress.

They asked a great number of questions, somewhat
bewildering the old lady, and at length they went off to
the Great Northern Railway Station, taking Mrs. Gray
with them.

Here they obtained corroboration of her story, but
little more.

After they had remained for some time making enquiries, the guard of the train in which Beatrice had
travelled was found, and he was plied with questions
and his memory refreshed with something more substantial than words or promises.

He remembered the young lady in question quite
well, for she would lean out of the carriage up to the
last as though she were expecting somebody to come
before she started, "and I remember you, ma'am," said
the guard, addressing Mrs. Gray, "and how many
questions you asked over and over again."

The old lady would have made some resentful comment, but Godfrey Lascelles was too impatient to allow
her to do so, and he asked sharply:

"Well, what became of the young lady?"

"I don't know, sir," replied the man; "she was all
right at Peterborough, for I saw her alone, the old folks
who were in the carriage with her having got out there.
But I never saw her again unless she was the lady as
was carried out of the train and through the station at
Scarbridge, but she'd got her husband with her and
had fainted, I was told."

"Did you see that lady's face?"

"The one as fainted—no, I didn't. I saw part of
her dress, and 'twas black, and the man who was taking
her away was a tall dark man, likewise in mourning."

"That could not be the lady we are seeking," said
Lascelles, decidedly; "she would have no gentleman
travelling with her."

"That might be, or it mightn't," said the guard
meditatively, "but I'd almost swear they got out of the

same carriage as your young lady was in, because you see they left the door open, and now I come to think of it, there was some things left behind—a shawl, and umbrella, and fan."

"Where are they? Can we see them?" asked Godfrey anxiously.

The man said he did not know, and there was much going about from one office to another, and asking of many questions, but at length the lost articles were found, and Mrs. Gray at once recognised them.

"The whole affair assumes a more serious aspect than I thought possible," said Lascelles gloomily, as he and Raynham drove back to the Temple.

"You think Miss Burnham has been taken to some place against her will?" asked the rector's son.

"Yes, I am sure of it. You heard the guard say that she was carried out of the carriage and through the station."

"Yes, but she might really have fainted," observed Raynham.

"Beatrice Burnham was not a fainting subject," returned Godfrey positively, "but it puzzles me to think who the man could be."

"He called himself her husband, the guard said," remarked Raynham.

"That he did to avoid question, no doubt, and you may be sure he wanted to marry her for the sake of her fortune. What a terrible curse money is!"

"It's a curse we are all anxious to get more than our full share of," laughed the young Yorkshireman. "I could very well do with a little more curse myself."

But Godfrey did not even smile; he was in no mood to take a light or cheerful view of any subject.

The forebodings that had hung over him like a dark cloud seemed to have been only too well founded, and though he was anything but a superstitious man, he felt that something very serious had happened to poor Beatrice.

Many men in his position would have taken the mysterious disappearance of his troublesome and ungrateful ward in a very philosophical spirit, and though they might have made some show of trying to find her, they would certainly not have exerted themselves to any great extent, for, by the terms of her father's will, Godfrey Lascelles became the heir to Beatrice Burnham's fortune if she died before she came of age or intestate, while half of her fortune was to become his if she did not marry him.

This will, of course, could not affect the Burnham Court estate, which would go to some distant relative, but the father of our heroine had been quite rich enough to satisfy the desire for wealth of most ordinary men.

Godfrey had not meant to marry Beatrice, or to take advantage of the terms of her father's will.

Over and over again he had told himself that not for ten times our heroine's fortune would he afford her the triumph of refusing him.

And that she would refuse him he had not the least doubt.

For the sake of her dead father, to whom he had been warmly attached, he had resolved to act as her guardian and look after her interests until she attained her majority; but when this time arrived, and he could hand over to her the property that he held in trust, he meant to politely raise his hat and bid adieu to his fair and ungrateful tormentress.

It was this mental determination that often made him patient and forbearing with the exasperating girl when he would otherwise have resented her persistent efforts to provoke him.

"Only a little while now," he would say to himself when more than usually tried, and then he would become more grave and more studiously courteous than ever.

All these trivial thoughts and feelings vanished now, however.

It may be a comparatively easy matter to guard oneself against the fascinations and even the caprices of a beautiful woman, but a man of generous impulses is apt to forget his shield and buckler when the woman in question is threatened by some positive danger, or is in any real trouble or distress.

So it was with Godfrey Lascelles now.

He would have held himself coldly aloof from Beatrice, and would have talked to her gravely and courteously, but without any spark of feeling, so long as she was safe and prosperous; but the moment she was in danger his heart and his imagination took fire till he was even himself startled by the strength and fervour of his emotions.

"I must find her! I owe it to myself as well as to her to find her. I am the man who would benefit most by her death, and her money under such circumstances would be a curse to me."

Such were his thoughts as he drove back to the Temple, and he was startled out of them by Archie Raynham, who was his companion in the cab, and who asked:

"What do you propose to do?"

"Find her," was the laconic reply.

"That, of course; but how?"

"I shall start off to trace her to-night, but first I must see a detective and make some arrangements for the transfer of my work. What do you propose to do?"

"I'd go with you, if you thought I could be of the least use," replied young Raynham diffidently.

"I don't know that you can help me," said Lascelles, who felt that he would much prefer being alone. "You see, you don't even know Miss Burnham by sight."

"That is true," assented the rector's son; "but I know the part of the country where, if the guard's theory is well founded, she must have been taken from the train."

"Well, come if you like," said Lascelles indifferently; "for my own part," he went on, "I am not inclined to attach much credence to the guard's story. I cannot imagine what man could have taken the girl away."

"That might easily be, for though you are Miss Burnham's guardian, you are not her father confessor, I presume," laughed Raynham; "and she might very well have a dozen admirers without your knowledge."

Godfrey frowned though he could not gainsay the truth of the remark, and he said briefly:

"Until I have seen a detective I cannot decide upon the steps I will take; if you like to call at my rooms in a couple of hours' time I shall be more clear as to my movements, and in the meanwhile you might telegraph to your father, and ask if any news of the missing girl has reached them."

Then they parted, Raynham to carry out his companion's suggestion, and Godfrey Lascelles to send for Mr. Longridge.

"It is odd," muttered the young barrister as he sat waiting for the arrival of the detective, "very odd, that Beatrice should have engaged this man to seek for a lost girl, and that I should have to send for him now to help me to find her. He knows her well personally, and he knows something of her position, and connections, and friends, otherwise I should engage somebody else, for I have not very much faith in Mr. Longridge."

At that moment, however, the detective was announced.

CHAPTER XXXII.

MR. LONGRIDGE GOES HIS OWN WAY.

 "OST! taken away by stratagem and violence combined; a strong-minded lady like Miss Beatrice Burnham, too! Well, this is what I call interesting; indeed, sir, it's as pretty a case as ever was placed in my hands."

And Mr. Longridge as he said this rubbed the aforesaid hands with great enjoyment.

"Confound you and your cases! have you any suggestion to make?" asked Lascelles, unable to repress his irritation.

The detective gave a slight start, and looked steadily at the barrister.

Had he been alone or had he considered it safe to express his thoughts in a manner peculiar to himself, he would have given a low prolonged whistle, but he knew from past experience that Godfrey Lascelles was a man who allowed no liberty to be taken with him, so the detective controlled the muscles of his face, and guarded the tone of his voice as he replied:

"I am not ready with a suggestion, sir, but I believe I recognise the hand of the prime mover in this affair. If my surmise is correct we shall soon find the young lady."

"Do you attach any value to the guard's story about a lady being carried out of a carriage at Scarbridge?"

"Of course I do, sir. I believe I recognise the man who took her away."

"You do?" and Godfrey's face flushed crimson, then became deadly pale.

"Yes, sir, but I'd rather not mention names if you'll excuse me. You place the matter unreservedly in my hands, I suppose, sir?"

"Yes, except that I shall also seek her myself."

"That of course, sir, and perhaps you'll do me the favour of not knowing me if we should meet. You might even go the length if you should find occasion for doing so of calling me an impertinent fellow, and a few more complimentary things of the same kind; them Yorkshire fellows are uncommon cute, it takes a Londoner all his time to best 'em."

"Very well, Longridge, but I had thought of going with you."

"'Twouldn't do at all, sir, not at all; but I ought to know where to send to you sharp."

"Well, that is a difficulty: Mr. Raynham, the son of the clergyman to whose house Miss Beatrice was going, wants to go with me; he says he knows that part of the country well, but I felt rather doubtful of the good we should both do."

"You can't do much harm, sir, and the gentleman's knowledge of the country will be an advantage to you, sir, though it wouldn't help me; and then I could make sure that a telegram would find you here or at Rawfell Rectory, couldn't I sir?"

"You might depend upon its being forwarded from either place," was the dissatisfied reply.

"That will do, sir, nicely, thank you. Perhaps you will give me Mrs. Gray's address, and—the—sinews of war."

Godfrey Lascelles made no verbal reply, but he took up a pen, scribbled down the old lady's address, then took out his cheque-book and filled up one of the blank slips for twenty pounds in Mr. Longridge's favour.

The detective took the cheque, examined it carefully, folded it up, and consigned it to his pocket, then he rose to his feet as he said:

"You'll hear from me, sir, as soon as I've any news to send, and you'll please to remember, if we meet, that you don't know me."

Godfrey bent his head, and then Mr. Longridge went away.

"Wants to go with me," muttered the detective as he walked along the Strand towards the bank upon which the cheque was drawn. "But I don't want his company," continued the man, talking to himself; "he'd spoil my little game, and he'd be known in no time, and any discovery I might make would go down to his credit. Besides, he don't suspect Mr. Frank Darlington as having run away with the young lady, and I do. I guess he's got wind of my little game and thinks to shut me up by nabbing her. I'll outwit you yet, Mr. Frank; but I don't want Mr. Lascelles to help me. 'Every man to his trade,' say I, and a barrister's trade is to defend a man or convict him, as the case may be, and the side he's engaged upon, but he ain't got nothing to do with hunting out the guilty parties; that is my part of the game."

When Mr. Longridge came out of the bank, however, with the money in his pocket, he felt more amiably disposed towards the young barrister, while his meditations took a more sentimental turn.

"He's in love with her," he mused, blinking his small brown eyes; "that's what he is, whether he knows it or not, or whether she knows it or not. Well, they won't make a bad-looking couple, and there'll be lots of tin between them; but I should like to have a little more of it in my pocket first."

Then the detective betook himself to his own home, there to make his preparations for the work before him.

"Confound that fellow! why couldn't he work with me instead of going off on the business alone?" muttered Godfrey Lascelles discontentedly when Mr. Longridge had gone. "I don't suppose I shall do any good by going alone or with young Raynham, but at the same time I can't remain here doing nothing. I wonder whom he suspects? It can't be Fortescue Grantly."

Then he laughed at his own suggestion, for he remembered that Fortescue had never shown even the faintest preference for Beatrice.

A short time later and both Archie Raynham and young Grantly came to his rooms.

Both had sent telegrams, as arranged, and had received replies, but neither had really learnt anything more than they previously knew about the missing girl.

Godfrey told them how he had set Longridge to work, but he did not mention the fact that the man had previously been in Beatrice Burnham's pay, neither did he repeat the detective's assertion that he thought he knew who the man was who had taken the girl away, for, in point of fact, he had himself put this assertion of Mr. Longridge down as worthless.

He, however, stated his intention of starting for Scarbridge the same evening, and he invited Raynham to join him.

"Yes, I will go by all means," was the reply; "we can make enquiries at the station and put up at the little inn. There we can hire a trap of some kind and drive over to Rawfell; the distance isn't above a dozen miles."

So the matter was arranged, and not long afterwards the young men started, Grantly parting with them as they entered the cab.

They were in ample time to catch the train at King's Cross by which they had intended to travel, and they had comfortably settled themselves in a smoking carriage and provided themselves with a variety of papers with which to while away the hours, when, just as the train was on the move, a man ran along the platform and sprang into their carriage.

Raynham muttered something that sounded like anything but a blessing, but Godfrey Lascelles made no comment, for he had recognised the intruder as no other than Frank Darlington.

When Darlington looked about him he gave a start of surprise and turned pale, but he soon regained his self-possession, and looking at the young barrister he said:

"Mr. Lascelles, I believe?"

Godfrey responded coldly and briefly, and after the few words that politeness demanded, he would have relapsed into silence, or have talked only with Raynham, if the last comer had not persisted in making conversation. For in truth, Darlington was alarmed at finding Beatrice's guardian travelling northward, and he was still more so when he heard him once address his companion as " Raynham."

Either they now knew of Beatrice's disappearance, or they soon would know, and in any case it was most desirable that he should divert all suspicion from himself.

So he began to talk about Clarrie Burnham, and the great blow her death was to him, and he talked so much of her virtues, her beauty, and her wealth that Godfrey Lascelles felt disgusted.

To him the woman's name would have been sacred who had been snatched from his side by death, on what was to have been her wedding-day.

Had he been in Darlington's place he would not have mentioned the girl's name before a comparative stranger, and though he had never cared for Clarrie Burnham himself, and had always thought her weak, insipid, and commonplace, though exceptionally pretty, still it jarred upon him now to hear her thus carelessly and glibly discussed.

This being his condition of mind, Lascelles said so little that Raynham, thinking the young barrister might himself have admired the deceased beauty, with a view of sparing him, joined in the one-sided conversation, told Darlington how he was a cousin of the Raynham girls, and then to Godfrey's intense vexation, the young fellow began to talk of Beatrice.

It would have been a great relief to Lascelles' mind if he could have well kicked the " cub," as he mentally termed him, but under existing circumstances this was impracticable, so he had to sit in grim silence while Archibald Raynham told Darlington how Beatrice was to have reached his father's house early on the previous Saturday, but had not arrived, and her friends were very anxious about her.

Of course Darlington was profuse in his enquiries and his expressions of sympathy, and when Raynham like-wise added for his comfort that he and Lascelles were now on their way to look for the lost heiress, he at once volunteered to join them.

But Godfrey Lascelles' patience had been strained to its very last limit, and he alarmed Darlington not a little by saying curtly and coldly:

"Thank you, there is not the least necessity for more help; we have a decided clue, and we shall no doubt find Miss Burnham and punish her cowardly abductor."

"I am sure I hope so," said Darlington, but he gasped as he uttered the words, his naturally pale face became paler than usual, his dark brows contracted, and his thin lips seemed to become more straight and more closely pressed together than ever.

He became silent too, and as the train neared Peterborough he said aloud:

"The weather makes one uncomfortably thirsty; we stay here ten minutes, don't we?"

"I believe so," was Godfrey's reply.

"You don't mean to get out?" was the next question.

"No," was the answer.

Raynham looked doubtful; he would have liked to stretch his long limbs, but something in Lascelles' tone and manner restrained him from going with Darlington, though he did get out on the platform and look around.

The stay was a short one, people got back into their places, the bell rang, time was up, and still Darlington did not return.

"He won't get back before we start," said Raynham.

"I hope he won't come back into this carriage," said Lascelles; "I don't like the man."

"So I thought," remarked the rector's son; "by the way, he has taken his bag with him."

On hearing this, Godfrey took up his post at the window, for the train was on the move, and he saw Darlington, bag in hand, making for one of the carriages further down in the train.

But the railway officials waved him back, he was too late.

So also was another man, who stood upon the platform gesticulating frantically, and pointing to a carriage, the distance between which and himself was rapidly widening.

"Except that the man is dressed so shabbily and is making such a fool of himself, I should say that was Longridge," said Godfrey carelessly.

"Who do you say it is?" asked Raynham.

"I thought I recognised a man who is doing some work for me," was the indifferent reply.

It had suddenly flashed across the young barrister's mind that it really might be Longridge, and he had already come to the somewhat hasty conclusion that his present companion was little better than a fool.

He forgot to make allowance for the fact that Archie Raynham knew nothing about Darlington and very little of his relatives at Burnham Court.

So the two young men made the rest of their journey for that night almost in silence, and day was breaking when they arrived at Scarbridge.

It was palpably useless for them to think of making enquiries at this hour of the morning, for the railway officials were sleepy, and they themselves were not particularly wide awake, so at Raynham's suggestion they went to the little railway inn, where they could be accommodated with beds.

Raynham went off to his own room cheerfully though sleepily enough, but though Godfrey Lascelles retired to the room allotted him, he could not sleep.

His brain was in a painfully excited condition, and his heart seemed on fire.

Over and over again he pictured Beatrice with her high spirit and her undaunted courage a captive dashing herself like some imprisoned bird against the bars of her cage.

If he could have credited her with some prudence and worldly wisdom, he would have felt less anxiety on her behalf, but he felt convinced that however bad her position might be, she would make it still worse by her uncompromising outspoken obstinacy.

And thus he tormented himself instead of going to bed and trying to sleep, until, fairly worn out with mental anxiety, he threw himself upon the bed, and fell into a deep dreamless sleep.

The consequence was that it was quite ten o'clock when he awoke, and he started up vexed at the loss of time, and began hurriedly to dress himself.

He had nearly finished this operation when an altercation in the yard over which his window looked attracted his attention.

Surprised at recognising the two men who were having the dispute, Godfrey Lascelles half hid himself behind a curtain as he stood and watched them, and listened to their voices.

"I tell you that my money is as good as his, and that I'm not going to be put off my bargain because the man as wants the gig is a gentleman. If he'd spoke first, he'd have had it first; as he didn't he won't have it, that's all."

"But surely another horse and gig can be found in the place," Frank Darlington broke in impatiently; "my business is pressing, I have already lost several hours by missing the train at Peterborough; come, my man, what will you let me have your chance of the gig for?"

"Where do you want to take it?" asked Longridge.

For a second or two Darlington hesitated, then he said:

"To Scarsdale."

"Well, now, that's what I call lucky, because I'm going through Scarsdale, so I'll give you a lift for a consideration, or you can give me one for nothing as far as you go, and I'll foot it the rest of the way."

Darlington hesitated, but the landlord remarked:

"That's the best way of settling it, gentlemen; all my horses are out for the day with the exception of this one, and I should be sorry to disoblige either of you."

Then the voices became lower, and the men moved away, but it was evident that Mr. Longridge had gained his point.

"I don't understand that fellow," muttered Lascelles as he turned away from the window to finish dressing; "indeed, for the matter of that I don't understand either of them. What does Darlington do here, I wonder. Surely he cannot think to find Beatrice and to so trade upon her gratitude as to induce her to marry him. He would sell his soul to get possession of Burnham Court, but he could scarcely hope to get it in that way."

With a view of speaking to Darlington before the latter went away, Godfrey hastened over the rest of his toilette, and hurried downstairs.

But the gig had started by the time he reached the inn door, and Darlington was looking straight before him.

The detective might have had eyes at the back of his head from the way in which he kept on the alert, for he seemed to know that Godfrey was watching them, and, just as the gig was about to turn a corner of the road, with Darlington driving, Longridge looked back and gave a significant nod in the direction of the man at his side.

In another minute they were out of sight.

"The fellow is more preposterous than ever," muttered Lascelles, as he turned on his heel and went into the room where breakfast and Archibald Raynham were awaiting him.

But he could not get the detective's nod out of his mind, until suddenly the man's meaning flashed upon him.

"Preposterous!" he exclaimed aloud; "the fellow is altogether on a false scent. The idea that Darlington could have had a hand in hiding the girl is as absurd as to attribute such an action to me. More so, indeed; for he has just lost the woman he loved, while I——"

He did not finish the sentence, and fortunately he was alone when he thus uttered his thoughts aloud; but he took up his hat, and then walked over to the railway-station, there to commence his enquiries.

And meanwhile Frank Darlington and the detective, Longridge, were driving along over the wild uneven road to Scarsdale, the name of the valley in which was situated the cottage of the two women in whose care poor Beatrice had been left several days ago.

CHAPTER XXXIII.

A STARTLING DISCLOSURE.

"'LL get down here," said Frank Darlington abruptly, when the gig in which he was riding with the detective was still half a mile distant from Scarsdale.

"Get down here," repeated Longridge, giving the reins a jerk that made the horse increase its speed; "we ain't come to Scarsdale; you said you wanted to go to Scarsdale."

"And now I say I want to get down here," returned the other angrily; "will you pull up, or shall I help you?"

Darlington looked as he said this as though he meant to grasp the reins, and the detective, who knew he had a desperate man to deal with, made a virtue of necessity, and, putting a smiling face upon his discomfiture, drew up, and said:

"You seem in a mighty cantankerous mood this morning, sir; I hope your young woman hasn't turned you up and bolted with some other fellow."

The frown on Darlington's face was black as night, but he made no verbal reply to what Mr. Longridge meant to be not only a piece of impertinent pleasantry, but calculated, as he thought, to provoke some incautious retort, but tossing the price agreed upon for his ride into the detective's hand, he strode along the road evidently intent upon making the rest of the journey on foot.

"Confound the fellow," muttered Longridge; "what am I to do now? By the time I have got to some safe place where I can leave this horse and trap, he will have given me the slip. But I have no time to lose. I believe he spoke the truth when he said he wanted to go to Scarsdale; in any case I'll risk it."

"HAVE YOU BEEN TELLING THESE PEOPLE THAT I AM YOUR WIFE?"

No. 13.

The detective whipped up his horse, and went off at a rattling pace, leaving his late companion trudging along the dusty road.

"At last," muttered Darlington in a tone of relief, as he saw Longridge turn a bend of the road which soon hid him from sight; "I was beginning to think that the man was watching me," he went on; "and that I had seen his face before. And I have seen him," he added, pausing abruptly and passing his hand over his brow; "yes, I have seen him, his face is familiar to me. But where have we met?"

For a second or two he stood still, pondering over the subject, then he gave up trying to solve the question, and went on his way.

But his pace was not a rapid one.

His heart misgave him as to the success of the plot he had laid with, as he believed, every probability of success.

It was not that he believed Beatrice's dislike to himself and determination not to marry him to be unconquerable, because he had great faith in the efficacy of time and isolation, and the pressure of a more powerful will than her own upon the mind of the girl whom he had deprived of her freedom, but there was an uncomfortable feeling upon him that was something stronger than a mere presentiment, and that seemed to warn him of danger and difficulty ahead.

"I certainly am the most unlucky beggar under heaven," he mused gloomily as he walked along the rugged though picturesque road, and caught occasional glimpses of the wild country on either side. "I seem to drift into so many scrapes without quite intending to entangle myself," he went on, "and then just as some move is going to save me, my ill luck comes to the front and I am baffled."

Again for a time he walked on in silence, then his thoughts seemed to need expression in words, and he muttered:

"There was that folly with Mary Trevor, but I got over it; then there was the entanglement with Fanny Raynham, but Clarrie's infatuation would have saved me from the consequences of that if she had lived; but now I am in a more desperate plight than ever; money I must have, and to get that money I must make Beatrice Burnham marry me. I could not accept the sum I require from her except as her husband, and I must get hold of six hundred pounds within a day or two, at any risk."

The consciousness of the overwhelming necessity that was closing in upon him made Darlington unconsciously quicken his footsteps, and it was not long after this last soliloquy that he stood at the garden gate of the white-washed cottage into which Beatrice had been taken the preceding week.

What had happened he could not say, but the cottage seemed to have a changed aspect to the man who was now about to enter it.

It was not that the place was deserted, for smoke was rising from the kitchen chimney, but still there seemed to be a certain air of desolation about the place which he had not observed before.

He walked so slowly up the garden path that he was surprised at having to wait at the door after he had knocked, but it was not until he had repeated his summons that the door was opened by Miss Jex in person.

"You have kept me a long time waiting," he said impatiently.

Then he stepped past her into the kitchen.

The tall, gaunt, forbidding-looking woman made no reply, but she closed the door silently, and with a sulky expression of countenance followed him.

Once in the centre of the room, Darlington glanced round him with apprehension.

Beatrice was not there, but Sall Jex was seated on a low three-legged stool near the fireplace, her elbows resting on her knees, and her chin supported by her hands, while her hungry-looking blood-shot eyes reminded the young man of nothing so much as the greedy glare of a she-wolf robbed of her prey.

The manner and appearance of the elder sister also was ominous.

"Where is my wife?" asked Darlington, turning to Miss Jex with something more than ordinary anxiety on his countenance.

It will be remembered that he had represented Beatrice as his wife, and said she must be brought to a reasonable and obedient frame of mind.

"She ain't your wife," replied the woman insolently; "she fairly laughed in my face when I said she was."

"Where is she?" demanded the young man with growing apprehension.

"What she?" asked Miss Jex in a mocking tone.

"The lady I brought here last week, and whom I left in your charge; tell me at once where she is, or call her to me."

"I might call a long time," grinned the elder sister; "she's gone away—gone back to her friends, we'd no right to keep her here when she didn't belong to you."

Oddly enough the woman's words created a feeling of anxious alarm rather than of anger in Darlington's mind, and he asked quickly:

"Where and when did she go, and why did you let her escape when I had paid you to keep her?"

"I don't know when she went," was the dogged reply.

"Yes, you do; 'twas Monday night," growled the younger sister from her seat on the stool.

"And where did she go" asked the young man, addressing Sall this time.

"You'd best ask her," was the significant reply, with a nod in the direction of her sister. "Ask her what she's done with her, and what she's done with her money," she added viciously.

"She went away, I tell you," snapped Miss Jex in mingled rage and alarm.

"Aye, she went where you led her, and you buried her safely, didn't you?" sneered Sall with a flash of vindictive hate in her brown-green eyes; "but you didn't bury her money with her, though you won't share it as you promised."

"I ain't got no money to share, and if you don't keep a still tongue in your head, Sall Jex, 'twill be the worse for you."

"No, it won't! I ain't such a fool as to walk with you near the old well; the girl didn't know you as well as I do, or she wouldn't have followed you like a lamb as she did."

"What does she mean? What have you done with the girl?" Darlington demanded in a threatening tone of the elder woman.

"I haven't done nothing," was the angry retort; "you mustn't take notice of what she says," with a contemptuous jerk in the direction of her sister, "she's soft," with a meaning tap on her own forehead.

Certainly Miss Sall Jex looked anything but "soft" as she regarded her sister and the young man, who was such a contrast in manner, dress, and appearance to either of them, and she said with a fiendish gleam in her eyes:

"Soft, am I? Well, I ain't so soft but I can pay you out; but I'll give you one chance more. Will you share the money with me?"

"I haven't got no money, you fool," cried the other woman furiously.

An incredulous jerk of the head was the only response to this assertion, for Sall Jex meant mischief.

She rose to her feet now, drew up her tall figure to its full height, and stretching out one of her long bony arms that was only half covered by the sleeve of her gown, she said to Darlington:

"You want to know what has become of the girl you brought here? Come with me and I'll show you."

Darlington's face was pale with terror, for the manner of the woman who spoke convinced him that some awful tragedy had taken place in which Beatrice Burnham was the victim.

"What has happened?" he asked nervously and fearfully.

"Come, and see," was the reply, and Sall Jex walked towards the door.

But before she and the young man could leave the
room the elder sister had planted herself in the doorway, and throwing herself into a threatening attitude,
she said :

" You don't neither of you leave this room till you've
both of you had a bit of my mind."

" We don't want any of your mind nor your tongue
neither," was Sall's disdainful response. "For the
last time I ask, are you going to share the money
with me ? "

" Fool !" cried the elder woman, irritated beyond
the bounds of prudence by this constant demand for
money. "What I've told you over and over again is
true. I ain't got no money. It went down the old
well with the girl."

Sall Jex stood convinced, but the conviction brought
anything but pleasurable sensations with it, for her
insatiate greed of gold, thrust aside for the moment,
left her mind clear to realise the uncomfortable consequences that might accrue to herself and her sister
from the accusations and admissions she had made
concerning the missing girl.

It was Darlington who naturally now demanded that
Sall should conduct him to the place where Beatrice
was to be found.

But that bony virago had changed her mind, and
she returned to her tripod-like seat muttering :

" If the money's at the bottom of the well, 'tain't
much good our trying to get hold of it, for I've heerd
our father say that if truth was only to be found at the
bottom of a well they'd have to go pretty deep for it
if 'twas our old chain well."

" I will stand this no longer," cried Darlington with
rising anger at finding his questions unanswered and
almost unheeded. "If you don't give me a satisfactory
account of the lady I left in your charge or lead me to
her at once, I will call in the police and hand you over
to the power of the law."

" Ah ; and you'll hand yourself over, too, I guess,"
hissed Miss Jex furiously. "What do you mean by
coming to us with such a white-livered face," she

went on indignantly, "when we've only done your work for you."

"My work!" echoed the young man aghast.

"Yes, your work," repeated the woman.

"I don't understand you," he said evasively.

"Don't you understand me?" she went on mockingly. "I suppose you don't remember that you told me the lady must be brought to reason or silenced for ever."

"I don't," was the audacious reply; "and if I ever did make such a foolish observation," he went on, "I never meant that you were to kill the girl."

"How was I to silence her, then?"

"There was no necessity for you to commit murder, and if you say you did so at my bidding you lie, and who do you think will believe you?"

"I don't want anybody to believe me; I ain't such a fool as to tell such a story. I ain't done no wrong to nobody. The poor girl you brought here begged and prayed me to let her get away, and went on her knees and said you'd taken her away from her true lover and wanted to marry her for her money, till at last I felt pity for her, and——"

"Rot!" cried Darlington passionately. "She as much went on her knees to you as you took pity upon her, and as for the rubbish you talk about a true lover, she hadn't any lover but me. Tell your story plainly, woman, and don't garnish it with more lies than you can help."

"Well, the long and short of it was, she promised me a great deal, and I agreed to let her get away to her friends before you came here again."

"Of course she paid you well for your treachery to me; but go on."

"She said she hadn't got but a pound or two with her, but she'd give me fifty pounds as soon as she could get to her friends."

"But we know she had got money," here interposed Sall, "for we peeped through the chinks, and saw her with it—heaps of notes and gold."

"Anyhow, we didn't get it," snapped Miss Jex.

"Get on with your story.   What happened to her?" cried Darlington with feverish impatience.

"Well, as I said, I agreed to let her go free," continued the woman; "but I wouldn't let her go in the daylight for fear of any of the folks living in the valley might see her, and wonder what we'd done to have such a visitor; but she said she wasn't afraid of darkness, so when it was quite dark I took her out through the back garden to the little gate as leads into the lane that by-and-by comes into the high road."

"Well?" asked the man feverishly, for the woman had paused.

"We walked along the garden, but 'twas rare and dark, and I took the girl's hand to keep her from falling, and I somehow forgot the old well, that hadn't been used since my father's time, and the girl stepped on the rotten wood that layed over the top of it, and fell down the hole, and that's the truth."

"But did you make no effort to save her?" asked Darlington with horror.

"Save her!" repeated the woman with callous scorn. "You don't know what you're talking about, man. I made a clutch to get hold of her other hand, for she'd got a little bag in it, and I think her money was in the bag; but she wrenched herself away, and down she went in the hole, money and all."

"But still she might have been saved," said the young man with horror.

"Saved!" repeated the woman contemptuously. Do you think she could have been saved, Sall?"

The younger sister shook her head ominously.

To her mind there could be no doubt as to the fate of the living creature who once fell into the long-disused well.

"But why was it impossible? Surely you could have called in the aid of some of your neighbours?"

"I tell you it was no use. The well's a rare deep one, and there's water at the bottom though it ain't fit for nothing, and there's plenty of foul air in the hole."

"Still you should have tried to save her, and even now it may not be too late. Take me to the spot at once; it is horrible to think that no effort has been made to save her."

"You can go if you like," was the sullen reply; "I sha'n't. I won't forget the horrible cry in a hurry, and if I was to see her white face staring up at me, 't would follow me day and night all my life."

"If you don't come and show me the spot, I will get other people to do so," said Darlington sternly. "I am not going to be an accessory to your crime."

"I'll show you where it is," said Sall, rising to her feet. "I didn't push her in; nobody can say I'd aught to do with it. Come along, sir."

"Hadn't we better take a light and a rope with us?" asked the young man anxiously.

"Best look at the place, then you can say whether lights and ropes will be of much use," said Miss Jex grimly.

This suggestion seemed to meet the approval of Miss Sall, for she led the way without another word through a door, from whence they emerged into a large straggling garden.

"Is that the well?" asked Darlington, pointing to a hole with a windlass close by.

"No, that's the one we use; come this way and look where you are going."

And thus picking his way with great caution, although it was broad daylight, Frank Darlington followed Sall Jex and her sister over the same ground that poor Beatrice Burnham had fearlessly trod in the dense darkness but a few nights before.

CHAPTER XXXIV.

THE MYSTERY OF THE WELL.

FRANK DARLINGTON and the two women stood by the side of the long disused well.

It was an ugly looking spot, suggestive of any amount of danger to anyone unwary enough to approach it too closely.

The top had evidently been covered over by some loose pieces of wood, which had become rotten with damp as much as with age; but some of these had been displaced, while one of the pieces which had been laid right across the mouth of the well had been broken downwards, having evidently given way under the sudden pressure of some heavy weight.

"Is this where she fell?" asked the young man, looking with loathing at the black pit at his feet.

"So sister says," replied Sall evasively; "I s'pose she walked straight on to the rotten wood."

Darlington bent down and listened, but he could hear no sound.

Then he knelt down by the side of the mouth of the well, and strove to pierce the dense darkness with his eyes.

In vain—he might as well have tried to look through a stone wall.

Once, as he knelt and listened, he thought he heard a groan, but though he waited a long time, with every sense strained to the uttermost, he could not be certain that the sound was repeated.

At length, wondering he had not thought of doing so before, he took a stone and dropped it down the well.

He listened to hear it fall, but no sound came; then he took a larger one with the same result, until, getting a little impatient, he took half a brick, and laying on the ground, he dropped it into the well.

Now he heard a noise like the striking of a stone against something which produced a dull heavy sound. then it seemed to rebound, and a few seconds later there was a faint splash, as though the piece of brick had come in contact with water.

"How horribly deep it is," said the young man with a shudder.

"Aye, it's deep enough," returned Sall Jex callously; "help wouldn't be much use to the man or woman who fell down there."

"And yet I should like to have more certain proof than your word that the girl I brought to your house last week has really met her death in this horrible way. Do you believe she did?"

"Aye, that we do," was the response.

"Is there any man whom you could trust in the neighbourhood who would help me to let down a light and explore the well?" was Darlington's next question.

But the women shook their heads.

"No man hereabouts; a stranger might do it. Why, there's a man on the stile yonder; mayhap he'd lend a hand," exclaimed Miss Jex, as she walked back to the house, leaving Sall to follow with Darlington.

The young man glanced in the direction indicated, then he quickly averted his head to avoid recognition, for his quick eye had recognised Mr. Longridge, seated on a stile at some distance from this cottage-garden, but on higher ground, so that he could command a somewhat extensive view of the valley.

"The fellow is looking for me," was Darlington's instantaneous conclusion; "I felt that he was watching me as I sat by his side in the gig; I must get away from this place without delay, and I must frighten the women into silence for their own sakes. As for poor Beatrice, she is past all human help, and—how I loved the girl!"

He covered his face with his hands for a moment; but he did not long yield to any feeling of sentiment, and he was about to turn away from the spot when his eye rested for a moment upon something lying close to the top of the well.

It was a piece of a jet watch-chain, and to it was attached a small locket of jet not much larger than a shilling, but that contained a portrait of Beatrice Burnham's late father.

Darlington had seen this before, and Clarrie had many months ago asked her cousin to show him the portrait of her dead father, so that the young man had no doubt whatever when he opened the small case as to who had once been its owner.

"There has been a struggle here," he thought gloomily; "else how should the chain have been broken if she fell in by accident? That female fiend forced her down this horrible pit, I am convinced, while she tried to rob her—tried, and, no doubt, succeeded."

He was turning slowly to return to the cottage, but Miss Sall's curiosity and cupidity were both aroused, and she insisted upon seeing what he had picked up; then she claimed it as belonging to herself.

But Darlington was getting alarmed and desperate, and anxious to get away from these women who seemed like two insatiable furies, and he now turned fiercely upon Sall, and said in a low threatening tone:

"This is not yours, it belonged to the girl whom you and your sister have murdered. I am going now to fetch the police, and have the well searched for the body; and before the sun sets, you and your vile sister will be in prison."

Before Sall Jex could recover from her astonishment at his changed tone and manner, or utter a word of threat or protest, he had sprung over the low wall that fenced off the garden, and was hurrying up the steep rough ground, where he was soon lost to sight.

The woman stood for a few seconds like one struck dumb and motionless with fear and wonder, then rousing herself with an effort she walked slowly back to the room in which her sister still remained.

"Well?" asked Miss Jex when she saw that Sall was alone.

A few words told her what had happened, and the elder sister's rage for a few seconds knew no bounds.

"He's gone without giving me the money he promised!" she screamed, "and now we're in his power, he can ruin us, and p'r'aps hang us, and all through your cursed tongue; but I sha'n't stop here, and you must shift for yourself, you sha'n't go with me."

"Yes, I shall go with you," said Sall decidedly; "if I don't you won't leave the valley alive. You know how the neighbours love you, and me too, for that matter, but they'll believe me when I tell them how you threw a girl down our old well when you'd robbed her.

"I didn't rob her, she was to sharp for me," insisted the elder woman.

"You tried at any rate; and you killed her, that's certain. A fine commotion there'll be if I go and tell the story to Will Jowett; why the folk will tear you limb from limb, and I'll do it if you try to throw me off; I know you've been making a purse for years, and you'll share it with me or 'twill go hard with you. Mind that now!"

For a few seconds the two women glared at each other like a couple of hungry she-wolves ready to spring at each other's throat, then Miss Jex lowered her head in sign of defeat, and she said with a grim smile:

"Of course we'll share and share alike, Sal; 'twould be hard after all these years if two sisters like us should part."

"Yes, 'twould be hard," assented the other dryly; "but we've no time to lose; I wish the night was come."

"So do I, but we'll have to go away in daylight, we've too much at risk to wait here till the constables come. 'Tis market-day at Seargate, and we'll just dress ourselves in our best, and take our baskets as though we was going to buy things, and we'll lock up the place and not come back again till we know it's safe. What do you say?"

"I say yes; but we'll take all that's worth anything with us, for who knows if we'll ever come back."

Miss Jex made no answer to this; the probability was that she had formed plans of her own for the future in which her sister had no share.

The two women were making their preparations for leaving their home when a loud knock at the house door startled them.

They had previously taken the precaution of locking and bolting the doors and putting up the shutters over the lower windows, in addition to extinguishing the fire, so that there was really no sign of life about the place, except the tabby cat that lay out in the sunshine, and that bristled up its back and swelled its tail to five times its natural proportions at the approach of a stranger.

The guilty creatures paused in their work and listened tremblingly, for the sound was repeated again and again.

With their sense of hearing quickened by intense fear, they waited and listened, becoming convinced at last that it was only one man who was demanding entrance.

"'Tain't the constables," said Miss Jex after a little reflection; "they'd never send one man to take us two women. Shall I open the door and see what he wants?"

"Not if you don't want to be taken away to gaol," was the terrified reply. "Hark! he's going round the house; and see if he ain't going to the old well."

It was true.

Mr. Longridge had believed he recognised his late companion Frank Darlington with the middle-aged woman in the desolate-looking garden, and after taking stock of the cottage from the outside, he had boldly knocked at the door, intending to make cautious enquiries concerning the missing girl, and with regard to the young man who was there or had been there that morning.

His failure to get the cottage-door opened, or to attract the attention of any living creature except the cat, that flew at his legs, and that he kicked away, emboldened the detective to walk round the house and explore the premises.

There was nothing peculiar about the place, and believing it to be deserted by its usual occupants, he went to the back of the house, and then cautiously made his way to the spot where he had observed a man and a woman examining something on the ground.

When Mr. Longridge came to the mouth of the old well, the covering of which had evidently been broken down by some heavy weight standing upon it, and probably falling into the deep pit below, he stood and looked at it with grave wonder and doubt.

An accident of some kind had evidently occurred here, but whether of a serious nature or not he could not easily determine.

Neither could he feel certain that it in any way concerned him or the object of his search, for though he thought he had recognised Darlington as the man who had stood on the spot half an hour earlier, he was by no means certain on the point, and he as yet had no evidence, and, indeed, no suspicion, that Beatrice Burnham had been brought to this cottage, still less that she had been lured to this spot to meet her death.

In point of fact Mr. Longridge did not think that any serious harm had happened to our heroine or was likely to happen to her.

He had formed two theories by which to account for the girl's disappearance, either of which he thought bore the stamp of possibility if not of probability about them.

One was that Darlington had managed to entrap her and was keeping her a prisoner somewhere with the intention of compelling her to marry him, so that he might get hold of her money.

The other was less to the young lady's credit, as he believed it not impossible that she had hidden herself from her friends simply to enjoy their anxiety and perplexity.

It is true that he laid very little stress upon this last hypothesis, still, he was not inclined to completely dismiss it.

But that any personal violence or any fatal injury had been inflicted upon Beatrice never entered his mind.

So now, though he examined the top of the well, looked carefully at the broken boards and grunted that somebody must have had an ugly fall, he never for a moment suspected that Beatrice Burnham's feet had ever rested upon that treacherous spot.

But a disused well with a broken cover is not a particularly interesting object to a person who has heard no story attached to it, and who is unconscious of either comedy or tragedy having been enacted upon the spot, and the detective soon turned away, and with the instinct of a sleuth-hound, though he had no expectation of discovering anything, he walked to the low wall over which Darlington had sprang when he left Sall Jex.

It is singular how the most careful criminal will, with all his caution, leave some evidence of his identity behind him which helps to unravel a mystery that would otherwise have remained unsolved.

In the present instance Darlington had hastily thrust the piece of jet chain with the locket that had once belonged to poor Beatrice into his coat pocket with his handkerchief, and there no doubt it would have been safe enough if his coat had not been caught in a projecting piece of the uneven wall, into which some nails had been driven.

The garment was torn by the sharp wrench, but it was the lining rather than the cloth that gave way, and it was not until he had walked at least a couple of miles from the spot that the young man, in putting his hand to his pocket, found that it was completely torn down.

When Frank Darlington discovered his loss, his brain reeled, his head swam, he seemed to lose the control of his limbs and muscles, and he sank down in a sitting posture by the roadside, helpless as any man suddenly stricken with paralysis.

What had he lost?

In that fatal pocket had been a pocket-book that contained notes and gold, but he scarcely thought of the money he had thus lost.

For that same pocket-book likewise held papers and a small diary, that any man with a moderate proportion of common-sense would have been very careful to destroy.

The piece of jet chain was in this pocket also, but that was a mere trifle in comparison with the compromising transactions which the contents of the pocket-book would reveal.

After a time he so far recovered from the shock as to be able to think, and to try to remember where the accident could have happened.

Step by step he mentally went back over the ground he had traversed since he last put his hand in his pocket, when Sall Jex demanded the piece of chain.

At last he recollected the wrench at his coat as he leaped the garden-wall.

The mischief must have been done then, though the contents of the pocket might not have fallen at that spot.

At any rate he must go back.

It was just possible, if he went over the same ground again, searching every inch, he might find at least something.

"And if not that diary, I may as well throw myself into the well with poor Beatrice," he groaned.

Then, more like an old man than a young one in the dejected weariness of his step, he rose from the ground, and with a feeling of hopelessness that he could not shake off he slowly retraced his steps looking for what he had lost.

CHAPTER XXXV.

A DESPERATE MOVE.

RANK DARLINGTON is again in London, but a decided change has come over the man, and he seems many years older than when he came away from Burnham Court after poor Clarrie's funeral, feeling himself a ruined man.

Looking back at that time, though the interval is but very short, he feels as though the troubles and misfortunes that then beset him were mere trifles compared with those that have since accumulated about him.

His search for his lost pocket-book and diary had been unavailing. He had spent most of that wretched day in the hopeless task, and then he had wandered away aimlessly until nightfall, when hunger and fatigue in a measure roused him to face his position, however bad it might be.

He had talked to himself of jumping down the deep well into which poor Beatrice had fallen, but his courage to take such a step had utterly failed him, and having worn himself out mentally and physically, he made his way to a railway station, and on the following morning reached London.

Tired and ill as he was, he thought it necessary to keep up appearances; so, having reached his lodgings, and bathed and redressed himself, he made his way to the City, though it only wanted half an hour of the time when he would ordinarily have left it.

To all appearance he might as well have remained away, for he saw no one of importance, did no business, and only excited the sympathetic comments of the clerks, who remarked how much he took the loss of his bride to heart.

One thing Darlington did learn, however, and it was that Cohen, the money-lender who had discounted the forged bill, was still abroad, and likely to remain out of England several weeks longer.

"That confounded bill will be presented at Sir Graham Grantly's bank, will be dishonoured, and then there will be the deuce to pay between the old man and his nephew; but, whatever fuss there may be between them, the result will be the same. My name is on the back of it. I had the money, and I shall be the one who will eventually suffer. However, they won't take me alive, I can promise them."

With this reflection he unlocked a box, took from it a case of pistols and began to carefully clean and load them.

They were not called into requisition that night, however, and the next morning another change came over this man's chequered fortunes.

By the early post he received a letter from his father, who but rarely favoured him with a written communication.

The present missive was brief and curt as it could well be, it only stated that his eldest son was dying.

"I suppose he wants me to come to the Mount," mused the young man gloomily. "Well, I am as well there as anywhere; if Arthur had only died a month, or even a week ago, I might have raised money to meet that cursed bill; but everything comes too late for me. I used to believe in my own good fortune, but now I know I am the most unlucky devil under the sun."

It was in this frame of mind that he sent a telegram to the office in the City to account for his absence, and then went down to Holly Mount.

The day was gloriously bright and warm, the country looked like an extensive garden, the full bloom of summer was upon the land, and any man less heavily weighted with guilt and disappointment could not have failed to enjoy the beauty of the scene.

As he entered the house in which he was born, however, his thoughts for a few seconds became less personal, for he saw by the face of the servant who admitted him that what he had hoped and others feared had come to pass; his brother, Arthur Darlington, was dead.

"You're just too late, sir," said the old servant, wiping the tears from his eyes; "half an hour ago poor Mr. Arthur fell asleep, and the doctor and the squire don't quite know when he passed away; but he's gone."

"And my father?" asked the young man, passing his handkerchief over his eyes to hide the satisfaction which would not look like grief.

"The master's awfully cut up, sir," was the reply, "he's gone to his room, and he says no one is to come nigh him. I'd leave him alone, sir, for a bit if I was you."

"I will," was the answer.

Then Frank Darlington went to his own room and shut himself in, not to mourn for the dead, but to try to realise that at last he was the person of most consideration in his father's house, and that if he could only tide over his other difficulties he would one day be owner and master there.

But even as he tried to realise the possible change in his fortunes the thought of Beatrice Burnham and of her tragic fate forced itself with horrible persistency upon his mind.

It seemed strange that he should think of Beatrice more tenderly than of poor Mary Trevor or of foolish, devoted Clarrie; for these two women had loved him, and the one whose death troubled him most had barely hidden her dislike and deeply-rooted distrust of him.

Later in the day he saw his father, but the old man was utterly prostrated with grief, and he took but little heed of the son who must benefit by this calamity.

So Frank found the time between his arrival and the funeral pass heavily and wearily, and his thoughts often wandered off to Burnham Court and Grantly Park.

"What was Lady Grantly about?" he wondered.

That mischief was brewing for him from that quarter he more than half suspected, for he was well aware that her ladyship knew of his intrigue with Fanny, and he also knew that she had espoused the cause of her sister.

"She will do me all the harm she can," he thought gloomily; "and, unfortunately, she may be able to do a great deal. I wish I could make friends with my lady, but she always laughed when I tried to be civil to her, and she told me over and over again to my face that I only wanted Clarrie for the sake of her money. Still, I always believe in being able to flatter a woman, particularly if she thinks herself more than usually clever, and I believe I could mould her to be of use to me if I only had time. But there it is again—the question of time."

He strode impatiently up and down his room like a caged animal.

His father had requested that he would not leave Holly Mount for town until after Arthur's funeral, and thus he was prevented from making any further effort to provide for the forged bill.

Once, in sheer desperation, he addressed his father, meaning to tell him of the ruin that was impending, but that might even yet be averted.

But directly the old man understood there was to be an appeal for money he silenced his son almost savagely, and the young man felt that no help could be obtained from that quarter.

And thus the time went by till the day of the funeral and a great number of friends and neighbours came to attend it.

Sir Graham Grantly's empty carriage came to swell the funeral procession, but the baronet himself was confined to his own room, and though no one seemed to quite know what was the matter with him, the general opinion was that he was in a very bad way.

In point of fact the successful man was at heart a disappointed man.

He was disappointed in his wife, and, worst of all, he seemed very likely to die without leaving a child of his own to succeed him.

These things and many others Sir Graham took to heart, and he at the same time caught a severe sore throat, about which he grumbled and growled for a few days, but would take no remedy.

His ailment got the better of him at last, however, and Lady Grantly at length sent for a doctor, who felt the pulse of his unwilling patient, asked many questions, ordered the baronet to keep to his room, and impressed everybody on the spot with the conviction that the matter was serious.

For a few days longer Sir Graham Grantly fought against doctors and disease, then he felt himself beaten and gave up the contest.

Very unwillingly did the old baronet submit when he felt that contention was useless, and even after he was unable to leave his room, and speaking was a pain to him, and reading and writing almost impossible, he still refused to let his wife manage his affairs, or conduct his correspondence.

Lady Grantly was alarmed, and sent for her husband's nephew, but Fortescue Grantly was out of town at the time and did not receive her summons.

Thus it was that the empty carriage came from Grantly Park to follow the earthly remains of poor Arthur Darlington to their last resting-place.

Funerals are melancholy ceremonies under the most favourable of circumstances, but to-day the very elements seemed to have conspired to mourn for the young man who had never enjoyed the healthy vigour of manhood.

For the rain fell in torrents, the wind shrieked and howled, and shook the trees as though it would dismember the strongest and uproot those that were most feeble, and when the mourners stood by the open grave it was with difficulty that they could hear the voice of the clergyman, it was so nearly lost in the noise of the storm.

There was no will to be read, and very soon after their return to the Mount the guests departed to their own homes, leaving the father and son together.

Now, Frank thought, his father must talk to him about money matters, but again he was mistaken; the old man shut himself up alone with his grief, and the younger one wandered about the house with the sensations of a man who was doomed to die for a draught of water while there was an abundance of the refreshing liquid within reach of his hand if he could but stretch it forth.

For on that very day the forged bill would be presented at Sir Graham Grantly's bank, and would be dishonoured.

The second event was as certain as the first, for the baronet would have given no orders to pay a bill that he had never signed, and of which he was completely ignorant.

Fortescue Grantly would naturally deny all knowledge of it when the matter reached his ears, and then, thought the guilty man, " the end cannot be far distant."

As night approached, Frank Darlington's restlessness and feeling of desperation grew stronger.

He must do something, he told himself ; then his tone changed, and he vowed that he would do something to avert the ruin that on all sides seemed crowding in upon him.

" What is my father's must one day be mine," he reasoned, "and therefore I shall wrong no one but myself by taking some of his property beforehand. Of course the old man won't take the same view of the case, but will say that I have robbed him, and for that reason I must not let him know who has emptied his safe. I believe I can manage it, particularly if this storm continues."

It was indeed a night suited for burglary, and any dark deed of robbery and violence.

The storm which had begun in the early morning and continued all day had increased in violence as darkness set in, and Squire Darlington's house, from its elevated position, came in for a more than ordinary share of wind and rain, and all the noises attendant on such a dirturbance of the elements.

The old squire was peculiar in his habits, and he trusted as little to banks as possible, keeping only a current account with a respectable balance to draw upon, but taking care to invest anything over a certain amount, and never trusting his title-deeds, his jewels, or securities of any kind to the bank cellars for safety in preference to taking care of them himself.

In consequence of this habit of his, there was always property of considerable value at Holly Mount, and this was usually kept in an iron safe in the squire's bed-room.

Frank was well aware of all this; but though he did not know what the safe contained, he had not the least doubt that he should find in it more than enough to help him over all his pecuniary difficulties.

However much he might talk to himself about only taking before his father died what must be his own property sooner or later, Frank was perfectly conscious that he was meditating a mean and cowardly action, and he could not hide from himself the fact that it was like-wise a dangerous one.

For his father not only kept the safe in his own bed-room, but he never slept without being well armed.

A pair of pistols always lay within reach by the side of his bed, and it was quite certain that if disturbed by the appearance of a robber he would not hesitate to use them.

"Still, I shall risk it," was the young man's desperate resolve. "But I must manage to get hold of his keys, and for that purpose I must see him."

It was with this object in view that he sent a short note to his father, begging him not to yield so completely to sorrow, but to show some fatherly interest in his re-maining son.

The letter was cleverly worded, and it came to the bereaved father at a moment when he was very forlorn and desolate.

He joined him in the library, where, after a time, he was persuaded to eat a little food—the first for the day—and drink some hot spirits and water.

Half an hour later the squire was helped to bed by the old servant who acted as valet and butler.

In the middle of the night the inmates of Holly Mount were startled out of their sleep by the sound of pistol-shots, the ringing of bells, and cries for help.

No. 14.

"I EXPECTED TO HAVE HAD A LETTER FROM HER YESTERDAY," THE OLD LADY WENT ON.

It was some time before even the men-servants could summon up courage enough to partially dress and go to their master's room.

When they got there they found the old man sitting up in bed, a discharged pistol in one hand, with a second one ready for use in the other.

"I've winged him," the squire cried excitedly. "I woke up and saw a man at my safe, unlocking it as though it belonged to him, and I called out and asked what he wanted, and took aim at him. He ducked his head and bolted; but I hit him—I know I hit him. Search the house, men; the fellow can't have escaped."

"Shall we call Mr. Frank to help us?" asked one of the servants.

"No, I'll call him myself if he isn't awake," was the growling answer.

Then Squire Darlington pulled on some clothing, took his own bunch of keys from the door of the iron safe, the contents of which had not been touched, seized a candle, and followed by the butler, went off to his son's room.

CHAPTER XXXVI.

AT HER MERCY.

"E'S sound asleep, sir. Mr. Frank! Mr. Frank!" So cried the butler at the Mount, as he shook the young man by the shoulder, while the squire, looking puzzled and suspicious, stood calmly by.

A yawn, a sleepy stretch of the limbs, and then Frank Darlington sprang up into a sitting posture, looked vacantly about him, and asked vaguely :

"Yes; what is it? What has happened? What do you all do here? Ah, father," as his eyes rested upon the squire, "what is the matter? Do you want me?"

"Aye, we want you to help us to search the house," was the reply, though the old man turned away his head as he spoke. "There's a thief in the house," he went on, "and I want to find him."

Frank instantly sprang out of bed and began to dress, asking numerous questions all the time.

The servants observed that the squire answered the questions curtly and abruptly, and that he watched his son closely as he moved about the room.

But whatever suspicions he might have entertained, he found nothing here to confirm them, and at length he went away, growling indistinctly.

He had misjudged his son most cruelly, or his son was an actor who ought to have made a fortune upon the stage.

The search over the house was fruitless, Frank being the most eager to look into every hole and corner where a thief might hide, and the squire very soon lost all interest in the matter.

Indeed it was not long before the old man returned to his own room, observing that he didn't suppose he should be disturbed twice the same night, and then, having secured the door carefully, Squire Darlington went back to bed.

"I don't think I could have been mistaken," he muttered, as he laid his head upon his pillow, "but I hope I was, I hope I was. I felt sure that I winged the fellow."

The next morning the squire found the bullet, which he thought had done some mischief to the would-be robber, embedded in the wall by the side of the safe, and he found that the fellow, whoever he was, had got away unscathed.

This, from the old man's point of view, was mortifying, but he derived some comfort from the circumstance that the attempt at robbery had been unsuccessful, and that not a single article of value had been taken from the iron safe."

"But I'll move everything of value to a safer hiding-place before the day is over," he decided; "I may not be so lucky another time."

And he carried out his intention, though he need not have been in haste to do so, for his worthless son was not likely to run such a risk again without much more likelihood of success.

Indeed, Mr. Frank Darlington had been a little bit scared.

The bullet from his father's pistol had passed unpleasantly close to his ear, and though in escaping from the room he had managed to hide his face, he felt convinced, from his father's tone and manner, that the squire suspected him.

"But he isn't certain," he assured himself, "and I must stay here a few days to let the suspicion wear away, but I am no nearer finding an avenue of escape for myself, so I must just drift with the tide, and go where fate or the furies take me."

In pursuance of this plan, he spent two more days at the Mount, and still no news reached him about the search for Beatrice, or about the forged bill.

The third morning after the funeral a groom came from Grantly Park, bringing a note for the squire's son.

"Lady Grantly desires to see Mr. Frank Darlington on a matter of importance to himself," the missive ran. "The business admits of no delay."

For a moment after he had read the letter, the young man stood bewildered by the conflicting thoughts, and by the hopes and fears that beset him. Then a feeling of satisfaction came over him. Lady Grantly had probably discovered something about the bill, but she would not have sent for him unless she had been prepared to make some terms with him, and the unprincipled wretch was ready to grasp at any straw in the hope of saving himself.

So he scribbled off a few lines saying he would be with her ladyship within an hour, and then he went off for a brisk short walk to fortify himself for the interview.

When he reached Grantly Park he found the knocker on the principal door muffled, and he observed that the servants walked about the house with careful steps and as silently as possible.

"Ah, I remember, Sir Graham is ill!" thought Frank; "I wonder if he is going to die just yet. Geraldine won't be a bad match as a widow, but it's of no use my thinking of her, that little affair with Fanny would effectually shut me out from anything of the kind."

He was still thinking in this strain when, on looking up, he saw Lady Grantly before him.

To apologise for his absence of mind was natural, but he was nervous, and he held out his hand to shake hers, and it happened that her ladyship either did not or would not see it.

This did not add to his comfort or increase his self-possession, and, looking at her, he could not help observing that Geraldine was greatly changed.

First of all she was much better-looking than she had been in the days when she had been Geraldine Raynham, for her features, and tone, and manner seemed to have fined down, while there was a certain dignity about her which she had not previously possessed.

In addition to this her ladyship was in deep mourning for her half-sister Clarrie, and black clothing suited her light hair, her fair complexion, and her pale blue eyes.

So she looked refined, elegant, and almost beautiful, as she stood before the man whom she had never liked, whom she now most thoroughly despised, and yet with whom, for the sake of a worthless girl who was dear to her, she was about to try to make a compact.

She pointed to a chair, as she sank into another herself; and then she asked how the squire bore up after the loss of his son.

"He doesn't bear up at all," said the young man with an affectation of sadness; "I am becoming quite alarmed about him."

Geraldine checked the sneering retort that rose to her lips and hastily changed the subject by saying:

"My note told you I wanted to see you upon a matter of importance to yourself."

The young man bowed his head in assent, but he asked no question, and the lady evidently found some difficulty in beginning the subject.

At length she said awkwardly:

"A very singular thing has happened, Mr. Darlington; some needy and evil-disposed person has forged my husband's name to a bill of exchange; there are two other names upon the paper in question, one of them being yours, and I thought it well to acquaint you with the fact before the matter passes out of my hands into those of the lawyers and police."

"Out of your hands," repeated Darlington, while his pale face and nervously working features showed the agitation under which he was labouring; "is the matter in your hands?"

"For the moment it is, though by little more than an accident. Sir Graham is too ill to attend to his own affairs, and this matter would have been passed over to the third person whose name is upon the bill, but for something that came to my knowledge some little time ago."

"Will you tell me what that 'something' is?" asked Darlington, speaking as calmly as he could, though he was labouring under great excitement.

"No," was the decided reply. "At present I do not know whether or not it is connected with the matter before us."

"May I ask, then, why you sent for me, and what you mean to do" he asked, while his throat grew hot and dry with suppressed agitation.

"Certainly. I want to know if your signature upon this bill is a forgery also. If it is, my course is clear before me."

"You have not given me any particulars concerning the bill of which you speak," he replied evasively. "Have you it here? Can I see it?

She looked at him a moment, with her large round eyes opened a trifle more widely than usual, then she smiled with a mixture of amusement and disdain as she replied:

"Certainly not; what should I do with it? I have simply received notice that a bill drawn by Fortescue Grantly, accepted by Sir Graham Grantly, and endorsed by yourself, lies dishonoured at a certain bank, the amount of the bill being six hundred pounds."

"But what makes you say your husband's signature is forged?" he asked seeking only for the moment to gain time so that he might decide upon the course he would take.

"Two things. In the first place, my husband would never sign a bill of accommodation. If he felt inclined to give or lend his nephew any sum of money he would have written a cheque for the amount. Next, I have asked him about it, and he denies all knowledge of the matter; and to add a third reason, if any further were necessary, Mr. Fortescue Grantly is not, and has not been in need of assistance from his uncle."

"Does Fortescue Grantly know of this?" asked Darlington with blanched lips.

"No, but he will do so before this time to-morrow. But I need not continue this explanation with you any

longer.   You have not answered my question : **Is your
signature on this bill also a forgery ?**

He rose to his feet, and despite the seeming rudeness
of such conduct in the presence of a lady in her own
house, began to pace the room with restless and troubled
footsteps.

"Suppose it is a forgery, and that I know nothing whatever about it ?" he asked pausing at length before her.

"In that case you will have as much interest as we
have in bringing the guilty party or parties to justice,"
Geraldine replied with a calm smile.

But she leaned back in her chair as she spoke, and
seemed to his excited fancy like a pretty cat playing
with a helpless mouse.

"And suppose my signature is genuine?" he next
asked, contracting his brows and tightening his thin
lips as he stood confronting the woman who was so
quietly and deliberately putting him to torture.

"In that case, of course, you know all about the
transaction," was the calm response, "and can put us
upon the track of the guilty person."

"Yes," he replied, throwing himself into any arm-
chair with a certain air of reckless bravado, "I can
put you upon the track of the guilty person; but that is
not why you sent for me, Lady Grantly."

"Indeed it is, Mr. Darlington," with an amiable
smile; "I wished to be quite certain that your father's
son would not be undeservedly compromised before I
allowed any steps to be taken in this matter.   Of course,
if I had known that you were a party to this transation,
knowing the nature of the affair, I should not have sent
for you."

"I don't think you would have sent for me if you had
not been very sure of having the game in your own
hands," he retorted brusquely, "for you are not a
woman to seek an interview of this kind without a very
definite purpose in view.   You have a plan in your
mind, and terms to offer me; tell me what they are,
and let us end this conversation."

"You jump at hasty conclusions, Mr. Darlington,"
said the lady coldly.   "I am not at all certain that I

have any terms to offer you, or that I am in the least degree inclined to compound a felony. Indeed, upon consideration, I shall not interfere in the matter. As yet, no one has been publicly compromised, and the bill, though dishonoured, may be paid and destroyed; but I should advise you to regard this narrow escape as a caution against a repetition of the crime."

And Lady Grantly rose from her seat and walked towards the door.

"Stay a minute," said Darlington desperately. "You have not said all you have to say. You tell me the bill could be paid, but the bill cannot be paid by me. All the powers of darkness seem to have conspired together to prevent my getting the money. If Clarrie had lived but an hour longer I should not have been in this hole; if—if my father were not the most selfish and unnatural of men, I should be able to get the amount required, but I have tried everything, done everything, that it is possible for a man to do, and all I put my hand to fails."

Lady Grantly slightly shrugged her shoulders, then she said:

"Men marry for many reasons besides love—women, too, for that matter—and it is possible that by an arrangement of the kind you might save yourself."

"You mean that I should marry your sister Fanny?" he asked in a tone of relief.

"I was thinking of Fanny when I spoke," replied her ladyship coldly, and with a certain dash of disdain in her tone and manner.

"But Fanny has no money," he objected. "How can a marriage with her save me?"

"I could raise the money required for this bill, and I would do so, even at great inconvenience to myself, to save my sister from the social ruin which you have brought upon her," said her ladyship with decision. "Not that I approve of the marriage," she went on, "or that I think it will conduce to my sister's happiness; but she believes that it will, and I am willing to help her and you to the extent of paying this bill, and keeping it from the knowledge of those whose names have been so unjustifiably used upon it."

"But suppose I do marry Fanny—how are we to live?" asked Darlington, hoping to make better terms for himself.

Lady Grantly shrugged her shoulders as she said:

"That is your affair and hers; but you must excuse me now, Mr. Darlington—my husband will want me. You can arrange details with Fanny herself. You will find her in the adjoining room. But let me know the decision you arrive at before you leave the house, and if there is to be a wedding, please remember that I shall make a point of being present at it."

Then her ladyship bowed and walked out of the room, while Darlington, who began to feel that he had been led into a trap, went to the room where Fanny was awaiting him."

"They mean to marry me off this time," he muttered bitterly. "There will be no slip 'twixt the cup and the lip on this occasion. By Jove! what a woman will do for a husband!"

CHAPTER XXXVII.

NOT USED TO THE BUSINESS.

GODFREY LASCELLES was not fortunate in his enquiries or in the manner in which he set about making them.

In the first place the station-master was away from his post on a few days' leave, and when after waiting a couple of hours for the ticket collector who had been on duty the night in question, Godfrey spoke to him about the matter he had at heart, the man at first professed the most entire ignorance upon the subject. The sight of a half-sovereign, however, sharpened his memory, but unfortunately it likewise set his imagination at work.

He said he remembered Saturday morning, and that only two passengers alighted from the London train, a lady and a gentleman.

Then he described how a carriage was waiting for them, and how the gentleman said his wife was faint, and so got assistance in carrying her.

But he had not noticed the lady's face at the time, and now, when pressed upon the point, he declared that she was very fair, with light blue eyes, a very white complexion, and pale yellow hair.

When questioned as to how he knew the colour of her eyes if she were faint and insensible, he asserted that she opened them and half smiled, and said to the gentleman who was with her, "Thank you, dear."

"There must be some mistake here; it could not have been the young lady I am looking for," said Lascelles decisively.

"You think not, sir?" said the man in a disappointed tone.

"No, the lady I am seeking had dark brown hair and dark eyes. I would gladly give ten pounds to anyone who could help me to find her."

The man looked wistfully about him, he was ready to do a great deal for ten pounds, and after all he was not very sure whether the lady's hair was light or dark.

"Would you recognise the man who was with the lady?" the barrister next asked.

The man's face immediately brightened, and he said at once:

"Yes, sir, he got out of an up-train here this morning; there were two male passengers, and he was one of them."

"Two," repeated Godfrey, remembering that Darlington and Longridge had both alighted here in the morning, having lost the train at Peterborough; "surely it could not have been either of the men who came to the Railway Inn yonder?"

"I don't know where they went, sir, but I know he was one of the two, for I wondered where I'd seen his face before, and your asking me these questions brings it back to my memory."

"Ah!"

This last exclamation was caused by the appearance of Mr. Longridge, strolling in leisurely upon the platform.

"That is not the man?" asked Godfrey in amazement.

"No, that is the other one, sir," was the reply.

The barrister made a sign to the detective to come to him, and the latter, not too well pleased at being obliged to defer to the wishes of a man whom he felt sure would muddle matters, came slowly forward.

Godfrey briefly repeated the man's statement, but it seemed to make little or no impression upon the detective, and he said carelessly:

"I should think it would be very hard to remember the colour of a lady's hair and eyes when you see so many ladies in the course of a week."

"Well, it is," assented the man, who felt this to be the weak part of his story.

"Likewise you must have a good eye for faces to be able to say for certain that the gent who got out of the train here this morning at the same time as I did was the one who said a lady he had with him was his wife, for to my certain knowledge he hasn't got a wife."

"I don't care whether he's got a wife or not, it's the same man that took the young lady away in the carriage, I'll swear to him," said the ticket-collector positively.

"Does he mean——" asked Lascelles.

But Longridge interrupted him before the name could escape his lips.

"He means the man who rode away with me this morning; isn't it preposterous?"

"It does seem incredible," assented Lascelles, speaking slowly and thoughtfully.

He remembered that the detective had himself expressed his suspicions of Darlington, and he thought he saw a gleam of mocking triumph in the man's eyes.

"Perfectly incredible," said Mr. Longridge with decision. "You have made a mistake, my man; we know the gentleman you speak of quite well. I have just returned from driving to Scarsdale with him."

"I don't care where you've been with him, he's the man that took the lady away in the carriage as soon as 'twas light on Saturday morning. I'm ready to swear to that anywhere."

"Swear away," laughed Longridge derisively; "but if the lady he had with him had light hair, she isn't the one we want. You don't happen to have a pinch of snuff about you, my man?"

"No, I don't take snuff," was the disdainful reply.

"Nor do I as a rule, but I'd give a shilling for a pinch now; my eyes swim so that I can't see. Do none of the men here take snuff?"

"Our signalman does," was the answer; "and if you mean to give a shilling——"

"There it is. I never wanted a pinch of snuff so much in my life."

The man took the shilling and went off to procure the snuff, a proceeding for which the barrister had evidently the most profound contempt.

But Mr. Longridge was quite unaffected by this.

He looked after the railway employé until the man was well out of hearing, then he said:

"This fellow can tell you nothing that I don't know, and I don't mind admitting that I've got a clue; but are you quite sure, sir, that Miss Burnham meant to go direct to Rawfell Rectory?"

"As sure as a man can be who is told by a lady that she intends going to a certain place."

"Yes, just so, sir; that's as far as it goes; but still it is possible that Miss Burnham may have changed her mind; you know she was a young lady who had a mind of her own."

"It's possible, of course," assented Godfrey unwillingly, "but it is by no means probable."

"Still, sir, as you admit, it is possible, and there is no accounting for what a woman will do; Miss Burnham may have gone off to get married.

"Preposterous! Whom should she marry?" said Godfrey Lascelles angrily.

"Well, there are plenty of people she might marry, sir," in a tone which aggravated the barrister to the last pitch of endurance. "And I shouldn't be surprised," he went on deliberately, "if the young lady hasn't eloped just to surprise her friends.

"I should be greatly surprised," returned Mr. Lascelles haughtily; "indeed the supposition is not to be entertained for a moment. Miss Burnham was her own mistress, and she is one of the last women in the world to do anything to produce a vulgar sensation. If your 'clue' tends to anything of the kind you may save yourself the trouble of pursuing it, Mr. Longridge."

The detective did not reply for a second or two.

Then he said in a less irritating tone and manner:

"My 'clue' doesn't tend to anything of the kind, sir, but it never does to tie one's faith to one theory in anything of this kind, and, as you admitted, it is possible the young lady may have changed her mind about going where she first intended. And she was going to several places to visit, wasn't she?"

"Yes, but as far as I can learn, she has not gone to any of them."

"Don't you think, sir, it would be as well for you to go to the people Miss Burnham was going to stay with and see if you can find out from them what her movements were likely to be? I think I once heard you say you were her guardian."

Now Godfrey Lascelles had not said anything of the kind to Mr. Longridge, or in his hearing, but as it was a fact that Beatrice was his ward, he thought the detective's suggestion worth consideration.

Moreover, he did not know what other step to take at the moment, and to a nature like his there was nothing worse at such a time as this than inactivity.

"Perhaps you are right," he said reluctantly; "and meanwhile what will you do?"

"I will follow up the clue I told you of, sir; what that clue is I would rather not say at present."

The barrister walked a few paces, then came back again, and looking up suddenly into the detective's face, he said:

"It is odd that your suspicions and this man's assertion should both point to the same man."

"It is odd," assented the detective dryly.

"Still, it seems so utterly improbable under the circumstances," pursued Godfrey.

"I usually find that it is the improbable things that really do happen," remarked, Longridge. "But it's useless speculating on the matter, sir. We are only wasting time, and time is precious. I mean to stay in this place for a day or two, and if I were you I'd go to Rawfell or to any other place where the young lady was expected."

"I can't help you if I remain here?" asked Godfrey dubiously.

"Not in the least, sir; rather otherwise," was the immediate answer. "You aren't used to the detective line of business and—and it don't come natural to you."

He was going to say, "You don't do it well," but prudence suggested a milder form of disparagement.

"No, I don't think it does," assented Lascelles. Then he turned on his heel, remarking: "I think I'll take your advice."

The consequence of this conversation was that as Dr. Raynham and his daughter Ursula were about to sit down to dinner that same evening a fly from the nearest railway-station drove up to the gates, and Archibald, with Godfery Lascelles, alighted.

"At last," cried Ursula eagerly, going towards the door, "they have come to tell us why Beatrice did not come on to us when she sent her boxes."

"Don't go to meet them, dear," said the rector gently, but firmly; "they don't seem like the bearers of good news."

This impression was confirmed when a minute or two afterwards, the two young men came into the room, and Godfrey looked round eagerly, as though expecting, or rather hoping, to see the face of another person besides those present.

"Miss Burnham has not arrived?" he asked anxiously.

"No; we hoped you had brought news of her," replied Ursula, who forgot her usual reserve in her present anxiety.

Then Godfrey explained how he had only heard the previous day that the girl was missing.

"While we are talking the dinner is getting cold," said the rector, who was himself hungry. "Ursula will excuse your making any change in your dress. Sit down and let us eat first; then we will take counsel together."

They did eat; but their counsel came to nothing. The rector's opinion was that Beatrice had met some friend, with whom she had been induced to stay, or that something had made her change her plans about coming direct to Rawfell, and that they should hear from her before long.

"It is needless working oneself into a fever of anxiety as Ursula had done," he continued, looking at his daughter; "grown-up young women are not kidnapped and made away with nowadays, and from the little I saw of Beatrice Burnham I should say that if ever a young woman could take care of herself it was she."

"I should have said the same," assented Godfrey; "but I am also convinced that she would never wilfully inflict needless anxiety upon her friends."

"That is what I have been saying," here interposed Ursula; "besides, papa's theory won't hold good for a moment; no woman in her senses would send her clothes to one place and go herself to another. I wrote to Burnham Court to ask how many boxes she brought away with her, and I find they have all come here. My opinion is that some terrible accident has happened to poor Beatrice, or that she is detained against her will.

"I am afraid your first supposition is correct," said Godfrey gravely. "Miss Burnham must have met with an accident; but even then one would have thought we should have heard of it; it is this suspense that is so terrible.

"How he must love her," thought Ursula, looking gravely at the handsome anxious face of the young barrister. "I wonder if she returns his love. Poor fellow! I hope he is not suffering as I suffer; but then, a man may speak of his love, while a woman must be patient and silent, and must hide the pain she suffers as though love were a crime."

Then Ursula sighed again.

She had sighed a good deal of late and her cheeks were becoming thin, and pale, and hollow; and though the weather was so warm a short dry hacking cough clung to her and made her father sometimes start with sudden fear, as though it were a voice warning him of some impending bereavement.

And yet Ursula was cheerful as of old, even if her vivacity were at times a little forced, and she laughed at her father's fears on her behalf, assuring him that she was as well as she had ever been.

But for all this, she half believed and even hoped that the days of her life were numbered.

For Ursula Raynham was a woman who could love truly, and faithfully, and patiently, but who could have but one love in a lifetime.

Hers was not an elastic nature, she could not give her love and faith away to one man, and then finding it misplaced and unappreciated transfer it to another.

Her affections were too deep and strong and steadfast to bear transplanting, and now when hope died out of her heart, and the conviction forced itself upon her that she had been trifled with by one who thought only of the amusement of the hour, and who cared not what looks and softly-uttered words might seem to imply to her who saw and listened to them, her spirit sank within her.

She was not angry with the man who had brought this blight upon her life.

"He had not meant what his looks and manner seemed to imply," she thought wearily. "A town-bred girl would have accepted his silent homage one day and have forgotten it and him the next; but I am not town-bred, and the poison rankles in my heart."

She talked to herself like this, which was by no means a sensible proceeding.

And she read sentimental poetry, and devoted herself more earnestly than ever to the welfare of the poor, and of those who were suffering from any kind of affliction.

As I have before said, the rectory was so isolated that the inmates saw but little of people in their own position in life, but even the little society she had previously cultivated Ursula now avoided.

She had made up her mind slowly but surely during the months that had gone by since Fortescue Grantly had last since her, that it was her fate to fill an early grave, and she was without doubt going the way to do so.

Only one thing she prayed for, and it was that she might never again meet the man who had given her the wound that was slowly sapping her life away.

But our prayers are rarely answered in the way we expect them, and the day after Godfrey Lascelles came to Rawfell, Fortescue Grantly likewise arrived.

CHAPTER XXXVIII.

LOVE AND BITTERNESS.

RSULA was not at home when Sir Graham Grantly's nephew reached it, neither was the rector, but his son and Godfrey Lascelles both happened to be in the house, and the former gave him a boisterous and hearty welcome.

The ostensible object of young Grantly's visit here was to see Lascelles and communicate a piece of information to him concerning Beatrice Burnham.

A man who looked like a groom or coachman had come to Mr. Lascelles' chambers the previous day, had expressed his disappointment at not seeing the young barrister, but had left a pencilled note, which he said had been given him by a lady.

He said he would call again, and he declined to leave any address at which he could be found, two circumstances that when reported to Fortescue made him suspicious, and induced him to read the paper which the man had left.

It was the same hurried scrawl that Beatrice Burnham had put with some gold under the carriage cushion, and had asked the driver of the brougham in which she was taken to Miss Jex's cottage to deliver or post to the barrister.

The note was brief and somewhat incoherent. The words were:

"I have been carried off by Frank Darlington, he is taking me to a whitewashed cottage in a valley a few miles from Scarbridge; he has dared to call me his wife. Save me if you can.

"BEATRICE BURNHAM."

This, with Godfrey Lascelles' name and address, was all that the paper contained, and if Fortescue Grantly had not known Beatrice's handwriting, he would have regarded the matter as a hoax.

As it was, he resolved to follow his friend in person, and see if he could in any way be of use to him.

Perhaps Fortescue Grantly had another motive in coming to Rawfell Rectory.

Certain it is that he had meant to come or to write to one of its inmates ever since Lady Grantly had given him the letter which several months previously he had written to Ursula, but that had never reached her hands.

He had felt, when he saw his unanswered letter, that Ursula must have thought his conduct strange, and he had meant to try to set himself right in her estimation without delay.

But the habit of procrastination, which was his besetting sin, made him put off writing day after day, until he felt that no letter could explain his prolonged silence, and that he must go in person to plead his own suit by word of mouth instead of trusting again to the post.

A long railway journey, however, is a serious consideration to a busy man.

Then there was the question as to how he would be received if he presented himself uninvited and unexpected at Rawfell, and in company with these thoughts came doubts as to whether he did love Ursula Raynham as much as he once believed, and whether if she accepted him she would make a good and suitable wife for him.

All these questions puzzled and tormented him not a little, but they did not spoil his appetite or blunt his interest in things connected with this life, which was the effect his conduct had upon poor Ursula.

It is such men as Fortescue Grantly who inflict more pain upon the women they love and that love them, than the most deliberately cruel scoundrel could do.

They are not bad in intention or in act—they mean no harm.

Their intentions are perfectly honourable, if definite intentions they may be said to have, and they drift along, winning love and returning it, meaning to propose one day, yet always putting off the day to a more convenient season.

Such men have no conception of the wearying pain they inflict upon the women who feel that they had better die than give their love unsought, or who, having given it, believe that the weakness should be hidden as though it were a crime.

But meanwhile, Ursula is visiting her poor and sick pensioners, with no thought in her mind that anything unusual is about to happen to her, or that to-morrow will not be as to-day.

The weather has been delightful, though the heat has been somewhat oppressive, and Ursula is wearily walking up the long ascent that leads from the valley to the rectory.

She is later than she intended to be, for she has been sitting by the side of a young girl whose earthly course is nearly ended.

Ursula is thinking of the dying girl, but her thoughts, after a time, become more personal; she thinks her own life cannot be a long one, and then her eyes wander over the wild and now beautiful country, clothed in the rich garment of summer, and as she seems to drink in the beauty of the scene, she murmurs audibly:

"What a beautiful world, and to think that we must so soon leave it!"

"Ursula!"

It is but her own name, but the voice that utters it seems to ring through her heart with an electric shock, and for one brief moment she thinks that the sound has come from afar, and that he who utters it is in grief or some great agony, and is calling for her.

The next instant the speaker is standing before her, and she is pale and panting, and almost dumb with agitation.

"Ursula!" said Fortescue Grantly, taking her cold listless hand, "you are not glad to see me."

She tried to speak, but her tongue refused to obey her will, and she gasped for breath.

Her appearance frightened the young man.

She had become paler, thinner, and more wan-like during the past seven or eight months, and now she seemed as though she were fading away from him.

He had wondered what he should say when he set out to meet her, and he was in some doubt as to how she would receive him after this long period of silence, but he was not prepared for the change that had taken place in her, and it frightened him out of all caution and prudence.

"Ursula, my darling!" he cried, clasping his arm round her as she seemed about to fall.

She had not regained the power of speech, though it was slowly coming back to her, but she had sufficient strength to disengage herself from his embrace and to lean against a huge block of stone which stood at the roadside.

Something in her silent manner seemed like a re-proach to the man and to put him on trial as it were to defend himself, and stung to impatience by her seeming repulsion, he thrust his hand in the breast-pocket of his coat, took from it the letter that Fanny had intercepted, and holding it before her, he said:

"Miss Raynham, I wrote you this letter directly I reached London, after leaving here last Christmas. Why did you not answer it? Did it never reach your hands?"

She looked at the envelope blankly for a second or two, then she shook her head and said slowly and with difficulty:

"You never wrote to me; that is not my letter."

"Pardon me for contradicting you, but I did write to you," said the young man firmly and almost angrily. "I could not find an opportunity for speaking to you alone the night before I left the rectory, so I wrote to you and naturally enough expected an answer to my letter. No answer came, and I was not only pained at your silence, but also surprised at your seeming want of courtesy. Three months ago Lady Grantly accused me of writing it to her sister Fanny, though she could see at once that it was meant for you, when I called her attention to certain expressions in it."

Ursula accepted the letter almost mechanically. It all seemed like a dream, only the man before her was very real, and she was so weak and so powerless.

But she read the letter slowly, almost critically.

She looked at the date it bore, and at the postmark, then she let it drop from her nerveless hand, and her head fell forward as she moaned:

"Too late—too late!"

Fortescue caught her in his arms and half led, half carried her a few steps to where a pure spring trickled its limpid stream from the side of a rock into a deep well beneath.

Some cold water on her face revived the fainting girl and brought a slight tinge of colour to her pale cheeks, and she opened her eyes and smiled, with a feeling of peace and contentment in her heart such as she seemed never to have felt before.

As soon as she was sufficiently revived to talk, Fortescue took her hand in his own, and asked tenderly:

"Why do you say it is too late, dear? Are you engaged to somebody else?"

The sad sweet smile that came over her face reassured him on this point, and she looked steadfastly and lovingly into his eyes, but there was a sad pathos in her face and voice as she asked:

"Don't you see that I have not long to live; that—that I am slowly dying?"

"Good Heavens, no!" he cried in breathless agony; "you are not well, perhaps you are ill, but you are not dying; you must not die, love; you must live for me. What makes you talk in this dreadful way?"

"I am weak, and I have not wished to live," she replied faintly; "and now I feel as though life were slipping away from me and I cannot grasp it."

"And all this pain and misery has been caused by that accursed girl," cried Fortescue bitterly. "She stole my letter, and she could not pretend that she thought it was meant for her, for she never answered it. I only wish I knew how to punish her."

"Leave her alone, dear; the way of transgressors is hard, and she has strewn her own path with thorns enough, poor girl."

"She has been very liberal in strewing the paths of others with thorns," said Fortescue bitterly; "but let us forget her. You have not answered my letter, Ursula."

A fond loving smile and a faint pressure of the hand were assurance enough of her love, but her words were not so hopeful as she said:

"If the doctors think I can live, my life is yours to devote to your happiness, but if not——"

"Don't speak of anything else as possible," he cried anxiously; "you are in a low morbid condition of mind, but I don't believe your health is seriously affected. You must go away from this place and have change of scene, and look upon life from a more sunny point of view than you have lately regarded it. You will try to be cheerful and to get strong, won't you, darling, for my sake?"

"For yours and for my own," she replied fondly; "I have now something to live for."

A kiss, the first that had passed between them, was the seal of the love that filled their hearts to overflowing, but even in their joy there was a certain tinge of sadness caused by the doubt as to whether their new found happiness had not come to them too late.

They sat together here by the unfrequented pathway talking of the months that were past, and of how each of them had thought the other cold and indifferent, and they forgot the flight of time until Ursula asked:

"Have you seen my father and brother since you arrived?"

"Your father was out when I reached the rectory," was the answer; "and that reminds me that your brother told me the way you were likely to return to the house, and that he said something about having dinner earlier than usual."

"Dinner!" Ursula had forgotten for the time that such a meal was ever served or needed.

She looked at her watch, then started up in something like alarm.

No. 15.

HE TOOK A STONE AND DROPPED IT DOWN THE WELL.

"They will be sending to look for me directly," said Ursula, blushing deeply; "it is past our usual dinner-hour, and papa will think something has happened to me."

"He will not be far wrong," laughed the young man, "you are beginning to look brighter and stronger already."

"Going without her dinner won't help to make her strong," growled a man's voice close at hand. "The idea of you two folks staying out here spooning while we are waiting for our dinner like famished wolves."

And Archie Raynham as he said this showed a face which exhibited anything but contentment.

"Wolves wouldn't wait, and it's a pity you didn't follow their example," retorted Ursula in a lighter tone than was her wont.

"That's what I suggested," said her brother, "but father wouldn't hear of it, and there is Godfrey Lascelles like a chained bear wanting to get away. He's had a telegram from the detective since you left him, Grantly."

"Ah! has anything been discovered?" asked Fortescue eagerly.

"I fancy so, and that the whole affair is more serious than any of us thought. But I can't give you particulars, and I am hungry enough to dine off a dog's hind leg."

"But can't you tell me what was in the telegram? Is Lascelles going away from here to-night?" asked Grantly.

"No, the detective is coming for him, that is one reason why we are in such a great hurry to feed. Do you mean to give us any dinner to-day, Ursula?"

Archie Raynham said this with all the unreasoning impatience with which brothers sometimes address their sisters.

"Ursula doesn't cook the dinner or put it on the table," said Fortescue, irritated by seeing the girl he loved so worried; "suppose you go back and tell the others to begin; we will follow you directly."

For a second or two Archibald Raynham looked at Fortescue Grantly in surprise, then with his good-natured cubbishness, he said:

"It's precious cool of you to talk like that; one would think that Ursula belonged to you."

"The person who thought so would not be far wrong," was the reply. "Take my arm, dear," he added, turning to the girl.

"Well, if that is the state of affairs, its of no use waiting any longer for dinner," said young Raynham. "I shall go back and order it to be served up at once; a ladybird's wing will be enough for you two."

Ursula smiled.

She was too happy to feel vexed with her brother, who was always hungry, but her sense of hospitality made her feel that she ought not to have kept Godfrey Lascelles waiting.

"Go home and order dinner to be served," she said, "and tell father I shall be there directly. I have been unwell."

"Shall I tell him anything else?" asked her brother with a grin.

"Tell him what you like," said Fortescue hotly, "only don't worry your sister."

A remark that sent Mr. Archie back to the rectory without another word.

"What can it be about Beatrice?" asked Ursula anxiously; "do you think anything very serious has happened to her?"

"I don't know what to think dear," was the reply; "the whole affair puzzles me. But let us follow your brother. Perhaps the detective has arrived, though why he should come here puzzles me."

"Yes, it does seem strange," replied the girl, leaning upon his arm.

Then she paused and asked suddenly:

"Do you believe in dreams, dear?"

"I don't know," was the cautious answer. "Why do you ask?"

"Because last night I dreamed that Beatrice Burnham was dead!'

"A very unpleasant dream," was the answer; "but here is Lascelles coming towards us, and, by Jove, how pale and troubled he looks!"

This was the case.

Godfrey Lascelles had received a second telegram from Mr. Longridge, and was coming to impart the sad contents.

CHAPTER XXXIX.

LASCELLES IS RIGHT.

THE last telegram which Godfrey Lascelles had received from the detective was alarming in its tone, and it likewise contained a request that the young barrister would drive over to Scarsdale without delay, and take up his quarters at the small beershop in the valley, that being the only place where he could get a night's lodging.

"Do you mean to go to-night?" asked Fortescue Grantly when he had read the message.

"Yes, and without any unnecessary delay," was the answer.

"I will go with you," said his friend.

But as he uttered the words he glanced at Ursula, as if asking her approval, and she smiled to assure him of her earnest and ready sympathy.

So, after a hasty dinner, the two young men started for their long drive, having first promised Archibald Raynham to send for him if he could be of any use in the matter.

Night had set in by the time they reached the long wide valley, and on driving up to the beershop in question they found Mr. Longridge awaiting them.

He had engaged the only private sitting-room for the use of Mr. Lascelles, and he at once led the way to it.

"What news have you?" was the first eager question from Godfrey.

"Nothing cheerful, sir," was the reply. "I'm afraid they've made away with the young lady."

"Made away with her? Good heavens! you don't mean that anybody has killed her?"

"Killed her, sir—that's just what I do mean. Of course I don't say positively that it is so, but it looks uncommonly like it."

"Preposterous!" cried Godfrey impatiently, "and who do you mean by 'they?'"

"You shall hear, sir."

And thereupon the man gave the substance of what he had discovered.

We will not follow him in the long-winded details with which he embellished his story; what he had really found out by dint of much enquiry in the neighbourhood was simply this.

Two women of the name of Jex lived in a cottage in this valley, and bore a bad character for cruelty and cupidity. To their house on the Saturday morning when Beatrice was lost a young lady was brought in a private carriage. This young lady was never seen outside the house again, but some curious neighbour prowling about the cottage a few days afterwards said she heard cries and groans from a disused well in the garden of the cottage.

Horrible stories were afloat in the neighbourhood about this well, as it was believed that it had been the receptacle for the victim of more than one crime of which the grim sisters were reputed to be guilty.

But no one had tested the truth of these rumours; it was the business of nobody, and the two sisters had inspired a certain amount of terror and of awe in the minds of their neighbours.

"I shouldn't have thought much of this gossip," Mr. Longridge continued, "if I hadn't followed Mr. Darlington to this very cottage the other morning, and if I hadn't seen him and one of the old women in the back garden kneeling down by the side of the well they tell such stories about. I couldn't make out what they were doing there, I was too far off at the time, and when I went a little later and examined the place I could make nothing of it. The mouth of the well had been covered over, but the boards were rotten and were broken down in the middle. I went to the house and knocked at the door, but I didn't get any answer, and I returned to

Scarbridge. But I came back to Scarsdale this morning and I ferreted about, and I picked up one story and another, and I found that the two women to whom the cottage belonged had gone away, and then I tried to get help to explore the well, but could arrange nothing till to-morrow morning, so I telegraphed for you, and did what little I could by myself."

"And did that amount to much?" asked Godfrey rather superciliously.

"Yes, sir; I found that the well seemed to be partly bunged up, choked like, and I fished up this."

And the man produced a lady's hand-bag, on the outside of which were the initials in silver, "B. B."

Godfrey Lascelles seized the bag eagerly and opened it.

There was a pocket-handkerchief, a pair of gloves, a scent bottle, and a small pocket-book, in which were several memoranda, and the numbers of some half-a-dozen bank-notes; there was also inside it a letter written from Ursula Raynham to Beatrice Burnham.

"How could you get hold of this if the well is so deep?" demanded the barrister incredulously.

"I tell you there's a lot of rubbish within a dozen feet of the top, sir. It seems to me as if pieces of wood had stuck in the sides, or had fallen across; at any rate, this bag seemed to be hanging to a rotten splinter, and I managed to hook it up."

"But you don't suppose that Miss Burnham has been murdered, and her body thrown into this well, do you?" asked Godfrey, in tones of horror.

"I did suppose it, sir, and that's why I telegraphed. This morning one of the two sisters came back to the cottage, and she went to the woman who first told me about the noises from the well, and she said that her sister had gone away, and was not coming back any more."

"But what has that to do with us?" asked Lascelles impatiently.

"This, sir.   She is angry with her sister, and is ready to reveal the cause of her absence. Her story is that Miss Burnham had bribed her sister to allow her to escape, that she had led her through the garden, induced her to stand on the rotten covering of the well, which gave way under her feet, and that she now lies at the bottom of the well—dead, of course."

"It isn't probable; it is scarcely possible," said the barrister incredulously.

"It's possible enough, sir," said the detective gravely. "The story goes that a man fell into this same well years ago, and that his body was never recovered."

"We will recover Miss Burnham's body if it lies there," said Godfrey in an excited tone; "but I don't believe the story; she isn't dead, I feel convinced."

"I hope you're right, sir," said the man; "but I'm afraid the woman's story is true; however, we can test it to-morrow. I have already made arrangements to begin work early in the morning, and communicated with Scotland Yard."

"Have you mentioned Mr. Darlington's name in connection with the matter?" asked Fortescue Grantly, who was present at the interview.

"No, sir; Miss Jex didn't know his name, and we always know where to pounce upon our man; besides, I think we shall have one or two other matters to settle with that gentleman before long."

"Moreover, you have no positive proof that Mr. Darlington had anything to do with the girl's death, even if there is no doubt that he brought her to the two women you speak of, and left her in their care," continued Fortescue.

"That is true, sir," assented the detective; "the woman Jex that I've talked to says he was very much cut up when he heard of the girl's death, and that he went off to communicate with the police. That's why she and her sister ran away."

"In that case, what made her come back again?" asked Grantley.

"Her sister managed to give her the slip and to get away with most of their money, it seems," was the answer; "and Sal Jex believed that a large sum of money belonging to Miss Burnham fell into the well with her, and this she thought to get hold of. The woman is more than half silly."

"I don't believe Beatrice is in the well," said Godfrey Lascelles positively.

He had been pacing up and down the room for the last few minutes, his brows contracted, and his head bent.

"I feel that she is not dead," he went on; "and nothing short of actually seeing her body would convince me."

"I hope you are right, sir," said Longridge; "but I confess I don't share your feeling."

Then it was arranged that at daybreak the two young barristers should accompany the detective to the spot where Sal Jex asserted Beatrice Burnham had met her death.

Longridge had already engaged a couple of men, who were to explore the dreaded and dangerous spot.

"That man's story doesn't seem probable," remarked Lascelles when he found himself alone with his friend.

He had taken a dislike to Longridge and was inclined to question all he did or said; and in addition to this feeling was another, which he did not care to recognise or to admit the existence of even to himself.

Other men would have called it love; but when it forced itself upon his consciousness and had to be designated by a name he chose to denominate it friendly interest and a sense of duty, since he had accepted the guardianship of this troublesome girl.

"The man believes his story, or rather, his theory," said Grantly uneasily; and it has one merit about it— its truth or accuracy can soon be tested. And now let us go to bed, though, by-the-bye, old man, I want you to congratulate me."

Then Grantley told his friend of his love for Ursula Raynham, and of the success his suit had met with.

It was only a little past five o'clock the next morning when a strange group assembled in the back-garden of the house of which Sall Jex was now the sole mistress.

The woman herself was present, telling over again the same tale she had told to Frank Darlington, the only variation in her narrative being an increased rancour and bitterness against her sister.

For Miss Jex had been too clever for Sall, and had managed to elude her watchfulness and get away from her, carrying the ill-gotten savings of years with her.

Besides the woman there was Longridge, busy and watchful, and a trifle too fussy in directing the two working-men as to how they should set about their investigation.

And then there were the two young men, Lascelles and Grantly, both looking very grave and the former rather nervous, but neither of them disposed to do more than look on.

The men set to work, expecting a long and wearisome piece of work—and work, too, not unaccompanied by danger.

And this is what they found.

A few feet below the surface the shaft was partly clogged with rubbish, and lower still a couple of broad pieces of wood had been wedged across the depth below, making a kind of insecure platform upon which a person could contrive to stand.

On each side of this was a half-circular aperture, large enough for a dog or a cat or an infant to fall through, but certainly not big enough to admit a grown-up person.

When the men made this discovery Godfrey Lascelles turned in triumph to Grantly and said :

" I told you it was impossible."

"Not so impossible as you seem to think, sir," said Longridge warmly ; "and, at any rate, the woman's story looked plausible. I dropped stones down here myself, and I heard them splash into the water, though they took a long time getting there."

"Of course it fell down one of the sides of these boards," was the reply ; "but though a stone might fall through there, a woman couldn't."

" Who fixed these boards across the hole, I wonder ? " asked Grantly of one of the workmen. " Is the wood very old, or is it new ? "

" Old, sir, and the boards have come there by accident more than by design ; they've been a cover for the well in their time, and I shouldn't wonder if they haven't got jammed in their present place by somebody standing on the top, as 'tis said the young lady did, and only falling a part of the way down. Don't you see, sir, that they ain't straight, and that one is more sloping than the other? I shouldn't much care to trust my own weight on it without a rope tied round my waist."

"No, nor I," assented the young man, bending to see by the aid of the light the man held down, the dangerous-looking platform in question.

"It is an ugly place," he went on; "but it settles the question that we wanted solved. No woman has fallen through there into the water beneath for the last month. It is satisfactory to be assured on that point."

"But I saw her fall," asserted Sall Jex positively. "Sister had hold of her hand, telling her to take care, for there was holes about, and I heard the girl cry, and I saw her fall; I did, as true as I stand here."

"You deserve to be hung for not raising an alarm and trying to save her," said Lascelles, turning fiercely upon the half-witted creature.

"But we have wasted time enough here," he added, turning to Grantly; "I must have fresh assistance, and must secure the aid of the criminal detective department in Scotland Yard; Mr. Longridge is all very well in his way, but this case is evidently too much for him. Here, my man, this is for your trouble," and he gave one of them a couple of sovereigns, then he turned and walked away, leaving the detective enraged and mortified."

"I confess it is a relief to my mind to find that the mystery of the well is not so tragical as we were led to believe," said Grantly as he and Godfrey walked away.

"Yes," assented the other, "I felt sure that Beatrice was not dead, but I do not feel so certain that the woman we have heard of did not try to kill her. Suppose she did fall down that hole, and afterwards scramble out again, what could then have become of her?"

"That is a difficult question to answer," said Fortescue thoughtfully, "so much would depend upon whether or not she was injured by the fall."

"Of course, and she would naturally be afraid to seek help from the woman who had meant to murder her. Her wisest course would have been to make her way to Rawfell Rectory, but that we know she did not do."

"No, I can't account for her absence from her friends and her silence except on the supposition that she was severely injured and is lying ill somewhere."

"In that case she ought not to be far from here," said Lascelles, "but we will leave no stone unturned to find her; hitherto I have tried to avoid publicity, but now I will engage some sharp detectives and publish a description of her far and wide; it is quite certain that she is in a terrible plight somewhere."

Grantly expressed his concurrence in his friend's opinion.

Although they seemed as far off as ever from finding Beatrice, it was such a relief to both of them to know that she had not been killed by falling into the well, that they felt as though they had made some pleasing and satisfactory discovery.

I shall have nothing more to do with that fellow Longridge," said Lascelles decidedly. "I have more than paid him for the work he has done, and he keeps one in a constant state of fever; he is always on the verge of some great discovery, which after all turns out to be little better than a mare's nest."

"I don't like the man myself," said Grantly, "but at the same time we should not know that Beatrice Burnham had been in such danger but for him; the story of the well without his aid would never have reached us, and we should not have known where to start from in our search for her."

"That may be, but I shall secure the aid of the local police, and I shall offer a handsome reward for information that will lead to our finding the girl."

Then the two young men returned to the beershop, where breakfast was awaiting them.

They ate their ham and eggs with a relish, and then at Fortescue Grantly's suggestion they called in the landlady and told her the reason of their presence there.

To the story of the missing girl she listened eagerly, and she added her testimony concerning the women into whose hands poor Beatrice had fallen.

But when Godfrey Lascelles told her he would give twenty pounds for information that would enable him to trace the missing girl, her interest took a much more practical shape.

"I'll find out for you which way she went if 'twas out of this valley," she said cautiously; "only you must give me time. Can you bide here till to-morrow?"

"We will if it's likely to be of any use," was the answer.

"'Twill be of use," she said positively. "The men will be in to-night to drink and talk, and I'll be bound to find out something from them."

She kept her word.

The next morning she informed Godfrey Lascelles that a girl answering the description that had been given, well-dressed, but rather strange in her manner, had been seen walking on the high road leading north from Scarsdale.

She had been walking slowly and painfully, as though one or both of her feet were injured, and she had been followed to a small roadside inn, where she had asked for and obtained food and a bed, paying for both in advance.

"P'raps she's there still, sir," the woman went on. "If she is you're sure to find her, and if she's gone, mayhap the folks that keep the house will know where she is gone to. The landlady of the Fox and Grapes is a second cousin of mine, and I'll go along with you to her."

The young men thanked her, and could have dispensed with her company upon the short journey, but prudence suggested that they should accept whatever help they could get.

Arrived at the Fox and Grapes, however, they discovered that the bird they sought had flown.

Flown, too, in a very lame condition.

She had evidently been here, however, and had remained for a night and a day; then she had travelled in a light cart belonging to a neighbouring farmer to the nearest town.

"The young woman would pay for her ride, but her head was uncommon light, and she didn't know what she said half her time," the landlady of the Fox and Grapes remarked. "But laws, she'll be all right," she added consolingly. "She'd got plenty of money, and she'd take care of herself."

Lascelles and Grantly were not quite so certain of her safety, however, and they set off to seek the farmer in whose cart she had ridden, and to learn from him where he had left her.

But they set out with hopefulness in their hearts, feeling assured that, sooner or later, they should find her.

CHAPTER XL.

AT THE ALTAR RAILS.

"GOOD-MORNING, Frank," said Fanny Raynham as Darlington came into the room in which Lady Grantly had told him he would find her sister.

He responded briefly, for there was a look of veiled triumph in the girl's eyes, and however much he might be made to feel himself contemptible by her ladyship, he had no inclination to submit to anything of the kind from Fanny, who never inspired any more powerful feelings than careless pity considerably tinctured with disdain.

"I ought to condole with you over your loss," she next said, glancing at his black garments.

"Thank you, it is quite unnecessary," he replied coldly; "there need be no pretence of being what we are not between you and me. My brother and I were never companions and were not always friends, and therefore it would be sheer hypocrisy on my part to pretend that I am heartbroken at his death."

Fanny shrugged her shoulders, made a little grimace, and then said :

"I think a little make-believe is a very comfortable thing; one doesn't always want to call ugly things by ugly names; pretty ones are no more trouble to utter."

"Make-believe as much as you like to the outside world," he said impatiently, "but don't let us deceive ourselves nor wilfully close our eyes to the truth."

"When people talk about not closing their eyes to the truth, they generally mean that they are going to do or say something particularly nasty," said Fanny, making a wry face; "but I suppose the truth is, Geraldine, has been sitting upon you, and as you couldn't punish her for it you are going to take it out of me."

Her statement was so near the truth that it goaded him to be as disagreeable as he possibly could be, and he said coldly:

"You may think your remarks interesting, I don't. I understand that you wish to marry me."

The words were offensive enough in themselves, the tone in which they were uttered was simply insulting, and Fanny Raynham's face flushed angrily, and for a minute or two she was in danger of losing her temper.

She soon recovered her self-command, however.

"Oh, I understood that you wished to marry me; Geraldine said she was sure you would wish it."

"Wish it!" he repeated contemptuously; "as though any man could ever be such a fool."

"If he were in your case he would be a very much greater fool if he did not wish it," retorted the girl angrily, "and it is not every woman who would care to marry you, even if she had compromised herself as much as I have done."

"Well, we have not met here to call each other by harsh names or to quarrel, have we?" he asked, feeling that in a war of words he would get the worst of it.

"I did not come for that purpose," she replied a little more meekly.

"You know what has happened," he went on, "and what has brought me here to talk with you?"

She bent her head and he continued:

"Your sister demands that I shall marry you as the price of her help in getting me out of a great difficulty, when do you promise that the marriage shall take place?"

"When would you like it to be?" she asked mildly.

"Like it!" he repeated, with a bitter laugh; "as though I should ever like it."

"Perhaps you prefer the alternative," she said, stung to anger by his unveiled insolence.

"It is a choice between two evils, and of the two, perhaps a marriage with you will be the most endurable," he said carelessly.

"Thank you, then you shan't have the choice of evils," she cried with rising temper, while a feeling of indignation made her determine to lose this man rather than submit to his brutal insults.

She rose to her feet as she spoke, and was walking out of the room, when he caught her round the waist and said:

"Come, Fanny, don't be disagreeable. I am irritable to-day, I know, but I have had a good deal to try me of late, and this marriage of ours is plaguy inconvenient, coming so soon after Clarrie's death, to say nothing of my brother being scarcely cold in his coffin."

"It may be inconvenient," replied the girl," but it can't be as bad as the exposure you would otherwise have to face, and I suppose I shall have to do without brides-maids or orange-blossoms."

"Yes, orange-blossoms would be rather out of place upon you," he said dryly; "but if there is a marriage it must be perfectly quiet, and it must be kept a profound secret while my father lives."

"I shall not consent to any condition of that kind," she said positively; "nor will Geraldine. We will keep the marriage secret for a few months if you like, but that is all. I may as well not be married at all, as wait for people to know it until your father dies."

"As you like," he said wearily; "it will make the difference of a good many thousands to us if I offend my father, but you have not answered my question, when is it to be?"

"Whenever you like. Geraldine will not pay the money you want until we are married."

"Then it will have to be done quickly," he returned, with a muttered oath; "for the matter will admit of no delay. Where do you propose to live afterwards?"

"With you, of course," was the answer. "But why do you talk like this, Frank?" she asked in a pleading tone, and with sudden gentleness of manner; "have you quite ceased to love me?"

"I never did love you," he replied, with brutal candour; "but let that pass. Shall we fix Tuesday next for this cheerful ceremony?"

"Yes, Tuesday will suit me as well as any other day," she said in a low tone, while tears of pain and mortification stood in her eyes.

"Then Tuesday it shall be," he said recklessly ; "I will let you know the time and place when I have made arrangements.   It will be in London, of course ?"

"I suppose it must be," she assented ; "but here comes Geraldine."

"Have you two settled matters ?" asked Lady Grantly, looking at the couple coldly.

"Yes, we are to be married on Tuesday next," was the answer.

"Very well, I shall arrange to be present, unless Sir Graham is much worse than he is to-day," said her ladyship ; "and now I must send both of you away."

A few details with regard to the forged bill and the money wherewith to meet it were then arranged, and Frank Darlington rode home from Grantly Park feeling more thoroughly depressed than he had ever before felt in his life.

To marry Fanny Raynham was a step which he considered fatal to his position and to his success in life, and to have her forced upon him in this manner was galling in the extreme.

Yet he had no choice ; it was his only avenue of escape from the consequences of that crime, which had seemed such a trifling matter when he committed it, but that now assumed such terrible proportions.

If ever a man endured mental agony amounting to positive torture, it was Frank Darlington during the time that elapsed between his last visit to Grantly Park and the morning of his intended marriage with Fanny Raynham.

During these horrible days all his victims seemed to rise up in judgment against him.

Mary Trevor, Clarrie Burnham, and Beatrice, each in turn or altogether seemed to rise up before his mental vision, till he felt as though he should go mad with thinking of them.

And then that lost pocket-book with its compromising contents.

If that were found by anyone who knew how to use the papers contained in it, then he might as well refuse to enter into this marriage and might defy Lady Grantly to do her worst, for ruin at no far distant period was inevitable.

The danger of his position seemed to grow upon him as the hours went on, until as a resource from thought and from memory, he began to drink largely of brandy.

Morning, noon, and night the fatal bottle was rarely out of his reach, until his senses became blunted, his reason clouded, and if he was never quite drunk, he was never quite sober.

He was in this disgusting condition on the morning of his wedding; maudlin, exacting, and apt to be irritable.

Lady Grantly had come up to town on purpose to be present.

She seemed to have constituted herself Fanny's guardian, and to have taken the place of a mother to her.

But low as was Geraldine's previous opinion of the man with whom her sister was so bent upon linking her own fate, she felt her contempt for him deepen this morning until she could scarcely tolerate his presence or be even ordinarily civil to him.

For, though he could walk steadily, he put down his foot each time with particular care lest he should fall, and there was a sleepy half-confidential expression in his tone and manner that was clearly attributable to alcohol.

"Pause a minute, Fanny," said her ladyship desperately as the small party entered the church in which the ceremony was to take place. "There is still time to turn back; think once again before you tie yourself for life to a sot."

"I mean to marry him," replied the girl, setting her teeth fiercely.

Her sister said no more, but she thought bitterly that after all the couple were not ill matched.

The clergyman had not arrived and they were shown into the vestry to wait for him.

It was not a cheerful wedding-party; Lady Grantly was silent and depressed, and the presumably happy couple seemed more interested in staring about them than they were in each other.

Fanny had suggested that Frank should ask some male friend to be present, but her sister had curtly replied that the pew-opener would be as good a witness as anyone.

She likewise scouted the suggestion of anything in the shape of a wedding-breakfast.

"You and your husband can take breakfast together," she said coldly. "As for me, I must hasten back to Sir Graham, whom I scarcely liked to leave."

So Fanny had to submit, though she chose to consider herself very much ill-used in doing so.

The clergyman came at last all in a bustle, profuse with apologies, and as soon as the clerk had helped him on with his surplice he took his place at the altar.

Frank Darlington and Fanny Raynham stood before him, while Lady Grantly took her stand by her sister's side.

Though the sun was shining through the painted windows, and the perfume of flowers was wafted in from the garden outside, there was something very chilly and desolate in the empty pews and the absence of anything like wedding festivities.

Lady Grantly felt this more than did her sister, and she contrasted this wedding with her own and sighed sadly, but whether for Fanny or for herself she scarcely knew.

But the ceremony has commenced, and to those who stand before the altar-rails it seems a long one, for the clergyman will miss nothing, but conscientiously reads every word.

He has just repeated the exhortation, "Therefore, if any man can show any just cause why they may not lawfully be joined together, let him now speak, or else hereafter for ever hold his peace."

There was silence for a moment.

Then a voice from the further end of the church cried :

"I can show cause. I am his wife!"

"His wife!" gasped Fanny and Lady Grantly in a breath.

"His wife," repeated the voice that had already spoken.

And then two women, both of them heavily veiled, came slowly up the centre aisle.

The clergyman paused and half closed his book.

Bride and bridegroom turned to confront the new comers, and they were dimly conscious that a small knot of people were gathered near the principal doorway.

The interruption has sobered the bridegroom, and his face is pale, though his voice is steady, as he says :

"I have no wife."

"This is the proof," said the woman who had first spoken as she produced a long blue slip of paper, which the experienced eye of the clergyman recognised as a copy of a marriage certificate.

At the same moment she threw back her veil.

Her companion did the same, and as Frank Darlington looked on the faces of two women whom he had counted among his victims he gave a low cry of dismay and horror, flung up his arms in despair and terror, and fell down senseless at the altar-rails.

CHAPTER XLI.

A WONDERFUL ESCAPE.

E must return to our heroine, whom we left a prisoner in the cottage at Scarsdale.

The story which Sall Jex told to Frank Darlington was substantially true.

After much beating about the bush, and trying to extort good terms from the captive, the woman had consented to accept the trifle which Beatrice declared to be all she had with her, accompanied by a promise to pay a considerable sum later on.

Unfortunately, for the girl, the old woman, who kept a close guard upon her, waited and watched, and finally discovered that her prisoner really had a considerable sum of money in her possession.

It was then that the sordid creature's cupidity and cruelty were aroused.

The girl had deceived her, she reasoned, and she should be punished for it.

That the deception was justifiable, was to this woman's mind, quite beside the question, and she proceeded to devise some scheme by which she could vent her spite, and, at the same time, get hold of the coveted money.

The plan she did form was as diabolical as any that could be invented.

She pretended to sympathise with her prisoner, and to believe her story, and she promised to release her.

But she asserted that she could not do this openly, or in the daylight, because the man who brought her there —meaning Darlington—kept a strict watch over the cottage, and Miss Jex not only asserted this, but said she was in his power, and she dared not let him know that she had betrayed the trust reposed in her.

Beatrice saw nothing improbable in this statement, and she was too anxious to get away from these repulsive women, and to feel herself beyond Darlington's power, to hesitate for a moment to escape by night, even though she had to walk through the country roads alone.

So she made no objection when Miss Jex suggested that she should leave the cottage when night had set in, and that even then she should get away by going through the back garden, and climbing a low wall, on the opposite side of which she would find a narrow path along the side of a hedge, by following which she would after a time reach the high road.

The directions were not very clear, but that mattered little, for Beatrice paid no heed to them.

Her one thought and hope was to get free, and, once away from this detestable cottage and its inmates, she felt that no great harm could befall her, and she had no doubt whatever about being able to take care of herself.

"I am not likely to be overcome by a powerful drug a second time," she thought as she tried to decide what her first step should be when she became free, "but I will make you pay for your daring outrage upon me, Frank Darlington, if I live long enough."

So she pondered till the time came when the doors of her cage were to be opened, and she was to be set free.

It was a dark night, though the air was soft and balmy.

The new moon, like a silver boat, seemed to float in the summer sky, and only a few planets and fixed stars were to be seen in the deep blue vault of heaven.

Beatrice looked at the crescent moon and at the stars, and thought how delightful it was to be out of the cottage, free to breathe the cool air and to enjoy the calm still beauty of the night.

Thus thinking, however, she stumbled over a piece of wood placed in her way.

But she did not fall, though she only just saved herself from doing so.

"Here, you'd best give me your hand to lead you," said Miss Jex in a surly tone.

The girl would have declined this seemingly well-meant suggestion, but the woman did not wait for a reply, she clutched her companion's arm and led her resolutely forward, more like one who was dragging a prisoner than helping a woman through kindness.

This idea flashed through our heroine's mind, and the fear that all was not right, and that treachery was meditated, set her upon her guard.

But she uttered no protest, in a few minutes she hoped to be free from the companionship of this creature, but she clasped a small bag she held in her hand more tightly than before, forgetting for the moment that she had taken her money from it just before she left the cottage, and had secreted it inside the body of her dress.

Miss Jex was as unaware of this transfer as Beatrice was forgetful of it.

She believed that this bag contained a large sum of money, and she meant to get hold of it.

And thus the two slowly walked through the garden, Miss Jex herself seeming to select her footing with great care.

Suddenly Beatrice felt herself violently pushed on one side by her companion, who at the same moment made a snatch at the coveted bag.

The natural instinct which makes one cling with more tenacity than usual to anything that another tries to take from us, made Beatrice Burnham give more heed to the security of the bag than it was worth, and in holding it firmly she failed to notice the insecure spot upon which she at the moment stood.

At the moment, I say, for it was scarcely more before the boarded space upon which she had been thrust, gave way beneath her feet, and the very earth seemed to open and engulf her.

"SUPPOSE IT IS A FORGERY, AND THAT I KNOW NOTHING WHATEVER ABOUT IT?" HE ASKED, PAUSING AT LENGTH BEFORE HER.

Beatrice uttered a shriek as she fell, and then consciousness deserted her.

How long she remained in this condition she could not tell.

She was aroused from insensibility by a feeling of acute pain in one of her ankles.

This became so intense that she tried to move, and then she felt as though she were walled in, for on whatever side she put her hand the cold damp earthy touch gave her a chill.

Where could she be? What had happened to her? were the natural questions that came to her mind.

And then the events of the last few days slowly and painfully returned to her memory, and she felt assured that the woman to whose care Frank Darlington had consigned her had brought her here and thrust her into this horrible hole to die.

She felt about her carefully and cautiously, and was terrified to discover that there were two spaces, one on each side of her, as it were, and that by her moving some loose stones seemed to be displaced and to fall, and after what seemed a great lapse of time, though it could only have been a second or two, there came up from the depth beneath a faint splash of water.

Then it was that the great peril of her position dawned upon the mind of the girl.

There was water down deep below her, and there was a wall round her.

She had been thrust down the shaft of a well, and by a merciful Providence had been saved from instant death by the well being choked not very far from the surface.

The question was, how far down was she, for to be here alive and to die slowly from starvation would be far more dreadful than the fate that was evidently meant for her.

She was afraid to move, because of the holes on each side of the place upon which she had fallen, and her ankle pained her dreadfully.

Looking up, she could just see one faint speck of light, which she knew to be a star, so she knew that it was still night, and that the night was dark.

The horror of her situation nerved her to exertion, for she felt that every moment she remained only increased her danger.

For aught she knew, the woman who had thrust her here might return and cover over the mouth of the well, and thus effectually prevent her escape, and as completely drown her cries for help.

Or, worse still, if anything could be worse, the boards and rubbish upon which she had fallen might give way under her weight, and precipitate her into the depth below.

This was not likely to happen after it had borne the shock of her fall, but the boards had been rather jammed in the shaft from the way in which she had fallen, and thus her weight had not had the effect which it must otherwise have had.

Intense terror gave the girl courage and strength, and she managed to move her cramped and bruised limbs, and with great pain and difficulty rose to her feet.

She was, as we know, above the medium height, and she stretched up her arms and felt cautiously and carefully over the walls of what was now her prison, and that might be her grave.

Standing upright, she was still some feet from the top of the well, and at first it seemed an impossible thing to climb up the straight sides.

Feeling about patiently and cautiously, however, Beatrice found that the sides of the shaft into which she had fallen were uneven, and in some places there were indentations where she could rest her toes while she sought a hold higher up with her hands.

It was a desperate effort to make, for the chances were that if she failed to climb up to the top, and fell down again, the frail support that had now saved her might give way, and then the end was certain.

Urged on by the consciousness that death would be the penalty of failure, Beatrice Burnham set to work to make her perilous ascent.

How she did it she could never afterwards explain.

But she would not have succeeded if some pieces of wood, which had become jammed in the sides near the top, had not given her something to catch hold of at a point when otherwise she must have failed.

It took a long time to accomplish, and the grey dawn was stealing over the valley when the agonized girl, with bleeding hands and clothes torn, scrambled out of the hole which had been meant to be her tomb.

For a few moments she paused to breathe a thanksgiving for her escape, then she rose to her feet and hastened to get out of this dreadful garden.

Not till she had put a good quarter of a mile between herself and her late prison did Beatrice pause, and then she only did so because her twisted ankle gave her such intense agony.

Indeed it soon became evident that she could not proceed far upon foot, and at this early hour of the morning there was little hope of getting any kind of conveyance.

She sat down on a stone by the road a little while, then she mustered up her courage and went on again until she could no longer stand.

Beatrice rested awhile, and then again ventured a little further.

By this time the grey dawn had given place to morning, and this gave the wearied girl fresh courage, for she felt sure that before very long she would come to some roadside inn where she could obtain rest, food, and shelter.

Her hopes in this respect were at length realized. The landlord of the Fox and Grapes was just opening his shutters when the exhausted girl reached his door, and asked for breakfast and a room in which she could rest.

How she remained here under the care of the landlady, and how the next day she rode away to the nearest town, we have already heard through the enquiries which Godfrey Lascelles succeeded in getting answered up to this point, and it is consequently from the time of her leaving the Fox and Grapes that we must follow her.

Poor Beatrice had received a great mental shock, and she was likewise suffering physically from her injured ankle.

A strange feeling had come over her that she wanted rest and quiet, and with this desire came a disinclination to return to any of her friends.

Beatrice felt a considerable amount of anger and resentment against many people for not having sought for her, and this feeling was particularly strong with regard to Godfrey Lascelles.

"One would have thought that common decency would have made him take some steps to find out what had become of me," she thought with unaccountable perversity.

Then she gave her proud head an impatient toss, and resolved that as her friends took so little interest in her welfare, that she would not be in a hurry to communicate with them.

In excuse for this seemingly unfeeling and ungrateful conduct on the part of our heroine, it must be remembered that she had no near relatives, and but very few intimate friends, while, whatever their true sentiments might be, there was always a kind of feud existing between herself and her youthful guardian.

She was in this frame of mind when she reached the outskirts of Woolerton, a large manufacturing town, the smoke from whose myriads of chimneys went up to heaven and hung like a heavy cloud over the place.

"Where do you want to get down," questioned the man who drove the light trap in which she was seated.

"I will get down here, please," was the reply.

Then she alighted, paid the trifle agreed upon, and the man who had been her companion went on his way.

It was now comparatively early in the day, and Beatrice had meant to walk into the town, look about her, and stay at an hotel or take lodgings for a few days while she rested and made up her mind as to the course she would pursue.

But walking was a difficult matter; at every step she took the pain in her ankle seemed to become greater, and it soon become quite evident to herself that she must find shelter speedily.

A row of somewhat old-fashioned houses, however, with long gardens in the front and rear, attracted her attention, and see limped past them, looking eagerly at the windows of each house.

She soon found what she sought for, a card with the word "Apartments," upon it, and she walked up the garden and knocked at the door.

The woman who answered her knock was a motherly kind of body, with a keen eye and a smiling countenance.

She never asked for references with her lodgers, and she often boasted that she never once had been taken in by accepting a tenant who could bring discredit upon her.

On the present occasion Mrs. Birch took stock of Beatrice as the girl spoke to her, and, being satisfied with her appearance, invited the girl to come in and look at the rooms that were to let.

Very glad of an opportunity that would give her some rest for her bad ankle, Beatrice complied, and as soon as she was shown into the small but pretty sitting-room, she determined that she would remain here for a time.

The bedroom did not lead out of the sitting-room, but it was on the same floor, and she would therefore have no fatigue in reaching it.

So she soon came to terms with the landlady and paid a week's rent in advance, though she was informed that such a proceeding was quite unnecessary.

Then, with a sensation of intense relief she threw off her hat and lay down to rest upon a couch which was drawn up near the window.

The view from this window was dreary and bleak enough in winter, since it only overlooked the gardens.

A very high wall, covered with ivy, faced the houses, and between it and the garden railings ran the flagged pathway, which gave access to all the houses in the row, through which there was no thoroughfare.

The advantage or disadvantage of this *cul de sac* arrangement was, that any persons living at the extreme end of the row must pass before all the other houses before they could reach the main street.

In summer, however, the scene was very pretty, for the gardens were well kept, and were full of old-fashioned flowers which gave a certain homely beauty that no mere carpet gardening could impart.

Now, the beauty of summer was upon the place, clothing the earth with a garment of rich hues, and Beatrice as she reclined by the open window breathed the sweet perfume from the stocks and mignonette, and half fell asleep with fatigue and the sense of rest and security.

She was thus resting, gazing half-dreamily out upon the flowers, when she heard the tip-tap of small heels upon a stone pavement, and looking to see who the owner of the heels was, she perceived a young lady coming down the row, evidently from one of the higher houses.

The girl must pass the window by which Beatrice reclined, but our heroine's interest in her had ceased, and she would scarcely have looked at her again if she had not heard a woman's voice that was peculiarly musical humming a tune in subdued tones.

Something in the voice or in the tune struck upon Beatrice Burnham's ear as familiar, and she half raised herself and looked eagerly at the stranger.

But the girl's face was turned away from her, and she was intently reading some music she held in her hand.

The entrance of her landlady with a tray on which was her luncheon, gave Beatrice the opportunity to ask :

"Do you know that girl? Can you tell me her name ?"

"Yes, miss," was the reply; "that is Miss Kate Villiers, the actress."

"Does she live about here ?" was the girl's next question.

"Oh, yes, she lives at Number Thirty," was the answer.

Then the woman arranged the meal upon the table, asked if anything more was required and finally left the room.

But though the luncheon was tempting and Beatrice had previously been hungry, she ate but little, for a new set of ideas were roused in her mind, and more than once she muttered:

"Kate Villiers! If such a thing were probable, I should say it was Mary Trevor. But it isn't probable—it is scarcely possible."

Then she tried to dismiss the subject from her mind, but it could not easily be got rid of.

CHAPTER XLII.

RECOGNITION.

EATRICÉ was confined to her couch by the window for many days with her injured ankle.

Indeed, she would not have been able to leave her bed and walk across a room had not the landlady and her servant assisted her.

Despite her reluctance to do so, she was obliged to send for a doctor, and also she had to commission her landlady to go out and buy for her such necessary articles of dress as she required.

The doctor came, and looked grave—so grave, indeed, that his patient jestingly asked:

"Will it be long before I am able to dance again, doctor?"

"I'm afraid it will," he replied seriously. "You have sustained a very severe sprain. It would have been almost better if you had broken the bone, for that could have been re-set."

"I don't agree with you in that," she said cheerfully, "for if I had broken my leg I should probably have been dead by this time."

"Indeed! How did the accident occur?" was the natural question.

"I fell down a deep hole, and my foot must have doubled under me; but if the bone had been broken I could never have climbed out again, and there I should probably have remained. But how long do you think it will be before I can walk, doctor?"

"I am afraid to say," was the dubious answer; "so much will depend upon your remaining quiet and following my suggestions."

"Oh, I will be quiet enough," she responded, with a little grimace at the twinge of pain she was suffering.

"I suppose there is a good circulating library in the town?"

Mrs. Birch hastened to assure her that she could quickly obtain any book she desired, and then the doctor went away, puzzled with his new patient, yet interested in her in spite of himself.

More than once, as she lay on her couch by the window, looking at the flowers, breathing their perfume, and listening to the songs of the birds, Beatrice thought she would write to Ursula Raynham, and explain her failure to reach Rawfell Rectory when she was expected.

But when she came to think of what she should say, and how she should say it, she found the letter a most difficult one to write.

Moreover, she scarcely thought it safe to commit her story to paper, or to let even Ursula know her present hiding-place, lest she should inadvertently betray it to Frank Darlington.

It will be remembered that when Darlington was in the railway-carriage with her, travelling north, he said he was going to Rawfell on a visit, and she had no reason to doubt his statement.

For aught she knew, he might even now be at the rectory, and if she wrote to Ursula he would be sure to hear of it.

"I must hide from him until I am strong and able to move about freely and without pain," she thought; "but when I am once able to take steps for your punishment, Mr. Darlington, you may, as a sailor would say, look out for squalls."

For fear of Darlington discovering her, therefore, she did not write to Ursula, and it scarcely occurred to her mind to communicate with anybody else.

She had plenty of money with her, otherwise she might have written to Godfrey Lascelles, as her guardian, for fresh supplies, but she was still angry with the young barrister for not having met her on the day she passed through London, and it never occurred to her that he would perhaps never know she had not reached her intended destination unless the driver of the brougham, whom she had bribed, had delivered her pencilled note to the young man, or had sent it to him at his chambers.

"If he received that slip of paper he should have taken steps to rescue me," she thought in her present unreasoning frame of mind, "and if he didn't there is no necessity for my writing to him. Besides, I couldn't very well tell him on paper that another man had run away with me, it would look so much like vanity, and if I did not give the true reason for my conduct he would think I had started upon some independent strong-minded course which would be sure sooner or later to lead me into difficulties."

Reclining on her couch by the window, and having so little wherewith to interest and amuse her, Beatrice watched curiously for the girl whose voice and general appearance had reminded her so forcibly of Mary Trevor.

But oddly enough she never properly caught sight of her face, though she more than once saw the girl pass down the row.

Curiosity and want of occupation made Beatrice question her landlady about the actress, but Mrs. Birch could give her little or no information upon the subject.

"A very little of this kind of thing will be quite enough for me," thought Beatrice impatiently the third day after her residence in Bolton-row; "I wonder who that lady-like woman is who lives in the rooms above me, and who plays so exquisitely. I wish she would take pity upon me, and help me to pass some of the long days more easily."

Strangely enough the next day Miss Gillingham did pay our heroine a visit.

She came purely out of kindness, and because she fancied, from what Mrs. Birch told her, that the suffering girl was lonely and often dull.

In person she was exceedingly tall and not bad-looking, and she had a way of seeming to patronize everybody she conferred her society upon, which usually had the effect of intensely exasperating them.

Miss Gillingham's manner, however, failed to irritate Beatrice; on the contrary, it rather amused her than otherwise.

Our heroine had not volunteered any account of herself to Mrs. Birch, but she likewise made no attempt at mystery or concealment.

She gave her own name, she spoke of the part of the country where her home was, and she behaved with so much ease and confidence that anyone talking to her and seeing her would think it was considered the most ordinary thing in the world for a young lady, not quite of age, to be wandering about the world alone without so much as a hand-bag in the way of luggage.

Her ease of manner, her beauty, and her evident refinement, puzzled and interested the doctor, who was a widower, and he found himself paying very much more attention to his new patient that her case required.

Miss Gillingham also took a great interest in the fair invalid.

This stately lady was a daily governess consequently her time was not entirely at her own disposal, but in the evening she was always disengaged, and it was then that Beatrice came in for the benefit of her company.

Our heroine had been in this place more than a week, and she was beginning to feel that her conduct in not communicating with her friends was not exactly what it ought to be.

The inmates of Burnham Court must have heard before now that she had not reached Rawfell, and they would naturally be anxious about her, while, though she still felt vexed with Godfrey Lascelles, she could make some excuses for him, and she remembered also that it was possible he was seeking her.

Her sprained ankle was very much better, and she could limp about the room without suffering any acute pain.

She was thinking about writing to Lascelles and to her aunt at Burnham Court when Miss Gillingham came in from her daily avocation, looking pleased and elated, and with rather more of patronage in her manner than usual she said :

"My dear Miss Burnham, I propose a treat for you and myself this evening. The mother of my pupils has made me a present of a private box for the theatre to-night. It is Miss Kate Villiers' benefit, and the entertainment is to be the best the theatrical company can provide, for she is their principal star. You will come of course ? "

"I don't feel inclined to go to a theatre, thank you," was the reply, "and don't think the doctor would approve of my doing so, though I should like to see Miss Kate Villiers," she added thoughtfully.

"Well, here is the doctor," said Miss Gillingham, who never liked to be thwarted in any little plan that she might make; "we will ask him if you can go, and, by the way, we'll ask him to go with us."

"Oh, no, don't ask him to go," protested Beatrice. But before she could say any more the subject of their conversation was before them. The doctor himself was particularly thoughtful this afternoon.

He looked at Beatrice steadily, even critically; he answered Miss Gillingham's question at random; and finally in an abrupt awkward manner he took a newspaper from his pocket, and, handing it to his patient, asked :

"Do you care to look at this, Miss Burnham ? "

His manner struck her as singular, and she took the paper almost mechanically.

The first paragraph her eyes fell upon was the following :

"Missing since the 16th inst., a young lady." Then followed a pretty accurate description of herself, ending with an entreaty that B. B. would communicate with her friends if she were able to do so, while a handsome reward was offered to anyone who would give information that should lead to her discovery.

The address of Godfrey Lascelles, at the Inner Temple, was appended to this, and it might possibly have been this fact that made the girl thus advertised for so furiously indignant.

"One would think I was a lost sheep," she muttered under her breath, "or a pet animal that had gone astray. I won't write to him, there!"

And she flung down the paper quite regardless of the possibility that the doctor might be looking at her.

He was looking at her earnestly through a glass which reflected her face, while his own back was turned to her, and his suspicions were at once confirmed; she was the missing girl who was entreated to communicate with her friends.

It was Miss Gillingham's voice, however, that recalled these two people to the immediate present, for she said:

"We have arranged it all, dear. Dr. Bond will go with us to-night, there will be plenty of room in the box, and he will take care that you do not over-exert yourself."

"Very well," assented Beatrice.

Her mind was too full of the thoughts suggested by the advertisement for her to pay much heed to what her present companions thought or said.

She showed very little interest in the process of dressing, an hour or two later; indeed, as she frankly said, she had only one dress to wear; but as she was in deep mourning that was a matter of very little consequence.

Some white roses fastened in her dark, wavy, shimmering hair, and a smaller bunch at the throat were quite ornament enough.

So the doctor thought when he called in his carriage for the two ladies, and he took so much care of his fair patient as she leaned on his arm that Mrs. Birch smiled meaningly.

But Miss Gillingham did not respond to the smile even if she saw it.

She had plans of her own with regard to Dr. Bond, and though Beatrice was the excuse for asking for his society she was not too well pleased to observe his attentions to her fairer rival.

They reached the theatre at last, though Beatrice had more difficulty in walking than she had anticipated.

It was not a large house, but the place was well filled, for the actress for whose benefit the entertainment was given was a popular favourite.

But Beatrice paid little heed to the crowd of faces in the theatre or to the people upon the stage.

She was too self-absorbed and too angry with Godfrey Lascelles for advertising for her to be able to fix her attention upon anything that was going on around her.

Suddenly, however, she was startled by the sound of a voice that seemed like a cry from the past, and looking in the direction from whence it came, she herself uttered a low cry of surprised recognition.

"Mary Trevor," were the words that escaped her lips.

The actress looked at her for a moment, while her face became very pale, but she quickly recovered her self-possession, and went on with her part as though no interruption had occurred.

"It is Mary Trevor!" thought Beatrice positively. "I have found her at last, and I won't lose sight of her again. I wish I knew where to find that detective Longridge; he would be invaluable to me now."

Even as the idea passed through her mind, her eyes wandered to the pit of the theatre, and there steadily gazing at her was the very man of whom she thought.

CHAPTER XLIII.

MARY'S STORY.

"ARY, I have found you at last!"
The speaker was Beatrice Burnham, and the time and place were the actress's lodgings on the morning following that visit to the theatre.

The girl thus addressed paused in her occupation of packing her trunks, became pale and even agitated for a moment, but quickly recovered her self-possession and said steadily, while looking at her strange visitor calmly:

"You are the lady I saw in a private box last night at the theatre, and who interrupted me in my part; did you fancy you recognised me as some one you had known elsewhere?"

"Fancy!" repeated Beatrice in a bewildered tone, "there can be no fancy about the matter. You are Mary Trevor as surely as I am Beatrice Burnham."

"I cannot vouch for your name," was the answer, "but I can assure you that my name is not Trevor. My professional name you probably know, my real name cannot in the least concern you."

Beatrice stood aghast, staring blankly at the girl to whose identity she herself could have taken oath.

"It is impossible!" she exclaimed, sinking upon a chair, "impossible that you can be any other than my old friend Mary Trevor."

"Had you once a friend of that name?" asked the actress in a sympathetic tone.

"Yes," was the impulsive reply, "and I loved her better than most women love their sisters; she left her home suddenly and mysteriously, and I have sometimes feared that she had met with foul play. But I am determined to find her if I spend half my fortune in doing so."

She fixed her eyes so steadily and so intently upon the actress as she said this, that the latter asked:

"Do I very closely resemble your lost friend?"

"You are the image of her, except that her hair was black while your's is yellow, and she wore it flowing loosely about her shoulders, while you have it coiled tightly at the back of your head."

"Then we could not have been so very much alike?" was the answer, uttered, Beatrice fancied, in a tone of relief.

"The difference could easily be accounted for," was the significant retort.

"Then, rising suddenly from her seat, the heiress threw her arms round her companion, and said in an earnest pleading tone:

"Mary, why will you deny yourself to me? I love you sincerely. Trust me, dear; no friend can be more true to another than I will be to you. Denial is useless; you are Mary Trevor."

"I assure you that my name is not Trevor," replied the girl thus appealed to.

But she spoke in a fainter and less assured tone, and she shrank away from Beatrice, and was evidently anxious to escape further questioning.

Beatrice, however, was not to be put off in this manner; she had sought Mary Trevor too long and too persistently to be put aside by a trifle now she believed she had found her.

That it was really Mary Trevor who stood before her, our heroine had not the shadow of a doubt, though she was aged and looked as though she had suffered much since they parted that summer night about a year ago.

"You may have been married since we last met," Beatrice said quietly and sadly, "but I should doubt my own sanity if I believed you were any one but Captain Trevor's daughter; but if you wish to remain unknown I am sorry that I did not know it, for I have had a detective in my pay seeking for you for some months past."

"A detective!" cried the actress in sudden terror. "A detective looking after me!"

"Yes, he is in this town; he was in the theatre last night. I have seen him this morning, and he knows where you are; so you see denial of your identity is useless."

But the girl she addressed shrank upon a chair and seemed convulsed with terror.

"You pretend to love me," she moaned, "and you hunt me down as though you were my bitterest enemy. Why can't you leave me alone; I never injured you, and I am earning my living honestly. Why do you persecute me in this way?"

"Persecute you," repeated Beatrice in amazement. "Why should I persecute you, indeed! Nothing could be further from my thoughts; I have sought you because I suspected you had met with foul play, and I wanted to restore you to your home and your friends, and to punish the man, who, I believe, has wronged you as greatly as he has wronged me."

"Wronged you!" repeated the woman, who despite her denial was the one we have known as Mary Trevor. "How has he wronged you? He has not married you, has he?"

"No, thank Heaven!" was the earnest reply. "It requires the consent of two people for a marriage, and I would die before I would consent to be Frank Darlington's wife."

"Hush!" said the actress, looking about her fearfully; "don't mention that man's name. "You don't know of what he is capable; it is fear of him that has kept me from my father and friends."

"I thought as much," said Beatrice sadly. "You fear him so much that you are not glad to see me."

For a moment the reproachful words were unanswered, then the girl to whom they were addressed threw herself upon her companion's breast, sobbing and weeping bitterly.

Beatrice kissed her and soothed her, assuring her of her love and protection, and of her determination to punish the man who had brought so much suffering upon them both, and at length Mary grew calmer, and Beatrice succeeded with great difficulty in getting her to explain why she left her father's house, and how she came to be a member of a company of provincial actors.

"You promise to help and protect me?" she asked tremulously as she held our heroine's hand in her own.

"I do. I will spend my last shilling in your cause if need be," was the reassuring answer.

Mary sighed, then she said:

"I am weak and nervous when I think of the past and of what happened to me the night we parted outside my father's house, when you went away from me angry and disdainful, your faith in me shaken if not quite gone. Do you remember, Beatrice, how you turned from me?"

"Yes, dear, and I have regretted my hardness many times since then, and I thought to atone for it by finding you and making your life as happy as possible."

"Happy!" repeated Mary bitterly; "I shall never be happy again, but life is sweet, and the thought of death is terrible to me."

"Poor dear! but we must all die," said our heroine sadly.

"Yes, but we need not all die a violent death," returned the actress impatiently, "and that is what I escaped, and what I fear may yet happen to me; but listen."

"I am doing so, dear, but don't excite yourself," urged Beatrice.

Mary took no notice of her words, however, as she said:

"Frank Darlington and I were married eighteen months ago."

"Married!" repeated Beatrice.

"Yes, married," in a tone of surprise. "What other tie could make me so afraid of him?"

"I don't know; but pray go on."

"Our marriage was kept secret," Mary continued, "because Frank was dependent upon his father, who

expected him either to remain single or to marry a rich
wife. I was very much in love with my husband, and
I accepted his reasons for secrecy, and I might, in
all probability, have been living in my father's
house an unacknowledged wife down to the present
day, if Frank had not made love to Clarrie Burnham."

"Poor Clarrie is dead," here interposed Beatrice, who
feared something disagreeable might be said of her late
cousin.

"Dead, is she?" exclaimed Mary. "Then to whom
does Burnham Court belong?"

"To me."

"Ah! I understand. Then you were marked down
for his victim?"

"Yes, but I have escaped him, and I don't think
he will try to drug me again; but get on with your
story."

"I was naturally angry that my husband should be
reputed to be engaged to another woman," Mary continued, "particularly so as I knew that he made love to
her, and I began to fear that my own marriage was not
legal, otherwise, I argued, Frank would not dare to act
as he was doing. Foolishly enough I expressed my
doubts, and I threatened to tell my father and have the
whole matter made public. I was frantic with rage and
jealousy, and you know, Beatrice, I have a most un-
governable temper."

Beatrice smiled and Mary went on:

"Matters were getting very strained between us when
you came to Burnham Court. I was madly fond of my
husband, and every day I grew furious at his attentions
to Clarrie. More than once last year I was on the point
of making you my confidante, and of acting upon your
calmer judgment, but Frank threatened never to see
me again if I did so, but to go away and practically to
disown me as his wife; and, as I tell you, I was his slave,
though often a rebellious one."

"Poor child," said her friend soothingly; "I can
understand now many things that used to puzzle
me."

"You remember finding me in tears," Mary continued. "Frank had just left me."

"I saw him go," interrupted Beatrice; "it was that which first raised my suspicions, and that afterwards made me connect him with your disappearance."

"We had been having a stormy scene," said Mary; "he insisted that I should go to London and live there quietly until he could acknowledge our marriage. I had refused to do so, and he had uttered terrible threats which sounded like so many empty words to me then. I know now that they were something more."

"You had not promised to go?" asked Beatrice.

"No; I flatly refused, and he had left me in anger, and I was crying over my misery when you found me. He came again the same evening after you had gone, and his manner was kinder and more gentle, but his purpose was the same, to get me out of the way of my rich rival. The news you brought me that my father had met with an accident played into my treacherous husband's hands; he expressed sudden sympathy and great anxiety that I should go to my father at once, and said he would take me to Brookfield, where I could get a train for London which would not stop at Burnham."

"But Brookfield was five miles distant," objected Beatrice; "he did not suggest that you should actually walk all that way, did he?"

"Yes, it was too late to get a conveyance of any kind without attracting attention; besides, five miles did not seem a great distance to me, for I was a very good walker. Often enough Frank and I had walked together to Brent Wood; indeed, that was our usual place of meeting, unless my father happened to be away from home."

"Then you started soon after I left you?" asked Beatrice.

"Yes; and I only took a small hand-bag with me," was the answer, "for I expected to bring back my father the next day, and Frank suggested that if he were too much injured to be moved, I could send home for anything I required."

"Ah! Excuse my interrupting you, Mary, but did you write a letter to your father some time after you went away, saying you were married and happy, and begging him not to seek you?"

"Certainly not; from that night I never wrote or spoke to a creature who had previously known me, until you came here to-day. But did my father receive such a letter?"

"Yes, and I felt sure it was sent as a blind to prevent enquiries and investigations. But go on with your story. You went into Brent Wood, didn't you?"

"Yes, but how did you know?"

"Never mind; but you wore the gold ear-rings I gave you, and you lost one of them?"

"Lost one!" repeated Mary; "yes, and I almost lost my life at the same time; but you shall hear. When we reached the wood, which you know we had to pass on our way to Brookfield, Frank suggested that we should enter it and rest for a time at our old trysting-place. I was tired, and I had a presentiment that this would be our last walk together for a long time, so we went to the spot where we had so often met, and I seated myself upon the trunk of a fallen tree.

"But I felt depressed and nervous, every trifling sound startled me, and I remember that I sprang to my feet suddenly and said, 'Frank, I must get away from here; I feel as though something dreadful were about to happen to me.' He made no reply, but he caught me in his arms—to embrace me I thought, but his embrace meant death.

"In a moment he pressed his strong cruel hand upon my mouth so that I could not breathe, and the next instant a painful pressure on the side of my neck just below the ear was followed by the sensation of some warm liquid flowing down, which I now know to have been blood, and I fainted.

"Hours must have passed before I again became conscious, and then my senses only came back to me by slow degrees, for I seemed to be lying under some weight which I could not easily throw off. Gradually I grew stronger, till I at length got my face free from the loose particles that covered it, and then to my horror I discovered that I had been buried alive."

"Buried alive!" echoed Beatrice in horror.

"Yes, buried alive. Not in a coffin nor in a deep grave, or I should not be here to tell the story, but I had been thrown into a trench which ran down to the river, the bottom of which was usually wet, as it acted as a kind of drain, but it was dry enough then, for there had been no rain for some time.

"I had been covered with gravel, and leaves, and broken branches from the trees close by, and there I had undoubtedly been left for dead by the man who had sworn to love and cherish me."

"Was it light when you came to your senses?" asked Beatrice almost incredulously.

"Yes, but it was quite early in the morning," was the answer. "Thank Heaven, darkness was not added to all else that I had to bear!"

"And the wound on your neck?" was the next question.

"The wound was not a very serious one, as it afterwards turned out," replied Mary, "though it was within the eighth of an inch of the carotid artery, and the flow of blood, which could not have been great, was stopped by some dried leaves which had become stuck to the wound."

"What a mercy!" ejaculated our heroine.

"Yes, it was a mercy," assented Mary, "though I scarcely regarded it as such then. Indeed my mind was incapable at the time of any sensation but that of absolute terror.

"Some women would have been filled with resentment, and would have punished the wretch, who had tried to kill them, but I had no feeling of the kind—my only terror was that my husband would find me, and that having previously failed to take my life, he would make the attempt again, perhaps with greater success. The fear clings to me still," she added piteously; "that was why I denied myself to you, Beatrice; he left me for dead, and I wish him to believe that I have ceased to live."

And she buried her face in her hands and trembled with agitation.

Beatrice tried to calm and console her poor friend, but it was some time before she succeeded, and at length, with the view of rousing her, she asked :

"But you have not told me how you became an actress, nor why you did not return to your father's house."

"Fear of my husband kept me away from my home and my friends," was the reply ; "but how I became an actress—such an actress as I am," with a smile of disdain, "is a long story, though I will try to tell it to you in a few words.

"Directly I could use my limbs, I made my way out of the wood, and walked along the high road to Brookfield railway-station.

"My one thought was to get away from any place where my husband was likely to come.

"I asked for a ticket for the first place that came into my head, for I was dazed and bewildered, and I got into the first train that came into the station.

"I don't quite know where it took me, and I think I rather lost my head at this time, for I am told that I was found at mid-day, sitting in a country lane by a hedge, plucking wild flowers like a second Ophelia.

"The man who found me like this is the manager and principal actor of our company. He took me home to his sister, who is also an actress, and when they heard me sing they pressed me to join them."

"Is that handsome young man who took the leading male character last night the manager ? "

"Yes, and the stout lady who did the sentimental business is his sister. She is married."

"Is he married also ? "

"No."

Before Beatrice could ask another question, there was a tap at the door of the sitting-room in which the girls were talking, and on its being opened, Beatrice saw, to her amazement, the handsome manager, while by his side stood Godfrey Lascelles.

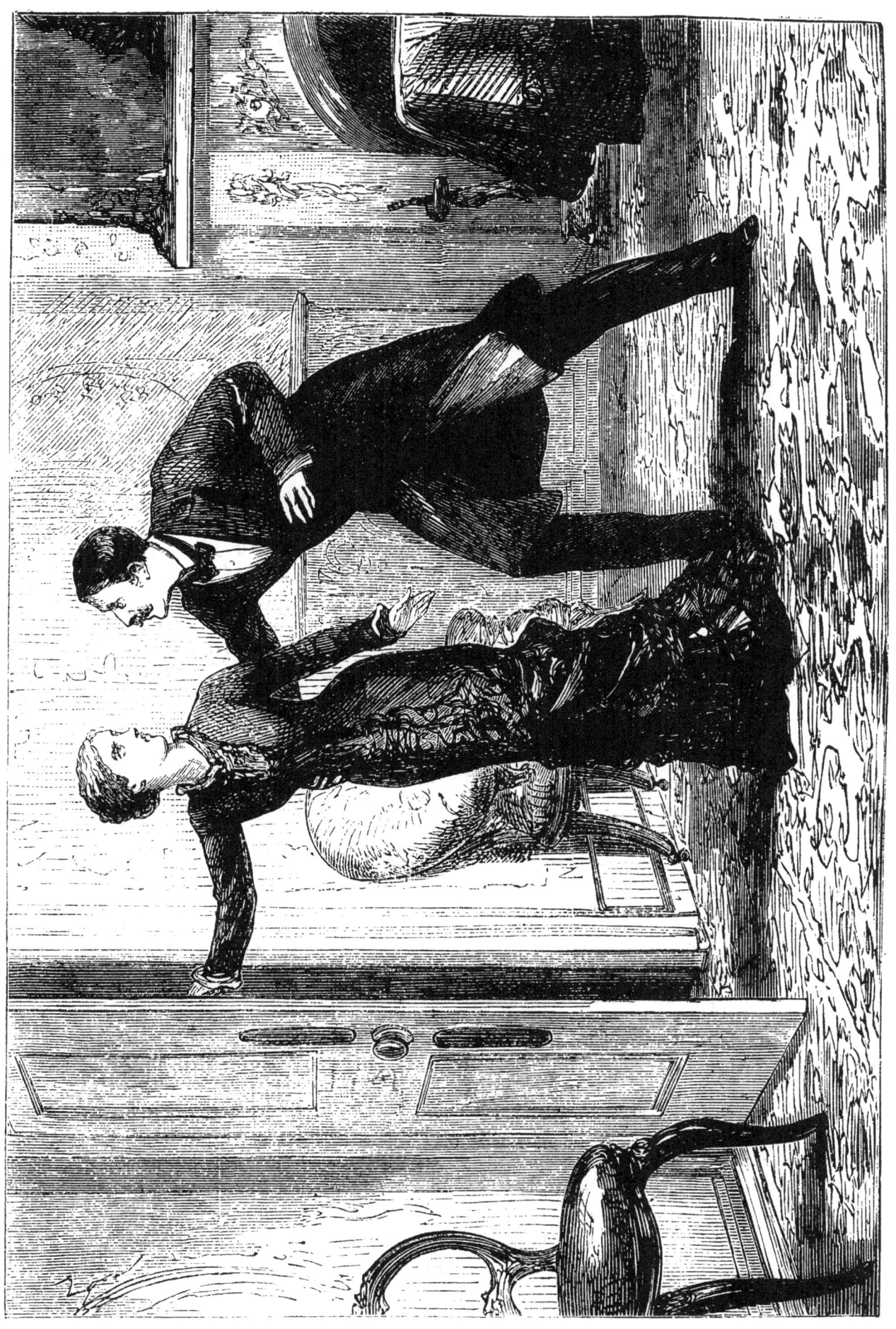

"COME, FANNY, DON'T BE DISAGREEABLE. I AM IRRITABLE TO-DAY, I KNOW, BUT I HAVE HAD A GOOD DEAL TO TRY ME OF LATE"

CHAPTER XLIV.

CLOSING IN.

"DO you think you have behaved quite fairly to your friends, Miss Burnham, and more particularly towards me, your guardian?" asked Godfrey Lascelles, some half-an-hour after he had appeared at the door of Mary's sitting-room.

"I think I have behaved as well to my friends as they have to me," was the retort. "None of them cared what had become of me, and none of them sought me; I was deprived of my liberty by a scoundrel, and I have to thank a merciful Providence and no individual friend for my freedom and present safety."

"You are rather rash in your statements," replied the young man, bitterly; "you say that none of your friends sought you, perhaps you do not count me among the number, but as I am still your guardian I thought it my duty to seek you, and I have neglected everything else to do so. Fortescue Grantly and Archibald Raynham have likewise spent their time in the same search ever since we learnt that you had not reached Rawfell."

"It was very kind of them," said the girl, disdainfully.

Then, with a sudden change of manner and with her usual frankness, she added:

"I don't think I have been grateful or considerate, Mr. Lascelles, but I feel so thoroughly desolate, there seemed to be nobody in the whole world upon whose affection or kinship I had the least claim, and I suffered so much that when I got to this humble refuge, without the aid of friend or foe, I felt as though I should like to hide myself from everybody. You don't know what happened to me, or how I was taken away by violence by Frank Darlington and kept a prisoner by two dreadful women, nor how I nearly lost my life by being thrust down a disused well."

" I think I do," he said, gravely.

And then he told her how he had sought her, and how he and young Grantly had traced her from Scarsdale after her escape from the well.

" I was beginning to fear you had fallen into some fresh trouble," he added, " for though we followed you to this town we could learn nothing more about you, but last night Grantly turned into the theatre for half-an-hour, and he came back to the hotel to me with the startling news that he had seen you in a private box with a lady and gentleman, and that the actress for whose benefit the performance was given was no other than Mary Trevor who had disappeared so mysteriously from Burnham a year ago."

" Oddly enough, as I was coming to call upon you this morning, I met Graham the actor and recognised him as an old acquaintance. I questioned him about Kate Villiers, as she calls herself, and he told me the little he knew of her and offered to introduce me. I accepted and accompanied him at once, as she and the rest of the company were going away from Woolerton to-day. The rest you know. I was saved any further trouble in seeking you by finding you with Miss Trevor."

" I am sorry you should have taken so much trouble on my behalf," said Beatrice, bitterly.

Godfrey Lascelles turned away to hide the pain and vexation that her words caused him.

It was strange how he and Beatrice seldom spent ten minutes in each other's society without jarring and getting into a skirmish of sharp speeches, which both of them regretted and resented afterwards.

And yet, though they were continually sparring and almost quarrelling, they each had a certain subtle attraction towards the other that they rebelled against and resolutely tried to ignore.

On the present occasion Godfrey was more pained than he cared to admit.

His anxiety for her safety had absorbed all minor considerations, and he had, he now told himself, been perilously near falling in love with her.

"She has saved me from that crowning folly, and the probable humiliation that would follow," he thought grimly as he turned away that she might not see how her words had stung him.

When he spoke again his voice was cold and business-like, as he said:

"Since you are so well able to take care of yourself, Miss Burnham, I shall return to London to-day. I don't suppose it is necessary for me to remind you that you will attain your majority next month, and that it will be necessary for me to see you on your birthday, so please let me know where you are when that time arrives, that I may set you free from the very slight control which I have exercised over your property rather than over yourself."

"Of course I will tell you where to meet me," said Beatrice, who was already beginning to repent of her ungrateful words, "but I wanted to talk with you about — about the conditions of my father's will, Mr. Lascelles."

"There is not the least necessity for any discussion upon that subject," he said hastily.

"But there is necessity for it," Beatrice quickly exclaimed; "half of my father's property was to be yours if—if—And Burnham Court has come to me since," she went on, overcoming her difficulty by leaving the words which she should have uttered unspoken.

"You will not be asked to pay such a heavy penalty for exercising a woman's privilege," he said with such grave dignity that the proud impulsive girl felt as though she had received a blow.

For Godfrey Lascelles' words and manner clearly told her that not for all her wealth would he ask her to be his wife, and that, to secure half of her fortune, he would not risk the chance of being accepted as her husband.

At another time she would have treated the matter more lightly, for she had always thought he cared for her, and she had presumed upon the supposition, and had often tried to torment him with a view of finding out the real state of his feelings towards her.

Hitherto he had baffled her, and all her little surprises had failed to tell her what she wished to know with absolute certainty.

Now she felt that there was no longer a question to be solved.

It was quite evident that she had deceived herself all along.

Godfrey would have nothing to do with her or with her money ; for her father's sake he had acted as her guardian, and she felt sure he was almost counting the days until he should be relieved of such a troublesome ward.

She was deeply mortified, and not a little pained, but she would have died rather than he should have read her true feelings, and she now roused herself with a great effort to say with some of her old smiling audacity :

"I wouldn't refuse the money that my father so clearly intended should be yours if I were you. I promise you that it will be perfectly safe for you to place yourself in a position to take it."

"Thank you, I don't doubt that it would," he replied coldly, "but we need not pursue the subject ; there is nothing that I can do in Woolerton to add to your comfort before I return to London, I suppose ?"

"Indeed there is," she replied, "I want to tell you Mary Trevor's story, and to ask your advice as to the punishment of the man who has behaved so imfamously to that poor girl and to me."

"I don't suppose that my advice will be of much use to you, or that you will follow it when it is given," he replied gloomily.

And he looked at his watch as though he would imply that time was precious, but he sat down on a chair nevertheless, and Beatrice without further waste of words told him what she had just heard from poor Mary, in addition to an account of her own abduction.

"Now, what course do you advise ?" she asked, when she had finished her narrative.

"What have you decided upon ?" was his question, with something like a smile in his eyes, though his face otherwise was serious enough.

"You think I make up my mind as to what I will do and then ask your advice afterwards, meaning only to follow it if it accords with my own sentiments," she said hotly.

"You would not be singular in taking such a course," he replied, "but tell me how far you are yourself inclined to go; do you wish to make the villain's conduct public ? "

"Well, no; I am not certain. I don't want to have Mary's name or my own connected with his in any way."

"You had better think only of yourself," said the barrister dryly; "if your friend is Darlington's wife, his disgrace is her disgrace, and she will get but little redress for his ill-usage of her. I suppose she can prove her marriage ? "

"She says she can; but here is Longridge the detective coming up the garden. We will take him into our council; he spoke very mysteriously this morning about certain things which he could prove against my enemy if desirable."

"I don't believe in the man," growled Lascelles. "I took matters out of his hands and started to seek you without him."

"Yet he found me first," retorted the girl with a smile; "but he is necessary to us at present, so pray tolerate him."

Before Godfrey could reply, Mr. Longridge stood before him.

There was a gleam of triumph in the man's eyes as he bowed to the barrister and said :

"You and I kept pace pretty closely, sir; you'd make a better detective than I first thought, when we started on this business together."

"It's very kind of you to say so," returned Lascelles sardonically.

The man never noticed the sneer, but continued in the same patronising tone:

"Yes, sir; you went about your work in a very tidy manner, but you see I'm an old hand at the business, and that's how I've got a march ahead of you. But we've no time to waste in talking; our quarry is in a tight place, and he may turn at bay or quietly make away with himself; there's no saying what a man like that will do."

"I thought you said we had no time to waste in talking, said the barrister significantly.

"No more we have, sir," replied the man; "so now, if you please, to business."

The business took a long time in discussing; the result of it was, however, that Godfrey Lascelles and Fortescue Grantly did not go to town alone that day, for our heroine and Captain Trevor's daughter travelled in the same carriage with them, where they arrived in due course.

The contents of Frank Darlington's pocket-book, which Longridge had found revealed several secrets which it would otherwise have taken the detective a long time to ferret out, and among these precious papers was the licence to marry Beatrice Burnham, of Burnham Court, which it will be remembered he obtained from Doctor's Commons a little less than a week before he carried her off.

Our heroine's indignation on seeing this was very great, and she was somewhat irritated with Godfrey Lascelles who remarked cynically:

"The fellow seems to be a second Bluebeard, and to go in for a large consumption of wives. I wonder who he will be trying to marry next?"

None of his companions caring to speculate upon the matter the subject dropped, and soon afterwards, the detective having previously gone, Godfrey Lascelles likewise went away, leaving the two girls together.

They had gone to Beatrice's house in town, in the dingy square where we first met her, and Mrs. Gray had been telegraphed for to come and stay with them since it was not our heroine's intention to return at present to Burnham Court.

The square was anything but dingy now, however; the fine old trees in it were covered with foliage, while bright flowers gave colour to the place.

Godfrey had been thoughtful enough to send telegrams to Rawfell Rectory and to Burnham Court announcing that Beatrice was safe, and thus our heroine after the exciting scenes she had gone through, seemed to have been thrown back into the old quiet life she had led immediately after her father's death.

Mary was her companion, but Mary was changed, and Beatrice was reluctantly obliged to admit that the change was not an improvement.

The roving life she had led as a provincial actress had unfitted her for the quiet everyday existence she had come back to, and she was always wondering how her old friends were getting along without her.

"I don't think I shall ever settle down to private life again," she said one day to Beatrice as the two girls sat in the drawing-room looking out into the garden of the square, waiting for a promised visit from the detective.

Beatrice looked at her friend and sighed as she said :

"I am sorry for it; you would be so much happier I think if you could make up your mind to live with me."

"Live with you dear," laughed Mary; "how long should I live with you? Of course you will soon get married, and then I should be in the way; that handsome barrister and you quarrel far too much not to be in love with each other."

"Indeed, Mary, I hope you will never breathe such a thought again," said Beatrice with flaming cheeks and a great assumption of dignity; "nothing is more improbable, nothing more impossible I might say, than a marriage between Mr. Lascelles and myself. I am the very last woman in the world that he would think of marrying, and I——"

But Mary's very incredulous laughter made the completion of the protest impossible.

Fortunately at this juncture Mr. Longridge was announced, otherwise something like an angry discussion might have followed between the two friends.

His information, however, was startling enough to drive all minor subjects from the minds of the listeners.

He came to tell them that Frank Darlington was going to marry Fanny Raynham on the following Tuesday.

"Good Heavens! the marriage must be prevented," cried Beatrice indignantly.

"Prevented I think it will be," said the detective grimly; "it's time we put a stop to my gentleman's little games. I think I've got evidence enough now to shut him up for a few years at any rate."

"I wish we could avoid a public scandal," said Mary nervously; "as far as I am concerned I only wish to get legally free from the man; he might then marry any woman he likes for me."

"I think you'll be able to get a divorce any way, ma'am, if you're so inclined," replied the man, "but I think it will be best to stop this marriage."

"Of course it will," said Beatrice decidedly; "Fanny is not a girl deserving of much sympathy, but she must not be deceived like this. Had we better try to communicate with her?"

"No, ma'am; best leave things to me. I'll arrange it all, never fear; there's just a little matter in the way of a forged bill that I haven't got quite clear yet."

Mary protested against delay, and she even pleaded for mercy for the man who had so deeply wronged her.

That her plea was selfish, because she feared the disgrace that might come upon herself, was quite evident, and Mr. Longridge was in no wise inclined to have what he considered a fine case spoiled by any sentimental nonsense.

But even detectives may be at fault in the way of time, and it was, as we have seen, only at the last minute that Mary, accompanied by Beatrice, appeared in the church to stop the marriage ceremony.

The bride would have protested, but the bridegroom was insensible, and when those nearest tried to lift him they looked gravely upon his white face for they thought he was dead.

CHAPTER XLV.

FANNY'Y FOLLY.

RANK DARLINGTON was not dead.
They carried him into the vestry, and after a while they succeeding in restoring him to consciousness, but by this time the clock had struck twelve, and it was quite certain that there could be no marriage that day, even if the ceremony had been interrupted without good cause.

But that there was good cause for it, Lady Grantly knew directly she saw Beatrice Burnham, while, at the same time, she was not a little mystified as to who her companion might be.

"You here!" she said, grasping our heroine warmly by the hand. "You are not married to him, are you?"

"No. I should have been glad to forget it if I had been," was the answer. "This is Mrs. Darlington."

And she turned to Mary, who lifted her heavy veil from her face and was immediately recognised by Lady Grantly.

"Ah!" cried the baronet's wife quickly, addressing Mary, "I always thought there was something between you and Frank, but this is no place for explanations; let us get away as soon as possible. Come, Fanny."

And she turned to her younger sister, who had been standing by, looking like a woman suddenly turned to stone; offering no protest and showing no excitement or emotion.

Lady Grantly repeated her words, and took a step forward, an action that roused the girl who was almost a bride.

A swift shudder passed over her frame, and her teeth chattered as if with freezing cold.

In another instant, however, this chill was succeeded by a rush of fiery heat. Her usually pale face burned, her pale grey eyes blazed with rage, and her whole form became dilated with over-mastering passion.

"Come!" she repeated hoarsely; "come with you and with those women who want to rob me of my husband! No; I will not come with any of you; my place is by his side, and none of you shall take me from him!"

And she turned to go to the man to whom she had given her whole heart, yet who in very truth cared less than nothing for the gift.

"Fanny!" said Lady Grantly, in a low stern tone, and taking her sister's wrist in her own with a firm grasp, "Fanny! recollect yourself. Frank Darlington has a wife living; he cannot marry you. To go with him now is to openly disgrace yourself before all the world."

The girl thus addressed wrenched her wrist from her sister's grasp, and replied in a low hissing tone of defiance:

"What do I care for disgrace, or for what the world may think of me? I care only for him, and I will not leave him; wife or no wife I will cling to him while I live."

And so saying she went resolutely over to Frank Darlington's side and quietly expressed her intention of going with him wherever he went.

Geraldine Grantly looked after the erring girl whom she had so patiently and earnestly tried to save, and her heart was filled with despair as the conviction forced itself upon her mind that the sister for whom she had felt so much love was beyond redemption.

For a few seconds she hesitated, wondering whether it would be of the least use to make another appeal; then she turned away sick at heart with pain and disappointment.

Beatrice and Mary had walked out into the churchyard, leaving the sisters together, and were holding a somewhat animated conversation with Mr. Longridge.

"Let me clap him in prison for eight-and-forty hours miss, and I ask no more," the detective was urging ; "you can withdraw the charge afterwards if you like, I shall have enough against him to give him a pretty spell of penal servitude by that time ; but I daren't take my eyes off him while he is free, and I can't trust my case to any other man to finish. Only let me know that he can't escape me, and I'll put a stop to his little game for another five years, I promise him."

But Beatrice shook her head resolutely as she replied :

"No; I will not go into a police-court to prosecute him, neither will I have my name in the newspapers if I can help it. I should like the man to be punished, but I have too great a regard for my own comfort to do as you propose."

The detective looked at the young lady with an expression in which rage and despair struggled with each other for the mastery.

He possessed all the natural instincts of the blood-hound, and having once scented his prey he would pursue him for the very love of the chase until he had hunted him down.

On the present occasion he was irritated beyond expression by what to himself he termed the sentimental nonsense of a couple of women who would not do as he wished them.

Finding it useless to waste further time in persuading Beatrice to prosecute the man who had carried her away against her will, Mr. Longridge turned to Mary and tried his eloquence upon her with the same ill success.

"No," she said nervously ; "I don't want to have anything more to do with him, but I will not injure him if I can help it ; it was to save Miss Raynham rather than to punish him that I came here and stopped the wedding this morning."

"I wish it hadn't been stopped," growled the man savagely, "for we could then have put our hands upon him for bigamy, though it might have needed somebody to prosecute him even then," he added thoughtfully.

"You had better leave the man alone, Mr. Longridge," said Beatrice decisively. "After the exposure of to-day, he will, in all probability, mend his ways. In any case, he is pretty sure not to trouble us any more. When a man like that is found out he ceases to become dangerous. Leave him alone; that is my desire, and yours, too, is it not?" she asked turning to Mary.

"Yes," was the reluctant reply. "If I could get a divorce from him I should be glad, but I fear that is not possible."

"It's quite possible, and I'll ensure your getting it, if you'll only follow my advice now," said the detective eagerly.

Mary looked at Beatrice, but perceiving disapproval on her face, she replied :

"No, I can't do it. A divorce would cost a great deal of money, and I have none."

Mr. Longridge was conscious that his countenance fell as he heard this.

Money was essential to the success of any case, let justice be ever so strong upon your side, and it was quite evident that Beatrice would not provide the sinews of war in this one.

"Lady Grantly came out of the church at this point, and joined the group, looking curiously at the detective who looked superior to a servant, and yet was evidently not a gentleman.

Beatrice observed the questioning glance, and she said to the man in a tone of dismissal :

"You had better leave matters as they are, Mr. Longridge."

And she was turning away to speak to Geraldine, when the detective said quietly but firmly :

"I can't do that, miss; it's against my principles to leave a case half-finished, so if you ladies won't help me, I must work alone."

Then he touched his hat and walked away, though he did not go so far as to lose sight of the vestry entrance of the church.

"What an odd-looking man!" remarked Lady Grantly, following Longridge with her eyes.

"He is a detective," replied Beatrice. "It was he who brought us here this morning."

"A detective!" echoed her ladyship in alarm.

Then she tried to collect her thoughts and regain her usual composure, though this was a difficult matter at the moment, for the unpleasant reflection occurred to her mind that she had engaged to compound a felony.

It was not a pleasant predicament to be in, and only her desire to save Fanny from further disgrace would have induced Geraldine to borrow so large a sum of money as to be able to pay and get possession of the forged and dishonoured bill.

But she had done so, and the bill itself was in a private drawer in her own desk at Grantly Park.

She had meant to keep the compromising slip of paper for two reasons; first of all that she might be able to have Darlington in her power in case be should be unkind to Fanny when he had married her; and, secondly, in her ignorance of all business matters, she thought it a kind of receipt for the six hundred pounds she had paid for it.

For she had very distinctly stated that she was only lending this money until old Squire Darlington died, and had not the least intention of giving it.

That the bill was safe enough she had no doubt, but she reflected that it would be an ugly story to come to light, that she had endeavoured to force a man who was helplessly in her power to marry her sister.

And she at once resolved that directly she reached home she would either burn the bill and sacrifice the money paid for it, or that she would send it to Fortescue Grantly and ask what he knew of it.

To take this last course would, she believed, result in the arrest of the man who could not marry her sister, and her ladyship would have had no hesitation in taking it, if she could only make quite sure of securing herself from blame.

But she dismissed the matter from her mind now.

There would be time enough to come to a decision when she reached home.

A few words made Beatrice acquainted with Fanny's resolve not to be separated from the man who was to have married her, and even as the ladies spoke together, Frank Darlington, with Fanny clinging to his arm, came out.

Impulsive as of old, and forgetful for the moment of how deeply this man had tried to wrong her, and of how intensely the girl by his side hated her with an envious, jealous hatred, Beatrice stepped forward, stood before the guilty pair, and said:

"Fanny, come with your sister and with me, I entreat you: if you knew half the wickedness of that man, you would shrink from him with loathing. He does not love you, he is utterly incapable of true and unselfish affection."

"You at least have no right to say that," said Darlington in a reproachful tone; "whoever else I may have been false to, I have loved you truly enough, and villain though you think me, I am more thankful than words can express to know that you are alive and safe."

Beatrice made a disdainful motion with her hand as she said:

"Now, Fanny, after what you have just heard, you cannot wish to go with this man. Do be persuaded; do come back to your sister or to me."

"Yes, go," said Darlington, letting the arm which Fanny clung to drop by his side. "Go with them; you will be safer and more comfortable than with me."

But the girl thus adjured stood sullenly by his side, as she said:

"I will not go with Geraldine; I will go with you. Your home shall be my home."

Darlington made no reply, he was looking at Beatrice with pleading eyes, but, gaining no response from her he turned away, silently allowing Fanny to accompany him.

And thus the two who should have been married entered a cab and were driven away, but not so rapidly that Mr. Longridge could not follow them.

"Come home with us, Geraldine," said Beatrice, leading the way to the brougham in which she and Mary had arrived at the church; "we have two such terrible stories to tell you, and it is but right that you should know them."

"I don't know how to spare the time," returned the baronet's wife with some hesitation; "Sir Graham has been very ill, but he is getting better, and he will think I am neglecting him."

"An hour can't make much difference," was the reply; "of course, he would know that coming to town would take up the best part of a day."

"He doesn't know that I have come to town," said Geraldine; "but to quote an old proverb, 'one may as well be hung for a sheep as a lamb.' I do want to hear what had become of both of you when you were missing, and in addition, I am so sad about Fanny, that I really don't like to go home without making another effort to save her."

Beatrice could not help thinking that if Fanny had been her sister, and acting in the same spirit, she would from henceforth avoid her name and utterly ignore the fact that such a woman existed, but she would not recommend this harsh course to another, so she made no comment, but led the way to the carriage.

Fully three hours afterwards, Lady Grantly rode in the same carriage to Victoria Station, hoping to catch a train for which she knew she was late.

She was just in time to see it go out of the station, and to have the pleasant consciousness that she had two good hours to wait before the next train started.

Mary and Beatrice had both of them told her of Frank Darlington's villainy and of their own narrow escape with their lives from him, or from those in his employ, and Lady Grantly's mind was so full of what she had heard, that she was scarcely sorry to be able to sit in a quiet corner of the waiting-room and think it all over.

"Such a man must not be at large," she decided at length; "one owes it to society to shut up such a wretch. I am glad now that I have the bill; I will send for Fortescue and leave him to vindicate himself."

Then she thrust her hand into her pocket for the small bunch of keys which opened her desk, her secretaire, and other private receptacles.

But the keys were gone.

This circumstance completely roused her, and she began to imagine a hundred things that might have happened.

Her first thought was that her pocket had been picked, but as her purse was safe this could not be the case, and at last she came to the conclusion that she had left the keys behind her when she left home in the morning.

"I hope my maid has not found them," she thought with a feeling of vexation at her own carelessness. "Happily Sir Graham is not likely to get hold of them."

But the very idea of such a possibility produced a feeling of discomfort, and she was nervous and anxious.

Not without good cause either.

CHAPTER XLVI.

AN EXPLOSION.

SIR GRAHAM GRANTLY was in his wife's boudoir when she returned home, and here he met her before she could take off her bonnet or her travelling-dress.

So little trace of his recent illness remained about him that her ladyship exclaimed in surprise.

"What can have happened to you, dear? You look better than you have done for months past."

"It is time that I felt well, whatever I may look, madam," was the chilling reply; "be good enough to take a seat and answer me a few questions."

Geraldine Grantly looked in blank surprise at her husband for a second or two.

The trying day she had gone through had completely unnerved her, while her husband's present tone and manner were such as he would only have dared to use in accusing her of some serious misconduct.

Her first impulse in this excitable condition was to sink into the nearest chair, and indulge in, to her, unusual exhibition of a fit of hysterics.

A moment's thought told her, that to yield to this weakness would be like pleading guilty to any charge that might be made against her, and she knew her husband's character too well not to be conscious that he would be merciless upon the weak, while he would shrink and hesitate before the courageous and strong.

But wearied and worried as she was, it required all the nervous energy she could command to steady her voice and control herself sufficiently to say:

"I will answer as many questions as you like when I have had some tea. Just ring the bell, will you; I have a splitting headache."

Sir Graham looked at his wife in amazement at her coolness, then he said hotly :

"You will have no tea in this house, for no servant shall obey your orders, and you shall not spend another night under this roof unless you can satisfy me that you have not been carrying on a shameless intrigue with my nephew Fortescue."

"Intrigue!" repeated her ladyship, passing her hands over her forehead as though she would press the idea into her head, then mechanically removing her bonnet. "Intrigue, did you say?"

"That was the word I used," returned the baronet, seeming to increase in size and stature as he felt his wife was at his mercy; "would you like me to put it in coarser language?"

"No, thank you, you are coarse enough at the best of times," she retorted with a sneer, as she quietly seated herself in her favourite chair, "but if I am not to have any tea until you have finished saying what you have to say, it will be well to make haste, otherwise I shall order it myself, and I should like to see the servant in this house who would refuse to obey me."

These last few words she said in a tone which told her husband she was not to be trifled with, while the light in her pale grey eyes made him feel that it was possible for her to be dangerous.

"There," he said, throwing the missing bunch of keys upon the table, "there are your keys, madam. You did not intend to leave them behind you, did you?"

"No; but when I discovered that I had done so, I had no doubt that you would use them if they fell into your hands," she replied disdainfully; "and you have used them."

"I have," he said, but he was taken aback by her coolness, and for the first time since he had ransacked her desk, he began to doubt the soundness of his own conclusions upon what he had found there.

"And what did you find?" she asked, guessing pretty well what the answer be.

"I found that, madam!" and he flourished the forged acceptance for six hundred pounds in her face.

"Precisely!" she said calmly. "You found that in the private drawer of my desk; what do you make of it?"

"What do I make of it?" he repeated aghast at what he considered her shameless audacity. "I make this of it, you worthless woman and faithless wife: my scoundrel of a nephew has forged my name, and you, to save him from the consequences of his crime, have provided the money. I have even ascertained where you borrowed this six hundred pounds."

"You might have known that by asking me," she replied calmly, though her anger was becoming every instant greater and hotter. "I did pay six hundred pounds for that bill," she went on slowly, "and if you had chosen to ask me quietly why I had done so, I should in all probability have told you. But instead of doing so you have in the most astounding manner made a shameful charge against me, and have called me a name which no woman with any self-respect would ever forgive her husband for applying to her when her conduct has been as blameless as mine. I shall not forgive it, and I shall leave your house to-morrow morning never to return, and now, perhaps, you will leave me. We have said all that it necessary we should say, the lawyers will do the rest."

"And you have no explanation to offer me?" asked the baronet, so completely astonished by his wife's words and manner as to change his own tone, and to be even ready for a reconciliation if she would only give him some excuse for it, and also allow him time to save his dignity.

"None," was the indignant reply. "If you had asked me for an explanation at first, I would have given it, but instead of doing so you offer me the greatest insult possible, and that too, without the least ground for the accusation.

"You have not found a love letter addressed to me from any man, nor have you discovered a single line that could in any way compromise me, and yet you have undertaken to play the *role* of the wronged husband, and that without first making a single enquiry. But further discussion is useless; henceforth you will go your way, and I shall go mine. Our marriage was a mistake from the first; I ought to have known better than to marry a man old enough to be my grandfather."

"The mistake was a terrible one on my part," cried the irritated baronet; "I married a girl without a penny, thinking to win her gratitude, and this is the result."

"Yes, this is the result," echoed Geraldine; "Beatrice Burnham was wiser than I."

Then she turned to leave the room, being well aware how any allusion to his rejection by Beatrice annoyed him.

He called after her, but she paid no heed to him; the more she thought of the insulting words he had addressed to her, the more bitterly she resented it, and she determined that she would give her husband a pretty hard lesson on the respect due to herself before she consented to forgive him.

That he had been slightly jealous of his nephew she had long since known, but that his jealousy should suddenly take such a decidedly unpleasant form rather startled her.

However, it was useless crying over what she could not cure, and she was in addition too completely worn out with the fatiguing events of the day to try to realise the position in which her dispute with her husband would probably place her.

She had taken one of the guest-chambers as her own room during her husband's illness, and therefore even those keen inquisitors, the servants, were not surprised at her retiring to it on this occasion.

Her own maid was a little annoyed the next morning by being called at an unusually early hour, and the coachman was not well pleased at being required to drive his mistress to the railway-station to catch the very first train to London.

But all this was done, and the coachman had returned with the carriage to Grantly Park before Sir Graham awoke.

He had been unable to sleep until daylight dawned, and then he had fallen off into such deep slumber that his servant had not cared to wake him.

The consequence was that his wife had accomplished more than half of her journey to London before the baronet knew that she had left the house.

Now that it was too late to recall her, Sir Graham would gladly have apologised for the expressions he had used on the previous night : but, though he would have taken Geraldine back to her rightful position, he now felt, if possible, more incensed than ever, against his nephew, who had, he considered, been the means of dividing them.

Had Sir Graham possessed his usual keen insight into character and circumstance, and had he not temporarily lost his good judgment, he would have accredited some other person with the forgery of the acceptance of the bill, if for no other reason than because his nephew was not a needy man.

But the baronet was incapable at this time of forming a cool and unbiassed opinion, and when he found his wife had left his house, he at once sent off a groom with a telegram for his solicitor.

Meanwhile, Lady Grantly reached town, and taking a cab, she at once drove to Beatrice Burnham's house in D'Eyncourt-square.

Here she found our heroine seated at her solitary breakfast, Mary Darlington, as we may as well call her now, being still in bed, where her breakfast was taken to her.

That her reception would be warm and sincere Lady Grantly had no doubt, and she had in addition great faith in Beatrice's good judgment; so, after a short time, she unfolded her whole story to her and asked her advice.

"Stay here with me until Sir Graham comes to his senses," was the answer ; "and, as for the forged bill, if I were you I should let matters take their own course.

You can't save Frank Darlington if you would, and I shall be glad to know that he will be punished for one of his crimes."

"But what will become of Fanny?" Geraldine replied by asking..

"What has become of her?" retorted Beatrice. "Do you think you could save a woman like Fanny, in spite of herself?"

Geraldine made no answer.

In very truth she thought Beatrice was rather inclined to be hard, and she was herself disposed to make one more effort to reclaim her erring sister.

But she thought she would say nothing about this. If she succeeded, well; and if she failed, few would be any the wiser.

"Would you send to Fortescue and let him know about the bill, so that he may be prepared for whatever happens?" she next asked.

"No, decidedly not," was the answer. "There could never be anything more unfortunate for you or for Fortescue than that you should be seen together."

"But he ought to be warned of what is likely to happen," urged her ladyship. "Sir Graham is so incensed against him that he is capable of having him arrested without further enquiry."

"I don't believe that he can do that," replied Beatrice; "and if he can, it doesn't much matter, for Mr. Grantly would obtain his freedom in a very short time. Take my advice, dear, and leave them alone. No one can find fault at your paying me a visit for a few days or weeks, and you may depend upon it that Sir Graham will soon come to his senses."

"Perhaps you are right," was the reluctant answer, "but it is very hard to sit down patiently, and suffer injustice, or witness it inflicted upon others."

"So it is, dear, but it is what we all have to put up with at some time or other. But now, try to forget your own troubles, and tell me what I shall do with myself. I shall be of age next week, and Mr. Lascelles will be relieved of his responsible post of guardian, but I am troubled about my father's will, and I am tired of the

aimless life I am leading; I want to do an act of justice,
and I want to do some good in the world.

Lady Grantly fell into the trap thus kindly laid for
her, and in discussing the best way in which an unmarried girl could live and spend her fortune for the
good of others, she forgot her own personal perplexi-
ties.

She did not forget her sister, however, and that very
same day she took an opportunity of seeking Fanny.

Though she discovered the house in which she and
Darlington lodged, she did not succeed in meeting her
sister, and it was three days after the thwarted wedding
that Lady Grantly once more stood face to face with
Fanny.

The change which had taken place in the girl during
this short space of time startled Geraldine out of all her
intended severity, and she asked with real anxiety:

"Are you ill, Fanny? Has anything that I don't
know of happened to you?"

"Has anything happened to me!" repeated the girl
with a loud harsh laugh. "Yes, much has happened;
much more will happen, too. Here, drink to my success.
There's nothing like brandy for keeping one's courage
up and driving away care."

"Brandy!" repeated her ladyship, recoiling in un-
feigned horror. "Are you drinking pure brandy?"

"As pure as I can buy it," was the reckless reply.
"You thought it was sherry, did you? Ha, ha! sherry
won't do for the work I have before me."

She laughed again, a wild, defiant, reckless laugh; a
laugh which made her sister remember the maniac
laugh of the patients in a madhouse which she had some
time previously visited.

"I wish you would see a doctor, Fanny."

"Doctor!" repeated the girl contemptuously, "what
can a doctor do for me? I am not mad, though I dare
say you think I am. I know what I am about very
well, and I know what I mean to do. Leave me
alone; forget that I am your sister; nothing that
anyone can say or do will make me alter my
purpose."

No. 18.

"I FOUND THAT, MADAM!" AND HE FLOURISHED THE FORGED ACCEPTANCE FOR SIX HUNDRED POUNDS IN HER FACE.

"And that purpose is?" asked Geraldine, somewhat anxiously.

"That is just what you have to find out. But go away now, Frank will be home presently and he won't want to see you; he doesn't even care to see me."

And she drooped her head and sank dejectedly back upon the chair from which she had recently risen.

Poor girl, with all her follies and failures she loved the worthless wretch who was so callously indifferent to her.

Geraldine tried to console her, hoping in this softened mood to make some impression upon the nature which she could not believe to be all bad.

But Fanny quickly roused herself, sentiment was never very much to her taste, and she was a little afraid of its effect upon her now.

"Go away, Geraldine, I don't want you here; nobody wants you here, and you are doing yourself no good by staying. Your words are wasted upon me, like water poured on sand. I shall go my own way in spite of all of you."

"I believe you will," was the sad rejoinder; "but let me entreat you, Fanny, to have some regard for your own safety if for nothing else."

"Oh, I shall take care of myself, and let others do the same," was the vague reply: "but I can't talk to you any more, so if you won't leave me, I'll leave you."

The next instant Lady Grantly was alone, for Fanny had walked into an inner room and had locked herself in.

It was with a heavy heart that her ladyship turned her steps towards D'Eyncourt-square.

She felt sure that Fanny meant mischief to others now, though up to the present she had only wronged herself.

"I fear she will attempt to do Mary or Beatrice some harm," she thought dejectedly, "and yet I am afraid to warn them."

Certainly she would have felt that a warning was necessary if she could have seen how Fanny was occupied the evening of that day.

Attired in a long cloak, with a small hat on her head and a thick veil on her face, the outcast from her family hung about the entrance of Beatrice Burnham's house, waiting till the carriage in which she and Mary had gone out some hours previously should return.

A policeman looked at her suspiciously once or twice as he passed her on his beat, but he did not address her.

He did not know that the hand she kept hidden under her cloak grasped an unsheathed dagger.

CHAPTER XLVII.

AN OLD OLD STORY.

ID you observe that woman with a thick veil on, who seemed as though she were going to roll against you?" asked Mary Darlington as she stood in the drawing-room of Beatrice Burnham's house un-buttoning her gloves.

Her question was addressed to Lady Grantly, who started and turned pale as she heard it, and she said nervously:

"No. A veiled woman? What was she like?"

"I am sure I can't tell you," was the answer; "she seemed enveloped in black from head to foot, and at one moment I thought she was going to strike you, but it must have been fancy on my part—your back was turned to her, and you were speaking to me at the moment."

"I didn't see any woman," replied Geraldine shortly.

Then she turned and walked towards the door, intending to go to her own room.

For she wanted to be alone to think and to calm her agitation.

She had had a presentiment ever since her interview with her that Fanny meant to do some injury to either Beatrice or Mary, and now she remembered that on leaving the carriage she and Mary had walked side by side into the house, while Beatrice, who was taller than either of them, had followed a second or two later, having paused to give some order to the coachman.

"If that was Fanny," thought her ladyship anxiously, "it is Mary whom she is most bitter against. I suppose she thinks if she were dead, Frank would be free and would marry her. I must get Mary away from here;

Fanny is dangerous, and as I cannot control her, I must remove the object of her fury."

So thinking, she had reached the drawing-room door with the purpose of going upstairs, when Beatrice met her, having loitered in the hall to tear open and read a letter which had arrived that evening.

"See," she said brightly; "this is from Ursula Raynham. She writes to accept my invitation to come and stay with me, as I was prevented from going to her, and she tells me, Geraldine, that she is engaged to Fortescue Grantly who is now at the rectory."

"Ah!"

It was all that Lady Grantly said, and her face was in shadow at the time so that its expression could not be read, but Beatrice could not help fancying that there was a note of pain and disappointment in the voice, and she thought sadly:

"Poor Geraldine! you made a sad mistake in your marriage, it was all very well to make up your mind to be married, but in singing 'Heigho! for a Husband,' you should have added 'but he must be young;' at any rate it would have been better not to marry the uncle of the man you preferred, for that places an eternal barrier between you."

But she uttered none of these thoughts; the matter was past cure.

"Yes, Ursula is coming here; she says she has been in bad health, and wants to see a doctor, but I suspect that, Puritan as your cousin is, Geraldine, she likewise wants to consult a fashionable dressmaker. But it will be very nice to have her here with us, won't it?"

"Very," replied Lady Grantly in a strained tone.

"We will stay here until my birthday is passed," Beatrice continued; "and then we will go to the seaside, or on the Continent, unless the marriage is to take place immediately."

"And Fortescue will be in town to-morrow?" asked her ladyship nervously.

"Yes, and he will be sure to come here to visit his *fiancée*, but you need not mind that now, dear; even

Sir Graham's jealousy must disappear under the circumstances."

"Very nice," responded Geraldine dryly; then she added with a yawn, "You must excuse me, Beatrice, I'm tired, and should like to go to bed. Goodnight."

A few minutes later, Mary also having retired, our heroine was left alone.

Then it was that she took out of her pocket Ursula Raynham's letter and read a certain portion of it carefully over again.

As may have been guessed, this part referred to herself.

"Fortescue left me in such haste with Mr. Lascelles, that we had no time to arrange anything," wrote Ursula, "therefore, he took the first possible opportunity of coming to pay us another visit, under less troubled circumstances. When Fortescue told me how Mr. Lascelles had found you after his long and anxious search, I naturally though that you two would soon be married, for that the young man loves you truly, my dear, I, who know but little of such matters, cannot feign to doubt. But Fortescue warns me not to hint such a thing to you, because you would only flout at his friend as you have flouted at so many suitors, thinking none of them good enough to mate with you, and he urges his friend to suffer any pain sooner than expose his heart to you to be made sport of. I should follow the advice of him who is to be my husband, my dear Beatrice, if I were not convinced that you have a warm and generous heart, even though you will not always show it to the sterner sex. But pray consider, my dear cousin, that it is not womanly to be so hard of heart to one who loves you truly, and who devotes himself to your service. Be not angry with me for writing in this strain, but it troubles me greatly to think that one in every way so sweet and amiable as yourself should use the gifts which Nature has bestowed on her as a means of breaking a true and manly heart."

Beatrice Burnham had only just glanced at this part of the letter as she walked upstairs; now, however, every word became impressed upon her mind, and her cheeks burned, and her eyes softened and drooped, while her hands fell loosely upon her lap as she murmured:

"She says Godfrey loves me, and that I flout at all my suitors, and that I should flout at him if he spoke to me of love. Perhaps she is right, for it is strange how his very presence seems to put me on my mettle, and to make me behave in such a manner that he cannot imagine it possible that I can care for him. And yet Ursula says that he loves me. I wonder if he does. But no; it is impossible. No man could ever tell a woman that he will have nothing to do with her money or with her so decidedly as he did to me the other day if he loved her. I can trust my own judgment better than that of Fortescue Grantly, and I know that Godfrey does not love me; if he did he could not be so hard and so cold. Do I wish that he did, I wonder? Heigho! I am glad I am not obliged to answer my own question. What is it, Mary?"

This to Captain Trevor's daughter, who had returned to the drawing-room, and was speaking somewhat excitedly.

"I have just received a letter from—from my husband," was the agitated reply. "He asks me to meet him, or, rather, he orders me to do so, and threatens to come for me if I refuse. What am I to do? Where can I hide from him?"

"Why should you hide?" cried Beatrice indignantly. "Who brought the letter?"

"A boy waits below, I am told, for an answer."

"Let me answer it," cried our heroine promptly.

Then, as Mary made no objection, she wrote upon a slip of paper, "Come if you dare," and signed it.

This was given to the lad who had brought the note to Mary, and who, on being questioned, said a gentleman at the corner of the street had given it to him with a shilling, and had promised to wait for his return.

"I wish we had a man in the house in addition to the servants," said Beatrice thoughtfully.

"I wish that Edgar were here," sighed Mary. "You may think little of him because he is an actor," she went on with burning cheeks and drooping eyelids, "but he is a gentleman, and he would protect me."

"His protection would probably do you more harm than good," said Beatrice coldly.

It had pained her to notice how Mary seemed to long to return to her wandering life, and how constantly the name of the handsome manager was upon her tongue and in her thoughts, and now she ventured to express her opinion upon the subject.

The clock had struck ten, and the two girls had just expressed their opinion that the man they both dreaded would not come, when a loud knock and ring at the front door startled them into the belief that Frank Darlington was below.

"I shall send for the police and give him in charge if he dares to lay a hand upon you," said Beatrice decidedly.

The next minute, however, she laughed at her own fears, for a servant came to announce that Captain Trevor had arrived.

"My responsibility is over now," said Beatrice gaily, as she left the father and daughter together.

And she felt a certain amount of relief in the thought, for Mary was anything but tractable, and their was always danger of her breaking through the mild restrictions of her present life and going back to her wandering career, fraught, as her position would then be, with so much danger.

But now Captain Trevor had come, his daughter would naturally be in his care.

He had accepted the invitation to remain in Beatrice's house, and he expressed himself ready to meet Darlington if he should put in an appearance.

But the guilty man did not come, though he was still, to all appearance, a free agent, for no criminal charge had been made against him, and he began to believe that the tide of good fortune, which had deserted him of late, was now going to turn in his favour.

The day following Captain Trevor's arrival Ursula Raynham and her father arrived at D'Eyncourt Square.

The rector's daughter was still pale and thin, but happiness had already produced a marked change in her, and there seemed every probability of her recovery to perfect health.

The London season was over, and the votaries of the world of fashion had betaken themselves to other scenes. Not that this could make much difference to Beatrice and her friends, for poor Clarrie's recent death made anything like amusement in the way of balls and parties out of the question.

One effect the time of year had, however, and this was to give up the garden of the square to the almost exclusive use of the inmates of No. 24.

Beatrice was very fond of the square-garden, for here she had spent many solitary hours during her father's lifetime.

Here too her father and Godfrey Lascelles would sometimes come out to smoke their evening cigar, and would there join her.

It was the evening of the day after the arrival of the Raynhams, dinner was over, and the drawing-room seemed hot and close, for the weather was heavy and sultry, and Beatrice suggested that they should all go out into the square.

"I think Fortescue is coming this evening," objected Ursula timidly.

"We can leave word with the servants asking him to join us," said Beatrice, and a few minutes later, the whole party, consisting of Ursula's father and Captain Trevor, with the four girls, were walking upon the soft grass under the large wide-spreading trees.

One advantage of this square was, that besides being large, it was so laid out that clumps of shrubbery were planted in a manner to make several nooks where one or two people could find a seat without being exposed to the view of the people in the street, and it was therefore a pleasant place to come to for a quiet smoke or a little chat with a friend.

Our party had not been long in the garden before three young men presented themselves at one of the gates, and Beatrice who perceived them opened it and admitted Fortescue Grantly, Godfrey Lascelles, and Archibald Raynham.

She shook hands with them in turn, then they all strolled off to join the other members of the party who were at a little distance.

Ursula's greeting of her lover was shy and timid, and neither she nor Fortescue observed the compressed lips and heightened colour of Lady Grantly, and even when the young man shook hands with his aunt, and enquired after his uncle, his thoughts were too pre-occupied for him to notice the vagueness of her replies.

The party soon broke up into groups of twos and threes, Beatrice attaching Archie Raynham to her side from the good-natured belief that he was a little bit of a cub, and would be neglected or quietly ignored by the other ladies.

But for Ursula's letter she would in all probability have kept Godfrey Lascelles near her, if only for the pleasure of sparring with him, but Ursula's reproof had made her self-conscious, and she wanted to get as far away from him as possible.

In consequence of this move on her part Godfrey after a time found himself alone, and he strolled towards one of the nooks already spoken of, and throwing himself upon a seat, fell into a far from pleasant train of thought.

He had during the late Mr. Burnham's lifetime spent many happy and many miserable hours on this self-same spot, and he was now thinking bitterly of the past rather than of the present, when the sound of his own name uttered by a woman roused him from his abstraction.

It was Mary Darlington talking to her father, Captain Trevor, and this was what she was saying to him:

"Godfrey Lascelles is clever, you think; well I don't, and I wouldn't pick him up with a pair of tongs, but here is Beatrice wearing her very heart out for love of him."

"Beatrice in love with him!" echoed Captain Trevor. "Impossible."

"Impossible or not, it is true," asserted his daughter. "She would die rather than he should know it, but that is the cause of her refusing everybody else, and that is what makes her always contradict him and seem as though she dislikes him, she is so much afraid of betraying herself."

"Well, I am sorry to hear it," said the old captain slowly, "for I don't think the young man is worthy of her. She is a noble, generous-hearted woman, always ready to consider the comfort and happiness of others rather than her own, and she deserves a better fate than to waste the best years of her life in loving a man who is indifferent to her."

"That is true, father, but for worlds do not breathe a word of what I have told you to anyone, least of all to Mr. Lascelles himself. Beatrice would never forgive me, and, though she were dying for love, she would deny that she did love the man her father wished her to marry. I know her so well, she is so proud and high-spirited she would never survive the humiliation of seeming to give her love unsought. Promise me that you will not breathe a word about what I have told you to anyone."

"Certainly I will not," was the reply, "but I am sorry for Beatrice, very sorry. I should have thought she would have been too wise to care for a man who does not love her."

Then the two passed out of hearing, and Godfrey Lascelles was left to ponder over the revelation that had just been made to him.

"Beatrice in love with him!"

The assertion had been made, but he thought it impossible that it could be true.

And he was unworthy of her, Captain Trevor had said. Well, that was true enough, no doubt, and yet if she loved him she would not think so.

But the idea that the proud beauty loved him was too startling for the young man to be able to grasp it, and when at length he left his retreat, and walked towards the subject of his thoughts, he felt like a man in a dream.

He would not have been a little enraged if he had known that Mary Darlington was quite conscious that he had heard every word of her conversation with her father, and that she had uttered each word with a purpose.

CHAPTER XLVIII.

DESPERATION.

ODFREY LASCELLES and Fortescue Grantly left D'Eyncourt Square together. Both were silent, each was busy with his own thoughts, and they walked slowly to Buckingham Palace, then through St. James' Park to Spring Gardens, from whence they made their way by Charing Cross down to the Embankment, and thence home to their chambers in the Temple.

A long walk for two men to take without a dozen words being exchanged between them, but they were old friends, and each appreciated the eloquence of the other's silence.

Fortescue was thinking of Ursula and of the life of happiness that he believed would be his with her for his wife, while Godfrey's mind was filled with the astonishing idea asserted by Mary Darlington with so much earnestness, that Beatrice Burnham loved him.

More than once during his walk he fell into a bitter cynical vein of feeling as he thought of his troublesome ward.

"If she loves me she has certainly taken some strange ways of showing her affection," he mused; "she has rarely missed an opportunity of irritating me when she could do so without being wantonly rude, and I am afraid I have not been too amiable myself towards her. But then excuses may be made for me, for if I told her I loved her she would think I wanted her money. Confound her money, I wish she hadn't a sixpence."

He had been uttering his thoughts aloud and Fortescue Grantly, who had been paying no heed to him previously, caught the word "money" and repeated it, asking, "What do you want of money?"

"I don't want it, you heard only half of what I said. By Jove! that's uncommonly like your uncle, Sir Graham."

He said this as a tall stout man with his head half averted passed rapidly by them.

"My uncle is safe enough in his own bed, sleeping the sleep of the self-contented," laughed Fortescue, "but I cannot understand his wife being in town while he is laid up at home. There is something more than is visible in my lady deserting her post after this fashion. Something decidedly wrong, I should say.'

"There is nothing wrong with her or she wouldn't be Miss Burnham's guest," said Godfrey, decidedly.

Fortescue was about to reply when two men who had been standing in the shadow close to the door that led to the young man's chambers, suddenly stepped forward and one of them said :

"Mr. Fortescue Grantly ? "

"Yes," replied Ursula's lover. "That is my name; do you want me ? "

"It's my duty to arrest you, sir, on a charge of forgery," was the answer as the officer at the same moment laid his hand upon the young man's arm.

"Forgery!" echoed the young man in amazement. "Who charges me with such a crime ? "

"The person whose name is forged, Sir Graham Grantly," was the answer; "but I warn you that anything you may now say will be used against you."

Fortescue Grantly stood in speechless surprise, unable for the moment to collect his thoughts or even to speak coherently, and it was Godfrey Lascelles who interposed, saying :

"There must be some terrible mistake here, but we cannot discuss the matter in the street; come up to my rooms and let us know the details of this conspiracy."

"It's of no use, sir," said the man who had made the arrest.

He spoke politely and even deferentially, but it was quite evident from his tone and manner that his conduct would not be influenced by anything that could be said to him.

"Perhaps not," assented Godfrey, "but where is your warrant for this arrest?"

The man produced his authority and the practised eye of the barrister saw that it was beyond dispute, so he said quietly:

"Your uncle must have taken leave of his senses, Grantly, but that is matter for the future and does not alter your present position. I will go with you now and will be ready in the morning with any amount of bail; it will only be a temporary inconvenience"

Fortescue tried to reply, but what he said sounded more like a groan than articulate speech.

The inconvenience he felt might be temporary, but the disgrace would be everlasting.

They got him into a cab and took him to Bow-street Police-court, and here his friend was at length obliged to leave him.

From all he could learn it appeared that Sir Graham Grantly had applied for a warrant for the arrest of his nephew that very afternoon.

"And it must have been the old coward whom I saw as we entered the Temple Gates," thought Godfrey savagely; "he has some bitter spite against his nephew, and he is venting it in this manner. I wonder if my lady knows about it, if so it would account for her strangely absent manner this evening; I could not help observing it."

So he pondered, not knowing any of the particulars of the case, and being unable to obtain his friends release that night, whatever bail he might be prepared to offer.

Early as possible the next morning Godfrey presented himself at the police-station, accompanied by a well-known solicitor, who was likewise a personal friend of the accused.

Time seemed to pass slowly until the case was called, but when Fortescue was brought before the magistrate, it was discovered that his uncle was not present to prosecute, nor was he represented by counsel.

Godfrey was indignant, more particularly so when the magistrate refused to dismiss the charge or to take bail until he had heard all the details, but he sent off an officer to try to find the baronet, and he put back the case till later in the day.

Just before the court was about to close, Sir Graham put in an appearance, and almost at the same time, Lady Grantly and Beatrice Burnham drove up to the door, and made their way into the crowded room.

Her ladyship's face was pale, and there was a look of determination about her lips that her husband, when he glanced at her, did not like.

She was evidently bent upon saving his nephew, even if by so doing she laid bare some of the discordant elements in her own married life.

Beatrice's face was slightly flushed, her eyes were bright with indignation, and Godfrey, who had not forgotten what he had heard on the previous night, thought he had never seen her look so beautiful.

Sir Graham frowned and seemed ill at ease.

Now it was too late he regretted the step he had taken, for if his nephew were guilty—as he sincerely believed—to punish him was but to bring disgrace upon his own name.

Thinking of this, after the arrest was made, he regretted what he had done, and he was explaining to his lawyer that he wished to withdraw the charge when the officer found him.

"You have gone too far to turn back now, Sir Graham," the lawyer was saying emphatically when the officer was announced, and then the hot-tempered baronet felt he had no alternative.

So here he is on one side, while his nephew, his wife, and his friends, are on the other, looking coldly and angrily towards him.

Once he made an attempt at conciliation, and he addressed himself to Beatrice, for his wife had turned her back upon him, but that young lady looked at him haughtily, and turned away her head mutely, declining even to listen to him.

Irritated at being thus snubbed all round, the baronet determined not to spare his nephew, and having been sworn, he told the magistrate how he had found the bill in his wife's desk, and how on making enquiries he found that his wife had actually paid the six hundred pounds for the bill in his name.

He further swore that he had never signed such a paper, and that he believed the rest of the writing to be in the hand of his nephew.

Fortescue's lawyer subjected the baronet to a severe cross-examination, and then called Lady Grantly.

"That bill is my property,' she said emphatically. "Mr. Fortescue Grantly never saw it before to-day.'

"But his name is upon it," objected the magistrate.

"I repeat my statement," said the lady.

Whereupon a whispered consultation ensued, and then the whole party retired to the magistrate's private room.

Here Lady Grantly gave a pretty clear account of what had happened.

She did not screen herself, but she spoke of Fanny as a relative, and she avoided mentioning the name of Frank Darlington.

Her statement was that the real forger had consented to marry a girl whom he had wronged on condition that he was saved from the consequences of his crime by this bill being met.

"It was met," argued her ladyship. "I paid the money out of my own private purse, and my husband had no business to touch that paper."

This assertion made even the magistrate smile.

Lady Grantly's ideas of the rights of a husband were certainly peculiar to her sex, if not to herself.

"The prisoner is discharged," said the magistrate gravely; "but Lady Grantly, by her own confession, has compounded a felony.'

Her ladyship bowed her head, but Sir Graham now began to look uneasy.

It was all very well to quarrel with his wife and to try to bring her to a condition of obedient subjection, but he had no desire to see her the inmate of a prison, and he said anxiously:

"If I withdraw the charge, your worship, and burn the bill, surely the matter may be allowed to drop?"

"I shall object to that course being taken," said Fortescue Grantly, who, now he was a free man, felt his wits returning to him. "My name has been forged as well as yours," he went on, "and I have been accused of committing a felony. Lady Grantly says she knows who manufactured that bill and obtained money upon it; I believe I also know; but it will save time if her ladyship makes her confession complete by divulging the name of the person she is so anxious to screen."

All eyes were turned upon Geraldine, who replied:

"The bill itself would tell you that I should think, and if there is any doubt upon the subject it can easily be traced to the man who discounted it. I should have thought these enquiries ought to have been instituted before any arrest was made."

"So should I," remarked Beatrice in a low tone to Godfrey. "Mr. Grantly might quite as reasonably have given Sir Graham into custody. I wish he had!"

Godfrey smiled and slightly shook his head, but he did not speak, for the magistrate was expressing a very strong opinion upon the whole proceeding, and neither Sir Graham nor his wife could feel flattered by what he said.

A quarter of an hour later and the whole party had left the court, and Beatrice and Lady Grantly were getting into the carriage of the former when the young lady said:

"You must come and dine with us this evening, Mr. Grantly; Ursula will not believe you are safe until she sees you."

"Ursula," grunted Sir Graham, who was close by.

No one heeded him, however, and the carriage door was being closed when he stepped forward and asked with more anxiety than dignity:

"Geraldine, where are you going, and where have you been since you left my house?"

"Lady Grantly is my guest at present," replied Beatrice with a defiant smile; "you cannot object to that Sir Graham."

Before he could reply the carriage had driven off, and he found himself standing alone on the pavement,

Fortescue and Godfrey having jumped into a hansom without a word of adieu.

For a few seconds he stood still, then he also hailed a cab and drove off to a club of which he was a member.

He remained here for some hours, speaking to no one but to the waiter who brought him his dinner.

All this time he was trying to bring himself to a frame of mind in which he could go to his wife and eat any quantity of humble pie, so that he could get her back again and be on good terms with her friends.

That his nephew would ultimately forgive him he did not doubt, but truth to tell he did not much care whether he did or not.

The mention of Ursula Raynham's name had recalled certain things to his mind which had previously escaped his memory, and the recollection of them, coupled with Beatrice's words, quite dissipated his groundless jealousy, while they also made him rather ashamed of the part he had been tempted to play, so he sat here trying to prepare himself for the humiliation he believed to be in store for him.

"I won't go to her to-night," he resolved suddenly; "I'll go into the card-room for an hour, and take a hand at whist if I can find anyone I know; then I'll go back to my hotel and have a good night's rest, probably we shall be all the better tempered in the morning.'

So thinking he went to the card-room and joined some acquaintances in making up a set.

He forgot the flight of time so interested did he become in the game, and it was quite late when he heard a voice that sounded familiar say:

"Luck is on my side to-night, and I mean to break the bank; I feel as though I had got my own luck and the devil's too!"

Then the speaker went on to play and to bet in a reckless manner, managing through it all to augment the pile of gold and notes that lay before him.

Suddenly the baronet became conscious that Frank Darlington was losing.

Quickly but steadily losing, and still he played and betted like a man whose life depended upon his success.

So it almost did, and success was resolutely turning a deaf ear to his appeals.

After awhile Sir Graham's interest flagged, for his own game was interesting, when he was startled to hear loud voices at the table behind him, and, looking round, he saw Frank Darlington standing up, gesticulating frantically, and with a loaded revolver in his hand.

How it happened, those who looked on could never tell, but before he could be restrained the young man fired several shots wildly and recklessly in various directions, then turned his deadly weapon towards himself and fired one shot more.

Men sprang upon him and wrenched the revolver from his grasp, and tried to staunch the self-inflicted wound, and just as they were getting him into a cab to send him home, two men came to the club door and asked for Mr. Darlington.

They were policemen come to arrest him.

"I hope I have cheated them," thought the wounded man bitterly.

He had no care for the injury he had done to others, and would only have smiled if he had known that one of his bullets had lodged in the shoulder of Sir Graham Grantly.

This was the case, however, and Lady Grantly, a couple of hours later, received a message to the effect that her husband was dying.

CHAPTER XLIX.

RETRIBUTION.

IT was the evening of the same day as that on which Fortescue Grantly had stood in the prisoner's dock at Bow street.

Beatrice and Lady Grantly had returned to D'Eyncourt Square, and as soon as the latter reached her own room, she threw herself upon a couch, and indulged in the very feminine luxury of "a good cry."

She was mortified beyond the power of words to express.

Her husband's behaviour had been such as to expose him to ridicule, and to cast doubt and suspicion upon herself.

"Why did I marry him?" she moaned; "I might have known that we never could get on together, and to think he should insult me as he has done; but I will never forgive him, never!"

She said this passionately, meaning it in all sincerity at the time, little dreaming how soon her resolution would be put to the test.

That evening her ladyship excused herself from going down to dinner on the plea of a sick headache, and only Ursula, Mary, and Beatrice sat down to table, Captain Trevor and Mr. Raynham having gone off for the evening together.

The ladies had only just re-entered the drawing-room when Fortescue Grantly made his appearance.

He had come to see Ursula and to tell her all that had happened to him since the previous night.

That the young man should be rather nervous and excited after going through such an ordeal was natural enough, and it was quite clear to the sympathetic eyes of our heroine that he would like to have a quiet chat with Ursula alone.

With the view of giving him an opportunity for this she said :

"Do you care to come into the square with me, Mary?"

"Yes," was the reply, "I should like to go."

Then the two girls went out of the house; and the lovers were left together.

"How considerate you are for people in love, and how awkwardly you manage matters," laughed Mary as she and Beatrice strolled under the trees; "one would almost think you were in love yourself. 'A fellow feeling makes us wondrous kind.'"

"I never have been in love," replied our heroine coldly.

"And are not now?" questioned Mary with an arch laugh.

"I wish you wouldn't always be harping on the subject of love," was the impatient reply; "going on the stage has quite spoilt you."

"I wish I were on the stage now," sighed the actress, "there is no life like it; I can't tell you how happy I was before you found me nor how kind my friends were to me. I saw Montgomery's name on a play-bill to-day, he is to appear in London next week; I must go."

"Is it wise?" asked Beatrice quietly.

"Wise or foolish I shall go," was the reckless rejoinder. "You are very kind to me, Beatrice, but I am getting awfully tired of this slow uneventful kind of life, while as for going back with my father and living with my step-mother and her two sticks of daughters, at Burnham Court or anywhere else, I simply can't and won't do it."

Beatrice made no reply.

"If Frank were only dead; or if I could get a divorce from him," sighed Mary, "I should know what to do."

Still Beatrice was silent.

She did not approve of Mary's words, for she knew that the girl desired to be free that she might marry the handsome actor, and she justly reflected that Frank Darlington's shortcomings were no excuse for Mary's love for another man while her husband was still alive.

Daylight had gradually disappeared, and evening had quite set in when the two girls decided to return into the house.

Mary came out of the square gardens in advance of Beatrice, and some temporary difficulty with the lock of the gate kept the latter for a second or two behind her companion, when suddenly, close to her own door-step, she saw the veiled and cloaked figure of a woman come swiftly behind Mary and lift her arm to strike her.

To spring forward, clutch the uplifted hand with all her strength, and to drag the assailant into the light was Beatrice's first and natural impulse; and then she saw that the clenched hand held a dagger, and that the face of the would-be murderess was the face of Fanny Raynham.

With a cry of horror and consternation Beatrice gripped the girl's wrist with redoubled tenacity, while the other twisted and fought and struggled to be free.

But Beatrice dared not relax her hold because of the uplifted dagger, and it was not until the weapon fell from the over-mastered grasp that our heroine loosened her own grip upon the frantic creature.

"You viper!" cried Fanny, shrinking against the wall with an expression of impotent fury mingled with abject fear upon her white and agonised face; "you always thwart me, Beatrice Burnham! sleeping or waking, you are my evil genius; and now you help that woman to stand between Frank and me; but I will kill her; I will have her life's blood yet!"

Then wrenching herself free from Beatrice's grasp she sprang with a wild shriek upon Mary, and Fortescue Grantly, who had that moment reached the spot, was only just in time to interpose.

But now the condition of the frantic creature was beyond doubt or dispute.

She foamed at the mouth and her body was contorted like that of a person in an epileptic fit, while she shrieked and uttered disjointed sentences with all the horrible abandon of raving madness.

Her wild behaviour had attracted the attention of several passers-by, and to avoid scandal as well as to take care of the miserable creature, Grantly and Beatrice half dragged and half persuaded her into the dining-room.

Then Lady Grantly was sent for, but her influence over her sister was gone; nay, her presence seemed rather to excite than to calm the unfortunate girl.

She screamed and raved and gave utterance to such wild incoherent reproaches, that only those who knew the sad history of her young life understood how she had wrecked her happiness through her passion for a worthless man, and how she believed that Beatrice had robbed her of her lover, and had thwarted her, until this last act had driven the poor wretch's tottering reason from its throne for ever.

She believed that the actress was the only obstacle to her union with the reprobate whom she so blindly loved—loved, though he had treated her coldly and cruelly, and was as indifferent to her sufferings as he was to her happiness.

She had heard him bemoan the tie that bound him to Mary, cursing his own ill fortune that he was not free, and she had promised in her wild reckless style to free him, believing that he would then make her his wife if only out of gratitude. But he paid no heed to her promise, he was making preparations to leave the country, and he certainly had no intention of taking Fanny with him.

He had even quarrelled with her this very day, and had when evening came on started for a club of which he was still a member, where play ran high and where he hoped to double the sum of money he had managed to scrape together from various sources.

If he were successful in doing this he meant to start for Spain immediately, and to remain there until his misdeeds were forgotten and his father was dead, or until he could make terms with his enemies.

With the instinct of incipient insanity she suspected something of this, but the dominant idea in her mind was that Mary Trevor—as she still called her—was the cause of Frank's intended flight and the only obstacle to her own marriage with him.

On the evening of Lady Grantly's visit to her she had watched the house in which her intended victim was for the time living; she had seen the carriage return with three ladies in it, but when she got close to the party and was about to lift her hand for the fatal blow the woman she was about to strike spoke to one of her companions, and the would-be murderess shrank back in fear and horror; she had been about to take the life of her own sister.

The shock which her narrow escape from injuring Geraldine gave Fanny, kept her away from D'Eyncourt-square the next night, but she came back again urged on by love and jealousy, and but for Beatrice Burnham's timely interference she would without doubt have accomplished her wild and wicked purpose.

A doctor was quickly sent for by Beatrice, but a glance at the patient told him her true condition and early the next morning Fanny Raynham was taken to an asylum, the medical verdict being that she was hopelessly insane.

"She must have been mad all along," said Ursula sorrowfully; "I more than once doubted her sanity when she was with us at Rawfell."

But even before the doctor had arrived that night, the messenger came for Lady Grantly to tell her that her husband was dying.

Geraldine was for the moment overwhelmed by the news; it seemed incredible that the man who a few hours ago had been so hard and vindictive, should now be near the end of his earthly career.

As soon as she could realise his condition, however, all her resentment against him fled, she only remembered his kindness and affection, and she at once declared her readiness to go to him.

The baronet was lying on a couch in his room in the hotel where he had been staying for the last few days.

He was calm and perfectly conscious and he knew that his hours were numbered.

"Will she come in time to forgive me?" was the thought that filled his mind; "and she does not know how much she has to forgive."

The remembrance of some wrong which he had done his wife troubled him now, more than the near approach of death, and he signed to those about him to bring pens, ink, and paper, and he managed to articulate :

"Codicil to my will."

They did his bidding, but when the materials were at hand he could not speak the words he wished to have written.

The very effort to do so weakened him, and he lay back on his cushions for a time with his eyes closed, looking as though his last struggle with life was over.

But after a while he rallied, and though he could not speak, he managed to take a pen and write :

"All my personal property is to go to my wife, and my real property to go to my heir-at-law."

Then he motioned to those around him to witness his signature, and this was only just done when Lady Grantly came into the room.

There was no anger or pride on her kind face as she came to the side of the husband from whom she was soon to be parted by that most terrible of all barriers—death.

There was no more room in her heart for other sentiments than those of wifely love and sympathy, and her feelings were expressed upon her countenance.

She took his hand in her own, pressed her lips upon his forehead, and by her very presence seemed to soothe him.

But she could not drive away the grim conqueror of life, and even her inexperienced eye could see that death was written upon the strong man's countenance.

And the end was not long in coming.

Several times he tried to speak, but the power of speech was gone for ever.

Once his lips framed the words "Dear wife!" and he pointed to the paper he had just signed, and then his eyes closed.

There was a convulsive struggle, and the hard worldly man started on that journey which we all must take, carrying with us no more of earthly riches than we brought at our birth.

To say that Lady Grantly was overwhelmed with grief at her husband's death would not be true, but she was greatly shocked at its suddenness, and when she knew that Frank Darlington's hand had caused it she could scarcely help blaming herself for not telling Sir Graham about the forged bill directly she heard of it, and thus by putting it out of Darlington's power of doing further mischief for a time, have prevented this last tragedy.

"I did it for Fanny's sake," she thought regretfully, "and what good have I done her, poor girl? None whatever. Better I had left her alone from the first; it is a mistake to palter with vice and crime, to do so is to soil one's own hands without washing other's clean, and I have done more harm than good by my weakness."

So the young widow blamed herself, though few would be found to blame her.

After the inquest was over, they took the body of the murdered man down to Grantly Park, and from there he was buried with much pomp and ceremony.

He was a man who liked show all the days of his life, and he had left behind him particular instructions as to what should be done with him after his death.

When his will which the lawyer had prepared was read, the reason for the last informal document was only too apparent, for in his anger at his wife leaving his house in the manner she had done, Sir Graham had made a will in which he carefully excluded her from any benefit beyond that given her by her marriage settlements.

"A pretty plight Geraldine would have been in if I had not been firm about those settlements," said Geraldine's mother when she heard this will read; and she expressed the same opinion when the last paper written by the dead man was brought forward.

"Fortescue Grantly will dispute it," was this shrewd lady's decision.

But for once she was mistaken.

The young barrister was quite satisfied that his late uncle's widow should have the whole of his personal property, as the estates would come to him, though the title would become extinct.

"I hope you will be in no hurry to leave the Park," Fortescue said to Geraldine as he was about to return to town after the will had been read. "I shall not want to live here until Ursula and I are married," he added with well meaning kindness.

But Geraldine thanked him coldly, and said that she should soon find another home for herself.

Sorry as she was for her dead husband, it grieved her bitterly to know that by her hasty marriage she had not only lost the man she loved, but the position she coveted had likewise slipped from her.

To be mistress of Grantly Park had been her ambition, and she had been mistress of the splendid mansion for one short year; but now she was to leave it, and her cousin Ursula would not only be Fortescue Grantly's wife, but would reign in the place that had once been hers.

"I suppose it serves me right," she thought bitterly as she wandered over the rooms of the mansion that had already ceased to call her mistress. "It is what novelist's call poetic justice," she went on gloomily. "I married for ambition and because I would have a husband without delay, and Ursula was ready to marry for love, and to wait for that love to come to her."

But even Lady Grantly did not know how tardy that love had seemed in coming, or she would have thought that Ursula's previous suffering had made the balance pretty even.

All this time, while his last victim died and was buried, Frank Darlington lay in a critical condition, and it was feared by his friends, and even by himself, that he would recover to stand his trial for the murder of Sir Graham Grantly.

That the baronet's death was the result of accident, as the wretched culprit asserted, no one would for a moment believe; for it was now well known that Darlington had first of all forged Sir Graham's name, and on the very day his crime was discovered had shot him; therefore, though he told the truth for once in his life, there was not one person found to listen to him.

As he grew better he was told of Fanny's hopeless condition, but he expressed no surprise and very little sympathy.

"It was bound to come sooner or later," was his remark, "and she had become an awful nuisance."

When asked if he would like to see his wife, he replied curtly in the negative, adding a little later that he had seen enough of her.

There was one person, however, whose presence he did desire by the side of his sick couch, and this was Beatrice Burnham.

But Beatrice would not come.

Had he been repentant for the past, or had he shown feeling and regret for those who had suffered at his hands, Beatrice would have forgiven her own wrongs, and would have yielded to his request for an interview in the hope that it might calm and prepare him for the dark future.

But he was hardened in his iniquity.

He only wanted her by his side to tell her of his burning passion, to look upon her fair face, and to assure her that she was the only woman whose love he had ever failed to win when he had once sought it.

This last gratification was denied him, and he grew morose and sullen, and when he was pronounced to be out of danger from his wound, and he knew that he would have to stand his trial for murder, and that even if he escaped from that he would have to meet the charge of forgery, a great change came over him, and it soon became evident to his gaolers that he meant to destroy himself.

At first he refused his food, but this failed; then he tried to smother himself, but again he was foiled; and they found it necessary to watch him day and night.

But despite all their vigilance he escaped them. A few days before his trial was to come on, they found him in his bed quite dead.

He had severed the artery in his arm, and keeping it under the bedclothes so as to hide it from the eyes of the watchers, had quietly bled to death.

"Thank Heaven I am free!" was his wife's first exclamation when she heard what had happened.

A manifestation of depraved feeling upon her part that made Beatrice look at her in anger and disgust, and that produced a breach between the two friends which never healed, though it did not sever them immediately.

"The only considerate act of his life was his manner of getting out of it," remarked Mr. Longridge when he had heard how the man he had hunted so long had escaped the legal penalty for his crimes.

"I should have liked to have seen him punished," added the detective reflectively, "but there are the feelings of others to be considered before mine, so perhaps it is best as it is."

Poor old Squire Darlington, in his big house with only servants about him and with no near relative to give him comfort, certainly thought it best as it was; the disgrace of having his worthless son branded as a felon would have broken the old man's heart.

CHAPTER L.

CONCLUSION.

MID these exciting and agitating events, Beatrice Burnham's twenty-first birthday came and went like most other days.

She had not expected it would be thus, indeed she had half hoped that some unpremeditated glance, some chance word would break down the barrier between Godfrey and herself, for that he did love her and that she loved him she was every day becoming more convinced.

On the morning in question, however, Godfrey did not put in an appearance.

Somewhat after the impatient fashion in which she had waited for him the day we first looked in upon her, so she paced the lone drawing-room now, thinking nervously of the approaching interview to which she was nevertheless looking forward with eagerness.

At length, when her patience was well-nigh exhausted, Mr. Rendal, her late father's lawyer, arrived, and with many apologies for being late, said:

"Mr. Lascelles will not be able to meet you to-day, and he has deputed me to explain your position and the manner in which your property is invested."

"Why could not Mr. Lascelles come?" asked Beatrice, unable to hide her vexation.

"An uncle of his, from whom I believe he has great expectations, was taken suddenly ill last night, and Mr. Godfrey Lascelles was telegraphed for this morning; he came to my house on his way to the railway-station while I was at breakfast, and asked me to come to see you and to explain the cause of his absence."

"An uncle," repeated Beatrice, thoughtfully; "he is a judge, isn't he?"

"Yes, and a very wealthy man; he married the daughter of a rich merchant, and she brought him a large fortune. They had several children, but they have died one after the other, and the last met with his death little more than a month ago; it is this last bereavement that has completely overcome the old man, and his nephew is now his heir."

"I am glad he will be rich," said Beatrice, turning away to hide her face from the keen eyes fixed upon her.

"Yes, money is always useful to a man," was the dry response, "particularly when for the sake of a crotchet he refuses to assert his undoubted rights. But now if you will give me your attention, Miss Burnham, I think I can explain the position of affairs as well as our absent friend could have done."

Beatrice bowed her head, and for the next hour the lawyer talked about shares and bonds and securities to ears that scarcely listened to him.

She was glad to hear that Godfrey would be a rich man. Glad for his sake, and perhaps too for her own, for if he had no need of wealth he might perhaps venture to confess his love for her, feeling assured from his improved position that she could not suspect him of fortune-hunting.

This hope, and all the possibilities it suggested, were so strong in her mind and filled it so completely to the exclusion of all other thoughts, that the lawyer, who knew but little of her, jumped at the conclusion that she was more than ordinarily stupid, and remarked to himself that it was very rarely that a beautiful woman like the one he had just left was possessed of an ounce of brains.

For the whole of that day Beatrice could think of nothing but of Godfrey's changed fortunes, and Ursula and Mary found her anything but an entertaining companion.

The following morning a letter came from the young barrister stating the cause of his absence from town, adding that Mr. Rendal would put her in possession of all necessary power and information, and congratulating her upon having attained her majority and her freedom from all legal restraints.

This letter was meant to be kind and almost tender, with a vein of bantering humour in it, but unfortunately, as so often happens with letters, it was read in a very different spirit from what it was intended to convey, and thus without exactly knowing where the sting in it lay, it galled the proud girl to whom it was addressed to the quick.

In this misread epistle, the writer said nothing about his probable return to town, neither was there any remark as to when or where they should meet again; it seemed, indeed, more like a leave-taking, as though a duty on his part was accomplished and henceforth their paths lay in different directions.

Beatrice first of all indulged in a good hearty flood of tears, then she roused herself, declaring that she was not going to break her heart for any man, and she like-wise exclaimed with some very natural indignation, that Ursula and Fortescue must, to say the least of it, have been mistaken, for it was quite clear that Godfrey did not care for her.

"And I have allowed myself to think of him, and I have taught myself to believe that I love him," she cried bitterly. "Well, I must unlearn the lesson; it will not be harder for me, I suppose, than it is for other women."

In this manner she braced herself up to endure and to hide the love she could not at once conquer, and she determined to seek change of scene, and to fill her life with as much occupation as possible so that she might have no time to brood over her disappointment.

As Ursula's marriage had to be delayed for a time in consequence of Sir Graham Grantly's death, it was decided that she and Beatrice should go on the Continent for a few months, with Mrs. Gray as their chaperon, while Mary went down to Burnham Court to reside with her father and step-mother.

"I don't want you to leave the Court until you find it quite convenient to do so," Beatrice had said to her aunt, and that lady had taken her at her word, and showed no sign whatever of any intention to move.

The next three months passed pleasantly enough, and the two girls with their companion would have spent the winter in Rome but for the urgent letters from England entreating their return.

Fortescue Grantly was getting impatient to claim his bride, and Mrs. Trevor wrote in a somewhat mysterious fashion to say that she hoped her niece would soon come home to take up her residence at the Court.

Mrs. Gray also was longing to get back to England, so a few days before Christmas Day the three ladies arrived in London, and went straight on to Burnham Court.

Everything seemed familiar and yet strange to our heroine as the carriage in which she sat rolled up the long avenue to the mansion that was now all her own, and she thought sadly and regretfully of poor Clarrie who had looked forward so eagerly to being absolute mistress here, and who now lay cold and silent in her narrow resting-place.

She was roused from this melancholy frame of mind by glad voices and bright faces welcoming her home, and then she and Ursula were almost carried into the house by the girls, who had so much to hear and so much to tell in their turn.

But the girls did not get it all their own way, for Fortescue Grantly was there as well as Dr. Raynham, and they put in a claim for some attention.

"I was very anxious that you should come back, and take possession here," Mrs. Trevor said some time later in the afternoon when the whole party was seated in the drawing-room sipping their five o'clock tea, "because Grace is going to be married, and I have promised to take Ruth to Italy."

"Grace going to be married!" cried Beatrice in surprise.

"Yes; to Mr. Langdale, the rector," replied the mother, with some pride in the good fortune of her off-spring.

"Ah me! they are all going the same way," sighed Beatrice with affected dismay; "all going to be married, but I am sunburned, and may sit in a corner and cry 'Heigho! for a husband!'"

"Will you have me?" asked Dr. Raynham with more earnestness than jest in his tone.

"No; your reverence is too grave; I should have to keep you for Sundays, and high days and holidays," was the smiling retort. "I want somebody more fit for this workaday world. What do you say Mary?"

"I say that you have not cried in vain," was the significant reply.

Beatrice looked up in surprise to ascertain what Mary could mean, and she saw Godfrey Lascelles standing in the doorway.

He must have heard what she said.

It was not often that Beatrice Burnham lost her self-possession, but she did so now completely.

Her face flushed, her eyelids drooped, and she rose to her feet, looking so utterly confused that Ursula could not help pitying her.

But Mary turned away to indulge in a low mischievous laugh.

She had always believed that under the assumed antagonism of these two lay a feeling that was very near akin to love.

Godfrey Lascelles saw the blush, but he himself was not quite as calm or as cold as it was his wont to be, and he came forward and took Beatrice's hand, holding it in his own, according to Mary's description of the scene, "an unconscionable time," and he said:

"I just missed you at Victoria. The train moved out of the station as I reached the platform, or I should have travelled down with you. I need not ask how you are, for you never looked better in your life."

"I am quite well, thank you," was the reply; "but look at Ursula, and tell me if I have not done her more good than all the doctors."

"Very clever of her," thought Mary, "to divert attention from herself; but you have betrayed yourself, Miss Beatrice, with all your caution. Minerva herself is vulnerable to shafts from Cupid's bow."

It was a very pleasant party that assembled at the dinner-table at Burnham Court this evening.

Everybody seemed cheerful and in good spirits.

Mrs. Trevor appeared to be unmindful of the fact that her long reign in this house was ended, and that she sat at the head of the table almost for the last time.

And as for the younger people, they were as bright and witty as though pain and doubt had never racked their hearts or wearied their brain.

Soon after dinner, the party fell into groups like the pieces of glass in a kaleidoscope.

Ursula and Fortescue had so much to say to each other that it was not to be wondered at when they seated themselves in the deep recess of the bay-window, within view but out of hearing of the others.

What took Beatrice into the conservatory, however, was not quite so clear; neither was it ever explained why Godfrey Lascelles found himself attracted to the same spot. Certain it is that, directly these two found themselves together, the young man clasped his arm round the girl's waist, and drawing her towards him, said:

"Beatrice our warfare is ended, and you love me."

"I have been told that you love me," she said with a defiant smile as she half resisted and half yielded to his embrace.

"I am afraid it is true," he replied with assumed regret; "but I should never have told you so if my fortune had not been equal to yours."

"Then your pride was really greater than your love," she asked reproachfully, still holding back from him.

"I don't know," he replied mischievously. "I don't think my pride would have been strong enough to resist your cry of 'Heigho! for a husband.'"

Beatrice's indignant protest was very indistinct by reason of the kiss that followed.

But this was their last mimic war of words; the spirit of contradiction fled when love became master of the field.

As Beatrice and Godfrey had no one to consult but themselves, and as there was no reason on either side for delay, their engagement, though made the last, was the soonest fulfilled.

"We will get married and come back from our honeymoon in time for your weddings," Godfrey said to Grace and Ursula laughingly; "then if we find we have made a terrible mistake you can take warning and not follow our example."

So no time was lost in making the necessary preparations and on the first of February the wedding took place.

The weather was too cold for any floral demonstrations, and poor Clarrie's death was still too recent for any great amount of festivity, but there was a good deal of quiet rejoicing, and when the happy pair went off on their wedding-tour the blessings bestowed upon them were deep and sincere.

For in the months she had spent at Burnham Court before the place became her own, our heroine's warm sympathy and ready purse had won her the love and gratitude of all who knew her.

At the end of a month the happy pair came back again more like lovers than ever, and, almost immediately afterwards, the marriage of Ursula with Fortescue Grantly and that of her cousin Grace with the Rev. Lawrence Langdale took place, both events being celebrated together.

For the first time since her widowhood Lady Grantly joined the family party and went to the church rather as a spectator than as a guest.

But she was present at the wedding breakfast, and her marriage gift to Ursula was more costly than any other on the occasion.

In point of fact, her ladyship had nerved herself for this day, and had been more cordial in her congratulations to her cousin than she would otherwise have been, because by doing so she thought she would more effectually hide the pain and mortification she was suffering.

But she need not have taken so much trouble, for not a living creature suspected that Geraldine Grantly had ever bestowed a thought of love upon the nephew of the man she had married.

Immediately after the double wedding had taken place, Mrs. Trevor, with her husband and her remaining daughter, went away from Burnham Court, which, henceforth, would cease to be their home.

But they went without regret, and the proud woman who had once looked forward to this step with such jealous dread, was now glad to go. She had no lack of this world's goods and she had suffered too much pain from Fanny's misconduct and Clarrie's death not to be anxious to get away from the place that reminded her so often of both of them.

When the party arrived in London, however, a fresh shock awaited them.

Mary announced her intention of not going abroad with them, as she intended to marry the handsome actor who had proved so good a friend to her.

It was in vain that her father pleaded with her and her step-mother spoke with scorn of such a proceeding, the self-willed girl had quite determined to go her own way.

She had been very quiet about it all, but every preparation had been made, and at the last moment what she had calculated upon really happened.

Finding they could not control her, her parents made a virtue of necessity, and with as good a grace as they could assume, were present at the ceremony and entertained the bride and bridegroom and the bridegroom's friends at the hotel at which they were staying.

"After all, it was an easy way of getting rid of Mary," Mrs. Trevor wrote to Lady Grantly. "I have always regarded her and poor Fanny as the two black sheep in the flock."

"Poor Fanny," that was the way in which those to whom she belonged always spoke of her, when, as rarely happened, her name was mentioned. She still lives, and may live for many years, but the light of reason is quite extinguished.

Beatrice and Godfrey are as happy as it is possible for mortal man and woman to be, and a juvenile Godfrey, who is the delight and the torment of the whole household, toddles about Burnham Court.

Certainly neither of his parents have as yet had cause to regret the day when Beatrice jestingly cried "HEIGHO! FOR A HUSBAND."

Nos. 1 and 2 of
"THE FAIR MYSTERY"
Will be Published on Wednesday, February 8th.

"YOU DID NOT EXPECT TO MEET ME HERE?"

Important Announcement!!

Now Ready. Nos. 1 and 2

OF THE

SPLENDID STORY,

ENTITLED

"THE FAIR MYSTERY."

THE TWO NUMBERS, PRICE 1d.,

Will be Enclosed in an Illuminated Wrapper,

AND

A BEAUTIFUL COLOURED PICTURE

WILL BE

PRESENTED GRATIS.

Order at once of your Booksellers to secure copies.

Office: 173, FLEET STREET, E.C.

www.ingramcontent.com/pod-product-compliance
Lightning Source LLC
Chambersburg PA
CBHW080330040726
47505CB00022B/2148